Praise for DUSK by Tim Lebbon
Winner of the British Fantasy Award for Best Novel, 2006

"Totally original. I've never read anything like it—new wonders at every turn. One might subtitle it 'A Riveting Work of Staggering Imagination.'"
—F. PAUL WILSON

"Lebbon has a way of throwing staggering images at you which you almost have to pause and think about before you can fully grasp. This is fantasy for grown-ups—and the ending made my jaw drop. This is an excellent book, and I would not say that unless I meant it."
—PAUL KEARNEY

"*Dusk* is a deliciously dark and daring fantasy novel, proof of a startling imagination at work. Lebbon's writing is a twisted spiral of cunning, compassion, and cruelty."
—CHRISTOPHER GOLDEN

"An exquisitely written, unique world is revealed in this novel. It's rare indeed to witness the conventions of fantasy so thoroughly grabbed by the throat and shaken awake. Even more enticing, this first novel in the series concludes with a jaw-dropping finale, and for what it's worth, such a reaction from me is not a common occurrence."
—STEVEN ERIKSON

"A gripping and visceral dark fantasy. Lebbon has etched a powerful new version/telling of the traditional magical quest, whose tortured twists and turns will (alternately) disturb and electrify its readers."
—SARAH ASH

"A compelling, if harrowing, read . . . dark, nasty, and visceral and yet a real page-turner. . . . Definitely worth reading."
—SFFWorld

"Well-drawn characters and a literate way with the grisly distinguish this first of a new fantasy series from Stoker winner Lebbon." —*Publishers Weekly*

"Dark, gripping swords-and-sorcery noir . . . A promising departure for horror novelist Lebbon."
—*Kirkus Reviews*

Praise for DAWN

"A terrific horror fantasy . . . The story line is action-packed and filled with the usual creative war gadgetry that keeps Tim Lebbon tales fresh. . . . A superior tale."
—*SFRevu*

"This sequel to *Dusk* again demonstrates Bram Stoker Award winner Lebbon's consummate talent for viscerally visual fantasy [with] strong and unusual characters and a plot of epic proportions." —*Library Journal*

"The relentless imagination and evocative prose that made *Dusk* such a thrilling read are still in evidence . . . Lebbon has shaken up high fantasy with his duology, and it was a pleasure to read." —*SF Site*

Praise for FALLEN

"Stoker winner Lebbon successfully combines quest adventure and horror in this gripping and disturbing tale. . . . Lebbon creates vivid and convincing major and minor characters, places and creatures, blending wonder and nightmare in this dark and memorable novel."
—*Publishers Weekly* (starred review)

Also by Tim Lebbon

NOVELS

Noreela
The Island
Fallen
Dawn
Dusk

The Hidden Cities (with
Christopher Golden)
Mind the Gap
The Map of Moments
The Chamber of Ten

Hellboy
Hellboy: Unnatural Selection
Hellboy: The Fire Wolves

Bar None
Mesmer
The Nature of Balance
Hush (with Gavin Williams)
Face
Until She Sleeps
Desolation
30 Days of Night
30 Days of Night: Fear
of the Dark
The Everlasting
Berserk

NOVELLAS

White
Naming of Parts
Changing of Faces
Exorcising Angels (with Simon
Clark)
Dead Man's Hand
Pieces of Hate
A Whisper of Southern Lights
The Reach of Children
The Thief of Broken Toys

COLLECTIONS

Faith in the Flesh
As the Sun Goes Down
White and Other Tales of Ruin
Fears Unnamed
Last Exit for the Lost
After the War

ECHO CITY

TIM LEBBON

BALLANTINE BOOKS • NEW YORK

Echo City is a work of fiction. Names, characters, places, and incidents either are the product of the author's imagination or are used fictitiously. Any resemblance to actual persons, living or dead, events, or locales is entirely coincidental.

A Spectra Mass Market Original

Copyright © 2010 by Tim Lebbon

Published in the United States by Spectra, an imprint of The Random House Publishing Group, a division of Random House, Inc., New York.

SPECTRA and the portrayal of a boxed "s" are trademarks of Random House, Inc.

ISBN 978-0-553-59322-8

Printed in the United States of America

www.ballantinebooks.com

9 8 7 6 5 4 3 2 1

For my sister Joan

In conclusion, my despair: the concept that Echo City could be all there is; the thought that we are alone; the conceit that humanity rose from one man, expanding into one place, shunning the beyond though dangerous it must be. This is abhorrent to me. It denies our nature, which has been proven again and again to be exultant and brave. It disregards the very idea of our progress as a race and the ultimate triumph that must come. But such ignorance is clasped to the heart of those who claim rule over us. And though I see glory in our future, before glory, I see pain.

BENJERMEN DAXIA,
Truth—An Exhortation to Revolt

Acknowledgments

Thanks once again to editor extraordinaire Anne Groell, who always sees the big picture and helps me find it. Also thanks to David Pomerico and everyone at Bantam, my ever-wise agent Howard Morhaim, and all those writers and friends who make sure it's never a lonely business. You are too numerous to list, but you know who you are.

Prologue

As it left the city, the thing did not once look back. It walked with heavy steps, looked forward with rheumy eyes, and its misted breath soon dispersed in the air. It did not look back, because its purpose was ahead, and large though this thing was, its brain was small and simple, its reason for being very precise. It moved away from the world and out into the Bonelands, and it would never return.

Darkness concealed the start of its journey. It was aware of people in the buildings and ruins around it, but Skulk Canton was a place whose residents would keep to themselves. If they did not, its maker had instructed it to force their attention away. In its rudimentary mind, the idea of violence was little different from the process of placing one foot in front of the other, or breathing, or blinking its eyes to clear them of sand.

For a while as it started across the desert, the ground still bore signs of Echo City. Rubble from tumbled walls marred its path, and it had to step aside or climb over. One spread of land was scarred with the evidence of digging, the reason and results long since lost to time. And here and there it saw the remains of a body.

The moon's pale crescent lit its way. Beyond the moon, countless stars speckled the clear, cold night. The thing had no concept of what moon and stars were, because they bore no connection to its purpose. But it looked up at them with curiosity nonetheless. Its maker had granted it that, at least.

Soon it was away from the outer limits of the city. It walked as it had been instructed, avoiding places where the sands looked thin and loose and keeping to harder, easier surfaces. No plants existed out here, and no animals—nothing but sand and rock and the dry, heavy air it breathed. Sometimes a gentle breeze whispered a skein of sand across its path, and it held its breath as it passed through the brief, scouring cloud.

Its body was clothed in heavy leathers. It had watched its maker constructing this suit, stitching together the garments of many normal people to create something expansive enough to cover its huge torso. The suit was tied around its bulky thighs, upper arms, and neck, and the exposed surfaces of its arms and legs had been sprayed with a thick dark lotion to ward off the desert's inimical influence. Woven into the layers of leather were fluid sacs, in a network of narrow tubes that merged eventually beneath a thin, hollow bone straw protruding beneath its chin. It took frequent sips of water, and it was not long before the sips were tainted by the salty taste of its own perspiration.

Its shoes were tied leather folded many times, spiked with iron studs to give grip. It carried no weapons. It bore no pack. The prints it left behind were wide, long, and deep, and they would command awe were they noticed in the days following. But by then the thing would be dead, and it would never hear the myths of its passing.

As dawn set the eastern desert aflame, the thing marched on. It glanced to its left only once, experiencing a brief flare of wonder and awe. Somewhere deep down basked shadows of memories that were not its own, in which the view of such sunrises was interrupted by the silhouettes of spires and walls, towers and roofs. Such a natural, unhindered view as this was something all but unique, but the giant creature was not here to pontificate. It was here only to walk.

The desert stretched before it. To the south, a low range of hills buckled the horizon. They were perhaps a day's journey distant, though distance here was difficult to judge, and there were no maps of the Bonelands. It focused on the hills as it walked. By the time the sun had passed its zenith and begun its fall to the west, the hills seemed no closer, and it had to re-assess its estimate of the time it would take to reach them. Beyond the hills, so every story said, there was only more poisoned desert. They were a meaningless marker at best. It might reach them . . . but probably not. Already it could feel the rot.

It paused to eat. Sitting on its huge haunches, the reduced weight of Echo City now many miles to the rear, it felt the rumbling, gnawing processes inside. There was a little pain, but it could compare the sensation only to the shimmering heat haze hanging above the desert far to the west—an insubstantial thing that would vanish as soon as it closed its eyes.

It closed its eyes, and the pain was warmth.

When it stood and started walking again, it looked down at its bare, sprayed legs. The skin was peeling, revealing a dark red rawness beneath. Its feet were blistered and swollen, and several of the tight leather straps had burst. It kicked off one of the folded leather shoes, and it flapped on the desert floor as tight folds unwrapped. And then the shoe was still, and there it would stay forever.

A while later the creature removed the other shoe, because wearing only one had been swinging it slowly around in a great arc across the sands. It corrected its direction of travel and set off once more.

It had passed several bodies on its walk, but just as the sun touched the western horizon it came across the first of the ruined transports. It was a rusted, rotten hulk, its wheels skeletons of metal wrapped in the brittle remains of parched wood. The creature walked close and touched one of the wheels, curiosity lighting a small flame in its limited mind. The wood came apart under its clumsy stroke, drifting to the ground in a cloud of dust and splinters. A gentle breeze that the creature had not even felt carried some of the wooden shards away, and they added themselves to the desert.

Before the ruined vehicle lay two great skeletons of the things that had pulled it this far. Pelts were draped across their bones in places, and within the stark confines of rib cages were the scattered remains of insides not yet burned to nothing by the relentless sun. Their horns were long and graceful, pitted now from the effects of the desert air.

Here and there it saw the mummified remains of human beings. They had been riding the wagon, and perhaps when their beasts succumbed to the desert's toxic influence, they had walked on until they all lay down together to die. The creature did not like to look at them. Though its maker had made it unique, somehow they reminded it of itself.

So it walked on and stared at that undulating horizon, and sometimes the texture of the ground beneath it changed. But it did not look down.

When dusk began to fall, it guessed that Echo City would now be out of sight behind it. But still it did not look back. The future lay before it—too far away to see, beyond its ability to feel—and as it considered what might come, the thing it carried inside seemed excited at the prospect.

It walked through the freezing night. Its motion kept it warm, but all the while it felt itself sickening. The desert's lethal, toxic influence was making itself felt upon the creature's flesh and bones, its blood and fluids, and though built strong it was now becoming weak. Darkness was its friend, though under the silvery sheen of moonlight it could still witness some of its flesh's demise. It was not worried, because it had not been made that way. But it did pause and stare up at the moon, and it realized that come dawn it would never see this sight again.

Sad, unsure what sadness was, it walked on.

When dawn broke on that second day, the creature realized just where the Markoshi Desert had gained its more common name.

The hills were still distant, and speckling the surface of the desert before them lay thousands of bones. There were skulls, some still bearing the leathery remnants of scalp and hair, and a few wearing the wrinkled skin of their hopeful, desperate owners. Beneath and around the skulls lay the skeletons. Older remains were all but buried by drifts, but more-recent escapees from Echo City lay atop the sand. Many of them were still clothed in the outfits they had believed would protect them from the desert's terrible actions, and beneath these, leathered skin was scarred with the rot. Most remains were whole, because not even carrion creatures could survive the Bonelands' poisons. Some had been scattered, however, and here and there the creature saw evidence of violence having been wrought. It knew that the only living things out here to perpetrate such acts would have been other people.

Their equipment lay around them where it had fallen. Bags, water skins, weapons, clothing, an occasional sled or wheeled vehicle, all had been heated by the relentless sun and cooled by the fearsome desert nights, and successive heatings and coolings had destroyed much. There was nothing here to aid the creature in its progress, and after a while it no longer paid heed to the strewn remnants of desperation and hope. It focused on the hills it would never reach, sucked water from the bone straw, and felt the thing inside it rolling and gnawing, making itself strong for the time to come.

It could feel itself weakening, but purpose drove it on. Flesh sloughed from its exposed limbs, and blood speckled the sand beneath it. Its large feet had spread since shedding the shoes, and had it looked back it would have seen the trail of bloody footprints. Sand worked its way into wounds, and the creature felt pain despite the way it had been made, and taught, and given life. It howled, but there was no one to hear.

Eventually it came to a stop among the bones and rocks and hot sands, sinking slowly onto its side and then its back, turning its head so that it could look across the desert at the low hills. They had drawn much closer, it thought, especially in the past few hours when it had been walking with the sun sinking to its right. It felt a sense of accomplishment and hoped its maker was pleased.

Its movements ceased, its eyes grew pale and dry, and its limited awareness of surroundings and purpose drifted away like dust on the breeze. Its only thought as things grew dark was that it had done its very best.

Hearing was the last to go, and the sound that accompanied it down into death was something tearing, and something wet.

The thing emerged from the giant corpse. It had been made with hooked claws and toes with which to rip, and it tore its way out through the weakened flesh. It had also been formed with a sharp ridge running down its forehead to the bridge of its nose, and it used this to saw and snap at the thick ribs that encircled its host's upper half. As it emerged, a bloody violent birth, it also ate and drank. The meat was warm and the blood thick, and strength coursed through its body.

Free of its confines, it remained there for a while as it grew accustomed to its surroundings. It had filled itself with its mother's flesh and blood, but already it could feel this desert's rot.

Its maker had warned it of this. Time was passing, the desert was exerting its poisonous influence, and it knew it had far to go.

Standing naked beneath the sinking sun, it looked to the sky and felt a sense of release that it could not accurately identify or understand. It had little to do with being away from the body now lying beneath and around it, because it thought of that only as meat. It had nothing to do with being able to stretch its arms and flex its clawed fingers at the glittering points of light. Looking back across the desert, marking the bloody prints stretching off into the dusk, it saw a smudge of light low on the horizon. Freedom, release . . . it thought it had something to do with leaving whatever that light represented.

Yet it knew that its destination lay in the opposite direction. It gathered folds of leather around its naked body, filled rough pockets with handfuls of meat from the thing that had birthed it, and started walking.

Daylight came, and night once more, and when it saw the sunrise for the second time it realized that there were no longer bones. The last set of remains it had passed had been wrapped in several layers of thick leather, a chain-mail body shell, and something that resembled the chitinous outer layers of a beetle. The mummified corpse had been lying with its right hand stretched out and finger pointing southward, as if indicating the place it wanted to be. Its mouth had been wide, and it had carried three obsidian teeth. On the corpse's skin, the creature had made out the dark smears of strange markings, and it wondered what that meant.

It had memories of something called Echo City, but they were very old, and they belonged somewhere else. It did not consider the strangeness of carrying such old memories when it had been born for only two days. It had a maker, and that maker's voice was the sole loud, clear thing in its fresh mind. *Walk*, that voice said, *avoid dangers, look south, and travel as far as you can*. It spoke in suggestions rather than words. The creature obeyed.

Though nothing lived in the desert, there were dangers. Around noon of that third day, it entered an area where great holes breathed dark fumes of gas and nightmare. Drawing in these fumes for the first time, the thing fell to its knees as its immature brain was racked with onslaughts of images dredged from some past it did not know. It saw faces and death, madness and war, and the release of an appalling disease that made it open its eyes again to look down upon its own body. It could not see its face to make out whether it resembled those in its nightmare, but its body was the same— and the abuse it suffered clothed it in the same sadness. Skin was weakening, flesh was rotting, and its insides churned as something sought release.

Farther, its maker's voice said, hardly audible through the nightmares. The creature stood and ran, ignoring the staggering pain that pummeled up from its legs as weakening bones crumbled. When they finally snapped, it crawled instead, hauling itself out of that region of holes and ventings, giving it the chance to breathe air that seemed clearer. Its mind settled, leaving it with the idea of its maker.

By dusk on that third day it could crawl no farther. Its fingers had worn away, and whatever ills the desert carried had turned its eyes to mush, its flesh to rotten stuff. It lay still as it birthed the thing it had been made to carry, and the maker had created it so that the pain was only slight.

As darkness came, it tried to imagine the maker saying, *Good*.

The smaller creature crawled from the remains of its mother. It had four legs and a hugely distended stomach, but the legs were long enough to lift it from contact with the sands and strong enough to carry it across the desert at startling speed.

It passed over a low range of hills, negotiating a dry ravine on the other side and continuing into the desert that lay beyond. Nothing lived here but it, though it did not find that strange. It carried vague and distant memories of life and plenty, but it did not suffer loneliness, because the maker was always there. It listened to the maker's songs, poems, and words of wisdom and humor, and though it could not respond, it knew that the maker was pleased. It ran fast and far, avoiding patches of lighter-colored sand, which would have sucked it down to unknown depths, and places where flames twisted across the landscape in defiance of the breeze.

At last night came, and in the deceptive shadows of dusk the thing tripped over a rock and broke one of its legs.

It lay quietly as death approached, feeling the desert's deadly influences now that it was down. It listened to the maker in memories, and even as its rounded stomach split and gushed forth innards, it did not feel the pain.

The thing that rose from the gore and steam walked on.

A day later, as noon scorched the sands and something slumped to the ground to die, the journey came to an end.

As the creature edged toward death, its legs fell apart and revealed the moist heart of itself. It growled as it obeyed what the maker had instructed it to do, defying the sun and the desert, the heat and the air, the dust and the winds. It felt its flesh withered and diseased, but it pushed harder as it birthed its son and willed itself to die, comforted that it was not the desert that had taken it in the end.

The child mewled as it squirmed in the sand. It poked strong fingers through the translucent film that enveloped it and blinked wet, intelligent eyes at the heat and sunlight that rushed in to bathe its soft skin. It tried to stand, but its legs were still shaky. It looked around, seeing only endless sand and sky.

And it imagined its maker growing sad, because there truly was nothing beyond the Bonelands.

Later, perhaps only hours before the child would have died, a shadow fell across it.

Chapter 1

"This is not my home," Peer Nadawa whispered as she came awake. They were the words with which she had comforted herself on the afternoon she arrived in Skulk Canton, and now their recitation was a natural part of welcoming a new day. They had started as defiance but quickly became a mantra necessary for her survival. And they were never spoken lightly.

She opened her eyes to see what sort of day it would be. The ghourt lizard that lived in a crack between her bedroom wall and ceiling was scampering across the wall in a series of short sprints. It was gathering flies and spiders early today, and that meant it would likely rain before noon. Great. Another day spent harvesting stoneshrooms in the wet.

Peer watched the lizard for a while, preparing herself for the morning ritual of rising through the discomfort of old tortures. The lizard shifted so quickly that it seemed to slip from point to point without actually moving, and there were those who believed that ghourts really belonged in the Echoes below the city. Peer was not one of them. It was a foolish idea to believe that such simple creatures could become phantoms. And, besides, her parents had taught her stillness. Relaxed from sleep, she calmed her mind and watched each tiny movement of the lizard—its fluttering heartbeat, lifting toes, and the darting streak as it ran from one place to the next. She pitied the people who did not have the time to see such things, because she had long ago stopped pitying herself. She had all the time in the world.

She sighed and scratched an itch in her left armpit. The little lizard flitted back into its hole, startled at her sudden movement. Propping herself on her left elbow, she grimaced as she started to sit up.

They'd used air shards to penetrate her right arm to the bone. Sharper than any blade made of stone or metal, the shards could never be removed, and they were a constant reminder of her crime. They were set in her bone and cast in her flesh, and it took a while each morning to warm them until they became bearable. That's all they ever were—bearable. Some nights, and on the very worst of days, she could picture the torturer's grin as he slid them in and see the virtuous expression on the Hanharan priest's face as he stood beyond the torture table, praying for salvation for her errant soul. Of the two, it was always that fucking priest she wanted to kill.

Grimacing, Peer sat up and started to gently massage her right arm. The pain from her left hip was flaring now, past the numbness of sleep. They hadn't been so creative with that; the torturer had smashed it with a hammer when she refused to acknowledge Hanharan as the city's firstborn. It was only thanks to Penler's skill with medicines and the knife that she was able to walk at all.

She closed her eyes and went through the pain, as she had every morning for the past three years. Each morning was the same, and yet she had never grown to accept it. She fought against what they had done even though the evidence was here, in pain and broken bones. Penler had asked her many times why she still fought when there was no hope of return, and she had never been able to provide an answer. Truthfully, she did not know.

Gorham's face flashed unbidden across her mind. Perhaps he was haunting her, though for all she knew, he was dead.

Gradually the pain lessened and she sat there for a while, as always, looking around the small room in the house she had been lucky enough to find. It had two floors, and she always slept on the top one. There was a ledge beyond the window that led to other rooftops if she needed to escape, a system of alarms and traps built into the single staircase—that had been Penler's doing as well—and if she stretched and stood just right, she could see the desert from her window. Some nights, if she could not sleep, she spent a long time simply looking.

One of the downstairs rooms still contained several paintings of the family that had lived there before the salt plague a hundred years before. Peer had no idea what had happened to them other than they had died. *Everyone* in Skulk Canton had died, either from the plague or from the brutal purging that quickly followed, ordered by the Marcellans. But she liked keeping their images in the house. It had something to do with respect.

"Time to leave," she muttered. "Important places to go, powerful people to see. Stoneshrooms to pick." She often spoke to herself when there was no one else to listen. In Skulk there were many who would understand, and probably many more who would consider her mad. There were also those who viewed her as fair game; Echo City's criminals were a varied breed.

After washing in a bowl of cold water and eating a quick breakfast, she set about arming herself. A knife in her belt, three soft widowgas balls in her pocket, and the wide, short sword on view. She had never grown used to the sword, but Penler assured her that it would scare off any casual aggressors. Up to now, it had seemed to work.

He often chided her for living on her own. *A woman on her own here in Skulk . . .* he'd say, shaking his head, then pursing his lips because he knew exactly what she thought of such attitudes. Still, she knew that he had only her safety at heart. After berating him with a playful punch, she'd argue that most criminals here weren't really criminals at all. *They execute the really bad ones*, she would say. *Some always slip through*, he'd counter. And so their little play went on.

Today, she and Penler were meeting for lunch down by the city wall. He said that he had something to tell her. As always for Penler, the mystery was the thrill.

When the sun was up and birdsong filled the air, and Peer was feeling sharper and brighter than usual, she often considered Skulk Canton as evidence of the basic goodness in people.

Since the devastating plague, it had become the place to which criminals and undesirables were banished by the ruling Marcellans. Murderers, rapists, and pedophiles were still crucified on the vast walls of the central Marcellan Canton, but lesser criminals—pickpockets, violent drunks, and political dissidents—now had a new place to be sent. The vast underground prisons in the Echoes below the city had been closed, because the abandoned Skulk was far easier and less dangerous to police. It was a city unto itself, and the criminals were left to make it their own.

Over the past few decades, they had done just that. It could hardly be called thriving—they still relied on regular food deliveries from Crescent Canton, and a new canal had been built from the Southern Reservoir in Course Canton to ration their water—but the majority of people in Skulk lived a reasonable life, and most contributed to making their community a bearable place to live.

Naturally, there were those who viewed it as their own private playground. Thieves ran rampant in certain areas; gangs formed, fought, and dispersed; and there were a dozen men and women that Peer could name who considered themselves rulers of Skulk. But as with elsewhere in Echo City, these gangs and gang leaders ruled only those who were at their own level. Violence was frequent but usually confined to rival factions.

Those who kept to themselves were mostly left alone.

Upon her arrival, Peer had been convinced that she would be raped and killed within days. Terribly injured, traumatized from the tortures she had endured and the fact that she was no longer considered an inhabitant of Echo City, she had scampered into a building close to the razed area of ground that marked Skulk's northern boundary with the rest of the city, and there she had waited to die. She drifted in and out of consciousness. Time lost itself. Day and night seemed to juggle randomly with her senses. And one day after passing out, she woke up in Penlér's rooms.

He told her that three men had brought her to him and then left. He did not even know their names.

Walking along the street toward the stoneshroom fields where she spent most of her mornings, Peer tried to deny the sense of contentment that threatened. She'd been feeling it for a while, as it sought to put down roots in a place that she had never believed she could call home. There was so much she missed—her friends, her small canal-side home in Mino Mont Canton, and Gorham most of all—that it felt wrong to be happy here. She had been banished from the world she knew, escaping execution only because the Marcellans knew it would be dangerous should she become a martyr. In Skulk she could fade away. She was a prisoner who was growing to like her prison, an exiled victim of an insidious dictatorship who was forgetting the fire and rage that had fueled her past. Often she would strive to reignite that fire, but it never felt the same. *Just let it come,* Penler would say to her, referring to the gentle contentment and not the righteous passion she had once felt. She hated him and loved him for that, the infuriating old man. He was trying to save her, and she was determined to convince herself that she did not want to be saved.

This is not my home, she thought again as she walked through the narrow streets, but this morning Skulk Canton felt just fine.

She passed through a small square and saw familiar figures setting up stalls for breakfast. She bought a lemon pancake and had her mug filled with rich five-bean, and she dallied for a while, enjoying the sights and smells of cooking, the sound of bartering, and the good-natured air of the place.

"You'll be late!" a big man called as he stirred soup in a huge pot.

"The 'shrooms will wait, Maff," she said. "What's cooking?"

He motioned her over, and Peer smiled as she negotiated her way through a throng of hungry people. Maff always enjoyed revealing the recipes to his top-secret brews.

"Tell no one," he whispered as she drew close, his breath smelling of beer and pipe smoke, his big hand closing around her long, tied hair. "I had a consignment of dart root delivered yesterday. I'm mixing it with rockzard legs, some sweet potatoes from Course, and my own special ingredient." He tapped the side of her nose and glanced around, as if they were discussing a coup against the Marcellans themselves.

Peer raised an eyebrow, waiting for the great revelation.

"Electric-eel hearts," he whispered into her ear. "Fresh. Still charged." She felt his bead-bedecked beard tickling her neck and pulled away, laughing softly. When she looked at him, Maff was nodding seriously, pearls of sweat standing out on his suntanned skin. He touched her nose again. "Tell no one."

"Your secret's safe with me, Maff."

"So . . . ?" he asked, lifting a deep spoon of the soup toward a bowl.

Peer held up both hands. "I'd like to wake up in the morning."

Maff shrugged and continued stirring the soup, and even as she bade him farewell, he called over a short, ratlike man. He whispered in the man's ear, nodded down at the soup, and his secret was told again.

In her early days here, Peer would have wondered what crimes Maff had committed to deserve banishment. Such thoughts rarely crossed her mind anymore. She left the square and weaved her way through narrow streets, the buildings overhead seeming to lean in and almost touch. The sun shone, though she still thought it would likely rain that afternoon, and Skulk Canton was buzzing with life.

She passed a group of men and women lounging on the front steps of a large building. They wore knives and swords on show, and all bore identical scars on their left cheeks—the unmistakable arc of a rathawk's wing. They observed her with lazy eyes and full purple lips, displaying the signs of subtle slash addiction, and one of them called to her softly. Laughter followed. She ignored the call and walked on, maintaining the same pace. She didn't want them to think she was running because of them, but slowing could have been seen as a reaction to the voice. They were part of the Rage gang—slash dealers and sex vendors—and she had no wish to be involved with them in any way.

She soon reached the first of the stoneshroom fields. There were already dozens of people at work, scrambling across the spread of ruined buildings in their search for the prized fungi.

Much of the wild plant growth had been cleared from the rubble, making the stoneshrooms easier to spot and giving them space in which to grow, and the ruins were stark and depressing in the morning sun. Some areas still bore the dark evidence of fire, even after so long, and to Peer the ruin seemed recent, not a hundred years old. She breathed in deeply, closed her eyes, smiled as she tried to drive down the dark thoughts that always haunted her, then went to work.

She knew most of the stoneshroom gatherers, and they were a friendly group to work with. They were all out for themselves—picking the 'shrooms was only the first part of the process, the next being their cleaning, preparation, and sale—but often, if a good spread was found, word would filter quietly to the several other harvesters in the vicinity. They were a prized plant because of their heavy meatiness, and they were one of the few foodstuffs harvested within Skulk Canton. *If ever we claim independence,* Penler had once quipped, *we'll all turn into stoneshrooms.*

Peer worked hard, delving down into the spaces between collapsed walls, shifting small blocks aside where she could, and spending long moments of stillness sniffing for the fungi. Some hunters sang, and the song was taken up by others, but Peer remained silent today. She was looking forward to seeing Penler for lunch, and she hoped to have several 'shrooms prepared for him by then.

As noon approached, storm clouds drifted in over the city to the north. Peer derived some small satisfaction from knowing that it rained on the rest of Echo City before it rained on Skulk Canton. She made the most of the final touch of sunlight, then set off for the city walls.

Penler was sitting on a wooden bench looking out over the Markoshi Desert. Peer saw something symbolic in that. The bench must have been placed atop the wall by Watchers long ago, because the Marcellans and their Hanharan religion looked only inward, and Penler knew her Watcher history.

"Penler," Peer said as she approached. The old man glanced up and smiled, wiping his lips. He nursed a bottle of Crescent wine in his lap, a good ruby red, and she smiled at his flagrant display of resourcefulness. Close though they had become, he had never told her how he still procured such produce from outside.

"Peer, my dear," he said, shuffling along the bench. "Been keeping it warm for you."

The first drops of rain spattered the stone paving around them as she sat down. Penler was wearing a heavy coat with a wide hood, and she pulled up her own hood. The sound of rain striking it made her feel isolated, even though she sat there with her friend.

"I brought some stoneshrooms," she said, taking the folded cloth from her pocket. "Not the best of the crop today, but I arrived at the fields late."

Penler nodded and ran his fingers across the proffered fungi. He moved his hand back and forth, then paused above one of the smaller, darker slices. He leaned in and sniffed, then grunted in satisfaction. He could always hone in on the best of everything.

"I have some fresh bread," he said as he chewed, "and the wine is good."

"They'll execute me for drinking it," Peer said, laughing and taking a swig from his bottle. He was right; it was excellent.

"Even the Marcellans themselves won't be drinking better wine today," Penler said, and beneath the humor lay the familiar seriousness. He'd been sent here many years before when he published a book exploring the Dragarians' beliefs. The prosecuting Hanharan priests had claimed it was not the publication that marked him as a heretic but his sympathy for the Dragarians and their dead prophet—murdered by the Marcellans' own Scarlet Blades, after all—that shone through his writing. Proud, stubborn, Penler had confirmed or denied nothing, and his future was set.

"Fuck the Marcellans," she said, "and get that bread out."

They ate in silence for a while, comfortable in each other's company without feeling the need to fill it with noise. Peer looked out over the flat, featureless desert, watching the line of rain progressing outward as the clouds drifted overhead. Sands darkened, and before long the rain front had moved too far for her to see.

"The weather knows no boundaries," she said, but Penler only laughed. "What?"

"You," he said. "Still watching."

"I was born a Watcher," she said. "It was in my heart, such belief. I can't bear ignorance. I can't understand people who *don't* think such a thing."

"You don't understand me?" he asked, a tricksy question. She glanced sidelong at him, and he was staring at her with raised eyebrows and a curious smile on his lips. For an old man, his mind was agile. That's why she liked his company so much.

"You're an explorer," she said. She'd told him that before, and it seemed to please him immensely. In Echo City—a place mostly known—true explorers had only their minds in which to travel. That, or down into the Echoes.

Penler smiled, but it did not quite touch his startling blue eyes.

"Penler?"

"My exploring days are long behind me," he said. "I'm getting old, and sometimes I wish I could . . ." He trailed off and looked at the stoneshroom in the palm of his hand.

"Wish you could what?"

But he shrugged and stared back out at the desert.

The rain fell around them, light but drenching, and soon they were huddled together, sharing warmth and closing in so they could hear each other speak. It was strange, sitting side by side talking, because their raised hoods meant that they could not see each other unless they turned. Peer spoke and, when Penler responded, it sounded like a disembodied voice. The Marcellans claimed that Hanharan spoke to them in their sleep. *We're ruled by ghosts*, Peer thought, but that could not make her angry. She believed in a larger world beyond the deadly desert—never seen, never known—and what was that if not a ghost of possibility?

"You said you have something to tell me," she said at last. She heard Penler sigh and take another drink of wine. The rain fell. The desert sands were dark and wet. She loved sitting here at the southern tip of Echo City with the whole world behind her.

"Whispers," he said at last. "Peer, you know I have . . . ways and means."

She turned to him, took the wine bottle, and lifted it in a casual salute. "*Something about you*, is how they say it. Dark arts. Bollocks, I say."

"Getting things is easy," he continued, "and the border is not solid. There's money, and people will do a lot for that, whatever their declared allegiances. But I've never dealt in money."

"No. You deal in information." Peer sipped at the wine. It was almost gone, and she wanted them to relish the final drop.

"Yes. Information. It comes, and it goes. Much of what comes is of no consequence or is likely false. Some of what I hear, I store." He tapped his head, gave her that lopsided grin once again. "And some of what I hear, on occasion . . . sometimes I try to forget."

"Now you're worrying me."

Penler pressed his lips together and turned away, and as he did so the rain caught his face and spilled like tears.

"What is it?" Peer asked, suddenly afraid.

"Murmurs from the Garthans," he said.

"The Garthans?" Peer had never even seen one. They lived way down below the city, in some of the earliest Echoes that were supposedly tens of thousands of years old. Some said they were pale and blind and so far removed from surface dwellers that they were another species. Others claimed that they were cannibals, fondly feasting on offerings of human meat presented by those eager for their strange subterranean drugs. The only certainty was that they were no friends of top dwellers.

"Rumors of something wrong," Penler said.

"You've heard such things before. You've told me, there are *always* stories from the Garthans."

"Yes, that's true. But this time they're afraid."

"Afraid of what?"

"I don't know. But the Garthans are never afraid of *anything*."

Peer waited. Penler felt the pressure of her stare and turned so that she could see his face, hidden within his coat's wide hood. She was concerned for him, because his voice had sounded . . . different.

"Why tell me?" she asked.

"Because you're a Watcher."

"And what does that make you?"

Penler smiled then, but once again it did not touch his eyes. Raindrops struck his face again as he tilted his head back to laugh, but his effort to lighten the heavy mood felt strangely false.

"I think that sometimes people need to build falsehoods for their own ends."

Peer bristled. For such an intelligent man, Penler often displayed an ignorance that she found shocking. She'd tried to see through it many times, but his opinion was a solid front, and whatever lay behind wallowed in shadows that perhaps even he could not breach. Once, perhaps . . . years ago. But now he was growing old. Maybe the fire had gone from him.

"That's what the Marcellans call any beliefs they don't agree with," she said coldly. "Falsehoods. They told me to deny my own false beliefs as they slid the air shards into my arm." She held her right biceps with her left hand, squeezing to feel a rush of warm pain. It always fueled her anger.

"Peer," Penler said, and his voice carried such wisdom and age. "I know very well what they did to you. And you know me better than that."

Do I? she thought. It had been only three years, though in truth it felt like more. In all that time, Penler had yet to betray his true beliefs, even to her. Sometimes she thought he was a secularist, sitting apart and observing while his friends expended time and effort on their own diverse philosophies. And other times, like now, she suspected that he might be a devout believer in something he craved to disbelieve. There were contradictions in Penler that scared her and an intelligence that she sometimes suspected would be the death of him. Even while he told her to be calm and accepting, he fought.

"So the Garthans are afraid," she said, "and the rain still falls where no one can walk." She stared out across the desert from atop the city wall. A hundred years ago this would have been a place for market stalls and street entertainers, but now the wall's wide top was simply another place to sit and wonder.

"I have to go," Penler said. "Will you eat with me this evening?"

"Are you cooking?" Peer asked.

"Of course."

"Hmm." She did not turn, even when she sensed him standing beside her. And she could not contain her smile. "Last time, you cooked that pie and I had the shits for a week."

"Bad pigeon," Penler said. He was already walking away. "I'll see you before dusk. You can stay, if you like."

"I will," Peer said. It was not wise to walk Skulk's streets after dark. She watched Penler leave, and as he reached the head of the stone staircase, he waved. She waved back. Through the heavy rain, she could not see his expression.

Chilled, she stood and walked to the parapet, chewing on the last of the stoneshroom as she went. She liked looking over the edge and down at the desert. Where she stood was civilization, order, comparative safety, and the whole world and history of Echo City. Down there, where the desert began, was the symbolic boundary of their world. People often walked the sands close to the city wall, of course. In places the wall had degraded and crumbled, and it was easy enough to work your way down to the desert, because where the wall was solid there were no doors or gates. There was no need. But those brave explorers never remained there for long; soon they were scampering back up the stone pile again, waving away the respectful cheers of their peers or the admiring glances of those they had set out to impress. The city drew them back.

The desert was death, and those who had ventured far out and returned had all died horribly. Some had time to reveal what they had seen—the Bonelands, the dead, those who had gone before them shriveling in the sun—but most died without saying anything, diseased flesh falling from their brittle bones and their insides turned to bloody paste, rotted by the desert's toxicity. Gorham had once told Peer that he'd seen two people die this way, and he would never forget the terror in their eyes.

The desert had always been this way, and such a terrible place attracted its myths and legends. There were the Dragarians, shut away and isolated in their canton for more than five hundred years now, who believed that their savior, Dragar, would emerge from the desert at the city's final hour to lead them into their mysterious Honored Darkness. There was the Temple of the Seventy-seven Custodians, who claimed that the desert was home to six-legged gods that watched over Echo City. But the Markoshi Desert—commonly known as the Bonelands—was the end of the world. And there were the Watchers, her people. They believed that there was something beyond and that their future lay in countering the desert's terrible effects.

She never grew bored of this. As the rain came down heavier, Peer leaned on the wall and watched.

At first, she thought it was a breeze blowing through the rain. The shadow shifted far out in the desert—a slightly more solid shape amid the unremitting downpour. She frowned and shielded her eyes, blinking away moisture. The day had grown dim, and the cold was making her hip ache.

The top of the wall remained deserted. Most people were sheltering from the rain or doing whatever it was they did to make their lives easier. Penler had probably reached the place he was happy enough to call home. Peer was alone . . . and the chill that hit her when she next saw the shifting shape made that loneliness even more intense.

There's something out there, she thought, and the idea was shocking. *Nothing* lived in the desert, because it was a place of death. She strained to see farther, leaning on the parapet in a vain attempt to take her closer. Curtains of rain blew from east to west, wiping the movement from view, but between gusts the shape was always there. *Something out there, and it's coming this way*.

She glanced frantically left and right. To her left, a tower protruded above the wall, but she knew that the staircase in there led only up, not down. She knew of a small breach to her right, maybe half a mile away, that had collapsed a hundred years before, during the purging of Skulk Canton. Many fires had been set back then, and it was said that a pile of thousands of bodies had been thrown from the wall and burned. The intensity of the flames had made the stonework brittle, bringing down a section of wall.

Peer ran. She paused every few heartbeats to glance out over the desert; the shape was definitely there, closing, resolving, and her heart started to pummel from more than exertion, because *it looked like a person*. The way it moved, the way it shifted behind the veils of rain, seeming to hunch over as if trying to protect its face from the unrelenting storm, gave it all the characteristics of a human being. ·

And then she saw something strange. The figure stopped, and perhaps it was the first time it had looked up in a long while, because it paused where it was and leaned back, looking at the great wall before it and the city beyond.

Even though it was impossible through the rain and over this distance, Peer felt that she met the person's eyes.

She ran on, finding it difficult to tear her gaze away, and tripped and went down. *Right arm*, she thought, *left hip*, and she fell awkwardly so that she jarred both. She cried out, then looked around to see if anyone had heard her. In the street below, a couple of people dashed from one building to another, but they seemed unaware of her presence, and she was happy to leave them to themselves. Biting her lip, standing, she concentrated on the cool rain instead of the heat of her old injuries.

When she looked again, the figure had started running.

It was a man in a yellow robe.

And past the hushing rain, past her thundering heartbeat, she heard his scream.

Peer reached the breach in the wall and worked her way down the precarious slope. The rain made the tumbled blocks slippery, but that shouting still reverberated in her ears, driving her. She stumbled once or twice, jarring her right arm again, but then she reached the bottom.

She paused on the final block, feet a handbreadth above the ground. *The desert is death*. This was drummed into everyone in Echo City, from birth to the moment they died, and though she was exiled for sedition and still in possession of her own inquiring mind, it was difficult to deny such teaching. She stared at her heavy boots, then past them at the sodden ground. It was muddy. Sand flowed in rivulets, shallow puddles were forming, and for the thousandth time she wondered where the death dwelled. In the sand? In the air she was breathing even now? Many had written and spoken of the Bonelands, but none had derived a definitive answer.

And then she heard a shout, and, looking to her left, she saw a man kneeling in the mud at the base of the city wall.

She stepped down onto the sand and ran. She slowed only when she neared him, then paused a dozen steps away. He looked up, his eyes wide and fearful, his face gaunt, and he seemed as terrified as she was.

Who? she wanted to ask, but she could not form words. His clothes were of a style she had never seen before, his robe a dirty yellow. Over one shoulder he carried a bag, and strange things protruded from it. The rain ran from his white hair and down across his face. And then he opened his mouth.

"Who . . . ?" Peer managed, because she felt it was important to say something first.

"You're not her," the man said. Then he fell onto his face and, somewhere over the city, lightning thrashed.

Chapter 2

Gorham stood at the border of two cantons and smelled the sweetness of freshwater. The rain had ceased, the storm passing to the south, and before him lay the Western Reservoir, three miles across and speckled with boats and canoes. He heard laughter from the beach, where a group of people were eating rock crabs cooked over a huge fire pit dug into the sands. One of them glanced his way. The young woman smiled, and Gorham tried to smile back, wishing only that he could abandon himself to such casual actions. But his life was far removed from this.

"Gorham. We need to go." Malia plucked at his sleeve and walked toward the border post, glancing back to make sure he was following. He smiled at her but did not receive a smile in return. Stern face, short severe hair, Malia was a widow who had never finished grieving, and though she was reliable in a fight, Gorham had never found her to be the most scintillating company.

"One more moment," he said, and leaned on the metal railing to look across the beach one last time. The picnickers were arranging themselves into three small teams now for a game of searchball, and the woman who had smiled at him skipped in the sand, hair floating, breasts moving heavily beneath her light shirt. Her joyous expression was absolute. She did not look his way again.

"For fuck's sake," Malia muttered.

Gorham turned and rested his back against the railing,

looking east at the imposing hills of Marcellan Canton. Echo City's rulers' huge home district had been built upon so frequently that it was much higher than the rest of the city, its Echoes below—those old places, forgotten streets, emptied buildings, and past times—deeper and more complex than elsewhere. Each successive generation of Marcellans seemed to want to stamp their own mark on the city, and they did that by building and naming a series of structures after themselves. Why they could not simply rename older places, Gorham did not know. He supposed it was all to do with ego.

But he heard Malia's impatience, so he nodded and started walking.

The lakefront was bustling. A waterfood restaurant was doing brisk business, the smell of cooking emanating from its open doors and windows and enticing people in. Gorham felt a rumble of hunger. Several taverns had opened their front shutters so that patrons could spill onto the street, and some raucous songs were already under way. The songs changed as Gorham and Malia passed each successive tavern, past tunes fading, newer ones increasing in volume, and it seemed they were fighting for dominance. Later there might be real fighting, but for now the revelers seemed good-natured.

If only they knew, Gorham thought, glancing across the road at a group of men and women seated outside a brothel. They were drinking cheap Mino Mont wine from huge clay carafes, and the air around them was hazed with slash smoke from the long pipes snaking down the side of the building. People took turns on the pipes, their eyes blank and soft with the effects of the burning drug. One of the women was chopped, her three legs spread to reveal two barely covered muffs. Twice the income. He saw the blankness in her eyes, which had nothing to do with slash and everything to do with amateur chopping. She was so not there that she did not even appear sad.

Malia had reached the border checkpoint, and she glanced back as she handed over her papers. The two Scarlet Blade border guards seemed tired and bored, and they opened and closed her lifecard without even looking at it. The taller of the two waved her on, and Gorham handed his card to the other soldier. The soldier yawned, looked at the card, glanced at Gorham.

"What's your business in Crescent?" he asked.

"We're sourcing a new supplier for plums," he said. "Our old one let us down."

The soldier nodded, scratching stubble that a Scarlet Blade should never wear. "Can't beat a good plum. Have fun."

Gorham nodded and passed through the border. *Have fun.* If they knew where he was going and whom he was going to see, they'd have pinned him down and slit his throat, then called reinforcements to interrogate everyone in sight. The people on the beach would be washing sand from their wounds for days. The drinkers would be thrown in jail until they were sober enough to be interrogated, and the whores and patrons would be exposed to their families, shame being a useful tool in gaining the truth. Only the three-legged whore would be left alone. Badly chopped people like her saw little and thought even less.

In Crescent Canton, the landscape changed abruptly. The buildings lining the road became more intermittent—homes and farm buildings now, rather than taverns and shops—and though they could still hear the revelry across the border behind them, Crescent was so obviously a different place. The reservoir marked part of the border, and the landscape beyond was a network of irrigation channels and pumping stations, with several great tusked swine pushing in circles at each pump to keep it working. A short fat man with bright red hair was waddling from one pump to the next, feeding the swine and singing songs of encouragement to keep them moving. He raised a lazy hand in greeting, and Gorham waved back.

"He'll remember us now," Malia said.

"Malia, thousands of people pass through the border every day. He probably waves to all of them."

"Still. Can't hurt to be cautious."

"There's caution and there's paranoia."

"Gorham, everyone *is* out to get us." Malia smiled, but it was a cool expression. He couldn't remember ever hearing her laugh.

There were many people on the road winding through the fields. Those coming from the opposite direction guided tusked swine pulling carts laden with fruits, vegetables, and plants with their root bundles bound with silk. Some hauled trolleys loaded with well-packed wine bottles, a few of these employing armed guards who eyed anyone approaching too close. Certain Crescent wines were worth more per bottle than the average Course inhabitant made in a week, and Gorham knew that most of it was destined for Marcellan Canton. Others walked alone, but their faces often displayed the contentment of a deal well done. Crescent Canton was the heart, lungs, and pantry of Echo City, the most fertile ground and the lowest part of the city, and the air here felt different. Gorham loved coming here, even when fruit and vegetables and other foods were the last things on his mind.

They walked for four miles. The landscape was given entirely to crops: fruit bushes, grapevines, vegetable fields, tobacco trees, and, here and there, the towering spires of mepple orchards, the red fruits as large as a person and jealously guarded against bird attack by vicious wisps. Farms dotted the gently rolling hills—some small, others spread over a wide area. Occasionally there were larger settlements where the farm workers lived, and the most expansive of these were raised slightly above the surrounding area. Below them lay their Echoes—old homes and streets and temples—but for as long as anyone could remember, Crescent had been farmland. Most of its subterranean Echoes consisted of long-dead fields, dried canals, and deserted farm buildings. On those rare occasions when its phantoms came to the surface, they haunted crops, not people.

"Almost there," Malia said. She'd hardly spoken for the entire walk, and though Gorham was used to this, it still irritated him. She was so focused on their purpose that she rarely let anything else in. He remembered her husband, Bren, well and could still picture the shocking sight of his body crucified high on the walls of Marcellan Canton. That had been almost three years ago. He'd long since rotted and fallen, but in Malia's mind his death was still on display.

If she'd had her way, they would have started a revolution long before now.

They stopped at the entrance to an old farm complex, sitting on the low stone wall. It seemed quiet. Gorham could just see a couple of figures on the road a way back, maybe a mile distant, and several miles beyond that was the imposing mass of Marcellan.

Malia was looking up, but the sky was clear of all but clouds.

"Time to go down," she said. It sounded as if she almost relished the idea of their descent. For Gorham, saying good-bye to the daylight was like ceasing breathing.

They walked along the overgrown lane to the farm. The main house was a ruin, its roof tumbled in a fire many years before, and the outbuildings had fallen into disrepair. It was said the place was haunted by more than phantoms, and though it was the Baker who propagated those stories, Gorham knew that he should believe every one of them.

After all, she had many more things at her disposal than ghosts.

Inside one of the farm's ruined barns, beneath a pile of fallen tools that had apparently rusted together into a single tangled heap, was one of the entrances to the Echo where the Baker maintained her laboratory. There were many ways in, Gorham knew, and perhaps fewer ways out, but this was the only one he and the Watchers had been told about, and he was quite certain it was theirs alone. As far as he was aware, the Baker—her name was Nadielle, but she had breathed that to him only on their third meeting—had not yet lied to him. The time might come, he knew, when events would start to prove more difficult, but he trusted her as much as he trusted any-one. Almost as much as he had trusted Peer.

He closed his eyes and thought briefly of his old love. When these moments came, he tried to imagine her as dead as Malia's husband—rotted away, gone. And he mourned.

"What is it?" Malia asked.

"Nothing. Here, help me." They grabbed a handle or blade each, and as they lifted, the tumbled tools rose in one solid mass. Beneath, when they kicked away the scattered straw, dust, and powdered chickpig shit, lay the trapdoor that led down into Crescent's Echoes.

"I hate this," Malia said. "It's the future we're looking to, isn't it?"

"And the Baker's going to help us get there," Gorham said. "So what better place to hide than the past?"

He lifted the trapdoor himself and started down the narrow wooden staircase. There were several metal torches fixed to the wall, and he took one and lit its wick with the flints supplied. He shook it and listened to the thick slosh of oil. It sounded full. As ever, Nadielle seemed prepared.

Malia descended behind him, picking up her own torch, and their journey down to the Baker's laboratory began. The wooden staircase ended in a short, narrow corridor, at the end of which was a metal door, bolted shut. Gorham twisted four bolts in a specific sequence and heard tumblers turning. He pulled, and the door squealed as it came away from the frame. A breath of air sighed out from beyond, carrying with it strange smells and the hint of faraway voices. They might have been phantoms or the whispered communication of the Baker's guards. Whichever, he and Malia would meet them soon.

Beyond the corridor was a slightly sloping cave. It had once been a field of grapevines, and some of the thicker stems were still visible protruding above the dust. Perhaps the old fields had been ruined by overuse or poisoned by some long-ago cataclysm. In places there were huge, thick columns supporting the roof, gnarled and knotted with the twisted metal and cemented stone used to build up from the land below. There were footprints here and there, and, with no breeze to shift dust, they could have been recent or ancient. Some of them were his own from previous visits. It disturbed Gorham that he could not tell which were which.

He and Malia walked across the underground plain, their torches setting shadows dancing in the distance.

With a hiss, the first of the Baker's chopped came in. It drifted low, trailing several long tendrils in the dust as though drawing energy from the ground. Gorham had seen this one before and thought it might once have been a woman, but now it was something else. Six arms, four thick legs, and two sets of light membranous wings made it unique, just as all of the

Baker's creations were unique. It dribbled something from its wide mouth as it hovered, and its obsidian eyes flickered this way and that—perhaps blind, or maybe possessed of a sight Gorham did not understand.

"Gorham and Malia," Gorham said. His voice sounded unnaturally loud, echoing into the dark distance.

The thing circled them, wings beating so fast that they were almost invisible. They were virtually silent, though their downdraft whisked up a cloud of fine dust that soon dimmed the effect of the torches. One set of arms reached forward—the hands were horribly human, fingernails blackened and sharp—and it came in quickly to touch their faces. Gorham was prepared, but he heard Malia gasp in shock behind him.

"It's fine," he said quietly. Her hand reached gently for his shoulder, seeking contact.

The thing flew away, and within heartbeats it was lost to view.

"I can never get used to this," Malia said.

"She's got a lot to guard against. A lot to be afraid of."

"With what she can do, I can't imagine her being afraid of anything."

"You'd be surprised." Gorham walked on, aiming for the far end of the field.

They passed through another door and started their descent through a maze of caverns and tunnels that confused him every time. They waited in the third cavern for what they knew would come, and the chopped man emerged from a crack in the wall within moments of their arrival. He was short and exceedingly thin, his head half the size of a normal man's, and his naked skin was constantly slick from some strange secretion. He moved with a disconcerting grace—almost dancing, like the troupes that performed on the streets of Mino Mont—and Gorham wondered how flexible his bones would be.

"My name's Gorham," he said. The small man glanced back, blinked softly, then continued on his way.

"I don't think he likes you, Gorham," Malia said.

"I doubt he even knows what we're saying."

The man led them from cavern to tunnel, cave to crevasse, and a while later they crossed a shifting rope bridge that spanned a dry canal. The bed was speckled with white shapes, and Gorham thought perhaps they were skeletons. He did not pause to make out whether they were human. He had never been this way before.

"How many routes are there to this damned place?" Malia said when she caught sight of the bones. Gorham did not answer, because he had been wondering the same thing.

They passed through an old village. Most of the buildings were in ruins, but there were a couple that still bore their roofs, almost fully tiled and with chimneys intact. Behind one of the glassless windows, in a building that might have been a temple to forgotten gods, shone a pale light. Gorham thought for a moment that torches had been lit to mark their way, but then he realized that was a foolish idea. This man had been sent to guide them in. And Nadielle would do nothing so obvious.

"Gorham," Malia whispered.

"I know." At the sound of their voices the light flared slightly, then blinked out. The phantom went to hide.

Beyond the ruined village they hit an ancient road, where wheel ruts cast thousands of years before were still visible. The man led them along the center of the road, and then without warning he turned right and ran into the dark.

"Wait!" Malia called. Her voice did not echo at all, as if the pressing darkness dampened it.

"Hey!" Gorham went to follow, but the man was already out of sight. *Slipped away into a crack in the ground,* he thought. He wondered how many of the Baker's chopped were watching them.

"So what the crap are we supposed to do now?" Malia said.

Gorham looked around, turning slowly and following the light from his torch. "Nothing," he said at last. "We're almost there."

"I've never come this way before."

"Nor I. Like I said, she's being very careful."

"Well, when she hears—"

"Hush."

Malia fell silent, and Gorham closed his eyes briefly. *Yes, when she hears what we have to say.* But right now he was trying not to look that far ahead. In the dark, in the coolness of forgotten times, he was simply looking forward to seeing Nadielle again.

"You must be hungry," a voice said. "Thirsty. This way. The Baker has a feast for you."

Gorham smiled, and five steps from them a chopped woman lit her torch. There were three of them in all, standing within striking distance of Gorham and Malia. Until that moment, none of them had been visible. They were naked, and their skin seemed to shift in and out of focus as the oil torches flickered. They each had a third arm protruding from between their breasts that ended in a wicked-looking serrated blade, and spines along their sides were raised and ready to spit. The Pseran triplets. Nadielle had told him about them—*Three of my best*, she had said, *three of my* most *perfect*—but this was the first time he had laid eyes on them. He knew now why the Baker was so proud. Beautiful, shapely, exquisite, intoxicating—and given cause, any one of them could kill him before he blinked.

"What in the name of Hanharan . . . ?" Malia whispered.

"No," Gorham said, "nothing to do with him at all."

The Pserans started walking, keeping far enough apart to avoid presenting a combined target, and Gorham and Malia followed.

He had been to the Baker's laboratory many times before this visit. Each time it had seemed slightly different—dimensions altered, design subtly shifted, the space it occupied flexed or folded—though the one constant was that it was filled with equipment that meant nothing to him. He knew some of what Nadielle did but never how she did it. That had always been the way of the Bakers, and the mystery was part of her allure.

The final door closed behind them and the Pserans slipped away. As Gorham glanced around to see where they had gone, he heard a low chuckle, and when he turned forward again the Baker was there.

"Gorham," she said. She seemed amused. "You look hungry. You like my Pserans?"

Nadielle was the only woman who knew how to make him blush.

"And Malia. It's nice to see you again." She sounded so sincere.

"And you, Baker," Malia said. "Your Pserans say you have a feast for us."

"They don't lie," Nadielle said. "Not unless I tell them to." She was staring at Gorham, enjoying his embarrassment, and she was more beautiful than ever. Last time down here, as they were rolling on Nadielle's bed, her legs wrapped around his back to hold him deep within her, she'd whispered into his ear: *They watch.* He'd known who she meant, because she was so proud of her chopped. They were like her children. It had given him a strange thrill then, and now that sensation returned. He glanced around again, feeling their eyes on him still, realizing that was what they were made to do.

Nadielle laughed out loud and turned, leading them deep into her laboratory.

Her seven womb vats were all full, condensation bejeweling their surfaces and dripping in a steady stream to the stone floor. The vats were made from metal or heavy gray stone—Gorham had never been entirely sure which, and he dared not touch one—and they stood propped with thick wooden buttresses wedged against the floor, giving the impression of a temporary placement. There were drainage holes around the vats to take any spillages, and bubbles of strange gas popped thickly from several of them. *I wonder what she's chopping now*, Gorham thought. The awe he felt each time he visited her down here was rightly placed, because she could do something that no one else in Echo City was able to do. Many *attempted* to copy, and the results were the twin-twatted whore, soldiers with clubs instead of fists, men with cocks like a third leg . . . and, sometimes, monsters. But no one could match Nadielle's talent or finesse, passed down to her from Bakers long past. No one ever had.

They left the vat room and entered a place of chaos. There were tables and chairs, cupboards and shelving units, baskets slung in chains that could be raised and lowered from the ceiling when required, boxes strewn around the room's perimeter, books piled high or pressed open on the surfaces, and many fine glass containers bearing all kinds of matter—some fluid, some more solid, and some that looked like heavy gas. Other containers held material not so easily identifiable.

Nadielle weaved across the room and through a curtained doorway. Gorham followed, and the smells of Nadielle's living quarters inspired a rush of memories. He glanced at her bed—blankets awry, pillows propped up, books strewn across its surface—and wished that Malia had not come.

But their purpose here was serious, and Nadielle was aware of that. She guided them to her table and sat down.

"I know you've come for something important," she said. "It's not just another visit to read my mother's books or to pore over the maps and charts I have down here. Not even . . ." She nodded toward the stacked bookshelf where the three Old Texts were hidden away. Gorham had read them, and the power and intelligence evident in books purported to be more than four thousand years old still staggered him.

"No," he said, "not them. Although what we came to discuss might concern them more than ever before."

"You Watchers," Nadielle said, a smile pricking up the corners of her mouth.

"What do you mean by that?" Malia asked defensively.

"Always so serious. Always waiting for the end—"

"Not waiting for it," Gorham said. "*Expecting* it. The city might have been here for five thousand years, or fifty thousand, but nothing lasts forever. We watch for Echo City's inevitable end so we can be ready for it."

"Don't mock our purpose," Malia added coldly. "When the end comes, we'll have our way across the desert."

"Maybe you will," Nadielle said, nodding, and the smile was still there. "For now let's eat. You've been on the road for a while, and no good decisions are ever made on an empty stomach."

So the three of them ate. The food was cold but delightful. There were breads and cheeses, smoked meats, dried fruit, yogurts flavored with some of the finest spices, and a sakefish whose pinkness and subtlety meant it must have come from the Northern Reservoir. Malia ate quickly beside him, eager to get to why they had come, but Nadielle savored each mouthful. Gorham wondered yet again how she managed to procure such good food. The bread had the taste and texture of the very best of the Marcellan bakers, and the cheese must have been matured for a long time. He could ask, but he knew that her answer would be misleading.

"How are you, Malia?" Nadielle asked. The question's meaning was obvious.

Malia shrugged, chewing a mouthful of mixed dried fruit.

Nadielle nodded slowly. "It heals, with time."

"You're twenty years old! If Bren and I'd had children, you could have been one of them." Malia trailed off, staring down at the tabletop but seeing something much farther away.

"My apologies," Nadielle said, but Gorham could see that she was not sorry at all. There was something about Nadielle that removed her from the world of Echo City. It wasn't even the fact that she chose to live belowground, with only the Echoes and her strange creations for company. Sometimes when he looked into her bright young eyes, there was such age there that it terrified him.

"It doesn't matter," Malia said, still staring down at the table.

They ate in silence for a while, Gorham trying to catch Nadielle's eye. But she looked down at her plate, cutting food very precisely, building meat on bread on cheese to gain the most of their blend of tastes. He watched her smooth hands and remembered them working at him with equal dexterity. Everyone who knew of her feared the Baker, and he wondered what his friends would think if they knew about their liaison.

When they had finished eating, Nadielle sat back in her chair and stretched her lithe body beneath the roomy clothes she always wore. Then she poured them each another glass of fine Crescent wine, raised her glass in silent toast, and waited for them to begin.

"We have people all over the city," Malia said. "Watchers, like us, and sometimes just people ready to earn a few shillings. They're instructed or paid to watch for certain things. Signs. Events out of the ordinary. Anything that might signify change. There are frequent false alarms, of course. Messages passed along that have already lost their meaning by the time they reach us. Lies, from people bored of waiting and wanting some money."

"But this is no false alarm," Gorham said.

Nadielle raised an amused eyebrow, but he saw a flash of something darker. Interest? Fear?

"*What* is no false alarm?"

Gorham glanced at Malia, and she nodded that he should continue. "It comes from three sources," he said. "First, Malia knows an explorer of the Echoes, Sprote Felder, and he has limited contact with the Garthans. He studies them, believes he has their trust, and he says there is concern among several of their deepest settlements. He wasn't specific, other than saying they were unsettled."

"Sprote is a mad old fool," Nadielle said, laughing.

Gorham blinked in surprise. *She told me she never leaves this place.* "He's a historian," he said. "His work on the Course Canton Echoes is well respected."

"Respected by some," Nadielle countered. "And I didn't say he was stupid, I said he was mad. He spends all his time down in the past."

"As do you," Malia said.

"You know nothing about me," Nadielle said after a pause, staring at Malia until she looked away. "So, the second source?"

"A priest from the Temple of the Seventy-seven Custodians," Gorham said.

Nadielle glanced back and forth between Gorham and Malia as if expecting a joke.

"They're harmless enough," Malia said. "And the Hanharans accept them."

"They *allow* them. It's different."

Malia shrugged.

"I trust him," Gorham said. "He's a good man, if misguided. And just because he thinks his beliefs are right, he doesn't insist that we are wrong."

"How magnanimous of him," Nadielle said.

"His elders are learned men and women. Intellectuals, not fanatics. Not mad. So I trust him, and he trusts them. And they say that something is coming."

Nadielle was silent for a while, blinking softly in the gentle glow of candlelight. She sipped her wine, picked at the remains of a loaf of bread, and hummed a tuneless melody.

"And the third source?" she said at last.

Gorham looked sidelong at Malia. They'd disputed whether or not to reveal their third source, not because of her privacy but because . . . well, because she *was* mad.

"Bellia Ton."

Nadielle laughed—a deep, throaty cough that did worrying things to Gorham's composure. She chuckled like that just after she came.

"The river reader?" the Baker asked. "You claim two sources that aren't mad but I say may be. And then you bring her into the tale? She's as mad as ten rockzards fucking a chickpig."

"Nicely put," Malia muttered.

Gorham held out his hands, palms up, and stood from the table. "Hear us," he said. "She's unreliable, but when she tells a story that meshes with others we've heard, we have to consider its veracity."

"And what story does the mad old hag tell you, Gorham?" Nadielle asked. Her eyes had grown icy, and he didn't like that. Neither did he understand it. He looked to Malia for support, but she was pouting as she picked the flesh from a slice of dried mepple.

"She holds court in a tavern in Mino Mont, right out by the city wall, close to where the River Tharin flows out into the desert."

"I know where she spouts her tales."

"One of our people was there."

"A Watcher?"

Gorham shook his head.

"A mercenary, then."

"Someone who sells us information," Malia said. "That doesn't mean it's false."

Nadielle was shaking her head, but Gorham went on, angry at her for dismissing something before she'd even heard it.

"She listens to the river, claims she can judge the health of the city by reading the waters that have flowed through it."

"The *dead* waters," Nadielle said. "Nothing lives in the river. It's as dead, and deadly, as the desert it comes from and goes to again."

"Maybe . . . but she heard *sounds* in the waters," Gorham said. "Noises from below, she said. Deeper than the Echoes, deeper than where any Garthans live, beneath Marcellan Canton where the Falls are, and—"

Nadielle stood quickly, her eyes growing wide and her glass tipping over. Wine flowed onto the bread platter and soaked in like spilled blood. "Do you know *how* she claims to read the river?" she asked, and Gorham thought he had never seen her so animated. "She dips her hands and feet in. She sits on the riverbank among the water refineries and touches the water. Sometimes she stays that way for half a day. So her madness isn't a weakness, really, but a strength. Do you know anyone else who could survive those poisoned waters for so long?"

"No," Gorham said.

"And have you any idea what that must do to her?"

"Why are you angry?" Malia asked.

Nadielle turned away, but not before Gorham saw that dark look in her eyes again. This time, he was certain it was fear.

"Because you're wasting my time," she said. "You've come here for what exactly?"

"To ask you to work faster," Gorham said. "The time might come soon when we have to attempt travel across the Bonelands."

The Baker laughed, and this time there was nothing orgasmic about it at all. This laughter was harsh, cruel, and tinged with a note of hysteria.

"You have no idea what I do here, so how can you ask something like that?"

Gorham glanced at Malia, who raised one eyebrow in an expression of defeat.

"We should go," Malia whispered, quiet enough so that Nadielle did not hear. "I've never liked this fucking place."

Gorham looked across the room at the large rumpled bed again, confused at why the Baker should act like this. Hadn't they secured her services for just such an occasion? Hadn't many people suffered because of this?

He closed his eyes, thought of Peer and that she would never be dead to him, even when one day she truly died.

"Nadielle, we're all sure that something is happening."

The Baker had reached the curtained doorway now, and she turned back to them, her face softening slightly. But there was still something very different about her. When they'd arrived, she seemed composed and perhaps amused at their discomfort; now there was a disturbing edge to her movements and voice. A *sharp* edge. "I'm busy, Gorham. I *am* working as fast as I can." And when she lifted the curtain aside, they both knew it was an invitation to leave.

Malia stood and walked to the door, glancing back at Gorham before stepping through. *Does she know?* Gorham thought, but right then it no longer seemed to matter. He was leaving again, and his heart thundered.

"Nadielle," he pleaded. She stood just beyond his reach.

"Gorham, now isn't the time," she said. She smiled sadly, and again he saw that strain behind her eyes, dulling them like the accumulated dust of generations on the finest oil painting.

He nodded, wished he could say more, wished he could touch her. And then the Pserans appeared from nowhere and stood around him, ready to guide him and Malia away from the Baker's laboratory.

"See you soon," he said, but Nadielle did not answer. He left without looking at her again, and Malia gripped his arm—a friendly touch that meant the world.

Chapter 3

By the time evening arrived, Peer knew that she could no longer remain in Skulk Canton. She might have been banished there, excluded from the rest of Echo City in its entirety, guilty of sedition in the eyes of the ruling Marcellans and blasphemy according to their Hanharan priests, and certain to be caught and executed should she attempt to return—but this was just too important. She could not place her own safety ahead of what this man's arrival might mean. So she would sit with the stranger through the night, nursing him as best she could, and come morning she would tell Penler goodbye.

Since helping the stranger up into the city from the cursed desert, Peer had tried hard to make sense of anything he had to say. The storm had intensified, and as she'd guided him through the streets, she was grateful because it kept most people under cover. The rain and lightning had stopped soon after she closed her door on the weather and offered him her bed to rest.

For a moment this afternoon, she'd believed that the stranger was stirring. He'd sat up on her bed, staring at the window and lifting his hands as if to push them through the glass. But then he'd looked around slowly, his wide eyes relaxing slightly as he saw her, and he'd rested again. He had been asleep ever since.

The man muttered in his sleep. He spoke broken, heavily accented Echoian, and that troubled her, because if he was from beyond, then where was his alien language? She could decipher little of what he said—random words, mumblings, and sometimes cries—but still she tried, because it gave her something to concentrate on, something to occupy her mind. . . .

This is the most amazing thing ever to happen to Echo City! she thought. She sat beside the bed, looking down at the frowning man, and in him she saw every hope the Watchers had ever expressed and every doubt that had ever been aimed at the Hanharans. He was special, and precious. If the Marcellans learned of his existence, they would execute him like every other Pretender they had caught—anyone who claimed an ability to travel the desert was treated the same way—and declare a day of feasting and celebration for the city. Peer closed her eyes, wondering whether any of those past Pretenders had been from the same place as this man.

And, if so, what had happened to those who helped?

"This is so much more than me," she whispered. The man stirred, turning his head as if looking for whoever had spoken, but his eyes remained closed. His breathing was ragged and dry, his dark skin burned by the sun and raised in countless minute pustules, his white hair clotted with sand. Those few times he had opened his eyes, she had seen how green they were. He was unlike anyone she had ever known.

She suddenly remembered that she was supposed to be eating with Penler that evening. For a moment she considered taking the stranger over there right away, but night in Skulk was dangerous. There were the gangs, and there were rockzards the size of humans living in the ruins, emerging only at night to feed. She could not risk him for anything. And, besides, she had never been the most reliable person. Penler would be annoyed at her absence but not worried.

Tomorrow she would make it up to him.

As the night drew on, and the man seemed to drift into a deeper, calmer sleep, Peer stood by her table, looking down at his shoulder bag. She touched it but did not recognize the material. Not silk, not canvas; it felt brittle but looked so strong. And those things she'd seen, protruding from the bag's open neck and still there now . . .

It felt so wrong, but she reached for the bag and loosened its string tie.

The man did not stir.

Guilt already weighing heavy, Peer opened the bag and emptied its contents across her table.

Later, staring at the man's belongings, terrified and excited in equal measures, she sensed that she was being watched.

She glanced at her bed and he was looking at her, blinking softly. He raised his left hand to his mouth to mimic taking a drink. She handed him a cup and he sipped at the water, then drank more greedily.

"Not too much," she said.

"More," he said, and his rough hand closed around hers to tip the cup farther. When he'd finished the water, he lay back onto the pillow, panting slightly and staring at the ceiling.

"You speak Echoian?"

"Echoian?"

"You do." She stood beside the bed, not quite knowing what to do. *He forms his words strangely. They* sound *different but mean the same.*

"I don't know," he said, but he did not elaborate.

"Where are you from?"

"Not here," he said, shaking his head. Desert dust fell from his hair, and Peer wondered whether she could die from that. But *he* hadn't died. What did that mean?

"What's your name?"

"Name?"

"My name is Peer Nadawa."

"Peer." He looked at her, and his mouth lifted in a faint smile. "You're not her."

"Not who?" she asked. He turned away. "Your name?"

The man closed his eyes, the frown returning. "No name."

"Listen . . ." Peer began, then she sighed and sat on the edge of the bed, relieving the weight from her aching hip. The man's hand was close to her thigh. She lifted it gently to examine his sunburn and the grit of his incredible journey collected beneath his fingernails.

"You're not scared," the man whispered.

"I'm fucking terrified!" She realized that she was crying, surprised at the aching nostalgia she suddenly felt for simpler times. Like yesterday. "I'm terrified because you're going to change everything. I need to take you to see some people, and they'll be amazed, and some other people will hate that you're here. They might even try to . . ."

"Why?" he asked.

"Why what?"

"Why . . . all of it?"

Peer shook her head. She'd lit some candles earlier, and now one of them went out with a gentle hiss. The room grew fractionally darker, but she did not notice the difference.

"Because that's just the way we are," she said. She kept hold of his hand. His eyes closed and his breathing softened. Peer looked down at where their hands touched. *He's from somewhere else*, she thought. *He's no wandering god, no straggler from Echo City gone out and come back again. If he was, he'd be growing sick by now, not getting better.* She tried to let go of his hand, but he squeezed.

"My name . . ." he said, frowning again.

"Let me give you one," she said, and the man nodded against his pillow. "Well . . . my father was called Rufus."

"Rufus."

"And for a second name : . . there are people who believe that seventy-seven six-legged gods wander the desert."

"I saw no gods," he said, smiling.

"It's just a belief," she said, shrugging. "One of them is called Kyuss. He's supposed to be the god of new things. It's his job to make sure Echo City moves forward."

"Echo City?"

"That's where you are."

"Where is Echo City?"

"It's . . ." Peer did not know how to answer. No one had ever asked her that before, because the question made as much sense as *Where is the air?* "It's here," she said. "It's everywhere. It's the whole world."

"No," the man she had named Rufus Kyuss whispered,

"there's more." And then he fell asleep and did not wake until morning.

Penler answered the door, bleary-eyed and with a knife in his hand.

"Peer? It's barely dawn. I was expecting you for dinner last night, and I—" He saw the shape standing behind Peer. "Who's this?"

"His name's Rufus." She ushered him through Penler's door, and the old man stood aside to let him enter. Penler glanced back and forth, confused, but Peer didn't give him time to object. By the time she was inside and closing the door behind her, throwing the bolts and checking through the peephole to make sure they had not attracted any attention, Rufus had disappeared into the house's shadows.

"Crap, Peer, what's going on?"

"Sorry about last night." She pushed past him and followed Rufus inside. He was in the large living area, standing in the center and turning a full, slow circle as he stared in wonder at the walls. Penler was a collector of maps, and he had some parchments that dated back many hundreds of years. One showed an area of Mino Mont that was now an Echo, built over seven hundred years before.

None of that would mean anything to Rufus. Yet Peer watched his amazement, and her heart skipped a beat.

"Who the crap is that?" Penler whispered behind her.

"He's a new arrival," Peer said.

"Oh," he said, raising his voice slightly. "Well, sorry. Welcome to Skulk."

"Skulk?" the man said, confused. "This is not Echo City?"

"No, no," Peer said, turning and placing her hands on Penler's shoulders. Exhausted though she was, and terrified, and in pain from the air shards in her arm, she could not contain the smile that warmed her face. "Penler, he's from outside. Out *there*!" She waved her hand in the general direction of the desert, frustrated because she could not properly voice what she had to say.

"Not Echo City," Rufus said.

The blood drained from Penler's face, and he swayed a little. Peer guided him to a chair, terrified that she'd sprung this on him too suddenly. He was an old man, and though he seemed fit, decades in Skulk had done him no good. She'd never forgive herself if—

"The Garthans," he whispered.

"What? No, no, Penler. They don't know about him. No one knows."

Penler looked past Peer at Rufus, who was now slowly pacing the perimeter of the large room, examining the maps.

"And no one *can* know," she said. She leaned down so that he had to look into her eyes. "Penler, this is what we've been waiting for all our lives!"

"We?" he said, still pale, shaking his head slightly. "Peer, it's a trick. It has to be. How can you be sure?"

"I saw him walking in across the Bonelands."

"When?"

"Yesterday, not long after you left me at the wall."

"No." He shook his head. "Impossible."

She was annoyed at Penler's reaction, and confused. He was the intellectual, the philosopher of Skulk, banished because of his great ideas. And yet here he was doubting instead of questioning, falling back on indoctrination instead of considering the fantastic possibilities that stared him in the face. He shook his head slowly, and she had never seen him looking so old.

"Penler, just listen to him, the way he builds his words, the way his voice twists around them—Echoian, but like none I've ever heard."

Penler was still shaking his head.

"Look in his bag! See what he carries, the strange things he's *brought*. Do you know what this means?"

"Do *you*?"

"Yes, of course! It changes everything, and—"

"Do you really believe this city can survive change?" he asked. "This city, built on the past?" And suddenly she knew what was wrong. *He* does *believe*, she thought, *and that's why he's so afraid*.

"Penler . . ."

A tear escaped his left eye and dribbled down his cheek. His face crumpled for a moment, then he seemed to gather himself again, wiping away the tear and standing up from his chair. Never once did he take his eyes off the man in his room.

"You believe," she said.

"I never had any doubt," he whispered, "but I never thought it would be in my lifetime."

"He can't stay in Skulk," Peer said.

"I know. But for now can I just . . . ?"

Peer reached out and brought the old man to her in a hug. He held his breath before hugging her back, his gasp warm and stale against her neck. She had not held anyone this close for a long time.

"I was going to get some breakfast anyway," she said. "But can't you leave Skulk with me?"

"Not me," he said, shaking his head against hers. "Not now. I've been here too long, and too many people know me. I'd slow you down. But I can help."

Peer pulled away so that she could look at him again. His eyes were moist, but she pretended not to notice. "How?"

"Oh, you know me. I have something about me."

"There's no such thing as magic, Penler."

He looked at the man from the desert again, as if to dispute her words. "Tell that to the magician's audience," he said. "Now go. Breakfast. We need a feast." He pressed five shillings into her hand and then walked past her into the room.

Peer watched Penler and the visitor for a beat. *He wants him to himself for a while*, she thought, and she could hardly blame him. Such a great man would have so many questions.

Outside, Skulk's morning air seemed fresher than usual, cleansed by the previous night's rain. Or perhaps it was the smell of potential.

She bought breakfast from a street vendor—fried chickpig in fresh bread sandwiches, a large carafe of five-bean, and a selection of dried fruits—and on her return to Penler's house she passed a body in an alleyway. The woman was lying on her back, her dusty eyes staring at the dawn-smeared sky and her slit throat gnawed at by rats and rockzards in the night. She was naked, and carved across her chest and stomach was the serpent sigil of one of Skulk's most powerful, brutal gangs.

Peer averted her eyes and walked on. It shamed her, but there was no way she could get involved. The woman must have offered some slight against the gang, and they always left their murder victims where they were for three days and nights before sending their lowliest members to clear away whatever was left. They liked to send a message, and anyone interrupting that message was likely to end up the same way.

It's so easy, Peer thought, and she felt a moment of terror the likes of which rarely visited her. *One wrong move, one sideways glance, being in the wrong place when a madman walks by. . . . Death is so easy, and life so precious. I could die here today. What would happen to Rufus then?*

Her whole world had changed, and there was plenty more to come. The future was suddenly a weight upon her shoulders, and she knew that she had to be strong. Life had never felt like such a precarious gift as at that moment. Peer hurried through the streets, one hand holding the bag containing breakfast, the other hanging close to her knife.

Penler was waiting for her in the hallway behind his front door. He ushered her in, took the food bag, and dropped it unceremoniously to the floor.

"What's wrong?" he asked, sensing the change in her.

"Nothing. Where's Rufus?"

Penler nodded back toward his main room. "He's like a child, Peer. Full of wonder, but he knows so little." He touched his long, wiry gray hair, twirling it around one finger. "The desert . . . it's burned something out of him, so many memories. Either that or he's lying."

This time she could see through his doubt. "What do you really think, Penler?"

"I think he's been through some bad times. And his words . . . strange. Echoian, but almost a different dialect. Almost as if he's relearning a language he hasn't used for some time."

"Did you look in his bag, like I said?"

The old man's face changed. The frown returned, but his eyes sparkled.

"I think I know what some of it is," he said, "but a couple of the things . . ."

"Did you ask him?"

"He's enjoying looking at my maps."

"Right," Peer said, inclining her head slowly. "And it's not that you want to figure them out for yourself?"

Penler laughed, and it was good to hear the old man sounding like himself again. "You know me so well, Peer."

Eager to see Rufus again, she picked up the breakfast bag and ushered Penler back along the hallway.

Rufus seemed pleased to see her. He pointed at one of the maps but said nothing, his incredulity evident in every crease of his face, every movement he made. She nodded and placed the bag on the large table, next to the contents of Rufus's shoulder bag. Penler stood close beside her, his arm touching hers. He pointed at a small round object, similar to a watch but marked differently.

"This finds direction," he said. "I don't know how, but it works."

"What do you mean?"

"Which way's north?"

Peer pointed without thinking. Most people in Skulk knew the direction of the world that had shunned them.

Penler pulled the small instrument close to them, opened the lid, tapped it, and a shard of metal floated inside, suspended in some viscous liquid. The arrowed end of the shard pointed north.

Peer turned the instrument around, and the arrow turned slowly to maintain the same direction.

"Clever," she said.

"Not clever. Scientific."

"All your city?" Rufus said, aghast. He was staring at a large current map of Echo City that took up most of one wall.

"Yes," Penler said.

"Here," Rufus whispered, moving closer to the area marked as Course Canton and pointing at the shadow of buildings. "Homes?"

"Some," the old man said. "Groups of homes, at least. The blocks in a grid you see spanning the river, they're water refineries. And the straight lines leading from them, they're the canals."

Rufus was watching Penler with his mouth agape, incomprehension clouding his eyes.

"It's a large city," Peer said. "Thirty miles across."

"Miles?"

Peer glanced at Penler.

"From here to Peer's home is less than half a mile," he said. "To walk from the south of the city, where you came in, to its northern edge would take two days and a night."

Rufus turned back to the map, spreading his hands across its surface, as if by touching it he could absorb every wondrous thing it displayed.

"What's that?" Peer muttered, pointing at a long, thin tube.

"I think it's a scope."

She stared hard at Penler, but he was not fooling with her. "A scope like . . . ?"

Penler picked up the tube and handed it to her.

Peer had first seen one of the Scopes when she was four. Her mother had been a tax collector, and she'd taken her on a journey into Marcellan Canton to consult with government officials over some proposed changes to the way tithes were gathered. The Scope had been sitting on the wall surrounding Hanharan Heights, casting its alien gaze down toward Mino Mont. She had stood amazed. Its naked, almost human body had gleamed darkly like the shell of a beetle, its deformed head elongated into a thick tube that ended with the curve of its massive eye. An intricate system of supports had propped the Scope's head, shifting with it, turning on well-greased gears and cogs. Long hair was tied back from its head in tight metal bands. Its genitals hung like shriveled dried fruits, and its arms had withered to nothing. It was not the first chopped Peer had ever seen—there were many deformed in Mino Mont—but it was the first of the Baker's originals, and the most amazing.

Peer took the tube now and held it at arm's length. "Rufus," she said, "what's this?"

"Long glass," he said. He came around the table and took the instrument from her, pulling at one end until it was twice its original length. He pointed at a small lever that had sprung from the tube. "Gear, for unblurring."

Peer took it back, held the narrow end to her left eye, and looked across the room at a map.

"No," Rufus said, laughing softly. "For outside. It brings things—*miles* away—near."

"Not something we'd have much need of," she said softly, placing it on the table. "And this?"

Rufus picked up the small knife she had touched. He turned it and showed them the flint hidden in the handle, then he prized out a curved blade concealed in its back. "For . . ." He frowned, staring at the blade. "For . . ."

"It doesn't matter," Peer said, touching the back of his hand.

"Whatever you've forgotten will return," Penler said. "The heat of the desert, the sun, must have . . ." He shrugged, because in truth none of them knew what the desert could make of a living person, other than a dead one.

"We should go soon," Peer said.

"But this place," Rufus said, pointing around Penler's room with wide, excited eyes.

"Skulk is not safe," she said, thinking of the murdered woman. "Anything could happen here. Any foolish, pointless death, and you . . . you're precious."

"I am?"

"Of course."

"Why?"

Why? she thought. *So much like a child, and yet he's not unlearned. Maybe he has forgotten much, or maybe the language is a barrier.*

Or perhaps he's holding back.

"Because . . ." And Peer realized that, through all this, she had not yet told him what he meant to them. His amazement at this place had blinded him to the astonishment she and Penler showed in return. And the only way to proceed was with trust.

"Because no one can cross the Markoshi Desert," Penler said, "and anyone who tries will die."

"Where do you *come* from?" Peer asked. "Where is your home?"

"I can't remember," Rufus said. "Only . . . bones." He stared between them and along the hallway.

He has so much to remember, Peer thought. *We have to give him the chance*. She turned to Penler and he nodded.

"I need to prepare," he said.

Rufus sat on the table and stared at a map on the wall, but he seemed to see much farther.

After the heavy rains of the previous day, the blazing sunshine cast a rainbow over Echo City. They left Penler's home in mid-afternoon, walking slowly north in a meandering, hesitant fashion that they hoped would attract no attention. Rufus was wide-eyed at everything he saw, and his childlike awe encouraged Peer to view things in a different light. The street vendors were familiar, but she looked again at all their wares. Usually she ignored them. Now she caught their eyes, smiled, and more than once she was dragged into a conversation about certain species of stoneshrooms, the best spices in which to marinate a chickpig's hooves, or the styles of silk scarves being worn in Skulk this season. Rufus watched and listened, smiling delightedly, and usually it was Penler who took his arm and guided him gently away.

Peer realized that she was saying goodbye to Skulk Canton, and the sadness in her came as a shock. She'd been forced here by banishment, tortured and wronged by the Marcellans, and everything she had ever considered home had been stripped away. Left alone and naked of hope, she sometimes wondered how the crap she had made anything of a life for herself at all.

Penler, she thought, and she looked at the old man's back. Yes, Penler. If it wasn't for him, she would likely have died, and her arm and hip ached in memory of the care he had given her. "And now I'm leaving him behind," she whispered. An old woman selling mummified wisps—considered lucky charms by some, though Peer knew that their stings often remained—heard what she said and reached out to her with a thin yellow wisp.

"It's yours," the woman croaked, the beginnings of negotiation.

Peer shook her head and walked on, and behind her the woman called, "Don't take it and you'll lose him for sure."

Penler turned at that, one hand still on Rufus's arm, and Peer had never seen such an expression on the old man's face. He looked like a young boy determined not to cry—cheeks puffed out, eyes swollen. She turned away because she was starting to realize what it all meant.

They moved away from the market districts and into an area of Skulk known as Pool. It was a relatively low area, its buildings ancient and not built over for many centuries, but no one had lived here since the salt plague. It was a haunted place. Peer had always poured scorn on those who let phantoms steer their decisions, but the fact that no one banished to Skulk chose to live there spoke volumes. Penler had said it would be a good place from which to approach the border.

Pool was a warren of streets, squares, and courtyards. Many of them were scattered with detritus from the decaying buildings—rotten window shutters, the glint of colored glass, chimney pots and clay bricks crumbled by decades of frost and sun—and here and there they found the bones of dead things. Most of the bones were animal, the cause of their demise always hidden. Some were human.

"Bones," Rufus said, and the sight of a fleshless skull seemed to terrify him. Penler and Peer calmed him, guiding him past, and Peer saw the ragged hole smashed into the skull by whatever weapon had killed its owner.

Around the next corner, bathed in sunlight and the melodious sound of red-finch song, they saw their first phantom.

It was a young woman, so faint that Peer could see right through her. She wore the formal silk attire favored by Skulkians before the plague, and she was kneeling by the side of the path, looking down at the ground. She reached with translucent hands and touched something, then sat back again and considered what she had done. She repeated the action, straightened once more, and never once did she appear to see them. Most phantoms did not.

Rufus caught his breath and backed up a step, but Peer stood fast, holding on to his hips and feeling the shiver going through him. "Beautiful," he breathed. It was a strange reaction to seeing a ghost.

"She won't harm us," Penler said. Rufus seemed unable to tear his eyes away from the young woman and her continuing attempt to arrange something none of them could see. The ground beneath her fingers bore only dust, and her fingers left no trails. "There'll be more, but phantoms won't give us away."

They walked by the hollow girl, leaving her to her past. Rufus kept glancing back until they turned a corner and continued across a small square. Peer tried to reassure him with a smile, but he did not meet her eyes.

There were several more phantoms, some obvious, some little more than blurs on the air. Sometimes all three of them saw, and once it was only Peer who seemed able to make out a tall man sitting in a broken chair in the doorway of an ancient home. She thought he nodded at her, but his head rose and fell as he slept. *How long ago?* she wondered. He was even older than he looked.

I will see Gorham, she thought, the idea hitting her suddenly and hard. *If he's not dead. If the Marcellans didn't hunt him down after taking me*. The excitement was tempered by caution; she could not afford to hope for too much. But the idea of meeting her lost love again was thrilling, and she tried to ignore the three years that had separated them.

Three years, and an escape from Skulk yet to be made.

They left Pool and started climbing a steep hill toward the border with Course Canton. There were few people here, as proximity to the border served only to remind those living in Skulk that they resided in a prison. Those people they did encounter seemed little more than phantoms themselves, and they rushed to hide away. These were the outcasts from the outcasts, those who could not accept Skulk as a place to live and who hovered at the border, as if one day they might go back.

But no one sent to Skulk ever returned. It had been a long

time since Peer had been here, and she'd forgotten just how heavily guarded the border was.

They called them the Levels. Once, before the plague, the dividing line between Skulk and Course Cantons had been difficult to distinguish. A street here, a square there, the banks of the Southern Reservoir, perhaps the edge of a park or the center line of a road. After the salt plague, there'd been a need to mark the border permanently. And so the razing had begun. In history books, the transcribers had gone to some effort to describe the methods used and the caution taken to prevent injury or worse to those innocents caught up in the chaos. In reality, the Marcellans had ordered the razing to be completed within two days. In such a short time, with so many fires set, ruin wagons dispatched, and buildings marked for destruction, the suffering of innocents was inevitable.

A fifteen-mile-long strip of land from southwest to southeast Echo City had been flattened of everything that stood or grew upon it. The Levels followed the old borders, up to a mile wide in some places, while here and there they were only a few hundred feet, one side still visible from the other. Following the razing and burning, almost two hundred watchtowers had been constructed along the northern edge of the Levels. For the next few years these were manned by Scarlet Blades, but as the public slowly forgot the plague and its consequences—or, if not forgot, at least put them to one side while they continued with their lives, content that the Marcellans had saved Echo City from its gravest, darkest hour—the Blades announced themselves as too important to spend their time on guard duties. A new branch of the Marcellans' army was therefore created. The Border Spites—brutal and barely trained—were employed from all levels of Echoian society, the only requirements being that they were strong, able to fight, and willing to kill if the need arose.

The need frequently did. Even since Peer had been in Skulk, she had heard of almost a hundred attempted escapes. They all ended the same way, and the rotting corpses were left across the Levels as warnings.

Facing the Levels, hidden in the shadow of a tall house, Peer could see three watchtowers. A gentle drift of smoke tailed from one of them as the Border Spites cooked their lunch. Between them and her were the sad, fire-blackened ruins.

"This is where we say goodbye," Penler said. He sighed heavily, staring anywhere but at Peer.

"You could still come," she said.

"No, I'll slow you."

She tapped her hip, aching a little after their long walk. "I'm not as fast as *I* was, you know."

"But I did a good job on that." He looked at her at last, and she saw tears in his eyes. Tears, and something else: regret.

And she wondered suddenly how she had been so fucking stupid all this time. *Old man*, she sometimes jokingly called him, but it *was* how she perceived him. Just what had he thought of those words coming from the woman he loved? She could never know. Even if Rufus had not come along, it was far too late, because they had become such good friends.

"I'll miss you," he said.

What do I say? She hugged him tight, confused, and angry at herself for being so selfish that she had never seen.

Penler held her. The three of them stood in silence, and Peer felt the pressure of that silence weighing on her. *He's waiting for me to say something.* But she did not know what to say. *I'm sorry* just wouldn't do, and time was passing.

"You need to give me an hour," he said, pulling away from her and staring back across the Levels.

"When will we know it's time to go?"

"You'll know." He'd strengthened now, looking forward, bringing himself back to what needed doing to get Peer and Rufus away. Out of his life forever.

"Penler . . ." she said.

He smiled softly. "You'll do fine."

"No, I don't mean . . . I wanted to say . . ." But she'd been blind all this time, and opening her eyes at the end would be pointless.

"Just remember me," Penler said.

"I will see you again," she replied.

His smile dropped, but only slightly. They both realized the likelihood of that.

Penler gave Rufus a one-armed hug before he went, then weaved his way back along the narrow street and disappeared into the blackened heart of a ruined temple. As well as letting go of Peer, he was saying goodbye to this remarkable visitor from the desert.

"Friends," Rufus said, looking after Penler.

"Yes, we are," Peer said. A sense of loss hit her in the gut, and she sat down heavily against the wall. They had a while to wait. And for her last hour in Skulk Canton, Peer reflected upon how self-obsessed she had been.

Chapter 4

The previous day's rains had turned the Levels to muck. Peer could see the black pools from where they waited, and she knew that the crossing would not be easy. The Levels were not actually level at all; the destruction a century before had been rushed, and here and there some remains still stood. Walls were piled with debris, and the dark pits of exposed basements led down to older Echoes. She hoped that whatever Penler planned, he gave them long enough.

Each of the three watchtowers she could see was manned. The guards in one were still cooking, and distant laughter came her way. In the second tower there had been movement as several Border Spites changed watch, and from the third she'd seen a guard pissing over the side.

"You'd better be who we think you are," she said mildly.

Rufus still wore that lost expression.

"You remember nothing from out there?" she asked.

"Bones," he said. "Sand. Dead desert." He looked down at his hands, twisted in his lap.

"And nothing from before?"

Rufus shook his head. "Maybe . . . there is nothing."

"No," Peer said. "I don't believe that. I *can't*. Do you feel sick, weak? No, you're fine. You're good. You're getting *better*! So there's something about you . . ."

Rufus looked at her and glanced away again, perhaps not understanding. He stared across the Levels at the beginnings of Course Canton beyond. The buildings were low and stark, most of them abandoned this close to Skulk, but they still carried a heavy significance. Over there was freedom and choice. Over here was imprisonment and necessity. The Levels were where everything changed.

"You told me I'm not her. So who are you looking for?"

"I don't know," he said, perhaps too sharply. And the first explosion came from the east.

Rufus jumped, scrambling to his feet, but Peer crawled across the debris-strewn alley and held him down. He was breathing hard and fast, but she held his jaw with one hand and turned his face until he was looking right at her. *His eyes are so green*, she thought, and she shook her head, shushing him as the noise echoed across the Levels.

When Peer was six, there had been a series of anonymous attacks on Mino Mont's water refineries. The authorities at the time had blamed them on the Dragarians, though there had been no such instances before or since, and the attacks had soon ended. What she remembered most was not the panic that had spread quickly through Mino Mont for those few days one summer—fear that if the refineries were destroyed, then the Northern and Eastern Reservoirs would quickly dry up— but the sounds of those few explosions. She had never heard anything like them before or since—until now.

Crawling to the mouth of the alley, she looked east and saw several plumes of smoke about a mile away. They did not seem to be rooted to the ground but floated on the breeze.

Three more explosions came, bursting in the air like rapidly blooming roses, spewing sparks followed by thin limbs of smoke. The colors were bright and varied, and each explosion flowered and spread differently. She had seen sky-fires before many times, during street parties to celebrate an important Marcellan's birthday or to mark the execution of another Pretender. But they were always a weak, sputtering affair. Never anything like this. These filled the sky.

"What?" Rufus said behind her. He'd crawled up close, and now he clung on to the leg of her trousers, shaking.

"Penler," Peer said. "Full of surprises."

She looked across the Levels at the three guard towers. Two of them were abuzz with activity as Border Spites climbed or slid down the rope ladders splayed around their legs. Atop the third tower—the farthest to the west—she could see three guards shielding their eyes as they watched the skyfires.

Go, she thought. *Relieve your boredom. See what's happening.*

"We'll give it a few moments," she said. "Then we go." Some of the guards started along the northern boundary of the Levels, the sun glinting from their weapons. *This is madness*, she thought, but she shoved that idea aside. Penler was doing this for her, and if he'd thought there was a chance of her being caught, he'd have suggested otherwise.

It was up to her to make sure his trust was not mislaid.

"Follow me," she said, turning to make sure Rufus understood. He nodded. "Stay close behind me. Stay low." She indicated what she meant with her hand. He nodded again. *He understands more than he says, or can say*. But that was another mystery to unravel later. *One breath at a time*, as her poor dead mother used to say. Peer took in a deep breath and left the cover of the buildings.

There were several heavy coughs to the east, and Peer saw smoke trails lifting objects high above the Levels. Upon exploding, they splashed a palette of colors across the sky, and the falling flames twisted around one another like dancing silk snakes. They were unlike any skyfires she had ever seen or heard of before. The sparks did not extinguish but kept spitting and dancing in the air, each one seemingly in concert with those around it. Shapes were formed and dispersed again, as if teasing—fighting rockzards, a diving rathawk plucking its prey from the air, wisps swooping toward and around one another without ever actually touching. For a second she stood amazed, before realizing that this display was not meant for her.

There was more movement way across the Levels, as guards streamed along the border.

Keeping low, Peer headed across, with Rufus following. She had been right about the rains—her boots quickly sank in thick mud. She felt it oozing over the boots' lips and touching her shins, her ankles, and she imagined it as the dust of history. So much was mixed up in this wet, rancid stew. The ruins of whole districts, the pulverized remains of neighborhoods where people had once lived, loved, and died on their own terms.

She heard Rufus behind her, his own boots sucking at the muck as he walked.

Of the three towers in sight, she aimed for the one in the middle. She'd seen the guards abandon that one, and though there were still Border Spites manning the tower to their left, she hoped they would be able to slip past unseen. *Keep them firing*, she thought, hoping that Penler had a long supply of whatever he was using. Hardly magic, but it was close enough.

They passed tumbled walls, where weeds had grown out of the dust and smothered a building's remains. Peer saw movement among the plants and kept her distance, in case they were biting or stinging things.

Penler's skyfires continued to dance. She stole occasional glances their way, awed and thankful. *He's not like us*, a woman had once told Peer about Penler, soon after she'd arrived in Skulk. They were drinking together in a tavern, watching the old man buying a fresh bottle of wine. *He's got something about him*. Peer had smiled at the time, not sure what the woman meant, and over the next couple of years she had mostly forgotten those words. But now the woman's voice rang back to her. It was how the most superstitious among them described someone who dipped into what were considered the darkest of arts.

Halfway across the Levels, she squatted behind a mound of weed-choked rubble, and Rufus did the same. He was following quietly and calmly, keeping low, and she wondered how terrified he must be.

"A rest," she said, rubbing her aching hip. Rufus nodded. She peered around the mound, and now that the other side of the Levels was close, she could scan it for movement. There was nothing. Gray buildings faced them, most of them low but a few consisting of several stories. The architecture here was sparse and functional, but the buildings all contained the familiar arched windows of old Course design. *There could be anyone watching from behind those*, Peer thought, but that way lay defeat. If she became overcautious, they'd never move again.

She was still quite certain that two of the towers were deserted, but she was no longer sure about the third. She'd seen no movement there for a while. It could be that the Border Spites had gone to witness the fantastical skyfires after all, or maybe they were hunkered down even now, scrutinizing the Levels for the movement one of them swore he'd just seen. If that was the case, they'd do their best not to be seen themselves.

Peer's heart raced, blood thumping in her ears. She'd heard stories about what the guards did to anyone caught trying to flee Skulk. She stretched her right arm, wincing as the air shards twisted against flesh, muscle, and bone. At least her hip was not too painful. Penler had been right; he'd done a good job with that.

"Follow me," she said, and without looking back she started again for the other side.

It did not take long but felt like forever. Three years before, Peer had been forced to watch as a Marcellan torturer shoved a selection of air shards through her arm, and the eyes she felt upon her now hurt almost as much. Whether they were real or imaginary she did not know, but that mattered little.

Panting, sweating, her heart racing at the certainty that they would be caught, she pressed up against the side of a building in Course Canton. *Three years*, she thought, but the stone beneath her skin felt no different.

The last of Penler's skyfires was fading as it floated slowly to the ground. Crimson sparks turned to a deep, rich blue, landing across the Levels and remaining lit for a while. Blue was Peer's favorite color. Penler knew that.

Her breathing slowing, Peer spent a moment looking back across at Skulk. She felt a curious sense of loss. Among the true criminals over there were wonderful people, whose imaginations and intellects had steered them to beliefs that resulted in banishment. She had been herself in Skulk. Now, back in Echo City, deception was to rule her life.

She nodded to Rufus, smiled, and led the way cautiously into a wide, empty street. And it was only as she began to believe they had escaped that they were caught.

The stupid thing was, she smelled the piss from thirty steps away. An hour earlier, she would have known what that meant and hidden. But her body could take only so much tension, and her sense of caution had given way to a sloppy belief in their good fortune.

We make it back, she thought, *and the first thing I smell is chickpig piss*. But it was not a chickpig pissing, and as the Border Spite stepped from a doorway farther along the street, still pulling up her trousers, Peer reached for her sword.

She had never killed or stabbed anyone in her life. The nearest she'd come to a fight had been with a drunken fat man, a year after arriving in Skulk, when he'd stumbled into her as she sat on the city wall. He'd drawn a sword and she'd pulled her knife, but he dropped his blade and started laughing before vomiting on her shoes. Leaving him in his own puke, trailing the stink behind her as she walked home, she'd wondered what the outcome would have been had he been not quite so drunk.

The Border Spite drew a short sword in her right hand, a triangular object in her left, and ran at them.

Peer unconsciously took a step back, nudging into Rufus. The sword handle felt cold and slippery in her grasp. "Hide!" she rasped.

The soldier brought the wooden object to her lips. *Poison darts*, Peer thought, but then a mournful whistling broke the loaded silence.

From behind her, a cough. She thought perhaps Rufus was gasping in fear, but then something struck the Border Spite's face. The Spite dropped her sword and wooden horn, took in a shuddery, loud breath, and started raking at her eyes. She went to her knees less than a dozen steps away, and Peer saw every degree of agony on the young woman's face. Her nails scratched ragged gashes across her eyelids and cheeks. Her mouth hung open, and pink foam bubbled from between her teeth. At last she fell forward, convulsing, hands now held just away from her face as if contact was too painful.

Peer turned. Rufus stood with his eyes and mouth open in shock, his arm held before him, and something in his hand. It was black and bulky, and a curl of smoke rose from its open end.

"Rufus, what did you . . . ?" She looked at the weapon and had no idea what she saw.

The shock slowly fading from his face, Rufus lowered his hand, never taking his eyes from the fallen Spite. She was still now, her chest motionless. Deep-red blood had replaced the foam issuing from her mouth.

He pulled something on the object and a small lid hinged up, revealing a huddle of egglike objects inside. "Wrathspider," he said.

Shaking, Peer started to walk, passing the dead guard and trying not to look at the mess her face had become. But she could not help glancing down. *Did her fingernails really do all that?* she thought. Probably not. Beneath the stench of blood was something like burning.

She heard Rufus following her. When she'd first seen him coming across the desert, she was shocked, excited, and filled with a sense of hope. Now she was afraid.

They left the body behind and hurried into Course Canton. After passing through a small park where yellow wisps flitted through trees surrounding a lake, they saw a group of normal people. No swords were on show; no panic or surprise crossed their faces. One young woman smiled at Peer, and Peer found it easier than she'd suspected to find a smile to return. *I'm free,* she thought, but immediately following that came the idea that had been forming since bidding farewell to Penler.

Free, yes, but now her life had become a lie. And with Rufus walking beside her, she began to suspect that made two of them.

Since hearing the sounds from below, Bellia Ton had spent more time than ever reading the river. The Tharin was wide here, just a mile from where it passed out beneath the city wall and back into the desert from whence it came. It was as dead when it left the city as when it arrived, but water carried knowledge, picking up a little of the ground it passed through. Most people could not understand this, and many did not believe. That suited Bellia well. Dead the river might be, but she was its disciple.

She knew the river and its banks well, and now she was down on a rock that jutted into the waterway, bare feet dangling into the flow. It parted around her ankles, churning a soft white against her old skin.

Bellia took one more look around. There were no residential buildings here, the area given over mostly to the tall water-refinery towers and their attendant structures, pools, culverts, and canals. The tower closest to her was also the newest, rebuilt after the attacks thirty years before, and like a youngster among older friends, it puffed steam and churned its parts with more gusto than the others. Its base was invisible to Bellia, hidden by a fold in the land, but she had walked past it many times before. The mountains of rotting extract stank. After all this time, still no one knew exactly what it was they filtered from the water. The mountain grew, just as the city rose, and in the Echoes there were hardened piles of that extract, still as mysterious as history.

She breathed in deeply and smelled the river: stale and dead, light and fleeting. It took the Tharin a day to flow through the city, and the waters that made it this far smelled and looked even more alien than where they'd entered.

And that was why Bellia chose this place to read.

She took in a deep, calming breath and closed her eyes. Imagining the water scouring away the flesh from her ankles and feet, then abrading the bones themselves, she became one with the river, the stumps of her lower legs barely touching the water. Her blood flowed with the Tharin, still linked to her through memory. She read its course into the city, along the steepening valley formed by the built-up land surrounding it. She frowned through the darkness where the river passed underground into the Echoes beneath Marcellan Canton, pulling away from the sense of endless space that existed where it split and poured some of itself down the Falls. That place was always so dark . . .

She gasped and fell back, striking her head on the rock.

Trying to lift her feet from the river, she found them held fast, the water pulling them down like wet sand.

"Something new!" she screeched, because she had felt a part of the city that should not be there. "Something *wrong*!" There was more to know, but she wanted to learn no more. That brief insight had been so cold, and through everything she had ever read of the city, its dark histories, its inhabitants, and the things that dwelled among them, she had never been so afraid.

Bellia managed to haul her feet from the river at last and scrambled up the bank, gathering her long skirts to her knees so that she could run. Craving the oblivion she would find in the End Wall Tavern, she sprinted through the deserted water districts of Mino Mont.

And all the while, an awful truth shouted something she had no desire to hear.

The thing that was coming is almost here.

Peer was exhausted. The sun had yet to touch the western desert, but she could go no farther, and she craved food. They had crossed several canals already, and when they reached the river valley she called a halt to their progress. No one who had seen them had called for the Scarlet Blades, and within sight of Marcellan Canton's walls she risked believing that they had got away.

Two miles to the east, the great dead River Tharin roared through Marcellan's wall and entered the city's Echoes. In her time with the Watchers, Peer had been down among the Echoes several times, though not too deep. It had always been a disturbing experience for her, leaving the world she knew and traveling through areas—streets, buildings, parks, and landscapes—where the city's past had played out. These Echoes were all but silent now, though history still hung heavy in their darkness. Once, in Mino Mont, she had descended with a woman who had known her mother, and the woman showed her a house where Peer's ancestors had once lived. They had been engravers, recording history on marble tablets for rich families, but that ruin had been empty of all but dust and dark things.

She knew others who had gone deeper. Some could not sleep for days after returning to daylight; a few wanted only to go back down.

"We'll stop here to eat," she said to Rufus. "Hungry?"

"Yes," he said, rubbing his stomach. He was looking around wide-eyed, and Peer was afraid that in itself would attract attention. But it was hardly surprising. The river valley was an amazing place—as newer layers of the city had been built upon older structures, the valley had both deepened and widened, its sides sloping back from the waterway. Looking down at the valley sides should have been like viewing the city's histories laid out in strata, but weathering and the actions of humankind had landscaped the slopes into something different. Here and there, evidence of architecture still remained, but mostly the steep slopes were either smothered with razorplant or oxomanlia, or had become refuse slicks where the city vented its waste.

This was especially prevalent beneath and around several bridges that spanned the Tharin's man-made valley. Most of the bridges were quite old—although there were rumors, no one knew for sure how the leg piles had been sunk through the poisonous river—and they had been built up along with the surrounding urbanized landscape, their own older Echoes on full view and deserted but for the occasional disoriented phantom. They were well maintained, and for some reason they had become centers of commerce and entertainment, wide enough to house all manner of shops and eating places. Each bridge had its own marshal, whose job it was to ensure the bridge's safety and success, and each marshal had his or her own gang of aides. The crossings were small towns in themselves, and in the past there had been skirmishes between rival bridges.

The one thing never permitted was bridge tolls. The Marcellan rulers insisted that the people of Echo City must be free to cross the River Tharin at any point and at any time, thereby defying the dead river with their own busy lives.

Peer had been to Six Step Bridge many times before, and she knew it to be a lively, cheerful place. Every second building was a tavern or restaurant, and its commerce was built around wine, ale, and good food. No one knew where its name came from, and few bothered to descend its structure to try to find out. *The past is below us*, the popular saying went, a statement of attitude as well as geography. The bridge was a place where people could remain anonymous, and Peer looked forward to a few moments of calm.

She also wanted to talk with Rufus. Since crossing the Levels and killing the Border Spite, he had not once asked where she was taking him or who they were going to see. His amazement at this place was obvious, but he was also an intelligent man—she could see that in his eyes, sense it in his bearing. He might be a visitor to Echo City, but she was certain he would never let himself be led blind.

They started across the bridge, the Tharin a pale snaking shadow far below, and Peer realized just how much she had missed the city. There were areas like this in Skulk, yes— places where people gathered to drink and party or to sip and discuss all the bad things in the world. But she realized now that, in Skulk, there had always been an undercurrent of exclusion. They had been partying in spite of no longer being part of the city. They had talked of the bad things, knowing that countless fellow Echoians thought of *them* as the bad things. They'd had something taken away from them—true criminals or offenders of the mind alike—and that fact was ever-present in that old place of disease and death.

Peer found a free table outside a bar called Hestige's. Sitting there exposed, starting to relax, the memory of the dying Border Spite shoved to one side—or at least smothered beneath the sights and sounds presented to her on Six Step Bridge—she ordered a bottle of cheap wine, and she and Rufus sat drinking it in sight of Marcellan Canton's distant wall.

Traders traded, drinkers drank, and people walked back and forth across the bridge. It had an air of bustle that no number of sedentary drinkers and eaters could dampen, and a whole selection of street performers added to the buzz. A woman juggled baby rockzards, her hands and forearms a network of scars old and new. A man seemed to be walking on stilts, until Peer saw that he'd been inexpertly chopped. His long legs were bony and bleeding, his desperate smile verging on madness.

Three children performed an ever-shifting play, a huge old woman following them and providing sound effects and prompts if they forgot their lines. They told of marriage and celebration among the ruling Marcellans, and ribald jokes and dangerous insinuations surprised the audience as they were muttered by the innocent-looking girls. Jokers told their amusing stories, painters strolled from table to table offering to capture moments in perpetuity, charm sellers preyed on maudlin drunks, and food stalls fought covert battles of smell and sense.

Peer lifted a glass and toasted Penler, and Rufus sat silently beside her, waiting for what would come.

"So who are you really?" she asked, and Rufus refilled her glass.

"Rufus Kyuss," he said.

"That's what I named you, but you have a name I don't know. A life I don't know."

Rufus nodded, looking around the busy street. "Will you help me find it?"

"I'll try," she said. "And if you tell me who you're looking for, I'll help you find her as well."

"I'm . . . not sure."

"But *I'm* not her!" Peer said, perhaps too loudly. After their flight from Skulk, this wine was quickly going to her head. She laughed over her embarrassment, then drank some more. "Don't worry," she said. "There's someone who'll help us both."

"Who?"

"An old friend." Peer thought again of Gorham, and the air shards in her arm drove pain through her bones, reminding her again who she was.

Chapter 5

As soon as he saw her, he left the street, pushing through a hustle of drinking men and women and entering a small water-food eatery. The smell of boiling fish and the crack of shells being ruptured grated—he hated fish—but he swallowed hard and went to the window to make sure. He had to lean over a small table, nudging a woman's arm as she brought a shrimp stick to her mouth. She mumbled, her companion bristled, and the man apologized. They quieted quickly. Perhaps they saw the knife in his belt and the scars on his face.

He wiped condensation from the window and looked across the bridge at Hestige's. He must have been wrong, it could *never* be her . . . but there she sat, sipping from a large glass, speaking to the weird white-haired man seated beside her.

He gasped, clouding the window again with his breath, then stood back from the table, staring at the wall.

"Are you . . . ?" the woman diner asked.

He looked down at her and the remains of her meal. His stomach rolled. "This is going to be interesting," he said. Then he turned and made his way back through the eatery.

People moved aside for him. He had that effect, but usually he did not notice. Today was different. In the kitchens, the sour reek of fish more intense than ever, he nodded at the two chefs and then kicked open the chute door.

Most buildings clinging to the edges of Six Step Bridge had a chute, through which all manner of garbage and waste was ejected, falling into the river or spattering the bridge's exposed Echoes below. Food, broken furniture, construction waste, ruined clothing—once ejected from the chutes, it was forgotten and cast aside. He had once seen a living man thrown into the river, and sometimes at night he remembered the weight of that man's left leg in his hand heartbeats before he fell.

Dead though the river was, in many ways it cleansed the city.

He edged through the chute, looking at the dark line of the Tharin way below. Then he started climbing down, from strut to support to crossbeam, until he hung wedged between two vertical timbers. Above him, he could hear the impact of countless feet and hooves on the bridge's surface. Around him, the dusty, abandoned structures of yesteryear.

Then he heard the squeals.

He took a small bag of powder from his pocket and spread some along a moldy timber beam. He also extracted a roll of paper and a charcoal, and while he waited, he wrote.

It never took long. He sensed the rats closing on him, hidden away for now but tempted by the bone powder. He'd once tasted the stuff himself—extracted and crushed from the skeletons of dead Garthans, so he was told—and he'd been sick for a week. Others often chided him about his sensitive stomach, and he berated them, claiming Marcellan blood. Bitterness and humor made good companions.

He watched from the corner of his eye as a rat the size of his forearm started licking up the powder. He waited a moment until its eyes started turning with the food frenzy, then he clasped the creature and tied the rolled note to its leathery tail. He splashed the fur on its back with rose stoneshroom extract—very rare, and visible only to certain creatures—whispered a few words into the creature's ear, then let it go.

It disappeared, jumping, running, and dropping its way north through the bridge's most recent Echoes, and his work was done. He climbed back up to watch the woman again, pleased to be among people once more.

The rat moved quickly, familiar with this underside and driven by the compulsion only recently planted within it.

Leaving the bridge behind, it stayed with the drains and sewers. Other rats saw it and cowered away, because there was something about it that smelled of death. It passed different creatures down there in the dark, and most of them also moved aside, though some sniffed after it, curious at the message it might carry.

It did not go *too* deep. It never went *too* deep—especially now.

It came to a place where the sewers vented, and here it left cover and ventured out into the open. It moved in slow, hesitant sprints, looking around for danger but forgetting where the worst threat actually dwelled.

The rathawk had a nest in the high walls of Marcellan Canton. It had nested in the same place for thirty years, mating with the same female, and together they had raised nineteen chicks that had survived to adulthood. It flew, ate, and slept, but implanted deep within its mind was some other compulsion that was fed only at the rarest of times. One of those times was today. Riding a thermal high above the walls, it spotted a glint in the shadows far below. Without thinking, simply following a set of instructions implanted when it was very young, the rathawk folded its wings and plummeted. For a few beats, it was the fastest thing in Echo City, other than thought. At the last moment it spread its wings to brake its descent, extended its claws, and the rat died so quickly that it uttered no sound.

Usually the rathawk would take such bounty back to its nest. It would rip off the head, tear out the poisonous innards, and throw them away for ghourt lizards to snap up from the wall's surface. The remaining dark meat would feed its chicks for another day. Sometimes it would even take some of the meat for itself. But today it clasped the rodent in its claws and did not rip.

The rathawk circled high and then flew north. When it saw and smelled the water far below, it rested its wings and circled down, singing a unique song as it went. By the time it reached the rooftop, there was a man standing there. The rathawk, usually afraid of people, alighted on the man's outstretched arm.

The man took the dead rat from the bird's claws. He placed the corpse gently on the parapet, noting the blood-speckled note tied to its tail, and picked up a chunk of swine meat for the rathawk. The bird took it with a gentle respect it probably did not understand, then lifted away. Within moments it was a speck in the sky, and when he blinked the man lost sight of it altogether.

"Now what's this?" he said, a little annoyed. A naked woman lay on his bed in the room below, and his mouth was still wet from her. But the rathawk call had shrunk his enthusiasm, and he had a feeling that he'd remain unspent for the rest of this day. A message sent in such a risky manner could mean only one thing: important news.

The question was, good or bad?

He snipped off the message roll with the tip of his knife and nudged the dead rat from the parapet. He unrolled the paper. His eyes widened.

"Oh," said the man. He rushed down the stone steps, and though the woman was still lying with her legs splayed, his mind was already far away. He waved off her objections, shrugged on trousers and a jacket, slipped on his boots, and left the room.

Out in the street, he looked around nervously as he hurried along. This felt like something that could bring only danger and upset with it. Danger for all the Watchers. And upset for Gorham. He never had got over that fucking woman.

Alert for any indication that he was being followed, he waited in a spice garden for a while, hunkered down among a profusion of bushes and vines, low plants and trees, breathing in deeply and trying to pass the time by identifying each spice. When he was certain he was alone, he slipped through the garden and emerged on the banks of a canal, startling a pair of mating ducks into flight. The female pecked at the male. *I know how you feel*, he thought, watching the drake take flight.

Farther along the canal, a woman lived in a boat. He knocked on one of the small round windows and her face quickly appeared, almost as if she'd been awaiting his arrival. She opened a hatch in the roof and climbed lithely out, sitting above him with a small crossbow in her right hand. He'd seen it before—crafted from the finest of metals, and it was whispered that it came from one of the older Marcellan Echoes, though no one had ever hazarded a guess as to how she came to own it.

"Malia," the man said. "I have a message passed down the route." She raised one eyebrow. He'd never felt comfortable around this one, even when her husband was still alive.

"Well?" she prompted.

"Peer Nadawa," he said. "She's back."

Malia's expression did not change. Her eyes glimmered as she shifted slightly. Her pale fingers grew pink again as they loosened around the handle of the crossbow. Then she slid from the barge's roof and landed a step in front of him, and wafting from her he could smell the intoxicating aroma of pure, unrefined slash.

"Forget this, Devin," she said.

He nodded, turned, and walked away, hoping that the angry naked woman would still be in his room when he returned.

Peer could have sat there forever, but she knew it was time to go. Gorham would know what to do. Even after she'd been caught and banished, the old network might have remained operative. Either way, she was certain that he'd still have contact with the Watchers.

Besides, she was desperate to see him, and every pause was another moment when they were not together. There were thoughts that had reared their heads but that she would not entertain: *He's dead; he's moved and changed his name; he's given me up for lost and is with another woman.* Though she had long ago given up hope of ever seeing him again, she had never stopped loving him. *He'll be just the same*, she thought. Yet a flicker of nervousness had seeded in her chest, and she could do nothing to extinguish it.

She and Rufus stood, and she left a couple of shillings for the wine. She glanced around for anyone who might be watching them. There was a group of women sitting in front of the next building along, all of them sucking on flexible pipes leading from a central smoke pot. Two of them were looking Rufus up and down, and one of the two had a hungry look in her eyes. Rut-slash smokers, out looking for men. Other than that, Peer and Rufus seemed to go unnoticed.

"Where now?" Rufus said.

"My friend used to live a couple of miles from here. If that's not changed, we'll see him soon."

Rufus started to follow her again, and Peer saw a flash of drug-fueled jealousy in one of the smoking women's eyes.

"Rufus," she said, "walk with me, not behind me." He smiled softly, but his eyes never stayed on her for long. They were drinking in the surroundings, flitting here and there and back again, and she envied him seeing all this for the first time. For her, returning here from Skulk, Six Step Bridge had a vital freshness to it. She could barely imagine what Rufus was thinking and feeling.

She wished he could tell her. *Soon*, she thought. *Gorham will know what to do and how to get him to the Watchers. Rufus is what they've been watching for forever. Proof of something beyond.*

As they left the bridge and started across a large park, the bustle faded away. There were still many people around them, but they were sitting or lying in the grass, eating or reading, staring or loving. The sound of a hooting heron came from the lake on the park's far side, and wind whispered through the numerous barch trees, setting their thin, heavy branches swaying.

In a grove of low trees halfway across the park, as Peer felt more relaxed than she had since escaping Skulk, a man stepped into their path.

Peer froze. Rufus's left hand reached out and grasped her arm.

The man glanced around quickly before moving forward, right hand resting on the hilt of his sword.

There's something . . . Peer thought, then saw a blur of movement from her right. Rufus dropped to his knees, letting go of her arm and bringing his strange spider-poison weapon up from his side.

More people appeared around them, emerging from behind trees and bushes, and Peer knew them. *Watchers.*

"Rufus!" she shouted, leaning sideways to try to knock him

off balance. It almost worked. She heard the gentle cough of his weapon as he fell, and the man before them looked down at the left knee of his trousers.

Peer staggered to the right but kept to her feet.

The others closed in quickly, knives drawn, and if Peer had said something different, perhaps the man would have lived. But her thought then was for Rufus. "Rufus, they're friends!" she said. And as the visitor from beyond Echo City lowered his weapon, she saw the man bending, reaching to his knee, touching the wet sticky patch there and raising it toward his face.

"No!" she shouted, but it was already too late. Maybe all it took was the smallest contact with skin.

He moaned a little, frowned, then started to shake. He stared down at his hand as if it was something he had never seen before. Then he began to scream.

"Gerrett!" one of the others shouted, pushing him so that he fell. "Quiet!" But Gerrett—and Peer remembered him now, a Watcher with whom Gorham had spoken a few times, a man whose children fished in the Western Reservoir and whose wife made the most amazing salted fish rack—was beyond listening. His screams were loud and high, and he was shaking his hand so frantically that it slapped hard against the ground, the crack of breaking bones almost hidden beneath his cries.

A woman clapped her hand across his mouth.

"Don't touch," Rufus said. "Poison."

The woman glanced from him to Peer and back again, then moved away.

Gerrett's screams died down suddenly, as though his throat had been clapped shut. The convulsions started then, and the bloody foam from his mouth, and the darkening of his eyes as something in there burst.

A man and woman beat Rufus to the ground. He let them.

When they came for Peer, they were not so rough, but the gag they forced into her mouth stank of chickpig and tasted of shit, and the blind they tied around her eyes was so tight it made her head ache.

"Gerrett . . ." one of them said.

"No time."

As Peer was led away, she could still hear the impact of thrashing limbs on the ground.

"They killed Gerrett."

"What?"

"Gerrett died. The one with her, he *shot* him with something. Some poison."

"Why?"

"I don't know."

Gorham walked faster. They'd taken Peer and her companion to a boathouse on the shore of the reservoir—a place with a hidden basement where they'd sheltered people before. But his initial enthusiasm about seeing Peer had been shattered. He had so many secrets to tell her, so many apologies to make—and now it seemed she had the same.

"Has anyone told his family yet?"

"Of course not," Malia said. "I only just found out myself."

"Keep it that way for now."

They hurried along the well-trodden path around the reservoir. It was seven miles all the way around, and it involved crossing the border with Crescent twice, but many people used it to exercise or walk away the excesses of every eighth-day feast. That was the reason why the boathouse was such a good hiding place: It was so close to activity. A row of vacation homes lined the road to their left, owned mostly by rich people from Marcellan Canton and used irregularly. But behind them were smaller buildings, retreats from the busier areas of Course and Crescent, and these were occupied for at least half of the time. Hiding people beneath the Marcellans' noses pleased Gorham immensely.

They slowed as they approached the boathouse, and Malia went ahead, disappearing through the door into shadow. Gorham looked out over the lake, trying to appear calm even though his heart was thumping hard. *Peer is back*, he thought. The idea seemed so surreal and alien to him, because he'd spent the best part of three years attempting to forget. Whatever confident face he presented to his fellow Watchers and the other people around him, deep inside Peer had always been a shameful scar.

I've got so much to apologize for.

Malia stepped from the boathouse. "Don't stand there with your head up your ass. Come *on*!" But even her brusque signal that the coast was clear could not raise a smile from him today.

Peer was back, sweet innocent Peer. And he wondered what secrets she had brought.

He went inside and followed Malia into the basement. The first person Gorham saw was the cowering man, tears streaking his bruised face and hands raised to protect himself. He had striking white hair and looked weak and thin, but looks could be deceptive. The three Watchers he'd sent with Gerrett to bring in Peer were there, and the air was loaded.

"Peer?" he asked.

"Here." She was on the other side of the basement, strapped against a wall.

His heart broke for her. She looked just as he remembered—her dark hair longer, perhaps, her face a little thinner and harsher—and right now her expression was one of misery. She looked at him with a naïve hope, and something else.

"Peer," he said awkwardly, "it's so good to see you again." He crossed to her and knelt, glancing at her bonds. They were tied well. Her left wrist had bled a little from where the rope had tightened and twisted in, but the dribble of blood was already drying. He scanned her face for any hint of abuse and saw none. Good. The Watchers were determined but not brutal. Not unless the occasion called for it.

"Gorham, what's happening here?" Her voice was soft and uncertain.

"I came to ask the same thing. Your friend killed Gerrett."

"That was an accident. He stepped out in front of us and—"

"You remember Gerrett," Malia said. "We haven't told his family yet. His youngest developed heart canker a year ago. The shock might just kill her."

Peer closed her eyes, and Gorham saw true sorrow there. *Careful*, he thought. *She's from Skulk.*

"So who's your friend?"

"Gorham, he's the only reason I managed to get out. I thought you might still have contact with the Watchers, even after everything, and I was bringing him to you so that—"

"Assassination," Malia breathed, the word like a revelation. "Those fucking Marcellans are hiring from Skulk now, are they? Can't do their own job because it would be too dirty?"

"Assassination?" Peer said, looking from Malia to Gorham.

"Of course," Gorham said. "You don't know."

"Know what?"

"We should get away from here," Malia said urgently. "Deal with him, take her somewhere safer for interrogation."

"Gorham," Peer persisted, "know what?"

Gorham looked at his old lover, whom he'd let go. He reached out and touched her face. She did not flinch, but neither did she lean into the caress.

"That I'm leading the Watchers now," he said.

Peer's eyes grew wide, and Gorham sighed deeply as he stood and turned away.

"Bring them both," he said. "We'll go down into Jail Ten. Then we can find out why they came."

"Gorham, I don't—" Peer's voice was high, confused.

"Quiet!" Malia shouted, then she grinned. "That'll be my job for the day."

Gorham was shaking, confused, emotions in turmoil. He forced himself to walk away, because he could not afford weakness. Not now. He knew how Malia found out things. And he hoped that, when the time came, Peer would tell the truth.

Twice in as many days. Gorham hated coming down into the Echoes.

Jail Ten was in the first Echo below Course Canton. It had been abandoned almost a hundred years before, soon after the salt plague and subsequent purge had turned Skulk Canton into a wasteland. The jail's prisoners had been moved to Skulk in stages, all three thousand of them, and legend had it that the brutal jailmaster had remained behind in Jail Ten, never to be seen again. The story went that he still considered it his duty to incarcerate anyone who wandered into the underground complex, whether by accident or on purpose. Gorham and his fellow Watchers had sensed phantoms down there, and some even claimed to have seen them, but no one had seen the jail-master.

It served them well to perpetuate the myth.

They carried oil torches similar to those the Baker used in her own underground retreat. There were no chopped down here to guide them, however, and Malia and the other Watchers navigated by memory alone. They had been using the jail for little more than a year, and they went there only when it was absolutely essential.

Gorham was feeling unsettled, uncertain, yet he could not let that show. The Watchers had almost been destroyed three years before, the crackdown by the Marcellan bullies and their Hanharan priests reaching deep into the heart of the organization and all but tearing it out. The memories of those times were still vivid and depressing, and he tried not to dwell on them too often. But seeing Peer walking ahead of him brought it all back. Her wrists were tied before her, and he wondered how painful her right arm would be. She limped slightly, and he wanted to ask about her hip. But he could not, of course. If he voiced his thoughts, guilt would break him down, and it was his job now to be strong.

We should be in each other's arms, he thought. *Normal lovers separated for so long would have swept each other away*. But they were not normal people and never had been. And these were not normal times.

They reached one of the few entrances to Jail Ten that was still functioning. Malia signaled a halt, and she and another Watcher, Devin, edged toward the heavy steel door. It was propped open by a bundle of rags. Malia whispered some words that hissed around that subterranean space, and beyond the jail door something moved away. The darkness in there was suddenly not quite so deep, and Malia nodded that the coast was clear.

The Baker had given them that. She said it was chopped from a razorplant and given a rudimentary mind, and for three nights after learning that, Gorham had not been able to sleep, terrified at what such a mind might think.

Peer stood fast, the tall man she called Rufus beside her. Gorham heard her breath coming harsh and scared, and the man seemed to be shedding a tear.

"This way, killer!" Malia said to the man, but Gorham stepped forward.

"Let me," he said. He stood before Peer and looked her in the eye, closer than he had yet been. He inhaled her breath, and it sent a thrill of nostalgia and recognition through him— a warmth that had been missing for so long. "We're not bringing you down here to hurt you," he said.

"Really."

"Things are changing, and the Marcellans think we're finished. We can't let them know otherwise."

"Why?"

"Because there's much to do. I'll tell you all of it soon, Peer, I promise."

"So we're down here for your own protection?"

Gorham almost smiled. *There, the strong-minded Peer still lives.* But she did not look strong right then, and he remembered the terrible truth he had yet to reveal. There was no way he couldn't, but he dreaded every word.

"And yours," he said. "You and your friend."

"He's more than you think," Peer said.

"Tell me inside."

"Bastard."

Does she know? he wondered. But, no, she could not, because there was no way she'd be able to keep such knowledge to herself.

"I never forgot you," he said.

"Nice way of showing it." Her voice broke on the last word. He went to say something else, but Peer shoved past him.

They made their way down through corridors lined with doors, all of them closed. There could have been anything in those small dark rooms, but the doors had been locked shut for decades, and whatever dwelled inside remained alone. Their echoing footsteps disappeared into the warren of rooms and corridors. The stench of stagnant water and old secrets hung heavy in the still air. It was a place never meant to be empty, and being so filled it with stark potential.

As they neared the center of the jail, Devin ran ahead and went about lighting scores of torches lining the walls. The huge room revealed what had once been an exercise area, three stories high and open to the sky until this part of Course was developed overhead. That was perhaps two centuries ago, according to Gorham's advisers' best guess. They trusted that this place was all but forgotten.

"Over here," Malia said. Peer and her tall companion were edged toward the far wall, and there the Watchers set about tying them fast. At Gorham's request, they sat Peer first, making her comfortable before securing her arms to the wall and her legs to the metal chair.

"I came to you because I trusted you," she said.

"You still can."

"Yes?" She was glaring at him now, and he wondered, *What the crap has she gone through these last three years?* He had no idea.

"You want me to start right away?" Malia asked. She was keen to begin. She'd already taken a folded leather pouch from her belt, and she was arranging its contents across an old mess table.

Something whispered in a dark corner of the massive space, and Devin and the others shifted nervously.

"Only phantoms," Peer said. "Already seen several today."

"No," Gorham said. "Not yet. I want to talk to her first." And he knelt before his old lover as if seeking her blessing and forgiveness.

But what he was about to tell her would surely damn him in her eyes forever.

"We gave you up," he said. "I was already higher in the Watchers' echelons than you knew. The part you worked with, the political arm, had always been intended as dispensable. It was a useless gesture, trying to give our ideals a political voice. You know the Marcellans: They sometimes allow beliefs disparate from their own, but they'll never grant them any sort of power. So your group was . . . expendable. A front. Ready to be given away to the Marcellans should they ever move on us. We hoped the time would never come."

Peer was staring at him wide-eyed. She said nothing.

"We were nurturing you and the others. Preparing you. And the time *did* come, when they heard rumors that we'd started using the Baker again."

"The Baker's dead!" Peer gasped, and Malia laughed bitterly.

"This is the *new* Baker," Gorham said. "She was killed twenty years ago, yes, but she chopped herself, knowing what was happening. It's how generations of Bakers have continued their line. So now we deal with . . . well, her daughter. And her mother handed down all she knew."

"So you betrayed me for your cause," Peer said, smiling. There was nothing behind the smile—no humor, no life. It was a rictus grin, and Gorham had to turn away.

"They took you and the others in the political arm. We hoped that dismantling our public face would satisfy them, but they came further. Bad times, Peer. We lost so many. We never suspected the ruin would run so deep. There were betrayals that led to scores of deaths—the Marcellan Canton's walls ran red for weeks afterward, and they announced a two-day feast to celebrate what they called the 'defeat of heresy.' But with you . . . we never knew—"

"Of *course* you knew what they'd do!" she shouted, but then she sighed and hung her head. "They tortured me, Gorham," she said, head still dipped.

"Yes."

"They made me hurt, demanded that I renounce my beliefs and accept theirs. And when I didn't, they smashed me."

"I know, Peer."

"You know?"

He nodded. "The tortures were made public knowledge."

"Do you care?"

How did he answer that? Of course he cared. "We need to make sure you haven't come here meaning us harm."

"And that's your answer?"

"That, and I'm sorry."

"Going to torture me now, Gorham?"

"No." And because he could not face watching this, and because he hated himself for not being able to say everything that needed saying until it was over, he turned away and left them all. Devin gave him a torch as he passed, and Gorham found a shadowy doorway and aimed for it.

"I came for you!" Peer shouted behind him. She sounded angry, but he still knew her well enough to hear the hurt.

Gorham could answer only silently and to himself. *When I'm sure that's true, I'll welcome you back.* The corridor closed around him and he slipped into a room, leaning heavily against a wall, sobbing.

From the large area he'd just left, he heard the hissing of Malia's truthbugs.

"My husband was one of those they crucified alive," Malia said. "You remember Bren?"

"Yes, Malia. I'm sorry."

Malia looked up from the table and stared at her, and Peer could see the sadness in her eyes. Anger tried to hide it, fury closed it in, but the sorrow was unmistakable.

"Thank you," Malia said. "I apologize, Peer. This won't hurt. But what Gorham said is right: We need to know. A lot has changed since you . . ."

"Since I was sacrificed?"

Malia sighed and came forward, several small bugs flitting across the palm of her hand.

Peer looked after Gorham, but he had not reappeared. Devin and the other two Watchers stood back, glancing around nervously as a whisper passed through the subterranean room once again. "I'll tell you the truth," she said.

Malia nodded, then held her hand flat in front of Peer's face and blew.

Peer felt the bugs strike her skin. They stuck for a while, speckling her face, and then they started moving. Some went for her mouth, some her nose, and one wormed into the corner of her eye. She opened her mouth to scream but could not. The breath was frozen in her throat.

"No," she heard Rufus say beside her, but she could not turn to comfort him. *He'd better be what I think he is,* she thought, and then something changed abruptly. The pain in her right arm grew distant, the ache in her hip faded, and the coolness of the air misted away into a comfortable warmth. Everything felt fine, and she relaxed down into the chair, her body taking the weight of her tied arms.

"Why have you come here?" Malia asked.

"To see Gorham."

"Why?"

"Because of Rufus."

"Who's Rufus?"

Peer glanced sideways at the bound man.

"Why do you think Gorham wants to see Rufus?"

"You don't need your little bugs for me to . . ." She frowned, feeling them on her, *in* her, and a terrible shiver ran through her body.

"Why?" Malia prompted.

"Because he's from beyond Echo City. I saw him walking in across the desert, and he doesn't know this place."

Malia's eyes went wide. Her mouth opened, then closed again, as though swallowing whatever she was trying to say. "That can't be . . ." she said at last.

Peer saw the others step forward, and all the attention moved onto Rufus. And then, below the terrible feeling of those bugs still shifting inside her, she realized the urgency of what Malia had to do next.

"Him," Peer said, shaking and feeling a terrible sickness rising.

"Devin, give her the drink," Malia said, and she returned to the table.

Devin came close to Peer and held a small goblet to her mouth, but he never took his eyes from Rufus. "Drink," he said. "It'll kill them. Is he really from the Bonelands?"

"I think so," Peer said weakly. The fluid tasted of rotten mepple, but it settled the rising vomit somehow, and she leaned back, exhausted, in her chair.

Malia was whispering to one of the other Watchers, and the woman ran off toward where Gorham had vanished.

"This is it," Peer said. "This is it, isn't it?"

Malia threw her a strange glance but then moved toward Rufus, her hand held out and swarming with a new batch of truthbugs.

"This is what we've all been waiting for," Peer said. "It's why I had to come." Rufus was looking at her, eyes wide and terrified, and she tried to offer him a reassuring smile, but it would not form. She was as fascinated as all of them in what he had to say, and she found herself wishing that Gorham was there to hear.

"There's more that you don't yet know," Malia said to Peer. Then she blew the bugs into the tall man's face.

And when she leaned forward to ask him her first question, he began to scream.

On the rooftop of the tallest building on the highest hill in Echo City, a Baker's child fed four Scopes and made sure their chains were secure. He liked these monsters, enjoyed the sickly wet sounds their mouths made when they opened, and breathed in the stink of them that even the stiff breeze up here could never completely carry away. He smoothed their thick, rough skin beneath their leathery covers. He scooped their shit and swept their piss to a far corner of the roof and into a chute that took it away. Sometimes he spoke to them, knowing that even if they heard they could never understand. His mother had made them well, while she had made him badly.

His name was Nophel, and he had named himself. She had never honored him with a name. He doubted she even gave him a glance before sending him to Bedmoil, the largest workhouse in Mino Mont. It had been the greatest moment of his life when he aided in her downfall twenty years before.

Nophel had taken his name from one of the six-legged gods of the Temple of the Seventy-seven Custodians. His Marcellan employers disliked that, and the Hanharan priests who occasionally visited him hated it. But these reactions interested him, and intellectually he knew that the name had become more than just a part of him. Nophel, so the temple's teachings went, was the god of quiet things, and he had spent his life keeping to the shadows, whispering while others shouted and ensuring that he could go where he pleased. Old Dane Marcellan had taken to using Nophel for some of his more covert activities, and Nophel liked that well enough.

Even so, alone up here with the Scopes was the only time he would reveal his mutilation to the skies.

He fed the Western Scope, the last of the four, using a wide spoon to scoop the chickpig and mepple stew into its drooling mouth. It made small, satisfied grunting noises as it fed—the only one of the four that did—and he heard its stomach rumbling as it swallowed the food. A thick membrane slipped down and up across its massive eyeball, clearing dust and renewing its view. While it chewed its last mouthful, Nophel knelt to check its gears, mountings, and cogs. They were well greased. He pulled a lever, forcing the thing to shift its weight slightly. The complex support system moved and flexed, but he heard nothing. That was good. Next he ensured that the reading tube's entry point to its body was not sore or infected. It entered at the back of the Scope's neck, and Nophel hated the bristly pink junction of silk tube with rough skin, because it reminded him of his own deformed face in the mirror. There was no sign of inflammation and it was dry. That pleased him, because it meant he would not have to apply any soothing cream.

Soon the time would come to move the Scopes around the roof, changing their positions to avoid resting sores. But not yet. That was a task he disliked because it revealed their true genesis: humanity. Covered in leather shrouds, they were monsters to him. When he moved them, seeing them walk, holding their shriveled hands to guide them across the rooftop because their eyes could see only far away, not this close in—despite all that, they seemed almost as human as he did.

He walked one slow circuit of the roof and looked out and down over Echo City. In some directions he could just make out the pale hint of the Markoshi Desert on the horizon, but mostly it was only city he saw, the great sprawl of ages. Towers rose here and there, and the spires of temples. The arches of the failed skyride network—the metal rusting, some sections fallen into memory, as had the dozens of people killed on its first and last ride—pricked the sky to the west. But none of them was nearly as high as Hanharan Heights. It looked so timeless, yet in a thousand years this view would be completely different. The place where he now stood would have been subsumed beneath the steady march of progress, and

whoever stood upon Hanharan Heights' summit might be five
hundred steps higher. *And what of forever?* he thought. He
often attempted to wonder that far ahead. The city could not
rise endlessly, and though he did not fear it—Nophel feared
little—eventual stagnation, then regression, was his predic-
tion.

He stood longest next to the Northern Scope. It was the
quietest of the four, the stillest, and there had been times
when he thought it dead. But if he leaned over the roof parapet and looked at its eye, he could see the moisture there and
the concentration as it looked past the spread of Crescent's
farmland at Dragar's Canton.

Though ten miles distant, the pale curves of Dragar's six
silent domes were clearly visible. Nophel appreciated a mystery, but this one troubled him.

"So let's see what's to be seen," he said, and the breeze
stole his words away.

He always bade the Scopes farewell, though they never answered back. Deep down, the root of their humanity must
still exist; the Baker bitch had seen to that. And he liked to
think that, even if they did not hear or answer, they sensed
that he cared for them.

He descended the winding staircase that led to the viewing
room, fifty steps below the exposed roof. Halfway down, he
tied his robe tight and lifted his hood, just in case one of the
Marcellans or, gods help him, a Hanharan priest had found
reason to pay him a visit. But the room was silent, other than
the steady rumble of brewing five-bean and the crackle of the
fire he'd set in the hearth. Warming already, mouth watering in anticipation of the brew, he glanced at the huge viewing
mirror set in the center of the room. The four wide reading
tubes hung down from a hole in the ceiling, and behind the
viewing mirror stood the complex apparatus used to select
tubes. The western tube was connected right now, and
Nophel saw the glint of sun on the Tharin's surface. It made
the river appear almost alive.

Nophel poured a large mug of five-bean and sat before the
viewing mirror. As always prior to seeing what *they* could
see, he needed to see himself. He pulled a lever and the

western tube disconnected with a soft hiss, the living image on the mirror fading and then flickering to nothing.

Nophel lowered his hood and smiled at his image. The single pale eye, his other eye a blood-red ruin. The dark skin split and bubbled with fungal growths; they would need pricking and bathing again later. His teeth were good, bright and even, and that made his smile the most monstrous aspect of all.

"Nophel, king of all the city," he muttered, laughing as he reconnected the western tube. Echo City's last king had been quartered and sent to the far corners fifteen hundred years before, and Nophel's utterance was an amusement only to himself.

For the next hour he controlled the Western Scope with a series of levers and dials. Rising within the reading tubes were the thin pipes that carried Nophel's hydraulic commands, and from his seat he could spur the Scope to turn its head left and right, up and down, and to extend its neck, thereby turning the great lens of its eye and bringing distant things in close. He imagined the chopped creature grunting as he turned dials and pulled or pushed levers, and perhaps it still had the taste of chickpig in its mouth as it obeyed promptings it did not understand. The Marcellans viewed the Scopes as little more than machines; Nophel alone acknowledged their spark of life.

From the expansive farmland of Crescent Canton to the water refineries of Course, he focused in and out, enjoying the sense of flying across the city. Smoke rose from tall chimneys close to the western wall, steam drifted southward from the refineries, canals flowed, streets bustled, rathawks drifted and swooped. He could see straight along the river from here, and he tweaked a lever, commanding the Scope to close along the Tharin as far as it could. The image on the viewing mirror grew, quickly passing the city walls and reaching far out into the haze of the desert. The image paused, Nophel nudged the lever impatiently, and the Scope stretched farther. The view was now simply a mass of hazy air and pale desert landscape, but he sat staring at it for some time. The Marcellans said there was nothing beyond the city, yet here he was. He reveled in this slight rebellion, realizing that it was foolish yet enjoying it nonetheless. If the Marcellans knew where he looked, he would be in trouble—yet nothing like that worried him. He sometimes believed that Dane Marcellan—the one who had taken it upon himself to look after Nophel—was even a little scared of him. One day that fear might serve him well, but for now he simply toyed with it.

Nophel worked for the Marcellans, but he lived for himself.

The image began to waver as the Scope grew tired, and he stroked the dial that gave it permission to draw back into itself. As it did so, its sight passed across the area to the north of Course where the Baker had practiced her monstrous arts until two decades before. Nophel smiled grimly and went about switching Scopes.

A hiss of escaping gas, the soft click of well-oiled gears, and he pumped the footrest that boosted pressure in the hydraulic systems. Draining his five-bean and going to pour more, Nophel felt the familiar thrill at what he would see next. Dragar's Canton was always motionless, quiet, enigmatic, yet he could watch its stillness for hours. *They're down there*, he would think, *or maybe not*, and both stark possibilities held him enraptured. The streets were full of rumors, of course, but there had been no verified sighting of a Dragarian for almost forty years.

When he returned to the viewing mirror and turned a dial, he dropped his mug of five-bean. He barely sensed the pain as the liquid scalded his foot.

Then he lifted his hood, closed his robe, and rushed from the room, heading down.

There were several Scarlet Blades in the corridor outside the Marcellans' rooms. They were lounging in wide leather seats, playing lob dice and laughing as one unfortunate lost more and more shillings. They glanced up at Nophel's approach, and the laughter chilled.

"I need to see Dane Marcellan," he said.

"Dane's busy," one of the tall female soldiers replied. Someone chuckled.

"Then I'll fucking un-busy him!" Nophel roared. One Blade stood and drew his knife; another took a step back. Nophel shook, his surprise at how he'd raged at them smothered by the fear and excitement that had taken hold.

."Fine," the woman said. "I'll pick you a nice spot on the wall." She kicked at the door handle behind her and shoved the door open with her boot. They all knew that Nophel would never hang on the wall. If and when the time came, he'd disappear quickly and quietly, and his body would float down into the Chasm with so many others.

I scare them, he thought, and he glared at the soldiers as he passed by. A couple of them glowered back, but their eyes flickered away before his did. The others did not watch him through the door at all.

He entered the long, wide corridor that ran the length of the Marcellans' living quarters, hurrying quickly past displays of rare artwork, sculptures, and religious artifacts from thousands of years of Hanharan dominance. As always, he spared a quick glance for the glass-enclosed finger bone— the priests and their more-devout followers believed fervently that it was the index finger from Hanharan's left hand—then paused outside Dane's door.

A moment of doubt gripped him. *Is it really Dane I need to tell?* But of all the Marcellans, Dane was the closest to a friend he had. And there really was no one else.

Heart thumping from exertion, eye wide as though it could retain the dread image of what he had seen, he thumped once on the door and then entered.

Dane was standing naked at a table in the far corner of the room, cooking slash and inhaling the fumes through a series of wet pipes. The flesh of his ample thighs and buttocks quivered as he breathed in, and Nophel heard the sighs of gentle pleasure. In the center of the room, reclining on the vast round bed, two naked women idly stroked each other. One of them glanced up, apparently unconcerned at being disturbed. And then she saw Nophel.

"Oh!" she gasped. She stared at his face, still shadowed by the hood, her brazen nakedness a sign of her sick fascination. *I'm not a person to her*, Nophel thought, and he felt the familiar flush of shame that he had spent his entire life trying to push down.

Dane turned around, taking a moment to focus. "Nophel," he said.

"We must talk," Nophel said.

Dane pulled the pipe to his lips again and pursed them around its end—a delicate action for such a fat man. His rounded stomach hung so low that his genitals were almost hidden from view.

"Poor man," the other naked woman said. She had slipped from the bed and stood, unashamed, scratching idly at her stomach with one hand while she looked at him.

"Leave us if you will, ladies," Dane said.

"But, Dane," the first woman began, "we were just getting—"

"It's important," Nophel said. He was looking at the women as he spoke, and he took several steps forward, knowing that the burning oil lamps would cast more light onto his face from this angle.

The standing woman stepped back, crossing both hands over her sex.

"Tomorrow," Dane said. He turned his back on the women and breathed in more slash, waving Nophel over.

The women left without dressing, exiting through a door hidden in an expanse of books lining one wall. Nophel had never been in there, though he knew it led to a series of stairs and corridors—Dane's own private route down into the vastness of Hanharan Heights. He felt a pang of jealousy that Dane would let two whores use this way yet not let him, but he shoved it aside. This was not about favors, or even trust. Both men wanted what was best for the city, and though their outlooks might differ, they came together about the bigger picture.

"It's been a while," Dane said. He turned and smiled. "You're sure I can't interest you in . . . ?" He nodded at the door through which the women had vanished. "Rebec really is very good. She does things with her lips and a mouthful of dart root that'll have you calling to Hanharan's divine cock for mercy."

Nophel shook his head. Dane's blasphemy never surprised him. "They pity me," he said.

"You interest them. They'd explore you."

"A gateway opened in Dragar's Canton."

For a moment Dane's smile remained as he blinked away the effects of slash, absorbing what Nophel had said. Then his face dropped and he became the politician Nophel knew so well.

"A gateway?"

"Or a door. Something. It was quick." Nophel breathed deeply, inhaling the scents of cooked slash, wine, and sex. He indulged in none of them, and the odors stirred little within him.

Dane waddled to the bed and lifted his gown, swinging it around his shoulders with a surprising deftness. Fat he might be, and cursed with many vices, but Nophel had long suspected that Dane was stronger and fitter than he looked. Perhaps deception came naturally to such a man, or maybe he had simply taken advantage of circumstance.

"You're certain of what you saw?" he asked.

Nophel nodded.

"The Northern Scope, it's fit and well? Healthy?"

"There was no fault. It wasn't a blur in the mirror or an inconsistency in the Scope's vision. Quick, granted, but I'm sure. Part of a dome slid open. Something came out. The dome closed again." He shut his eyes for a beat, remembering what he'd seen to ensure it tallied with his description. Something came out—that was the part that still confused him.

"*What* came out?"

"I don't know."

"Hmm." Dane regarded him for a moment, then came closer and touched his shoulder. "Sit with me." He walked around the bed to an area of floor seats, the table in the center bearing several opened wine bottles and a scatter of glasses and goblets. There was also the remains of a meal. "You're well?" he asked.

"I'm as fine as I can be," Nophel said.

"Then we have a problem that needs investigating."

"You'll take it to the Council?"

"Of course." Dane eased himself into a seat, the upholstery expanding and stretching to take his weight. Nophel sat opposite, uncomfortable as ever in such plush surroundings. He preferred his own rooms lower down in the vast sprawl of buildings that made up Hanharan Heights—book-lined, simple, with the smell of the past hanging in the air from old manuscripts and older maps. Nophel had once met Sprote Felder, the renowned explorer of the Echoes, and the two had talked for hours about things most Echoians would never even know. Nophel respected that man—perhaps envied him too— but he was as much an explorer as Felder. The only difference was, he explored history through his mind. And the history he sought was all to do with the Bakers—those damned women who had cursed him so.

"And what will they do?" he asked.

"They'll want to talk to you. To ask exactly what you saw." Dane sighed and poured himself a large glass of ruby wine. "Then they'll debate the veracity of your account, argue once again over your control of the Scopes. Express their continuing mistrust at your heritage."

"I *gave* them the Baker."

"Some don't see it that way, Nophel. You know that well enough." He sipped at the wine, nodded, then clunked the glass down on the table. "They'll argue and agree, then dispute and call for more meetings, and it'll take them three days to get to where I've arrived in two heartbeats."

"Where you've arrived . . ."

"Knowing that we can take no chances." Dane shook his head, the metal bonds in his tightly tied hair tinkling together. "Dragar's is given its privacy, and most have forgotten it's even there. It's a blank spot on the city, Nophel, but you know as well as I that we keep a good watch. That's partly what they're for." He nodded vaguely at the ceiling. "And also part of the reason why you and I are such good friends."

"Maybe it happens a lot," Nophel said. "Maybe they're always slipping in and out, and it's just that I happened to see it today."

"Do you believe that?"

Nophel thought about what he'd seen, trying to make it clear in his mind. "No," he said softly.

"No. That's why you need to go and investigate."

"Me?" He was shocked, but pleased as well. Nophel knew he was a monster to most, but he had never denied the presence of his own ego. It was something to do with fitting in.

"You're quiet," Dane said. "You can move well. People . . ." He shrugged. "You know."

"People avoid me."

"Yes. So while I take this to the Council and let them bicker like old women, go and look for me, Nophel. Find out what came out and what it means. And bring it to me."

Nophel nodded, running his fingers around the rim of an empty wineglass. When he looked, a fine line of lip paint slashed across his finger, and he thought of where else those lips had been. He felt no longings and never had.

"I'll need something from you," he said. "Something to help me."

Dane raised his hands in a whatever-you-want gesture.

"I need to be more than quiet and unseen. More than unnoticed. I need to be invisible."

"Blue Water?" Dane gasped.

Nophel nodded again.

"But . . . there's very little left. Only drops. And nobody has ever survived it." Dane stood and paced around the table. His robe knocked over his wineglass and it spilled, dripping onto the pale carpet. *That stain will always be there*, Nophel thought, *long after I'm gone*. "You know we tried it on some of the Blades, Nophel, and . . ."

"They died."

"They disappeared. Everyone who took it—just gone."

"Everyone who took it wasn't the Baker's blood son."

Dane stared at him, and for the first time ever, Nophel saw fear in that fat politician's eyes. *He called us friends*, he thought, *and we have been for a long time. But sometime in the future, he'll become so afraid of where I came from that . . .*

"Have it," Dane said, nodding slowly. "I'll take you down myself."

. . . *that he'll have to kill me*. When that time came, Nophel would need to be ready.

Dane led him through the hidden bookcase door. It seemed that today was filled with privileges.

Chapter 6

Peer could not help watching Gorham as he prepared drinks for them. The way he moved, his smallest mannerisms, the subtle twitch in his left eye when he was concentrating, all belonged to the man she had once known. Yet here he was now, that same man—leader of the Watchers and a stranger to her all over again.

And he had given her up. Their loving and caring for each other, their tentative plans for a future, all had been discarded when the need of the Watchers grew too great. He'd sacrificed her to the brutality of the Marcellans and their religious pogrom. She thought of that grinning torturer, sweating and slavering as he drove the air shards into her arm, knowing that they could never be withdrawn. Her screams had barely covered his grunts, or the chanting of that bastard Hanharan priest. *You're supposed to love everyone!* she'd pleaded between long sessions of torture, but he had been only too keen to put her right.

Hanharan loves everyone, he had replied. *All he asks is that you love him back.*

I love him! Peer had screamed. *I love him; I love Hanharan.* And then she'd seen that priest's self-righteous, sad smile and noticed that he was actually rather beautiful.

I think we both know you don't mean that deep in your heart, the priest had whispered. And then the grinning man, and the air shards, and later the hammer when she realized she could *never* mean that, could *never* really love the myth of Hanharan. And neither could she pretend.

"I left a man in Skulk," she said. Gorham paused in his movement—only briefly, but it was there. "He's been there for a long time. He wrote about the Dragarians and how they were wronged long ago by the city and its rulers. He expressed pity for them, and the Marcellans banished him. A good man." She wondered what Penler was doing now and wished she could be with him. They would talk and argue, debate and agree, and sometimes they'd discuss only the quality of the evening's wine or what the weather might do tomorrow. But with Penler, it was always deeper. *Those vines draw such goodness from deep down where no one goes,* he might say, or, *Imagine the things that weather saw before it reached the city, and the things it will see beyond.*

"I'm sorry, Peer."

"It doesn't matter. Only Rufus matters."

"So he comes out of the desert without a name, and you name him yourself. He speaks Echoian, though not fluently."

"He *is* fluent," Peer insisted, "but it's a child's fluency. Haven't you noticed? He speaks Echoian like a child."

"A murderous child." He brought her a drink and, despite everything, she felt her whole body relax slightly when she smelled the five-bean.

"That was an accident," she said, remembering the Border Spite Rufus had killed after they crossed the Levels. She had not yet told Gorham about that and wasn't sure she would. Perhaps the time to tell had passed. And maybe she didn't trust him.

"But it shows he's dangerous. If he really does come from elsewhere—"

"How the crap can you still doubt it? You saw how he reacted to Malia's truthbugs. He screamed and gibbered, as if whatever he saw was just too terrible." She shivered at the memory, wondering how many others had been subjected to their intrusion. "Has anyone else you've used those things on ever acted that way?"

"No. The bugs usually cause calm, not fear."

"His clothing? The things he carries?"

"There are people in Echo City who might have made all that."

"Really?" She drank some more, looking at Gorham through the steam and trying to read his face. *I should hate him*, she thought.

"You must hate me," he said. Peer laughed softly. "What?" he asked.

"Gorham," she said, and they both heard the echo of old affections in how she spoke his name. *We should be asking about each other, filling in those missing three years, but we're dropped into the importance of the here and now.*

Malia entered, her stern face different. She was frightened and amazed, excited and nervous. At least one Watcher now believed in Rufus.

"He's asleep," she said. "I gave him some vinegared stone-shroom to help him rest."

"Thank you," Peer said. Malia nodded and offered the beginnings of a smile.

"So now we need to talk," Gorham said.

"Is this it?" Malia closed the door behind her, pouring a mug of five-bean for herself. The room was an old administration office for the jail, sparse and bleak, but the Watchers had dragged some comfortable furniture down here over time. It felt damp and had soaked up the atmosphere of the place, but it was somewhere to rest.

"I'm not sure we can—" Gorham began, glancing at Peer.

"Hanharan's cock, Gorham! After what she went through because of us, and what she's put herself through for Rufus? Honor her with your trust, at least."

Peer glanced at Gorham, and he lowered his eyes, abashed. He swilled the five-bean in his mug and seemed to study the dregs, like some old seer trying to read the future.

"There's something happening," he said, still not looking up from the mug. "Noises heard deep down. The Garthans are worried."

"How can you know that?" Peer asked cautiously, thinking of Penler's haunted words: *The Garthans are never afraid of anything.*

"You've heard of Sprote Felder. He's . . . a friend of ours."

"A Watcher?"

"He doesn't call himself that."

"What sort of noises have them worried?" Peer asked. *This is what I heard from Penler . . . these same rumors . . .*

"Something unknown."

"And one of the Custodian priests," Malia said. "We've talked to him as well. He and his people believe something is coming."

"Maybe they mean Rufus Kyuss," Peer quipped, but there was little humor in her voice, and neither of her companions smiled.

"God of new things," Gorham said. "Maybe he's here to welcome in the future."

"You can't be—"

"Of course I'm not serious!" he said, standing and turning his back on Peer.

"Others in the city are nervous as well," Malia said. "Bellia Ton?"

"I don't know her," Peer said.

"River reader. Her, others, all sensing something. And now you come to us with Rufus, and . . ?"

"And the Watchers may not have to watch for much longer," Gorham said. "We've never known exactly what it might entail, and we *still* don't—but the end-times we've long expected for Echo City might be here at last."

Peer shook her head, confused at what was being said.

"This *is* it," Malia said. Peer had never heard fear in the woman's voice before, but it was there now. "This is what the Watchers have been waiting for forever. Even *before* you came, we were starting to suspect."

"How does Rufus figure in this?" Peer asked.

"He changes everything!" Malia said.

Peer looked from Malia to Gorham, and he continued staring into his mug. But his eyes were alight. Her heart thumped, and she felt a queasy excitement.

"Your friend from afar might just be our salvation," Gorham said. "And I can't believe his appearance is a coincidence. If Echo City ends, we have to leave to survive. And if he truly came from across the Bonelands . . ." He looked up at Peer at last. "We have to get him to the Baker."

"Yeah," Malia said.

"But we should tell someone, shouldn't we?" Peer asked. "There must be people we should tell?"

"Who?" Gorham asked. "Nobody in power. After they took you, the Marcellans crushed the Watchers down. You already know what happened to Bren." He glanced at Malia. "The whole upper echelon of the Watchers' organization was wiped out, imprisoned, or—"

"Driven underground," Malia finished for him. "Some of them—the cowards—ran. Never seen them since."

"So here I am," Gorham said. "Leading the Watchers. Making decisions that might affect everyone."

"I won't pity you your position," Peer said quietly. "I can't."

"And I respect that. But I need you to understand why this has to remain secret. We can't risk anyone finding out about Rufus. If word of this gets to the Marcellans . . ." He shrugged.

"They know they can never destroy our beliefs and aims," Malia said, "and they suspect there are still Watchers in the city. They'd kill Rufus as a Pretender and proclaim a day of celebration the moment they laid hands on him."

"Aren't there people you can trust?" Peer asked. Something seemed so wrong here—a visitor who had crossed the Markoshi Desert, one of the most incredible things ever to happen to Echo City, and they could tell no one.

"With this? I trust Malia," Gorham said. "Devin. A few other Watchers." He looked around, stroking one cheek as if searching for someone else.

"The new Baker?" Peer asked.

Gorham did not answer.

"Her name's Nadielle," Malia said. "And we have to take Rufus to her *now*!"

No, Peer thought. But she knew they were right: Rufus might have come to the city as a lost, confused man, but circumstances she knew nothing about were turning him into a potential savior.

The three of them sat for a while, drinking their five-bean and relishing what was left of silence.

"We're taking you to see someone," Peer said. Rufus lifted his head, and he was still terrified. She saw the potential for further screams in his eyes, and he suddenly looked much older. *I thought he was thirty*, she thought. *But now maybe sixty.*

"Who?" he asked.

"Her name's Nadielle. I've never met her. She's . . . we call her a flesh artist. The Baker."

"Artist," he said softly.

"We think she might be able to help."

"Will she hurt me?" Rufus asked, and Peer felt her throat tighten, her eyes burn.

"No, she won't," she said. "But you must realize that my friends don't trust you yet. You killed Gerrett."

"But I thought he was—"

"I know, Rufus. I know." She lowered her voice to a whisper. "But I still haven't told anyone about the Border Spite."

"Why? I was . . . protecting us both."

Is he really so innocent? she thought. His eyes said so, and his voice, and the way he was almost cowered down before her, like a submissive hound. But she could not shake that poison gun from her mind, nor the way he'd swung into action so smoothly when he thought it necessary. As if he'd been prepared rather than aimless.

"I don't want them to see you as a killer," she said.

His face relaxed a little and he nodded.

Peer looked around the small cell where they were holding Rufus. They hadn't locked the door—the mechanism was rusted and jammed—and Malia told Peer they'd taken him there to recover. But Devin had been standing outside the cell ever since, a sword on his belt. He'd said nothing when she came to see the visitor, but Peer could feel his eyes on the back of her neck. *I can hardly blame them for guarding him,* she thought, and she remembered Gerrett and his easy laugh.

The cell wall was damp with moss, and in the corner the hole in the floor that had once been the latrine was filled with dead rats. A hundred years before, real murderers might have inhabited this cell. She wondered what these walls had absorbed—confessions, tears, shouts of rage. Now, perhaps, they were witness to the beginning of the end.

"When are we going?" Rufus asked.

"Soon," Peer said.

"Now," Gorham said as he entered the room. He glanced at Rufus, then fixed his attention on Peer. "There's no time to waste."

"Where is she?"

"She's in her laboratories. We'll take you."

"What are laboratories?" Rufus asked.

Gorham looked at him, and Peer could not tell whether Rufus's expression was expectation or fear. Probably a bit of both. "It's where she chops," Gorham said. "Where she makes things."

Malia came in behind him, crowding the small cell. "It'll be almost dark," she said. "Now's a good time."

"How far?" Peer asked.

"Just follow me." Gorham could not hold her gaze. *He still doesn't trust why I came here*, she thought, and she motioned to Rufus to follow them out, Malia bringing up the rear. A flush of anger hit Peer again, aching her head, driving her heart. The bastard had lied to her, had given her up to die! She shook her head to try to clear it, but that only seemed to confuse things more.

Maybe it wasn't that he mistrusted her. Maybe it was guilt. *I forgive you*, she thought, but she could not imagine saying it, could not *mean* it—not to this man who was so different from the one she thought she'd known. Perhaps given time. But if what the Watchers had been awaiting for generations really was coming true, time was something none of them had.

Sprote Felder went back down. He never spent more than a few days aboveground, because he found it claustrophobic and constricting, and the sky took his breath away. He discovered his greatest freedom belowground, where the undersides of later times formed the skies, and phantoms from the past whispered to him like the dregs of old dreams. Sometimes he understood what these whisperers were saying; other times their words formed exotic and unknown shapes, like vague mumblings of the mad. He had spent much of his life down in the Echoes, exploring and recording, and the histories of Crescent Canton especially were a source of constant pleasure and fascination. He was always cautious and alert, and occasionally he had been scared. But he had never been terrified—until now.

His father had once told him, *To most people, history is a dead thing, but in reality it still exists—but is forgotten.* Down in the underside of Echo City, he strove to remember.

His porters had fled. He hired them from the taverns and slash dens of Mino Mont's Southern Quarter—a place that many thought of as a stepping-stone to Skulk. Most people in the quarter were involved in crime in one way or another, be it as perpetrators or beneficiaries. It was a way of life there, with children introduced at a young age and given the only choice of their pitiful lives when they struck adulthood: which branch of crime to enter into. The possibilities were endless, the uptake huge, and few people escaped the circle of life that persisted in that place. The only reason the Marcellans allowed the quarter's existence was that it provided many things that they and their families and friends enjoyed. The city's best slash was refined in the quarter, in dens deep in Mino Mont's newer Echoes, where sunlight could not damage the stock. Some of the larger brothels ran schooling camps, where young girls were taught the ways of sex by an array of visiting dignitaries, Scarlet Blades, and Hanharan priests. And if a dirty deed needed performing that was below even the Marcellans' guard of Scarlet Blades, the quarter was the place to look. Countless taverns held countless shady corners, where killers beyond number drank and waited.

It had not always been that way. Seven hundred years before, Mino Mont had produced some of the finest musicians, artists, and writers that the city had ever known, and there was still no consensus on why the area had become so corrupt and violent. Some said it was creativity driven back to its basic, wild core. Others suggested that creativity and insanity went hand in hand, and the Mino Mont of today was certainly a product of some sort of madness. Whatever the reason, Sprote found that the people of the quarter produced the best porters. In almost twenty years of exploring the Echoes and employing hundreds of people from Mino Mont, he'd had only one turn on him. That man was way down in the Echoes, his eyes put out by his companions, and sometimes Sprote had nightmares that he was still alive.

But now his helpers had gone. Strong men, hard women— only half of those who had come down with him previously had returned on this journey. And of those, only three had crossed the deep Echo border between Crescent and Marcellan Cantons. They had all heard what the Garthans had to say last time, though Sprote was not convinced that anyone but him could speak Garthan well enough to truly understand. And when they had felt the first distant vibrations, like the secret heartbeat of the city itself, those remaining had turned and fled.

"You should come with us," the last woman had said.

"I can't," Sprote Felder had replied. "This is where I live."

He'd watched them leave, walking along a dusty street buried beneath progress for maybe five thousand years, then he'd entered an old dwelling and lit a fire in the hearth. For a long time he had sat there, feeding the fire, snaring ghourt lizards and spitting them over the flames, and thinking about where he was going and what he might find. Shadows moved where there had been no movement for a hundred generations. In another room in the house, a phantom whispered in an old language. And Sprote had known that the only way for him to go was down.

He knew the Echoes, and the sounds that reverberated there, as no one else did. Heading deep beneath Marcellan, passing through Echoes that were still talked about in hushed tones—sometimes awed, sometimes feared—he heard the sound of the River Tharin. It was the city's endless sigh. He was used to the sound from his times beneath Course Canton, but there the river was still on the surface, where some of its power was expended to the sky and the water refineries added their own booming accompaniment to the river's whisper. Here, where the river itself had been built over, its power was contained. Its voice echoed. And as he finally left that dwelling and started deeper, memories of his one and only visit to Echo City Falls began to surface.

He'd been there fifteen years before and vowed never to go again. The Falls carved their way through the rock of the land, the foundation of the place that had become Echo City, and those caves and caverns had been a stark reminder to Sprote that there was a time *before* the city. He had never been a great believer in Hanharan and the associated creation myths, but during that time down by the Falls, he had understood where some might find comfort in such beliefs. It was a basic, wild place, where the only sign of the city and its Echoes was the steady stream of bodies that the Falls carried away. He'd seen dozens in the short time he was close—the dead swept away by those dead waters, arms and legs waving goodbye to someone who should never have been watching. His porters at the time had been terrified, and the torches they carried had cast dancing reflections across the Falls as they shook in fear.

Below the Falls . . . even Sprote had not gone that deep. He'd heard tales of the bottomless pit—the Chasm—swallowing the river and its grisly cargo into a darkness that was home to a thousand fearful myths. Some said that the city was built on nothing, and that one day the Chasm would consume it whole. Others claimed that the Echoes made up some vast, mindless creature's face and that the Falls carried the city's dead down into its endless gullet. But explorer though he was, some things were best left unseen. Sprote believed that the sight of this Chasm would swallow his sanity, sucking it down like the countless dead of Echo City over the eons.

Now he was breaking his own promise to himself and returning. Fascination, and also a vague sense of duty, drew him. He'd made himself the authority on these deep places, and now that something was here, he felt that he should be the first to know.

He was deep and had to go much deeper. And already, as well as the whisper of the dead River Tharin far above and the rumbling of the Falls a mile or two to the west, he could hear something else.

Something rising.

Nophel sat naked in his rooms and looked around at what he had. Each book held worlds, but all those worlds were aspects of Echo City. Some volumes could be construed as Watcher material—highly imaginative texts concerning what might be beyond. He had an illicit copy of Benjermen Daxia's *Truth—An Exhortation to Revolt*. But even these were inextricably bound to the city. Nophel had read nothing of their persuasion that made him believe anything other than that they were written by good fictionalists. If the Council knew he had these tomes, he would likely be in trouble. But that was what Dane was for. Protection.

Other books and objects concerned his mother and those generations of Bakers before her. Reading them was an exquisite torture.

He rolled the small metal flask back and forth across the fingers of his right hand. He felt the liquid in there shifting with the flask and played with its weight. *I won't see that water*, he thought. *I'll barely even feel it.* Nophel breathed deeply. He loved the smell of his rooms. If he drank Blue Water and disappeared, like everyone else who had ever tried it, he would miss the scent of books and maps and olden times.

But he had to try.

They had found it in his dead mother's rooms. She had already destroyed him by the time he was old enough to talk, so he had no fear of her now.

He opened the flask and sniffed at its contents. There was very little smell, only the sharp tang of metal. Taking one last look around his rooms, Nophel put the lip of the flask to his mouth and upended it.

His saliva drew back, something pushing it across his tongue and around the insides of his cheeks, and his mouth flooded with cold. He gasped and dropped the flask, leaning back in his metal-framed chair. When he breathed out, his breath misted before him, quickly dissipating in the warmth.

Speckles of moisture clung on to his wispy mustache and beard. *Blue Water*, he thought, and when he tried to hold his hand up before his face, his arm would not work. *There's something wrong*, he thought, closing his eyes to hold down the panic. Death had never been a fear for Nophel, but he was no lover of pain.

He tried once more to lift his arm and hand, turn it before his face . . . but again it did not work. "Am I paralyzed?" he asked, and as his mouth opened to speak, the words came out. He tapped his feet against the floor, and the impacts were clearly audible. Leaning forward in the chair, he stood smoothly, feeling no impingement in any muscles or joints.

Lift again, he thought, and this time he knew he lifted his hand. He felt air moving against the tiny hairs on his forearm as it shifted position. Sending the command to bring his hand closer to his face so he could see, he slapped himself across the nose.

"I can't see my hand," he said. Nophel looked down, and he was no longer there. At least not completely, though there were shadows in the air where none should be cast, and when he moved those shadows shifted. He ran both hands across his chest and stomach, down across his groin, bending so that he could run them all the way down his legs to his feet. He felt the cool air touching his body and stirring at his movements, but he saw only a hint of himself.

Nophel laughed. His mother had touched him again, from the distance of twenty years and through the veil of death. He only hoped that wherever her body and soul were still falling into the bottomless Chasm, she felt his derision and hatred more strongly than ever before.

He shrugged on a long, heavy coat. For a moment it hung on nothing, then slowly it faded until it, too, was little more than shadow. He had not been sure, but he was pleased that he could go clothed, and armed, and ready to face whatever might be out there. It wasn't often that Nophel ventured into the city, and even unseen he felt danger pressing down on him already.

"Good," he said, standing before a tall mirror and not seeing himself. And he began to concentrate. *I am there*, he thought. *That's me, I am there . . .* It did not take very long. The Blue Water acted on the minds of those around him, rather than on his own physiology, and knowing that enabled him to control its effects upon his own mind. The initial shock had rendered him invisible to himself, and that had been comforting. It meant that the strange fluid was working. But now he focused upon those shadows in the mirror, shifting left and right so that he could see them becoming thicker, stronger, until the shadows had gone and he saw himself. It was unsettling, but Nophel had been ready for it. He manifested out of surprise, formed from nothing, and by the time he could look in the mirror and no longer see bookshelves through the back of his head, he knew that it was time to go.

He left his rooms and locked the door. Walking softly through the darkened corridors of Hanharan Heights, he headed down ramps and staircases toward the wide courtyards surrounding them. He passed a maid, a whore, and a group of Scarlet Blades playing nine-sided dice against a wall, and the only reaction he saw was from the whore. She paused before him, gathering her robes around her and pressing her forefinger across her tattooed lips in the familiar Hanharan blessing. Frowning, she moved quickly on.

Outside, the setting sun cast his shadow across ancient pavings as he started his journey north. He knew that few people would see that long shadow, and if they did they would run in the opposite direction.

I'm safe, he thought. *My bitch mother has made me safe.* The streets of Marcellan Canton were busy as dusk approached. People rode toward home in one of the seven giant steam wagons, their faces wan and tired from a day spent working in whichever bank, government office, or shop employed them. The wagons rolled on circular tracks around the canton, moving every hour except one each day, when their reservoirs were refilled and their engines rewound. Nophel stood beside the track as one passed by, and if anyone noticed the man-shaped hollow in the steam cloud, they made no sign.

Many other people chose to walk or ride in tusked-swine-pulled trailers. The streets smelled of cooking food, dust-tainted steam, ale and wine from one of the taverns doing a brisk dusk trade, and swine shit. Nophel walked confidently, enjoying the looks of befuddlement as he passed people by. Perhaps some glimpsed a flicker of what he was, but then the Blue Water influence would work its mystery upon their senses, and he'd be gone before they knew why they felt so confused or unsettled. More than one person stopped in their tracks and started to talk to him—but found themselves muttering into thin air. Some blushed and hurried on, heads bowed so that they did not have to see any observers' smiles or looks of concern. Others headed straight into taverns or restaurants, where the food and drink would divert them. Only a few turned and watched him leave, not seeing, not knowing, but watching nonetheless. These, Nophel guessed, were the ones most likely to suffer nightmares.

He had no wish to inspire nightmares. He bore no ill will toward anyone alive. But this disguise would soon become a necessity, and he kept that in mind as he walked on. And there *was* that subtle feeling of power that he had experienced only once before.

Then, he'd been alone in his rooms. The walls had been lined with fewer books, the furniture slightly less worn and shaped to his bones and flesh, and he'd waited while they went to find his mother.

Nophel was the god of quiet things, and though cloaked in the Blue Water's strange effect, he still kept to the shadows beside buildings, seeking out streets and alleys that were quieter than most. Once he slipped on some damp cobbles and went sprawling, crying out as his elbow struck the ground. He looked around to see who had noticed and rolled into the mouth of a recessed doorway. Breathing hard, his heart thumping, he rubbed his elbow as the tingling pain lessened.

Someone laughed.

Nophel caught his breath and looked around. The darkening street seemed deserted. It was lined with residential buildings with tall windows and closed doors, and there was a series of scaffold towers where these old places were being built over. The laughter came again, high and gleeful, and he leaned out of the doorway and looked along the street. Three children were playing catch a few houses along, bouncing the ball off a building's façade and seeing who could catch it first. The smallest and youngest of the three laughed each time she threw or caught. The other two played silently.

Nophel did not understand children, but for a beat this sight gave him pause.

He moved on, the feeling of power subdued now, driven down by the force of expectation hanging over him. Dane had sent him out on his own—no one from the Council's famed and brutal Inner Guard to accompany him, and no Scarlet Blades—and he'd done so because he trusted Nophel. *You have their ear*, Dane had once said, standing on the roof and watching Nophel tend and turn the Scopes. *They're my brothers and sisters*, Nophel had replied, and that was one of the few times he'd ever seen a look of fear on the fat politician's face. Cosseted from reality, such a man rarely had to confront such mystifying truths.

Nophel walked through the night, traversing the wealthy areas of Marcellan, where huge houses were surrounded by gardens so vast and lush that the buildings were almost invisible from the streets. Many Scarlet Blades patrolled these areas, their garb more refined than most Blades' clothing, their weapons polished, their attitude one of reserved watchfulness rather than the casual superiority exuded by Blades elsewhere in Echo City. They walked in pairs, conversing quietly as they passed from one splash of oil-lamp light to the next. Nophel stood aside in the shadows, thrilling at the feeling of being so close. A couple of Blades paused in their stride and conversation, looking around with hands on the handles of their renowned weapons—the knowledge to cast and fold such swords was long-lost, though many attempted to re-create their qualities—but eventually their companions urged them on. *You're seeing shadows,* they said, or, *It's just the breeze, the wind, a phantom*. And Nophel passed through, the god of quiet things, still finding shadows to his liking, though he went unseen.

Close to dawn, nearing Marcellan Canton's sheer outer wall, he waited patiently while a street trader set up his food stall and started cooking diced chickpig and pancakes for the breakfast trade. When the big man sauntered off to piss behind a tree, Nophel snapped up a pancake, smeared the steaming meat across its surface, spooned on dart-root sauce, folded it, and tucked it beneath his coat. He hurried past the pissing man, unsure whether the food would be visible. Rounding a corner, he saw the canton wall, and he climbed fifty-six steps to its ramparts to eat. Relishing the first hot mouthful, he sighed and took in the view.

Beyond the wall began the gorgeous green farmland of the northern arm of Crescent. Three miles away, beyond the haze already rising from the rashpoison canal the Dragarians had built hundreds of years before to protect their privacy, he could see the massive domes that made up Dragar's Canton. They seemed to float above the haze, like giant stoneshrooms sprouting from the heart of the land. Just to the east, the rising sun glanced from the surface of the Northern Reservoir.

I saw something open, something come out, and it closed again, and what I saw . . .

He shook his head and took another bite, and that was when he noticed the woman sitting to his left. She was perhaps fifty steps away, seated on one of the many stone benches that littered the head of the great Marcellan wall. Long, loose hair, a pale face, the worn, tattered uniform of a Scarlet Blade who had seen one too many battles or drunk through one too many nights of decadence. She was alone. And she was looking directly at him.

Nophel paused with the last chunk of pancake held against his lips. He glanced in the other direction. *No, fool, don't pretend, she's looking at* you!

When he glanced back, she was already walking toward him. She was tall and thin and ragged, but her stride was strong and confident. She paused a few steps away, staring directly at his disfigured face without reaction.

Nophel leaned to his left, and her eyes followed him. She frowned, then smiled slightly. Amused, but only a little.

"New?" she asked.

"What?"

"You. New? Yeah, a new one. So what did they tell you?"

"I'm sorry . . ." Nophel said, shaking his head.

"The Marcellans—what did they offer you if you drank that fucking stuff?"

They died, they all died, he thought, but already he knew that was wrong. *No . . . they* disappeared.

"Doesn't matter," the woman said. She held out her hand, and with a wry, cynical smile said, "I'm Alexia, of the *other* Echo City. Welcome to the world of the Unseen."

He followed her along the head of the wall to a stone spiral staircase leading down to the street. A woman turned at the sound of footsteps, but Nophel was sure it was only his that she heard. Alexia was as silent as she was invisible.

At the foot of the wall, she headed back into the warren of Marcellan streets. There was no explanation, no glance over her shoulder. Nophel followed, and even if he decided to follow no more, he was not entirely sure he could simply stop. *How many?* he was wondering. *How many have tried the Blue Water over the last twenty years? How many have been forced to try it?*

They stopped outside a sunken door leading to a building all but subsumed beneath a new structure. Not yet an Echo, this was a place soon to be forgotten. He supposed it was an apt hiding place.

"Here we are," Alexia said. "We go downstairs. Quietly." She spoke in the clipped, brusque tones of the military, but though she still wore a tattered uniform, the dyed armbands of rank had either faded or been deliberately bleached away. As she pushed open a heavy wooden door and entered a large, low-ceilinged room, Nophel found himself facing a dozen frightened people.

"There's no breeze," one of them said. Nobody responded. They were all looking directly at Nophel, and he felt naked and insecure, baking in their regard.

Alexia walked into the room, between several seated people. They were playing a tabletop version of lob dice, the dice now abandoned. She paused at the head of a staircase, glanced back, and smiled. "Come on," she said, and they didn't even hear her. "You'll get used to it."

Suddenly I don't want to, Nophel thought. He walked through the room, stepping lightly, careful not to nudge past anyone. The people remained staring at the opened front door, and as Nophel reached the staircase and started descending after Alexia, a man stood.

"I'll do it, then," he growled, striding to the door and slamming it shut. "You're all chickpig cocks."

"Yeah, and you're so brave, Mart," a woman said, snorting like a chickpig. The forced humor lifted the atmosphere a little. As Nophel went down the curved staircase out of sight, he heard the clatter of dice once more.

Alexia turned left and walked along a narrow, tatty corridor, then entered a doorless room where four other people sat. They looked up as Alexia entered, their eyes going wide when they saw Nophel.

"Got a new one," Alexia said.

"That's the dead Baker's son!" one of the other Unseen gasped. "He's the one that tends the Scopes."

"I know who he is," Alexia said.

Nophel paused in the doorway and looked around the room. There were a few broken chairs but no other furniture. No food. No water bottles. This was nowhere near a home, and he wondered what these people were doing here.

"Are you dead?" he asked, the question unforced and unconscious.

They laughed, some more than others. Alexia smiled.

"No," she said.

"Yes," someone else said. Another Unseen shrugged.

Nophel focused inward, sensing the solid part of himself that had never let go since his mother had abandoned him. It was strong, this part, and rooted in the real world, because even back then he'd known that he would need a solid foundation to survive. When he opened his one good eye again, the people were all looking at him.

"Still here," Alexia said.

"You all drank the Blue Water?" he asked. They nodded. *My mother's Blue Water*. He wondered if they knew, and if they'd blame him if they did. He hoped not.

"Did they force you?" Alexia asked.

Nophel shook his head. "I'm here to find something."

"Something from out of Dragar's."

Nophel could only nod. *How does she know so much?*

"We've been watching," she said. "Sometimes . . ." She trailed off, her thin face falling slack.

"Sometimes what?" Nophel asked. Alexia stared at him.

"New?" she asked.

"You've already asked me that."

"I have?"

Nophel took a step back into the corridor. The walls were rotting here, the plaster damp and weak, and the joints between floorboards were wide and decayed. Small insects crawled in and out of the space between floors, appearing, disappearing again, and most of them had probably never been seen.

"We've seen what you want," Alexia said from the room. There was no plea to her voice, and no hint of threat. Simply a statement of fact.

"Who are you all?" Nophel asked.

"The Unseen," Alexia said. "I told you that. We're like you."

"No, I can go back. I can—"

"Is that what they told you?" She came and stood at the doorway, the others shifting slightly behind her, moving in a strange, fluid way.

"I know it," Nophel said.

Alexia only nodded. "It's how most of us thought, to begin with. It's a way to try to handle it."

"You *are* dead," Nophel said, and Alexia chuckled at that.

"Sometimes we wish," she said, "but no. Not dead. Just . . . faded."

Nophel leaned against the door frame and looked into the room. The other Unseen were still there, but the room seemed hazy, incomplete.

"And we fade more and more," Alexia whispered. "Some become invisible even to the Unseen, and who's to say . . . ?" She shrugged, as though loath to consider her future.

Dane would never have lied to me, Nophel thought. *Not if he'd known about this.* "My mother made the Blue Water," he said.

"We know." For the first time, there was a sliver of ice in the Unseen woman's eye.

"So you'll know that she was my mother only in blood. In every other way, she was nothing to me."

"Defending yourself?" Alexia asked, then offered a humorless smile. "It's widely known you helped kill her."

Nophel nodded. "So, Dragar's Canton. Tell me what you saw."

"I can do better than that," Alexia said. "We captured it. Come with me and I'll show you."

Chapter 7

When they reach the surface, the sun casts its light on the sheer tiled steeple of a Hanharan temple. A man is standing on the precarious iron balustrade around the temple's summit. He's reaching up for the stone birthshard—Echo City's outline balanced in the palm of an outstretched hand—which is the eternal symbol of Hanharan's birth and continuing love for the city. He's stretching, and Rufus—

(*that's not my name, not here, not now, but it's all I know it will do it will suffice*)

—can see the slashes and cuts on the man's back as his shirt rides up. And even from this distance—the birthshard stands proud on the steeple's summit, perhaps a hundred steps above the street—Rufus sees that they are still bleeding. The man is raging.

People in the crowd around Rufus are shaking their fists at the man, throwing stones that barely reach halfway and cursing his and his family's name to the pits of the Chasm. Four Scarlet Blades are battering at the temple's main door, but though they have it open and Rufus can see a sliver of flickering light from the thousands of candles always burning inside, the man must have barricaded it. So the soldiers push, and soon other people join them in attempting to break in.

But Rufus has eyes for only the man. *He's going to die*, he thinks. *He might fall, or if he doesn't they'll get in and shoot him down with a crossbow. Or if he grabs the birthshard and gets back into the temple, they'll stab him to death when he's on his way down the staircases. . . .*

The man stands on the edge of the balustrade and leans against the spire, gaining himself a vital extra reach. He shouts in triumph as he closes his hand around one of Hanharan's fingers, and the street crowd gasps at such blasphemy.

It's only a statue, Rufus whispers, and he looks up at his mother. She smiles down at him, and he sees surprise in her eyes, and pride. And something else. Sadness? He's not sure, but it's something he'll ask her about later. There's *always* something to ask later, because Rufus is an inquisitive little boy.

The man tugs, his blood spatters onto the temple spire—red rosettes on the spread of familiar pale gray pigeon shit—and Hanharan's index finger snaps off in his hand.

This time, the crowd cannot even gasp. It holds its breath, and for a moment that congested scene is utterly silent. It terrifies Rufus, and he has the staggering idea that he is seeing a moment between moments, as if time itself has been stretched to the breaking point by this man's blasphemy and Rufus is the only one to exist in and *through* that moment. It's something else he will ask his mother about later, and when he does she will stare at him for a long, long time and then shake her head and whisper to herself that he *has* to go.

The man breaks the silence and moves time on. After climbing so far and dooming himself to perform such a useless protest, his trust in the strength of Hanharan is his downfall. Still clasping the stone forefinger in his fist, he tilts backward and falls.

Around Rufus, people turn away or cover their children's eyes. He and his mother watch. *Learning never ends,* she said to him once, *and watching feeds knowledge.*

Rufus notices that the Scarlet Blades have disappeared inside the temple. *Too late,* he thinks, and he takes confused delight in the fact that the man has denied them their kill.

The blasphemer strikes the steeply sloping spire on his back, then slides to its edge. Several tiles come with him as he falls, and he turns slowly so that he strikes the cobbled street on his front. The sound is heavy and wet, and Rufus hears snapping. People pull away, but he and his mother stand still. The man spasms.

Someone from the crowd—Rufus knows him as a baker from three streets over, a cheery man with bright white teeth and rosy cheeks—runs to the body, pulling a huge knife from his belt. He hacks off the dying man's arm and shifts it aside with his boot, careful not to touch the blood-soaked stone finger still clasped in the hand.

Why did he do that? Rufus asks.

Because he's a fool, his mother says. And later she will tell him about false gods and idolatry, all the while watching him with her sad, tragic eyes.

"Rufus?" Peer said. *"Rufus?"* She grabbed the tall man's arm as he leaned against her, pushing her back against the wall. He raised one hand and pointed up at the temple roof.

"Finger . . ." he whispered.

"Yeah, it's gone." She'd noticed the birthshard's fault years before, but no one could tell her how it happened. *Entropy,* Gorham had suggested, and, *progress.* Now she looked at Rufus's startled expression and wondered.

"What is it?" Malia asked. They'd only just emerged onto the street, and the last thing they wanted was to draw attention. They had to cross the border into Crescent at night, and they wanted to be in the Baker's labs by dawn. A holdup now would be a bad start.

"He's fine," Peer said. She grabbed Rufus's upper arm and squeezed hard, and his head snapped around.

He looked at her blankly for a moment, then said, "He fell."

"Fine, but we have to go." She moved off, still holding his arm, and Rufus followed. As they left the street, Peer glanced back up at the temple spire and the damaged birthshard; the moon cast a weak red glow across the tiles, like the smudge of old blood. *He fell,* Rufus said. She shook her head and decided to ask him about it later.

Few built-up districts of Echo City were completely quiet at night—if they did not sing to the tune of revelers, they groaned to the sound of streets and buildings settling into their foundations, as if enticed down by the past beneath them. But here was less bustle, because most of the businesses in shop areas were closed, and much of the manufacturing trade worked mainly during daylight hours. Nighttime walkers were also more relaxed, because generally they were out for enjoyment or leisure, eating and drinking at some of the hundreds of taverns and restaurants dotted around the city. Different areas specialized in disparate food and drink, and it was not uncommon for dusk to see a vast emigration of people from one canton to another.

But the night also brought dangers. Peer was Mino Mont born and bred, and she knew that the Southern Quarter of that canton was a no-go area after dark unless you wanted drugs, illegal drink, or had a mind to sell your sex. There were gangs that made the Rage gang back in Skulk look like an orchid-arranging class, and she'd heard many stories in her youth of youngsters who ventured there searching for adventure, never to be seen again. She'd asked her mother why the Marcellans allowed the quarter's continued existence, and her mother's reply had been pointed: *Do you think they have any choice?* For a young Peer, that idea—that the Marcellans were not as all-powerful as the image they liked to project—had been a revelation. She wasn't sure that her interest in the Watchers had begun at that point, but she had always credited her long-dead mother with planting in her mind the concept of doubt and the inclination to interrogate rather than accept blindly.

Gorham went first, chatting casually with Devin and Bethy, another Watcher. Behind them, Malia, Peer, and Rufus walked together. Malia had produced a bottle of wine and she passed it back and forth. Peer enjoyed the deep fruity taste. Rufus would lift it to his mouth, but she was certain he never drank; he just let the wine touch his lips, leaving a blush there afterward. Peer sensed the tension around them all but hoped that no one else would.

I'm going to see the Baker's daughter, she thought. Back before she was arrested, tortured, and banished, stories of the Baker had terrified her. The Baker had been hunted and killed by the Scarlet Blades when Peer was a teenager, but she was a legendary character throughout Echo City, and many of her chopped constructs could still be seen. There was the Scope that Peer and her mother had once seen, and the larger Scopes that watched from the top of Marcellan Canton. There were Funnelers that drew air into the tunnels and routes passing through the higher parts of Marcellan. And, as a child, Peer and her friends had delighted to rumors of a series of monstrous chopped that existed within the many water refineries dotted along the riverbank in Course and Mino Mont Cantons. They eventually came to learn that the refineries were driven by rather more mundane technologies, but the memory of that belief persisted, as did the sense it had imbued within her that anything was possible. Sometimes she dreamed of the dead Baker and her creations, and *anything* was a dangerous thing.

They stopped for food and drink at a street restaurant close to the Western Reservoir. Lights bobbed out on the water as lantern fish leaped for night flies, and farther to the west they saw electrical storms out in the desert, lightning scratching out from places no living person had ever seen. Such displays had always disturbed Peer, because it made her realize that there *was* a land out there. Blank, featureless desert was easy to look at, because it was dead and barren and motionless. But a landscape where lightning struck was one in which something happened. She tried imagining the place where the lightning bolts hit, what they touched, whether they fused sand into glass.

Rufus stared out across the water and said little. Gorham and Malia chatted with the other two Watchers, and Peer was left sitting alone, drinking imported Mino Mont ale and letting the taste flare a surprising nostalgia. Her mother had drunk this brew, and she'd given Peer her first glass when she was twelve. *Lots of growing up to do yet,* she'd said, *but this is a good place to start.* She died a year later.

Peer was suddenly cold, and she laid a hand on her lower abdomen. Once, she had sensed Gorham's seed taking life within her, but the next moon had proved her wrong. And now, watching him trying to affect casualness while his eyes and expression remained stone-serious, she wondered whether that would have changed anything at all.

No, she thought. *He'd have given me up despite that*. She finished the ale and nudged Rufus, and they started walking away from the restaurant.

Gorham and the others hurried to catch up, and Gorham fell in beside her.

"What the crap are you doing?" he asked.

"We've dawdled long enough," she said. She had a headache from the pressure, and sweat coated her skin beneath the thick overshirt and coat.

"Peer—"

"You bastard," she said. "You fucking bastard."

Gorham fell back, silence betraying his shock. But some things can never be forgiven, and Peer hoped he realized that. She hoped he understood.

They crossed the border into Crescent soon after midnight, with the moon throwing their shadows before them. Gorham led the way, eyes darting left and right to ensure his peripheral vision scouted the route ahead. Since leaving the old jail, he'd had a sense of being watched and the idea that catastrophe was weighing heavily on all of them. With Peer following close behind, such a sensation brought back terrible memories.

He'd shut her away. That realization was slowly dawning on him, and each time he looked at her, his guilt bit in harder. They'd taken her and tortured her, then sent her to Skulk, and deep down—maybe deeper than he knew, and perhaps in primeval places where his humanity held little sway—he really had thought of her as dead. It was simpler that way, and any other concept, he knew now, would have made it impossible for him to function. There was a void of loss within him, true, and he remembered her smile, and sometimes the taste of her flooded back to him and the sound of her groaning against his neck as she came. But if these memories manifested when he was asleep, her groan would turn into a cry of pain, and however hard he looked he would not be able to find her. And so, awake, he had tried to ignore the fact that she was still alive. Guilt and pain had fed his delusion: that Skulk was an afterlife, a place where people went when they were dead, and there was no way back. Souls as well as corpses fell into the Chasm, so it was said. But Peer had never taken that fall, and so he had created his own mythology surrounding her departure.

And now here she was, as alive as he was, and in as much peril as all of them. He wanted to hug her and whisper that he was sorry—she had returned expecting to find her lover, not a man who had betrayed her—but that would never do. Worse than giving her up to the Marcellans and their Hanharan torturer, worse than sacrificing his love for what everyone told him was the greater good, was persuading himself to think of her as dead—and he was becoming more and more certain that she knew exactly what he had done.

And now they were going to see the Baker. If his overwhelming guilt could have a name, he would call it Nadielle.

The fields of Crescent were mostly deserted at night, home only to the wildlife that hid away during the day. As they followed the road that he had walked so recently toward the Baker's laboratories, cries and howls drifted across the fields, crops wavered and whispered where things passed by, and an expectant silence accompanied them from very close by. Things fell quiet when humans were near.

They met only a few people coming from the other direction, mostly traders hauling wagons laden with fruit and vegetables. One man walked alone with only a tall staff in one hand, a small bag in the other, and he did not glance at them as they passed on the narrow road. Peer tried to offer him a greeting—Gorham smiled at that, because she had always been garrulous and friendly—but the man did not even turn his head. Looking back as the stroller passed them by, Gorham caught Peer's eye and offered a tentative smile. She looked down at her feet. Garrulous once, yes, but now there was a caution to her that he had never seen before.

Of course, you fool. You caused that. He sighed angrily and marched on, picking up speed so that the others had to hurry to catch up.

A mile before the abandoned farm complex that hid their route down to the Baker, Gorham called a halt. To the west towered several mepple orchards, dark smudges against the moon- and starlit sky, and the vague lights from night wisps drifted in and around them as the creatures patrolled against fruit eaters. Other than the glow of Marcellan Canton to the east, theirs were the only lights visible in any direction. The landscape here was completely given to farmland, and the scattered farmsteads were shut down for the night, families resting for the next day of toil.

Gorham sat on a low stone wall at the side of the road, ignoring Malia's questioning glance.

"What is it?" Peer asked. Rufus sat on the ground against the wall, head rested back and eyes filled with moonlight.

"Not too far from here," he said, frowning slightly at Malia. *Say nothing*, that frown said. Malia looked away, taking a pipe from her pocket and thumbing it full of tobacco.

"So why are we stopping?"

"Because this way down to the Baker is a secret," he said. "It's the Watchers' way. Maybe she sees other people—with Nadielle, nothing would surprise me—but if she does, they'll have their own route to her laboratories."

Peer sat beside him on the wall. Not close enough for contact, but they could talk without having to raise their voices. On the ground beside her, Rufus had closed his eyes.

"I *am* a Watcher," she said.

"Peer—"

"You want to blindfold me? In case I'm caught and tortured and—"

"Please!" he said, and his voice sounded more beseeching than he'd intended.

She offered a weak smile that the starlight barely illuminated.

"Not you," he said. "Rufus. I don't want him seeing where we're going, and if you think about it for a minute you'll understand. Don't you understand?"

Peer looked at the tall man—he seemed to be dozing now, the rise and fall of his chest even and calm, even though he frowned deeply—and then rubbed her hands across her face. Gorham saw her wince as her right elbow bent, aggravating the air shards buried there.

"Of course," she said. "None of us really knows . . ." She

rested a hand on Rufus's shoulder. He mumbled something and leaned against her leg.

"Nadielle will know what to do," Gorham said. *She has to*, he thought. And for a moment he almost told Peer about Nadielle and him, their confused and confusing relationship, but perhaps right then that would be a betrayal too far. *I left a man in Skulk*, she had told him, but he didn't believe she was talking about a lover. For all he knew, she had waited for him and there had been no one since her torture and banishment. He hoped there *had*, but it was a selfish hope, seeking only to assuage his own guilt.

"I'm looking forward to meeting her," Peer said. Gorham could not make out how honest his old lover was being. Her eyes, silvered by pale starlight, betrayed nothing.

He hears them talking, and then the feeling of the cold wall against his back is replaced by warm sheets, and blankets cover him against the cold coming off the womb vats in waves.

He sits up, stretching the sleep from his limbs and rubbing his eyes. Dawn peers in the row of high windows along the eastern face of the old warehouse. Dust motes dance in the sunlight, and several small birds flit back and forth between metal bracings high in the open roof space. Rufus stands from the bed—

(*that's not my name, this is not my home*)

—and looks around for his mother. As far as he can remember, he has never woken before she has. Even in the night, when screaming nightmares rouse him or illness shivers him awake with fever and sweats, she is already sitting on the edge of his bed, offering comfort. He is used to always having her with him, and whenever she is not in sight, he grows nervous.

There are no memories older than a few months, and the absence is one of his greatest fears. It is also the fear his mother does least to calm. *There, there*, she says when he talks about his lost years, *it doesn't matter, only the now matters*.

He dresses quickly and descends the ladder from the raised sleeping platform at one end of the warehouse. The stone floor below is cold, even though he wears thick-bottomed sandals, and a light mist plays around his ankles. If he concentrates, he can feel the cold mist kissing his skin. His mother will never tell him what she is working on next. Sometimes, the things she makes scare him. And sometimes they scare her as well. Once he asked why she did what she did, on an evening when tiredness seemed ready to wither her to nothing and tears hung suspended in her eyes—held back, he knew, only by her love and concern for him. *Because it's all I can do,* she had replied, and he had never heard her so low. The next day she'd been bright and cheery, as if the sun had reignited her optimism.

"Mother?" he calls. His voice echoes around the cavernous warehouse. It was once home to produce brought from Crescent on vast barges across the Western Reservoir, but when more people started crossing the border to select their own, the barges ceased sailing. Sometimes the room still stinks of rotten mepple and dart-root leaves. "Mother?"

There is no answer. He walks toward the vats, keeping close to the wall and sunlight because he never likes going too close. They're strange. Sometimes they vibrate as if something is turning around inside too fast to see; other times they drip water and tick, expanding and contracting as the processes work away. And occasionally he hears *sounds*. The scraping of bony, sharp things across their inner surfaces. Bubbles breaking surface. Whispers.

There are four large vats and then eight smaller ones, and by the time he's passed them all, Rufus is aching for a pee. This end of the warehouse is home to his mother's workrooms, several smaller areas partitioned off from the main hall by timber walls barely higher than her head. In one there is a toilet and a huge iron bath, and he heads there now to relieve himself and wash sleep and dreams from his skin.

"He's not yours yet," his mother's voice says. That's all. The silence that follows is heavy, like a bubble ready to burst or a claw about to scrape up the inside of a vat. Rufus—

(*what* is *my name, what does she call me other than son . . . ?*)

—freezes, breath held and one foot raised. He lowers it gently, glancing down to avoid stepping on anything—grit, paper, an insect—that might make the slightest sound. He lets out his held breath, then opens his mouth to slowly draw in another.

And then the voice comes, and it sets his skin tingling.

"All for us, *Baker*. Our commission, *Baker*." It's a horrible voice, wet and guttural, and each word is formed by someone or something that does not usually speak the language. And though awkward and forced, its disdain for his mother is palpable.

"He's not quite ready," his mother says. She sounds weak. Rufus is not used to that.

He sees most of the people his mother works for, and though he does not really understand the forces of commerce when applied to his mother's gifts and talents, he likes the fact that they have visitors. Smiling Hanharan priests with their soft hands and ready smiles, Scarlet Blade soldiers wearing smart uniforms and swords, businessmen from Marcellan Canton with strange ideas that his mother nods at, adapts, and re-creates; they all provide color and variety to the days, now that . . .

Now that she no longer takes him out. *It's too dangerous*, she said recently, and that was after she'd been drinking wine and sinking lower and lower in her wide seat. Since then she'd forbidden him to ask why.

Rufus moves softly, slowly, heading for the door leading to a small storeroom. It is always left open because his mother says, *Stuff in there needs to air*. He touches the cool wood and waits for that deep, strange voice to come again before pushing it open. He cannot quite hear the words this time—the voice is lower and quieter, a burgeoning threat. In the room, he breathes easier and looks around.

None of these partitioned rooms has a ceiling. He looks at where the sloping ceiling of the great hall meets the outside wall at the far end of the storeroom. There are shadows there, and heavy spiderwebs. And, piled in the corner, wooden boxes that he can never recall seeing opened, moved, or touched.

The conversation continues, his mother's voice steady but afraid, the stranger's deep and difficult. Neither voice is raised, but Rufus has seen enough to know that there is nothing friendly here. *It's too dangerous*, his mother said, and he wonders whether, after this, staying inside will be too dangerous as well.

He climbs the boxes, taking his time. They creak and groan, but no one seems to hear. On the highest box, lying almost flat, he lifts his head slowly to peer over the top of the partition, and when he sees the thing talking to his mother, he draws in a sharp breath, ignoring the spider that is crawling across his forehead toward his left eye, not seeing his mother's startled look as she spots him . . . seeing nothing but the thing turning its head and fixing him with its piercing indigo eyes, then lowering slowly to its knees and stretching out its spidery hands for him—

"Rufus!" Peer was shaking him, slapping him softly around the face.

"What is it?" Malia asked.

"Nothing." She shook some more and Rufus started awake, pushing away from the wall and wiping at his left eye, his right hand held out before him to ward off something none of them could see. "It's fine," she said softly, grasping his seeking hand and squeezing tight.

"What's wrong with him?" Gorham demanded. "He was acting strange back in Course, and now this?"

"He's confused," Peer said. She resisted talking slowly, as to a child, because that would be petty. "He's overwhelmed and afraid."

"Well, try to calm him," Gorham said. "If he's worried now, when we go down to the Baker . . ." He trailed off, but the implication was clear.

"What's down there?" she asked, looking up at Gorham. *He liked to stand that way*, she remembered, *while I took him in my mouth. Maybe it always* was *about dominance with him.*

Gorham squatted close to her, glancing up at the Watchers and nodding along the road. *Keep watch*, that look said. Peer had yet to ask him how many Watchers there were left, and whether they all ever met, and what exactly he was now leading.

"She's careful," he said, glancing back and forth between

Rufus and Peer. "She has to be. Not many people know about her, and as far as she's aware, the Marcellans think her mother died and left nothing. They think they ended the ancient line of Bakers, and she likes it that way."

"What happened to her work?" Rufus asked, and there was something more than curiosity in his voice.

"The old Baker? After she was killed, they destroyed everything. I can still remember the fire, though I was a teenager then. Didn't know what any of it meant, only that the Scarlet Blades had caught and executed . . . I think they called her a 'threat to the city.' The fire burned for three days, and by the time it started dwindling, they'd set up food stalls and ale wagons for the curious."

Rufus nodded, still holding Peer's hand. His own was slick with sweat.

"Why?" Gorham asked.

"I'm interested," Rufus said. "You're taking me to see this important woman, whom the rest of the city knows little about. The rulers of your city killed her mother. I'm wondering . . ." He looked away, and Peer thought, *Just what is he wondering?*

"The rulers of the city will kill *you* if they know about you," Gorham said. "Reason enough?"

Rufus nodded, smiled, and touched his forehead—a curious gesture that none of them recognized. "Sorry," he said.

"No need to apologize." Gorham stood. "We'll go down soon. Malia and I will go first. We know what to expect."

"And what's that?" Peer asked.

"Nadielle protects herself well. We'll meet chopped people on the way down. Just warning you."

Peer felt a thrill of fear and excitement, and Rufus nodded. He did not appear at all concerned.

When Gorham stood and chatted to Devin and Bethy, Peer leaned in to Rufus to help him up. "What did you dream?" she whispered.

"I don't know," he said. "A nightmare, I think. I don't like nightmares."

"Something from the desert?"

For a while he said nothing. They stood together against the wall, and he was still clasping her hand, like a frightened child hanging on to its mother.

"No," he said at last. "The desert is still a blank to me."

"Come on!" Gorham called. "A short walk this way, a short wait, and then say goodbye to the stars."

"Nice way of putting it," she mumbled, and, when she looked up, Gorham was looking at her as if he'd heard. Once, lying naked on the rooftop of her old family home in Mino Mont, the sweat of sex drying on their skin, they had each chosen and named a shape in the stars. She could remember neither shapes nor names—too much had happened since, her desire to forget too strong—but that sense of contentment and peace washed over her briefly now, surprising and powerful.

Then Gorham turned away, and she remembered what he had done. And even that memory felt as though he had abused her, not loved her, on that long-ago roof.

Chapter 8

Markmay believed in that cruel mistress Fate, and he also believed that she could be read and predicted—translated from the meanderings of a beetle in a maze, the viscous drip of poison from a wisp's leg bladder, the sway of hanging chimes in a breezeless place. He traced the veins in a rubber plant's waxy leaves, then drew maps with the tracings, applying them to a book of shapes and shades handed down from his great-great-great-grandmother. By the time he reached the end of a mug of five-bean, he felt ready to read its message, discerning truths in the spatter of bean dregs. His mother had taught him how to do that, and he had many fond memories of sitting with her before a roaring fire, reading Fate's path in cooling bean shells. Some called him fool, but he would merely pass them by and content himself with seeing their deaths in a slab of shattered ice.

Today, Fate was telling him that something was coming.

Markmay's home was in the lower levels of Hanharan Heights—a complex of rooms, corridors, and staircases that wound around, above, and below other dwellings. He had no windows in his home and only one doorway, but the places where he ate, slept, and fucked were twisted around and through the daily life of Echo City. Those around him were not aware of the shape of his home. They put occasional scrapings and thumps down to the mass of buildings around them expanding and settling with the sun. But Markmay knew better. His home was a maze, and when he watched those beetles in their smaller mazes, he saw himself. At the end, when he killed them and took them apart to read the truth of their insides, his own guts ached in sympathy.

In one room, seven heavy bone chimes hung from knots of chickpig hair cast into the plaster ceiling. He sat among them for a while, trying to still his thumping heart lest it transfer to the chimes and spoil his reading. He closed his eyes, breathing slowly and deeply, but the excitement was there. *Something coming*, he kept thinking, because as yet he had no idea what. Stilled at last, he opened his eyes slowly and looked around.

Six of the bone chimes were swaying, too slightly to set their parts colliding and singing but moving nonetheless. There was never any air movement in Markmay's home—that would spoil so many readings—other than when *he* moved. He watched the chimes, then looked closer at the bone that did not move. It was the longest of them, its knuckle weight closest to the floor.

Markmay leaned slowly to his side and crawled from the room. He left a trail of sweat on the wooden floor behind him. His home was not hot.

He hurried up a curving staircase to a circular room. This was the highest part of his home. Its walls flickered with the light from seventy-seven candles—one for each of the six-legged gods supposed to wander the desert, though Markmay held no allegiance to any such foolish superstitions—and when he closed the heavy door behind him, they danced like excited puppies. He sat in the center of the room and repeated his calming process from before: slower breathing, settled heart, motionless.

When he opened his eyes, the candles were still agitated. Those that danced the most burned with a purple flame, and Markmay knocked several over in his panic while leaving the room. He slammed the door shut behind him and knew he must refer to the book.

Back down the circular staircase, across an empty room, along a doorless corridor, down another twisting staircase that wrapped a Hanharan priest's home like a secretive snake, and in a wide, low-ceilinged room Markmay sat at a table and opened the huge book it held. He went to one page, back to another, forward almost to the end, and all the while he was making notes with a rockzard-spine pen on a pad of rough paper. Sweat dripped from his nose and chin onto the paper, and he wiped it away. It smudged the ink, but that did not matter. This was recording, not reading, and the next person to read this would not be concerned with smudges.

Markmay had the ear of Wendie Marcellan, one of the more senior members of the Council. She told him that none of the others knew of her predilection for Markmay's unusual readings—indeed, she had hinted more than once that some would find it blasphemous—but Markmay knew the Marcellans to be not quite so virtuous as they seemed. He was almost certain that there were other readers informing other Council members, but that did not concern him. He was the best, Wendie paid him well, and whenever he asked, she sent one of her whores to keep him company for the night.

When he finished his notes, he sat back and stared at the filled page. He was shaking his head.

"Not good," he whispered. He rarely spoke to himself, and his voice was loud in the normally silent dwelling. A feeling of dread had settled upon him, and his insides were in revolt— heart thundering, stomach churning, and a pain in his right side like a hot dagger driven between his ribs. It was as if his body and home were so closely linked that he mimicked the upset of swaying chimes, the heat of agitated flames . . .

And one more thing to check. If this read true, there was much to tell Wendie, and she would have to reveal his knowledge to the Council. How she would do this—tell the truth, make up lies—he did not care.

But they would have to be warned. Perhaps then they could prepare, plan, protect the city from what was about to befall it.

"Please, no," he said as he descended staircases, squeezed through small rooms he rarely frequented, and climbed down a vertical metal ladder. "Please, no. Please, no." He imagined the people living in the homes around which his rooms and corridors were wrapped, and what their reaction would be if they heard the faint echoes of his voice. *Phantoms!* they might say to one another. Or they might say nothing at all.

Finally he reached the deepest room in his dwelling, one that intruded into the first Echo beneath Hanharan Heights. He had been down here only three times before, and each time he had climbed those stairs again with a sense of relief that things had not gone badly. This time, lighting candles around the room and kicking out at several large sand spiders that had made this space their own, those relieved retreats inspired a nostalgia for good times past. Before even taken his final reading, Markmay knew that everything was going wrong.

"How in the name of Hanharan are the priests going to account for this?" he muttered. The last sand spider scuttled away, melted down, and flowed into an impossible crack, and Markmay set about making the marks.

He trailed handfuls of dust across the floor from a bag hanging on the wall, creating spirals, straight lines, and other patterns with distinct edges. A pile of dust here, a carefully scooped bowl there, and if he dripped sweat he removed the affected area. There must be nothing here that would mislead his reading. Nothing to skew results.

Before he announced the doom of Echo City, he had to be certain.

Several people sitting outside a tavern saw the panicked man burst from the doorway and dart out into the street. His eyes were wide, his hair standing on end, and his hands were clawing at the air as if to grab some down or to haul himself up into the sky.

"It's coming!" he shouted, and his voice was torn with terror.

"There's that reader, Markmay," one of the drinkers said. "I've heard he's mad."

"Coming! Rushing! *Rising!*"

"Well, he certainly looks—"

A combined gasp went up from the crowd of drinkers as the mad Markmay rushed headlong across the street, straight into the path of a runaway dray. Weighed down with thirty full barrels of fine Marcellan ale, the wagon was hauled by four tusked swine. One of them had died in its harness, and the other three were running in a blind panic, shit and blood streaking from the suspended dead beast as their hooves trampled it.

They ran Markmay down. Even as the dray's front left wheel rolled across his neck, he was still shouting, "Rising. It's—"

Such is Fate. The cruelest mistress.

I can't be like this forever, Nophel thought. *It's like living among phantoms.* But, of course, here *he* was the phantom. And he had seen what had become of Alexia and the other Unseen.

Where do you live? he'd asked her as she led him out through the gaming room and back onto the streets.

Here. There. She'd seemed confused.

Where do you sleep? Eat?

Some of us . . . we don't need food. We're removed from the world.

You told me you weren't ghosts, he'd said.

She'd frowned at that, averted her eyes, but not before he saw her fear and doubt.

So he followed her as she weaved through the streets, avoiding people with an expertise that looked effortless but, Nophel discovered, was hard-won. Several times he breezed too close to someone, his arm brushing theirs or his hair stroking the exposed skin of their neck. These people would glance around, startled, and at least twice he was convinced that they saw him, their pupils dilating as they focused, their brows creasing as they tried to make sense of things. Then their eyes grew hazy and their frowns deepened as they turned and hurried away. Once, he walked right into an old woman carrying a basket of fresh silk snake eggs, knocking her to the ground. She cried out as the eggs spilled and broke, spewing their bright yellow innards across the pavement. Alexia glanced back and only smiled, and as Nophel rushed away, he saw the startled old woman's gaze focusing on the footprint he'd left in the yolks.

He caught up with Alexia and grabbed her arm. "How far?"

"Almost there," she said. She pulled her arm away and walked on. He raised his hand to his nose, smelling only himself. *It's more than just the Blue Water*, he thought. *That*

*started it, but she's moved on from there, disappeared some
more.*

Alexia marched from a street, through a narrow alleyway
stinking of something dead, and into a courtyard enclosed on
four sides by tall, windowed walls. None of these windows
was open, and Nophel had a feeling that few people ever
looked down into this place. She walked toward the far corner,
skirting around a dry fountain erupting with purple knotweed,
and opened a low wooden door set into the moss-covered wall.
It creaked on rusted hinges, and Nophel caught a whiff of
something stale and wet.

"We're going down," she said.

"The Echoes?"

"Not that far. Just down. These buildings are a warren, and
the Unseen have the time and inclination to explore. We
found this place after we caught . . ." She trailed off.

"Caught what?"

She stared over Nophel's shoulder and into the distance,
and for an instant she seemed to fade from his view.

"Alexia!" He reached out to grab her, his hand slipping
from her arm. Then she grew more visible again, smiling uncertainly.

"Yes?" she said.

"You were going to show me." He felt a cold chill at what
he had seen, what she had become. *Are there deeper levels?*
he thought. *Do they fade, and fade again, until they're little
more than memories wandering these streets?*

"Yes," she said, nodding slowly. "Oh, yes." She turned and
entered the dark doorway, and immediately Nophel saw her
dropping out of sight.

The steps were steep and slick, turning tightly around their
central column, treads worn by use. He counted twenty before the first sounds reached him—the clank of metal, and
the sniffle of something sobbing.

"It's awake," Alexia said.

The descent ended, the stairway opening into a small low-
ceilinged room. One wall was lined with empty wine racks,
the wood rotten and slumped toward the ground. In a corner
lay a pile of roughly folded canvas that could have hidden

anything. In the center of the room, a creature was fixed to the floor with a series of heavy chains.

It growled at their approach. It looked almost human.

It sees us, Nophel thought, but the idea did not surprise him. What did surprise him was what he saw on the creature's back.

"It has wings," he said.

"We tied them folded shut."

"But . . . it's a Dragarian. With wings."

"Surprised me too," Alexia said softly.

Nophel had heard so much about the Dragarians, but he had never thought he'd see one. They were apart from the world, the six giant domes enclosing their canton simply part of the landscape now for most Echoians. When they'd withdrawn five hundred years before, they were human. Now . . .

The thing before him *was* humanoid, though it was thinner than most people, and its piercing indigo eyes were disconcerting. Its broader facial features, body shape, all but the wings marked it out as a human being. Nophel thought it wore leather clothing before realizing the wings folded around its torso gave that impression.

"How did you catch it?" Nophel asked.

"It didn't see us," she said. "Now it does. It learned of us when we brought it down, and the Blue Water has a different effect on its mind. It doesn't forget."

"Brought it down?"

Alexia pointed, and then Nophel saw the dark slick beneath the Dragarian's chest.

"Crossbow?" he asked. She nodded.

The thing stared at Nophel, its eyes blazing in the weak oil lamplight as if focused upon him.

"It's concentrating," Alexia said. "Bringing you into being."

I need to talk with this, he thought. *I need to find out why it came out, where it was going, and what it was looking for.* He looked at the Unseen, in her faded and stained Scarlet Blade uniform, and wondered at her allegiances. She'd faded into invisibility, and some of those she waited with seemed to have gone further. He had heard many stories about the phantoms inhabiting the Echoes and how they could not be relied on to know anything but the exposure of moments from the past. Could he really trust such a thing?

"Why did you catch it?" he asked.

"Sport," the Dragarian said. Its voice was a growl, like flesh across grit. It ended with a grunt of pain, and for the first time Nophel considered it as a living thing.

"You didn't tell me it speaks Echoian," Nophel muttered.

Alexia chuckled darkly. "Sometimes we can't get it to stop."

"They shot me down for sport," the Dragarian said. "And because it's in the nature of humanity to destroy what it does not know."

"And what do *you* know?" Nophel asked.

The Dragarian averted its eyes, wincing slightly as it shifted position. Chains clanked, its wings flexed against their bonds. "More than you, ghost."

Dane charged me with bringing this thing back to him, Nophel thought. But it had teeth, and its fingers and toes ended in claws, and even its wingtips were bony and sharp, glittering with moistness that could have been poison. He looked to Alexia, considering asking her for help. But her eyes had taken that faraway look again, and she seemed even less substantial than before.

The Dragarian looked at him and grinned, exposing too many teeth for a human.

"What are you?" Nophel asked. The Dragarian did not respond, but Nophel already knew. He was one of their soldiers. The Marcellans had their Scarlet Blades and the specially trained units within their ranks used to infiltrate, kidnap, or murder. The Dragarians had this. Before they had built their domes and retreated, they vowed that the prophesied return of the murdered boy they had proclaimed their god would bring war. It seemed that under cover of their domes, they had been preparing.

"You've come to spy," Nophel said.

"No," the Dragarian replied.

"Then why?"

"Seeing the sights." The thing sniggered, shifting position again to move weight from its punctured chest.

"What has it told you?" Nophel asked Alexia, but she frowned, appearing not to have heard or understood the question. She looked at Nophel as if she had never seen him before, and when he stepped forward and reached for her, she shrank away, fading as she moved. "Alexia!"

The flying thing laughed some more. Nophel glanced at it, anger seething, and when he looked back, Alexia was climbing the stairs. He grabbed for her leg but missed. As he ascended, she faded from view completely, and he knew then that she was climbing these stairs somewhere else, seeing a different view, and perhaps he was nothing in her memory at all.

He paused on that tightly curving staircase, leaning on a step and catching his breath, trying to work out what to do. Dane would expect him to return with *something*—and Nophel could not help feeling that there was more to the Blue Water than Dane had told him. It had been easy drinking it down, but perhaps the antidote would be more difficult to procure.

Mother, he thought, *have you doomed me again?* The old anger bit in—rage at what she had done to him—as well as a desperate fear that he had willingly invited another Baker-inspired tragedy into his life. He slowed his breathing and calmed his mind, knowing that panic could never help. She was dead. Anything that happened now was up to him.

The thing in the basement had called him *ghost*. He had to show it that ghosts could bite.

Nophel moved quickly. As he stepped down into the basement room again, the Dragarian turned its attention upon him, confirming that he could still be seen.

"Has your friend left—" it began, but Nophel gave it no chance to continue. He stepped on one stretched chain, forcing the creature low to the ground and crushing its injured chest against the stone. As it screamed in surprised agony, he straddled it, pulled his knife, and sat heavily on its back. He felt the wings against his thighs, warm thin things with blood pumping visibly through thick veins.

He grabbed the Dragarian's hair—it was greasy and slick, and he had to twist it around his hand to maintain a grip—and pulled its head back. He nestled the knife against its exposed throat. Its cries and struggles ceased. The basement became very quiet but for the rhythm of blood pounding through Nophel's ears.

"You will find," he said, "that this ghost is not as ineffectual as you might believe."

"You're just like them," the thing said. "You'll fade to nothing soon enough."

"They might fade, but they still shot you down."

"Unfair advantage."

It speaks as though it knows of the Blue Water, he thought. Perhaps it was bluffing, hinting at knowledge it could not own. He would have to be cautious if he was to expose the information he sought.

"It's been a long time since you opened your doors to the rest of Echo City," Nophel said.

"You'd be surprised." It spoke carefully, cautious not to increase the pressure of the blade against its throat. Nophel pulled a little harder, feeling the warm drip of blood on his fisted hand. The Dragarian caught its breath.

"What have you come for?"

"What have you?" the thing replied, and for a moment Nophel wanted to slit its throat. If it thought it could *play* with him, enter into word games while *he* was the one with the knife—

But, game or not, its question rooted in Nophel's mind. What had he come for? To question this thing and serve the Marcellans? Or to seek out something for himself?

"I've done this before," Nophel said, pulling the knife harder. He felt a slight give as it split the thing's skin, and he swallowed the sick feeling rising in him. He could not betray his lie for a moment, or else the Dragarian would never give him anything. It had to believe completely that he was ready to torture and kill it, and once that belief was implanted, he might have a short while to dig for real answers. "I usually start with the eyes, but with you, strange thing that you are, I think the wings will have to go first. You'll fight. I'm sure of that. You're a soldier, after all. But these chains will contain your fight. And I have all day."

There were no snappy answers, no clever retorts, and when he leaned slightly to the side he saw the Dragarian's strange eyes blinking softly as it considered its predicament.

"I was sent out to search for someone," it said.

"Who?"

"Someone . . . who will save us."

"Save you from what?"

"Doom," the Dragarian said. Nophel felt its fear, the shiver of terror that could not be affected. "The doom of Echo City, rising even now."

"Rising?"

It started to breathe more heavily, shaking. "Please don't make me—"

"What is rising? What doom?"

"The doom that has brought Dragar back to lead us—"

"Lead you into Honored Darkness. I know all your Dragarian swineshit. But I'm not here to listen to your religious crap, and I know you're not here to spout it."

"No," the thing said. "No."

"So what are you looking for?" It did not answer. "What? *What?*" He jerked back, tugging at the thing's hair even as he pulled on the knife, the sudden movement and violence startling one word from the terrified creature's mouth.

"Baker!"

"Baker?" Nophel whispered. *My mother is dead*, he thought, and he felt the Blue Water slithering across his tongue once again, smelled it sharp in his nose.

"Our spies tell us that he's back. He will go to her. And he was always ours."

If he had not been distracted, Nophel might have sensed what was coming next. He would have felt the thing's shaking lessen, heard its breathing slow, sensed the rumblings deep inside as it entered into some sort of internal prayer. And he might have taken the knife from its throat. But his mind was on his dead mother, that Baker bitch, and why the hell had this monstrosity come out of Dragar's Canton looking for—

It flicked its head from left to right and back again, pulling forward at the same time. Its slick hair, grasped in Nophel's fist, tightened around his fingers, and he felt the gush of warmth across his other hand as its throat opened.

The Dragarian cried out in pain, slumping as Nophel fell from its back. He released its head and the knife at the same time, and both thumped to the stony floor. It landed facing him, those stunning indigo eyes fading already as a puddle of blood spread quickly beneath it. The blood was black in the lamplight. Its eyes reflected little. Even as Nophel reined in his shock and crawled to the Dragarian, determined to ask more, why, who, he realized that it was beyond answering anything.

He knelt beside the dying thing and tried to deny the last word it had spoken. But it was beyond denial.

Baker.

Nophel spent a while in the enclosed courtyard. Oxomanlia clung to the sides of the buildings, and usually its sweet perfume would permeate the air at this time of day. But not today. He'd slammed the door behind him, cutting off the dead thing down in that basement, and he held his breath, paused in the moment between past and future.

Baker . . . Baker . . .

He had helped them destroy her. Brought them evidence, gathering it through the Scopes, aiding them in building a case, until in the end the Marcellans had decided that it was not in Echo City's interest for her to *answer* any case. They had wanted her work halted and her voice silenced, and over one terrible night they had done just that. He'd stood beside the Scopes that his mother had chopped to serve the Marcellans and watched as they destroyed everything she had ever done. In that fire, so Dane had assured him, her remains were turned to ash. They had not even wanted her body crucified on the walls as a warning to others, because there *were* no others like the Baker. Not anymore. Their actions—and his efforts, investigations, and betrayal—had ended the long line of Bakers once and for all and closed a page on Echo City's history. It had been the greatest day of his life.

And now this flying thing from out of Dragar's Canton had come looking for the Baker. *He will go to her. . . . And he was always ours.* Did they really believe that their old prophesy was coming true?

Nophel touched the deformed ruin of his face. *None of the Unseen seemed to see this*, he thought, but he knew that was not true. It was simply that the physical meant so much less to them than it did to normal people. A bird called somewhere, startling him and moving the moment on. Behind him was the closed doorway, ahead the narrow alley that led back to the main street. Once on that street, he would have no choice but to return to Dane Marcellan, taking what little information he had. He did not belong out here. He had never killed except at a distance, and the real blood on his hands made him feel sick.

So he walked through the stinking alleyway, soon finding himself standing at the opening where it vented its stench onto the street. He watched the people passing by, and they did not see him. *I just killed a man*, he thought, though the Dragarian was like no man he had ever seen. It intrigued him that only in death did he think of the flying thing as a *he* rather than an *it*.

"New?" a voice asked. Alexia closed her hand around his wrist.

"You've already asked me that."

"Oh. Come and see." She led the way, and even though she had let go of his arm, Nophel found himself following. She weaved through the oblivious crowd, and, unlike before, he found it easier to follow. He still brushed past a fat man and a little girl, but they barely noticed, wiping away a floating spiderweb or the breath of an errant breeze. And as they walked, things began to change.

At first it was Alexia who was different. He saw her fading again, becoming less substantial and showing refracted, distorted parts of the world through her body. Then he felt a shifting of perceptions, something drawn out of him and hauled in by Alexia's closeness and his compulsion to follow, and her body manifested again. This time, it was the world around them that grew vague.

"No," he said, but he kept walking. "Leave me, I have to

go." But Alexia turned and smiled at him, mouthing something that seemed to drift in from a great distance: *I'm only showing you.*

The people around them faded away. Life left the street, color was leached from the buildings and plants as if exposed to a decade's sun in moments, and soon Nophel and Alexia were standing in an Echo City that held no life at all, not even their own. This was a place frozen between times, its plants motionless and lifeless, the sky above wan and empty, and even though the sun hung overhead, it was a pale echo of its true self, unmoving and cold.

"What is this?" Nophel asked, surprised that his voice sounded so normal. He stepped across the street and touched a building. Stone, cool and gritty, just as it should feel.

"The final existence of the Unseen," she said. "This is what awaits us all. I come and go, but every day brings me closer to being here forever."

"No," he said. "It won't be like this for me. My mother would have never meant it to be—"

"Your mother was an experimenter in arcane things!" Alexia spat, and such passion seemed incongruous in this neutral place. "For every thing she got right, there were five that were wrong."

"How do you—"

"The Marcellans gave us her Blue Water—me and many others. They wanted us to be their secret fighting force." The anger left her as quickly as it came. "This is what we became."

"Not me," Nophel said. "Not me."

"Because you're her son?"

He turned and started walking away from Alexia. *Change back*, he thought. *Take me back, I can't be like this* . . . His walk turned into a run, and when he glanced back, Alexia had vanished. His was a lonely, endless gray street in a gray city, and for a moment, until he rounded a corner and saw the blur of movement returning, he thought he might be there forever.

He cried out in joy as the world came to life around him, fading in from some distance until the people were close enough to touch. He did so, startling one woman into a scream, rushing farther until the colors were all there again, the smells and sounds and sights of the city he both loved and hated. As he ran as fast as he could toward Hanharan Heights, all that was left to return was him.

Chapter 9

Gorham sent Devin and Bethy back to Course. Peer saw him whispering to them before they left. Maybe they'd simply come this far as a guard, but she thought not. Gorham was planning things moment by moment, and now he had something else for them to do.

"Where are they going?" she asked.

"Spreading the word. Come on." He led the way down into the shadows. Malia descended through the hatch next, and Rufus and Peer followed. It was a strange feeling, leaving the cool open air and feeling the pressures of the land crushing in, and the darkness was complete. *Say goodbye to the stars*, Gorham had said, and Peer found herself glancing up at them moments before Malia closed the hatch. She had never appreciated the beauty of the sky more than at that moment.

Gorham moved confidently, handing them each a torch from clips on the walls and guiding them along a short corridor to a metal door. He twisted some bolts and the door hissed open, a rush of air pulling past them as pressures equalized. *So they can smell what's coming in*, Peer thought, and the idea was deeply disturbing. Gorham had warned them about the things they would see down here, the chopped that the Baker used to guard her laboratories, and she was terrified.

He barely paused when they were through the door, even though the space around them opened out so that the walls were way beyond the reach of their torches. Peer had the impression of wide open spaces, and the occasional gnarled

columns that the torches danced across did little to alleviate
that. Rufus glanced back at her, and the light reflected in his
wide eyes. *Green eyes, greener than I've ever seen.* The more
time she spent with him, the more she was beginning to believe there was more to him than met the eye. Breaking out
of Skulk, he had been so willing to kill, and now he carried
his bag of strange things once more. Gorham had even returned the weapon with which Rufus had killed Gerrett. *We
all have to trust one another now*, he'd said, as if trust could
get them far.

Well, perhaps it could. She wondered whether Gorham
trusted her or, when he looked at her, did he see only hatred
and the potential for revenge? And with what had happened,
could she even trust herself?

After a while Gorham came to a halt, hand raised. "Here
they come," he said. "Stay calm and—"

Something knocked him to the ground and flitted away
into the darkness. Peer heard the gentle flap of huge wings
and saw something unknowable flash through the puddle of
their torchlight.

"It's Gorham!" he shouted, scrambling to his feet again
and raising his torch. "It's Gorham and Malia, and we bring
two friends!"

"Friends to the Baker?" a voice said from the darkness,
and Peer winced when she sensed something closing on
them again. She pushed Rufus to the ground and fell over
him, and moments later something rushed by overhead.
Things lashed across the back of her neck and head, and she
cried out.

"Yes!" Gorham said. "And someone she'll want to see."
He was standing again, crouched low and aiming his torch
about them. He glanced at Malia, Rufus, and Peer, trying a
smile to indicate his control of the situation.

It did not work. Something drifted in from the shadows
and plucked the torch from his hand. It doused the flame and
shoved him to the ground. Then it sat astride Gorham's chest
and whispered, "Wait!" At last, Peer could see the thing.

It had been a woman, but now it flew. The wings were thin
and membranous, and many long tendrils drooped from her

legs and lower body. A queasiness rose in Peer. This thing was unnatural, a bastardization of what should be, and however clever it might be, she found it disturbing. The Baker made the natural order of things her own personal playground. Yet through the fear and disgust came another thought, and Peer could not help smiling. *Penler would love this*.

"Tell Nadielle I've—"

"Wait," the flying thing whispered again. It looked at all of them, eyes resting the longest on Rufus. It hissed softly.

"But—"

"Wait."

"Best wait, I think, Gorham," Malia said. And they did, but the wait did not last for long. At a signal none of them heard, the thing lifted from Gorham's chest, disappearing into the darkness before Peer could blink.

"There's something else here," Peer said in a low voice. Never before had she sensed being watched as strongly as this. Watched, observed, analyzed—she felt eyes all over her, and whichever way she turned, the sensation grew.

"The Pserans," Malia said. "They'll guide us in now."

"Or kill us," Gorham said. He stood, brushing himself down.

"I don't *see* anything," Peer said.

"That's how I know they're there." Malia was turning a slow circle, and then she paused, pointing into the murk. "There."

A pale shape emerged from the darkness—a naked woman with a wickedly sharp appendage protruding from her chest. Down each side, spines flexed and stretched.

"The Baker isn't expecting you," the Pseran said. Two more appeared, materializing as if from nowhere. Rufus did not reach for his weapon. Peer wondered why.

"We've some important news for Nadielle," Gorham said. "And someone she needs to see."

The first Pseran moved quickly, seeming to flow rather than walk as it approached Peer and Rufus. It brushed past Peer as though she was not there at all and halted within kissing distance of Rufus, eyeing him and sniffing with a delicate nose.

"Ahh," she whispered, nodding and stroking one long finger down Rufus's cheek. "Chopped."

"What?" Peer asked. "What did you say?" But the Pseran continued to ignore her. Instead, it moved past the group and ahead, indicating with one backward glance that they should follow.

"Come on," Gorham said. He sounded flustered for the first time, and Peer wondered how close they had all come to being killed.

"Chopped?" she asked Rufus. "You? Chopped?" Rufus only frowned, bemused.

Gorham was looking back at them as he walked. Peer caught his eye. He shrugged, looked at Rufus, and faced front again.

Chopped? she thought. Confused, scared, she followed, because that was the only way to go.

The Pseran guided them through this Echo of Crescent Canton, over an unstable bridge spanning a dried riverbed, and past a ruined village, where Peer caught sight of strange lights from the corner of her eye. All the while, the Pseran's two sisters— Gorham whispered of them, dropping back slightly so that the four visitors could walk and talk together—followed behind. They kept to the deep shadows, and Peer caught sight of neither, but she always knew that they were there. They watched her. But, more than that, they watched Rufus. She saw the tall man glancing about him many times, and he never once met her eyes.

They followed an old rutted track, and here the ceiling was low enough to be partially illuminated by their oil torches. Peer had been down in the Echoes before, though only a few times and always in built-up areas. Here, she could not help but be amazed at what she saw. Perhaps only two hundred steps above them were the crops that would help feed the uncountable inhabitants of Echo City, while down here the dead past was home to phantoms and dust. Some roots showed through and hung like dirt-caked spiderwebs—the deepest roots of the tallest trees. At irregular spacings were the unimaginable supports and struts laid ages ago, upon which the current Crescent Canton had grown and become the fertile area it was today. Here and there were hollows in the underside, and once Peer saw the red twinkle of blinking eyes staring back at her.

The Pseran halted at last. "Wait," she said, staring only at Rufus.

"Tell Nadielle—"

"I'll return to inform you whether she will welcome you in," the Pseran said.

"You'll . . ." Gorham shook his head, sighed, and nodded. "Tell her it's important."

"Isn't it always?" the Pseran said with a wry smile, and Gorham glanced back at Peer as the chopped woman drifted quickly into the darkness.

"So now we just wait?" Malia said.

"Yes." Gorham sat on a raised bank of dried soil, taking a drink from his water skin and splashing his face. He rubbed with his hand and wiped it dry with his sleeves, leaving a smear of dirt across one cheek.

"I'm tired," Rufus said. He sat in the center of the rutted road. "Why won't the Baker see us?"

"She will!" Gorham snapped.

"Are you sure she's really on our side?" Peer asked.

Malia laughed, without humor. "She's on *her* side."

"She has her own rules," Gorham said. "She works on her own time frame, and living down here . . . she's strange."

"Strange," Rufus said. Peer moved closer and sat beside him, noticing that he'd already closed his eyes and regulated his breathing. *That Pseran called you chopped*, she wanted to say. *What does that mean? Where are you really from?* But she said nothing, because now did not feel like the time.

Instead, she got up and went to sit next to Gorham. Malia had wandered off, still keeping within the circle of torchlight and kicking at the dusty ground. Peer thought she was a woman who would never look right sitting still.

"Still talking to me?" he asked.

"No." They sat in silence for a while, and when Peer breathed in she caught a whiff of Gorham's familiar smell. She had inhaled that scent so many times—lain with it, loved it—that she would know it anywhere. It gave her a deep pang of regret for what had passed, but the anger was still stronger. She tensed to stand, and the air shards scraped against her elbow.

"Peer," he began, but she could not let him continue. However much he had changed—become the leader of whatever was left of the Watchers, a true rebel as opposed to the safe protester he had been before—the parts of him she had loved would always stay the same. Their past was a wide foundation, and betrayal and separation had been built upon that. Right now she did not feel capable of finding her way back to the solid base of their relationship. And letting him talk about it would only confuse her more.

"I can't," she said. "There's too much happening here." She looked at Rufus where he seemed to sleep, thought of his piercing green eyes and that Pseran's single word: *chopped.*

"I need to tell you—" Gorham began.

And then Rufus was gagging, coughing, choking, scratching at his throat with long nails, and even though his eyes were squeezed shut, Peer was certain that all he wanted was to open them.

It's dark, and very cold, and a wind whips in from the desert, bringing only a stale, slightly burned smell. There was a lightning storm out there the previous evening when he and his mother had arrived, and Rufus—

(*that's not my name, but that* is *me*)

—had watched from the flat roof of the empty dwelling they'd found close to a tumbled section of the south wall. She had called him down after a while, hugging him close when he came to her and bestowing affection that he was not used to. She'd been sad since that strange visitor, though there was still something about her that at times made her seem very far away. He'd walk into a room to see her staring at something he couldn't see, her fingers slowly stroking her chin, mouth working ever so slightly as if she was saying something much too quiet to hear. And after those times, she'd be quiet and distracted even when she did start talking to him again.

It was because of the thing that came to visit several days before. She'd been different ever since then. It was a man, though unlike any man he'd ever seen before—incredibly thin, long-limbed, with those indigo eyes that seemed to burn right through him. And when it reached for him, then lowered its head and started mumbling . . .

He shivers, and his mother hugs him tight.

"It's going to be fine," she says, kneeling and pulling him to her. He can feel her tears on his face, and he wonders why.

"I'm hungry," he says. "I'm thirsty."

"I know," she says, because she has not fed him or given him water for a whole day. "There'll be something soon, don't worry."

"When?"

"Soon."

"What are we doing here?" They were in Skulk Canton. He'd watched his mother speaking with people and breathing stuff in their faces, like she sometimes did. The people—he thought they were soldiers, but scruffy and dirty, not like most of the Scarlet Blades he saw around Course—slowed down, drooping to the ground while he and his mother passed. It was all part of the strangeness that began two days before, when she left for the day. *Stay in,* she said, making him promise. He did what he was told and spent the day wondering why the womb vats were all silent and empty.

Now here they are, and Rufus knows that something is about to change. There is an air of moving on about the way she speaks to him, touches him, looks at him. It is as if she's trying to remember every part of her boy.

"I'm sorry," his mother says, and when he asks what for, she only shakes her head and cries some more. He has never seen his mother crying before now. She is strong. It makes him cry too, and then he sees something out in the desert.

"There's . . ." he begins, because he has read all his mother's books about the Markoshi Desert, how everything is dead out there and nothing can live upon its sands.

"Yes," his mother says, and she has already seen it. Far out, a dark-gray smudge on the light gray of the starlit desert, a shape is moving toward them. "It left Course before we did, and now it's coming back to Skulk. As I instructed it." She sounds vaguely angry, as if she wishes her mysterious instructions had *not* been obeyed.

"What is it?"

"Something I had to make. Because I'm not *sure* what you are, but if you *are* what they say, then this needs to be done. And one day you'll return to me."

"*What* needs to be done?" he asks. "I'm scared."

"Don't be," she whispers. His mother looks around furtively, then pulls her hood up over her head. He doesn't like it when she does that; he can no longer see her beautiful green eyes. *There were precious stones called emeralds*, she once told him, *buried deep in the ground that is now buried beneath the domes of Dragar's Canton. People used to go there many hundreds of years ago and dig them up.*

Why? he asked.

Because they were beautiful.

So are your eyes, but people don't dig them up.

She nodded for a while, staring at him, until finally she said, *It's all about having something for yourself.*

"I have something for you," she says, producing a silvered metal flask from her pocket.

"One of your magic drinks?" he asks.

"It's *not* magic!" she says, almost spitting. Her sudden anger could have frightened him—but he knows she will never do anything to harm her son. She loves him. "It's only magic because people don't understand it, that's all, and people are *scared* of what they don't understand. They have to give it names to protect themselves from it." She holds him hard, staring into his eyes, and he thinks, *She really wants me to listen*. This is how she speaks when she has a lesson to teach. "People try, but they never get it right. I know how to do it, because of . . . knowledge passed down to me. If you'd known my mother, and hers, you'd understand. But this is *not* magic."

"Yes, Mother."

"If anything, it's a curse." She looks past him at the thing approaching across the desert. "A curse on me, and a curse on . . ."

"Mother?"

"You," she whispers. Then she uncorks the flask, holds the back of his head, and tips it to his lips. He drinks, because she wants him to and she'd never do anything to hurt him. And as he sits on the cold wet stone, watches the huge lumbering thing walking in from the desert, and sees his mother going out to greet it, something starts to happen.

First he forgets his name.

"Grab his hands!" Peer shouted, and when Gorham did so she felt that she was taking control. She held Rufus's head still, whispering and soothing, and when he opened his eyes at last he looked lost. There was nothing there—no knowledge of where or even who he was. Then he focused on Peer, and she felt the fear slowly draining from him.

"I forgot my name," he said.

"I called you Rufus."

"Rufus. That's not my name."

"I know," she said sadly. "Maybe the Baker can help you remember."

"The Baker . . . she's . . ." He squeezed his eyes closed again, but the thrashing and scratching did not return.

"What's wrong with him?" Gorham asked, speaking as if Rufus wasn't even there. Peer glared at him without answering.

"Someone's coming," Malia said. She was standing several steps away from them, staring into the darkness in the direction in which the Pseran had disappeared.

"Her?" Peer asked.

"I doubt it," Gorham said. "She rarely leaves her laboratories."

"How many times have you been down here?" Peer asked.

Gorham glanced at her and away again, off into the darkness. "A few," he said.

A shape emerged from the shadows—the naked Pseran walking smoothly toward them. She was both beautiful and monstrous, and Peer wondered what else she would see that day.

"The Baker will see you," she said, and Peer noticed that

she was looking only at Rufus. There was a slight smile on her face but also a creasing of the brow, which could indicate confusion—or fear.

"Which way—" Peer began.

"Gorham knows." The Pseran drifted in closer to Rufus, circled him once, and then, without another word spoken or a glance at any of them, she disappeared into the Echo once again.

"Come on," Gorham said, and he led them from the track and across ancient fields.

Peer walked behind Rufus, trying to keep her eye on his back but finding herself distracted by what they were walking across. She had never been able to envision whole landscapes of dead fields and gentle hills cut off from the sun and sky like this. It seemed unnatural, and walking across ruts tooled into the ground generations ago made her sad.

"Here," Gorham said. He stood before a door cast into a steep hillside, the stark gray stumps of old trees stubbling the ground all around.

Rufus took a deep breath.

"Are you all right?" Peer asked.

"Yes," he said. "Hungry."

"Good," Gorham said, and his smile seemed genuine. "The Baker always has a feast to hand." He pushed the door open and entered, and Peer followed the others into a new world.

She had never imagined anything like this. She'd heard tales of the old Baker and her incredible warehouse laboratory and how the Scarlet Blades had destroyed it all twenty years ago. The Watchers had always held the Baker as one of their own, though even before her banishment, Peer had known the lie in that. The Baker was unique, last in a long line of freak geniuses among Echo City's scientists, experimenters, and charlatans. At least, most of Echo City *believed* she was the last.

And now here Peer was, about to meet the Baker's daughter. *Really?* she thought. *Daughter?* This woman had been chopped, not born. Grown in one of the womb vats she saw in the huge room before her, or one very much like them. Created, somehow, by her mother's strange art.

The vats were huge and bulbous. They seemed to cast shadows where the many oil lamps should shine. Moisture trickled down their sides and splashed on the stone ground, and when it hit it took on a sickly viscosity, spreading red as blood before slipping into floor drains. Pipes and tubes hung overhead, converging and spreading again from several points where cogs turned, gears scraped, and steam escaped from vents and flues. The steam fell instead of rising, dispersing to the air and giving the whole room a heavy, humid atmosphere.

The closest vat was a dozen steps away. Peer could hear noises from inside—mewling, scratching, and a grumbling so low that, rather than hear it, she felt it low in her guts.

"Gorham . . ." she began, but her old lover had already walked on ahead. There was a woman standing beside one of the vats, tending to an array of tools laid out on a wide table before her. She glanced up at Gorham's approach, offered him a half smile, looked beyond him, caught Peer's eye . . . and then she saw Rufus and dropped the curved metallic tool she'd been holding. The noise as it struck the table and clattered to the ground brought home the relative silence of that place. This was not a noisy factory but a quiet laboratory, its processes proceeding with a calm confidence.

"Who are you?" Rufus asked, and Peer noticed a change in him. It was as if he were a held breath, and with every glance around that amazing chamber he was about to scream.

"My name is Nadielle," the woman said. She was quite short and unassuming, but as Peer walked close to meet Nadielle, she sensed the power in her. Nadielle's eyes were fixed on their tall visitor, her mouth working slowly as if chewing words she could not utter.

"This is Rufus Kyuss," Peer said.

"Named after a god," Nadielle said.

Rufus remained tense, glancing from the Baker to those vats and back again.

"You're the new Baker?" Peer asked.

"New?" Nadielle glanced at Peer, her eyes instantly harsh and threatening.

"Yes," Peer said. She did her best to hold the woman's gaze and silently thanked Gorham when he spoke.

"This is Peer Nadawa," he said.

"Oh," Nadielle said. And she smiled. *A smile?* Peer thought. *As if she knows my name.* And then she saw the way Gorham was looking at the Baker, and she understood all at once. *Oh, Gorham, after all this time you could have warned me.*

"This man says he's from beyond Echo City," Malia said. "He says he walked in across the Bonelands. Peer was at the city wall in Skulk, and she found him. Brought him to us."

"From out of Skulk?" Nadielle asked. The surprise had gone from her face now, and she was hiding her excitement from the others well. Peer could see that.

"A friend helped me," Peer said. "It's not as difficult as you'd think."

"Oh, I know that," Nadielle said. She glanced at Rufus again, then turned her back on all of them. "You'll be hungry," she said quietly, before heading past the vats toward a door in the far corner. "If I'd known you were coming—"

"Nadielle!" Gorham said. "This is *important*!"

"Yes," she said, looking back over her shoulder as she walked. "It is. So what better way to discuss the end of Echo City than over a feast?"

Nadielle passed through the door without saying anything else, and Gorham looked nervously at Peer. But she could not find it in her heart to hate him anymore.

They entered a chaotic room where tables and benches were strewn with all manner of equipment and containers. A strange smell hung in the air, but Peer could not identify it. She saw Rufus sniffing, his nostrils flaring, his eyes half closed as he took in the scent. He saw her watching and smiled.

"That's not her," he said softly, and as Peer started to ask what he meant, Nadielle spoke again.

"Nowhere to sit," she said. "Perhaps if I'd known you were coming, but even then . . ." She waved her hand around the room. "I'm very busy."

"What are you working on?" Gorham asked.

"Many things."

"You don't seem surprised by Rufus's claim," Peer said.

Nadielle reached a table in the corner of the room, spread a pile of plates, and then went to a cupboard. Cool air misted out when she opened it, followed by the enrapturing smells of cheeses and fruits.

"You found him?" she asked.

"I saw him coming across the desert, yes."

"And you named him?"

How does she know that's not his real name? Peer thought, but she nodded.

"Why those names?"

Peer told her. Nadielle smiled.

"What does this mean?" Malia said. "After what we discussed last time we were here and—"

"Malia," Nadielle said, "calm. I've sent out my eyes and ears. I've seen and heard. And that's why I'm busy, because what you brought me last time is all true. It's been a long time coming, but I'm able to help at last."

"What's in the womb vats right now?" Gorham asked.

"More eyes," she said. "More ears. Better ones, and they'll be ready soon."

"So quickly?"

She shrugged, putting a slice of cheese into her mouth. "Some processes have been accelerated, yes, but they'll work fine." She looked at Rufus again, watching him take tentative bites from a chunk of bread, a slice of cheese. He was looking around cautiously, and every few beats his eyes would flicker back to the Baker.

"What's wrong, Rufus?" Peer asked.

"That's not her," he said again. The small group fell silent, but Peer saw no sign of confusion on Nadielle's face. She knew exactly what Rufus meant.

"He's been having dreams," Peer said. "Waking from them upset, disconnected. It's as if he's been here before."

"Of course," Nadielle said.

"And your Pseran called him chopped."

Nadielle smiled and nodded, waving a chunk of cheese at the air while she chewed. "I made *them* perfectly, for sure."

"Then tell us what you know," Gorham said. And in that

plea, Peer saw the landscape of the bond between these two, and it pleased her. Gorham and Nadielle were lovers, yet she held him in the palm of her hand. Perhaps she welcomed him into her bed purely for the physical gratification, or maybe there was even a trace of affection or love about her for the Watcher. But the Baker was a woman removed from Echo City and in complete control of her own life. She was superior here, and she held the reins wherever their relationship went.

Nadielle finished the cheese and rubbed her hands. None of them had sat down, and an expectant air hung heavy. "I'll tell you," she said, nodding at Peer. "You seem to be his friend, and that's what he needs right now."

"What about—" Gorham began.

"Eat," Nadielle said, and she headed for a spread of tall bookcases against the far wall.

Peer glanced at where Gorham and Malia stood bristling, then she touched Rufus's arm lightly and guided him after Nadielle.

The Baker slipped a book from the case, plucked a key hidden in its pages, and went to a darkened corner of the room, behind her bed and hidden from view.

"We won't wait for long!" Gorham called, and Nadielle chuckled softly.

"Yes, you will," she muttered, and Peer realized that Nadielle didn't care whether Gorham heard or not. She and Rufus followed the Baker through a low doorway, waiting as she closed and locked the door behind her and lit several oil lamps. It was a small room, rarely used, musty and rich in cobwebs. Pushed against the far wall was a table, and on the table sat two bulky old books and a spread of large paper sheets. At first they looked like maps, but as the three of them stood around the table, Peer realized that they were schematic drawings of some vast . . . thing. She saw legs and arms, a head and a heart, but nothing else made sense.

"Oh," Rufus said.

"You weren't supposed to remember at all," Nadielle said softly. "It's not like my mother to make mistakes."

Peer closed her eyes, absorbing what had been said and realizing that it all made sense. Perhaps she'd even known it for a while now but had been unable to come to terms with what it meant.

"Maybe it *was* no mistake," Rufus said.

"You remember her?" Nadielle asked, with a passion and need that she obviously rarely displayed.

"Yes," Rufus said.

"Your mother made Rufus," Peer whispered.

"The previous Baker, yes. Who chopped me when she knew she was being hunted, using essence from her own body, growing me in a hidden womb vat, nurturing me with as much care as if I was in her own womb."

"So how did she . . . ?" Peer asked, looking at Rufus. His eyes were wide, but she also sensed a growing anger about him. *Where is that from?* she thought. *What is it for?*

"The same way," the Baker said. "Which makes us, Rufus Kyuss, brother and sister."

Rufus did not react. He moved one of the books aside and traced his fingers over the images on the large sheets. *He's seen those shapes before*, Peer thought, and she wondered where and when.

"She sent me out."

"Yes," Nadielle said. "She left me many books, and these are the ones I've always kept hidden away. No one can see them, in case . . ."

"In case?" Peer prompted.

"In case he comes back."

"She sent me out, in this. Made me drink something to . . . forget. But I'm remembering now."

"I should be writing this down," Nadielle said. She reached for a pencil and a sheaf of paper, starting making notes, but Rufus went on as if neither woman was there. His dreams were coalescing into memories, and Peer began to fear the reaction this seemed to be engendering. He was becoming more animated, though not with joy at the revelation of his genesis but with anger at something different.

"She *abandoned* me."

"No, Rufus," Nadielle said, setting down her pencil. She

reached for him and he waved her back, raising his arm to fend off her touch. *How quick he was with that venom weapon*, Peer thought, looking at the bag still hanging from his shoulder. Gorham had returned the weapon to him, and now she wondered why. It was clumsy of someone so used to secrecy and caution.

"Sent me into the desert . . . a place where people die . . . in this *thing*."

"What is it?" Peer asked, but neither answered her. She watched Rufus's fingers tracing the lines and shapes on the paper, heard the grit of dust beneath his fingertips, and felt the temperature of that place rising.

"You were a hope she always had," Nadielle said. "The hope *every* Baker has. The city changes and grows—a living thing—and, like all living things, Echo City's time will come to die. We have always known that."

"*How* have you always known?" Peer asked. "What have you—"

"Because the Bakers have always lived one step back from the city," she said. "Isn't it obvious? So many believe so many different things, but if you consider things from a distance, you can see all the foolishness and lies. They stink like rotten things, those lies, and people lap them up and live by them."

"The Watchers don't."

"Not all of them, no. But even they live life under a cloud of superstitious prophesies and predictions. I see the fault in this, as did every Baker. Nothing lasts forever, the city least of all."

"What did you bring us back here to show us?" Peer asked.

"This," Nadielle said. "Her charts, her books. These designs. She chopped a construct to take Rufus out into the Bonelands. She knew he'd survive out there—"

"She *can't* have known for sure," Peer said softly, because Rufus's anger was a palpable thing now. She tried to hold his hand, but he pulled away.

"Well . . . no, she wasn't *sure*. That's why she built this thing to carry him as far as possible, toward whatever *must* be out there. And she hoped he'd return in her lifetime."

"She made me to return?" he asked.

"Of course. And whatever she did to ease your memories, perhaps she designed it to fade as soon as you came home."

"Rufus is not my name," he said. "This is not my home. What did she name me? Sister—Mother—what did she name me?" And in that *Mother,* Peer realized another staggering truth: Nadielle, chopped from the old Baker when death was stalking her, was as much a mother to Rufus as she was a sister.

"She . . ." Nadielle said. She touched a book, stroking dust from its surface. They had not been touched for a very long time.

"Nadielle?" Peer asked.

"She did not name you," Nadielle said.

"But I grew into a young boy. With her. My mother. She *must* have given me a name."

"She made you that age." Nadielle kept her eyes averted, though her voice held little emotion. "You were with her for perhaps thirty days. The Dragarians provided material from Dragar's remains, and she chopped you as a commission for them. But she never intended to hand you back. They wanted the Dragar of their prophesies, and she wanted the truth about that name."

"She listened to myths?" Peer asked.

"Here," Nadielle said, touching the other large old book. "There's so much in here. It's written that Dragar was born to illicit lovers, one tall with white hair, the other with the greenest of eyes. Their love was forbidden—they were from different Dragarian castes—and they chose to meet in the desert, where no one would see. The child was conceived out there, and when born he was immune to the desert's effects. The Dragarians took him to themselves as a god, *named* him after their god, and soon after that the Marcellans killed him as a Pretender. So long ago, all of it so uncertain, unproven. But when they came to my mother with the commission, she saw the chance of discovering the truth. They offered a shred of Dragar, his essence."

"I might have died," Rufus said.

"But you didn't," Nadielle said. "You were her greatest experiment."

"I'm *not* an experiment!"

"Rufus," the Baker said, excited, "you have to—"

"That is not my name!" he screamed. The sudden noise was shocking in that confined space, his fury startling. He swept the books from the table, and clouds of dust dimmed the air.

"Rufus," Peer said softly, because she saw his tragic history.

He struck her. She fell against the wall, hand landing on one of the books. Its cover split from the spine; her arm shifted beneath her and spilled her to the floor, setting her hip aflame. She banged her head. The air darkened even more, ringing with shouts and a scream and the frantic shuffling of a struggle from somewhere beyond the room. Silence, the beating of her heart, and then another scream from much farther away, androgynous in its agony. It could only have been the cry of someone close to death.

Peer stood and swayed, closing her eyes to regain balance. She felt the warm trickle of blood down the back of her neck. Moving carefully, she left the small room and found the larger room beyond empty. Even in the disorganized chaos of that place, she saw that things were toppled across the floor, one smashed jar steaming as its strange contents spat and jumped as if to escape the cool touch of stone.

More shouts, raised voices, and two more screams filled with rage and grief. Peer rushed out into the womb-vat chamber, pausing to see where the cries came from. The vats bubbled softly, indifferent to the drama being played out around them.

Another cry—less a scream and more an exhalation of hopelessness. It had come from outside. She ran across the chamber and through the door that had been left ajar, into the wide dark Echo of fields and farmland from decades or centuries before, and highlighted before her in an oasis of torchlight she saw what had happened. One of the Pserans was dead, her hand clasped to her neck and bloody foam on her lips. *He killed her*, she thought, but she was not as surprised as she should have been. The two remaining triplets stood close to their sister, but not close enough to touch. They looked on as Nadielle knelt beside her creation and stroked the skin of her face, closing her eyes and weeping gently.

Gorham and Malia stood to one side, their torches lowered and turned off. Peer wondered why. She went to them, trying not to make a noise, and Gorham looked up at her approach.

"He's mad," he whispered.

"What happened?"

"Isn't it obvious?" Malia asked. Even this stern, harsh woman spoke quietly. She was no stranger to grief.

"What did she tell you in there?" Gorham demanded. He grabbed Peer's arm, the potential violence almost surreal in the silent shadows. She owed him nothing.

"That Rufus has come home," she said. She pulled her arm from Gorham's grip, fisting her hand, ready to punch. And she could have punched him, happily. She could have swung her fist into his mouth and felt his teeth loosen beneath knuckles hardened by years of stoneshroom picking.

But Gorham sighed, looking back at the dead woman—the dead *thing*—as her sisters picked her up at last.

Nadielle stood back as the Pserans carried the body into the darkness.

"Which way did he go?" Peer asked.

"Does it matter?" Malia said. "He's gone, and even if we find him again, he'll be no help. How can he?"

"He holds this city's future in his hands," the Baker said, walking toward them.

"You think you can . . . ?" Gorham trailed off.

"Maybe," the Baker whispered, looking past them all at places none of them could know. "It's been tried before, with rackflies, spreading a harmless germ. But that was long ago, and . . ." She blinked, snapping back to the present. "You have to bring him to me."

"We *have* to?" Malia asked, attitude spilling from her.

"Yes, Malia," Nadielle said.

"Can't you help—" Gorham began, but the Baker was already walking away.

"I have work to do," she said. "Find him. Bring him. Nice to meet you, Peer."

Peer almost laughed out loud. *Nice to meet you*. But she smelled blood, and the air was still thick with the violence perpetrated there.

He was ready to run, she thought. *As soon as the moment came, he was ready to run.* And as she, Gorham, and Malia began the lonely journey back up from the darkness and into the night, Peer knew that there was so much more to Rufus Kyuss.

Chapter 10

He went back into Hanharan Heights as he always did: silently, discreetly, slipping through shadows and pools of light without disturbing either, and all the way Nophel tried convincing himself that it was his stealth that kept him unseen. He knew that was not the case—it was a nightmarish kind of knowing, like the certainty that when you woke up you would find yourself dead—but all the way up the urbanized hillsides of Marcellan Canton, through the well-guarded gates of the Heights, and into the warren of corridors and staircases that led to Dane Marcellan's rooms, he maintained the illusion.

Standing before Dane made it all real.

The fat man squinted as Nophel entered his huge bedroom. There were no nubile young women on his bed this time, but the table of slash in the corner still exuded its sweet fumes, and Dane was piled naked on his bed like a heap of bled swine meat. He sat up and turned his head this way and that, frowning. Then he nodded and waved in Nophel's general direction.

"Even knowing you're there, I see only shadow."

Nophel stood silently, wondering.

"Don't mess with me, Nophel." His tone was serious, and his eyes were no longer out of focus.

"Make me whole again," Nophel whispered.

Dane laughed. It shivered his rolls of fat and set him coughing, which shook his body even more. Nophel wondered how long it would take him to stop moving. He might have laughed, had he not felt so wretched.

"You *are* whole!" Dane said. "Touch yourself. Feel!"

Obeying Dane's words was almost a subconscious act—Nophel touched and felt. His skin was slick and cool with sweat. He held his hand in front of his face and barely saw it.

"I met the Unseen," he said.

Dane's laughter drifted away, and he was serious again. Shuffling to the edge of the bed, he slipped his feet into leather sandals and shrugged on a robe, tying the cord with a surprising dexterity. "I don't know what you're talking about," he said.

Nophel smiled and wondered whether Dane could sense it.

"Everyone who has ever tried the Blue Water," he said. "They exist—like me. And some are more invisible."

"*More* invisible?"

"They watch you, Dane," Nophel said, feeling a thrill of power and danger. *This is a Marcellan*, he thought, but Dane stood amazed before him. "They watch all of you. Perhaps they're too far gone for revenge, or maybe not. I couldn't tell."

"But they died. They went away and died, and you're the one it was always meant for. Your *mother* made that stuff!"

"I don't believe she knew the real power of it," Nophel said. He walked across the room and sat on the end of Dane's bed. The fat Marcellan took a step back, looking down at where the bedclothes were dipped beneath Nophel's weight.

"You really can't see me," Nophel said.

"It seems not."

"I can't . . . I don't want to be Unseen," he said. "There are the Scopes to consider, my duty to them, and—"

"Let me think," Dane said, and already the command was back in his voice. He turned his back on Nophel and walked to the slash table, picking up a flexible pipe with a bone tip and breathing in a huge draw of the drug's smoke. *That's how you think?* thought Nophel. But he knew that Dane had a good mind, and whether or not the drug improved that seemed unimportant now.

For a few moments Nophel looked down at himself and

concentrated, and the shadow of his limbs and body slowly faded. He closed his eyes and focused, and when he looked again he could see the shine of metal buttons on his shirt. They seemed to wink at him. When he looked up, Dane was walking back and forth before the wide window. Beyond, Nophel could see only sky, but if he went closer he could look out over Marcellan Canton and the hazy Course beyond.

I should tell him everything, he thought. But news of the Baker felt like power.

"Do they scheme?" Dane asked at last.

Yes, Nophel wanted to say, because a frightened Dane would be easier to manipulate. But he suddenly saw real fear in this man, and he felt something he usually felt only in the presence of the Scopes: pity.

"I don't think so," he said. "Not against you or the city. But I think they do still maintain an interest."

"How?" Dane asked. He was looking out the window now, his back turned on the unseen man, and perhaps he was picturing Nophel as he remembered him from the last time they'd met: disfigured, scarred, unsettled.

"They caught the thing that came out of Dragar's Canton."

"*Caught* it?" He spun around and advanced on Nophel, and Nophel realized that Dane's fear was not for himself. It was deeper and richer and composed of things Nophel would likely never be privy to, however much he asked and however much he thought of himself as almost the Marcellan's equal. "Caught it *how*?"

"Crossbow," Nophel said. He stood and held his ground. Dane stopped a couple of steps away from him, nostrils flaring.

"What was it?" Dane asked. "I need to know. You must tell me now."

"A Dragarian. A flying thing."

"And it spoke?"

Here we are, Nophel thought. *Here is when I play the only card I have.*

"It spoke," Nophel said. "Before killing itself, it spoke."

Dane's eyes widened a little, then he sat down on the bed, hands resting on his knees. His head turned left and right, as if scanning the room for something invisible. *The Unseen*, Nophel thought, smiling. *I've made him uncertain, at least.*

"What did the Dragarian say?" Dane asked.

"Make me whole again."

Dane paused in his movements, staring at the floor between his feet. Even his massive frame stilled, as though that sway of flesh could rest in a held breath.

"You dare to bargain with me?" he said quietly.

"I merely—"

"You dare to withhold something from me?"

"I can't *be* like this. I've seen what *happens* to them."

Dane stood quickly and reached out, his meaty fist closing perfectly around Nophel's throat. He squeezed, his face remaining calm and composed. He raised one eyebrow. "Don't take me for a fool!"

"I *know* you're no fool," Nophel croaked, and Dane released his hold, turning away. He wiped both hands on his robe as he strode back to the slash table.

"You have such a power now," Dane said, "but you're too weak to see it and too scared to use it. Look at you!" He turned again, long pipe hanging from the corner of his mouth. Dragging on the smoke, his eyes widened and glittered as he dropped the pipe and raised his arms. "*Look* at you! You're Unseen, Nophel, even more than you were before! Your dead hog of a mother gave you nothing, but her talent has made you what you are now."

"And what is that?" Nophel demanded. He was proud at the edge in his voice, the challenge he could still muster in the face of this man's intimidating authority and power.

"Mine," Dane said, tails of slash smoke still curling up from the corners of his mouth. "That's what you are. Completely. Mine."

"No," Nophel said, but he knew it was true.

"I have the White Water," Dane said. "The antidote. If those fools you say you've seen had come crawling back instead of losing themselves in the city, maybe I would have given it. Maybe."

"Then let me—"

"After you tell me what the Dragarian said."

"You swear?"

"No, Nophel," Dane said. "I swear nothing." He drew on the pipe some more, a gentler draw this time, and then he sat on a giant floor cushion, his robe falling open and displaying the rolls of fat covering his genitals.

He thinks nothing of me, Nophel said. *Such disregard. Such disdain.*

"It said, *Baker*," Nophel said. "Then, *He will go to her. And he was always ours.*"

Dane closed his eyes. Sighed. And when he stood again, purpose in his stance and expression, Nophel knew that his drink of the White Water was still not assured.

"You're looking for anything unusual," Dane said. "Anything strange."

"I see a lot of strange things," Nophel said.

"Stranger, then." Dane stood behind Nophel. The mountain of a man smelled of perfumes and sweat and was still panting from the effort of their ascent.

The pretense of their relationship had been shredded; Nophel was Dane's servant. And yet . . . as they watched the Scope's images presented on the viewing mirror, Nophel sensed that Dane still held him in some regard. Several times as they'd climbed staircases and opened and closed doors on the way to the viewing room, Nophel had almost asked the Marcellan something plain and cutting, a question he had believed he'd known the answer to for some time: *Do you truly believe in the will of Hanharan?* But such talk might elicit punishment. Still possessed by the effects of Blue Water he might be, but Nophel had no doubt that Dane could bring him down.

"We're looking north," Nophel said. "I'll try to find the place on the wall where I met the Unseen."

"What was his name?"

"*Her* name. It was Alexia."

"Ah."

"You knew her?" Nophel turned dials and cogs, pulled levers, and a hundred steps above them the Northern Scope was lengthening its skull, projecting its one massive eye farther out over the wall beneath its chest.

"A Scarlet Blade. She took the Blue Water . . ." He whistled softly, thinking. "Maybe three years ago, during the Watcher crackdown. She was a good soldier."

"She's bitter now."

Dane did not answer, but Nophel sensed no gloating, no anger. Perhaps the Marcellan was sorry.

"There," Nophel said. The screen was filled with an image of the northern wall around Hanharan Heights. He tweaked a wheeled button beneath his left hand and the image shifted left, pausing again at the seat where he had met Alexia.

"If they're all out there, there must be dozens," Dane mused.

"I saw only a few. But the Blue Water continues to work. The removal is . . . progressive and deeper as time goes by." He shivered, remembering those gray, empty streets. He never wanted to see them again.

Dane rested a hand on his shoulder. It surprised Nophel so much that he jumped, knocking a cog and jerking the Scope's view to the right. *That might have hurt it*, he thought, but then he felt Dane's breath close to his right ear, and the Marcellan whispered, "I've no wish to hurt you, Nophel. But you're far more useful to me as you are, for now." He stood and pulled his hand back, coughing lightly, perhaps even embarrassed at the contact. Nophel thought that it was the only time the man had ever touched him, other than when he grabbed his throat.

"I need to see the Council," Dane said.

"To tell them what the Dragarian said?"

"That would be the very *last* thing I'd tell them."

He's trying to say something, Nophel thought. Dane's tone of voice had changed, become quieter and lower, as if something heavy bore down on him every time he went to speak. *Desperate to reveal something to me.*

"You can trust me to watch," Nophel said. Dane was silent, unbreathing, unmoving. Nophel winced. *And now the knife in my back for such presumption?*

"Thank you," the Marcellan said, and he meant it. "Now look for me. The Baker is dead, but that Dragarian was out there for someone connected to her. Help me find him."

"Who is he?"

"That's not your concern."

"You'll destroy him like you did the Baker?"

"Destroy?" Dane laughed softly. "Nophel, I know the hate you still carry for her, and it might disturb you to know this, but we weren't guilty of your mother's death."

Nophel closed his eyes, trying to will away the sudden nausea. *I gave her up to them.* "But—" he croaked, then cleared his throat. "But I spied on her, gathered evidence of her heresy. *Presented* it to you. So who killed her?"

"The Dragarians," Dane said. He walked away, and Nophel tried to make sense of the revelation.

I'm more useful to him as I am, he thought. And as he heard Dane opening the door to leave, Nophel stood, tumbling his chair over backward.

Dane glanced back across the dimly lit room toward the man he could not see.

"I don't believe in Hanharan!" Nophel blurted. His heart was thumping so hard that blood thrummed in his ears, and he had to strain hard to hear Dane's reply.

"Just keep watch," the Marcellan said. And he closed the door on the blasphemy.

The Baker was waiting for them at the end of the rickety bridge. There was someone with her, and even from a distance Gorham could see that the shape was wrong. Human, yes, but changed. Chopped.

They'd been running, desperate to reach the exit up from this Echo before Rufus did. They knew that once he was out in the city, he'd either be lost forever or he'd reveal himself and the Scarlet Blades would capture him. After that, it would be a short walk to the crucifixion wall.

"Has she come to—" Peer began.

"There's no guessing with her," Gorham cut in. He felt his old lover glaring at the back of his head, but he walked on ahead.

"Have you found him?" Malia called.

"No," Nadielle said. "I sent the Pserans deeper to search."

"If they find him?" Peer asked.

"They'll take him back to my laboratory and keep him safe," Nadielle said. "They're grieving, but they're also mine."

"Is she yours too?" Gorham said. The five of them were standing in a rough circle now, and the small, misshapen form at Nadielle's side was blinking at Gorham with big, wet eyes. She was a woman, but beneath her simple clothing her chest was flat, and her body seemed almost formless. Her long hair hung bound with fine bone clips, her mouth was slightly open, and she looked back and forth between them all, never settling her gaze on one of them for more than a heartbeat. She could have been thirty years old or eighty.

"Yes," Nadielle said. "And she's very special."

"So what can she do?" Peer asked. "Fly? Burrow? Juggle?"

"She can help us find out exactly what's going on," Nadielle said, not rising to Peer's bait.

Gorham glanced at Peer and shook his head, but then he saw how scared she was. *Nadielle's blocking our way across the bridge*, he thought, and he listened for the flap of leathery wings, looked for the pale skin of a surviving Pseran manifesting from the gloom. *He* wasn't scared. But there really was no guessing with Nadielle.

"We need to find Rufus," Peer said. "That's the absolute priority, so if she can help us with that—"

"She can't," Nadielle said.

"Then why are we all standing here like spare cocks?" Malia asked.

"Rufus has left the Echoes," Nadielle said. "Another exit, half a mile from here. He's gone up into Crescent, and last I heard he was heading north."

"How do you know?" Peer asked.

"It doesn't matter how I know!" Nadielle snapped, and for the first time Gorham saw fear in her eyes. *She's not grieving for the Pseran*, he thought. *She's terrified!*

"What do you need?" he asked.

"You. Come with me. We're going down, way down, to find out whatever it is that's got the Garthans so agitated. You told me about Bellia Ton, the river reader. After that

I . . . investigated further. There are other readers realizing that something's terribly wrong."

"But Rufus—" Peer began.

"Is a part of it all," Nadielle said, more gently now. "So you're right, he's a priority. But something incredible has begun, and I need to know. I need to check."

"Know what?" Malia asked. "Check what?"

But Nadielle ignored the question. Instead, she stroked the small woman's hair and smiled at her. The woman's expression did not alter.

"Why do you need me?" Gorham asked.

"To read me when we get there."

"*Read* you? I'm no reader. I've never done *anything* like that. I wouldn't know—"

"I can teach you. We have to go. Peer, you and Malia need to find Rufus. Malia, use your Watchers, however many are left. Find him, and bring him back down to my rooms. Do it any way you can, but it's important—it's *imperative*—that you keep his existence from the authorities. The Marcellans can't know about him. *Nobody* can know about him. Do you understand?"

"Yeah," Malia said.

"Do you understand?" Nadielle was almost shouting now, and Gorham took a step back, frightened for her, frightened *of* her.

"Yes," Peer said. Gorham looked at her, but she would not meet his eye.

"Because he might be the answer," Nadielle said, muttering now. "My mother wrote that she wasn't certain, but it seems it was all true. There's something in him that meant he survived. Out there, in the Bonelands. Something in his blood."

"And you can copy that?" Peer asked.

"I can try," Nadielle said. "But only after this."

"You're going with them?" Malia asked Gorham.

"Yes," he said. *The Baker's uncertain, and more than that—she's scared.* He was cold and felt the weight of Echo City's present bearing down upon him. He looked up at the dark ceiling of this place, invisible in the gloom, and imagined all those people up there going about their lives with no concept that everything could be about to change. And then he thought of Rufus. *He lived out there for more than twenty years.* The idea of that was shattering.

"We should go," Nadielle said, and Gorham felt a rush of pure panic. He went to Peer, stood before her, and waited until she met his eyes.

"I'll see you soon," he said. She only nodded, and he resisted the compulsion to reach for her, to hug her until she could understand. "Peer, there's so much I should say to you."

"Starting with sorry again?" she said, glancing at Nadielle and back to Gorham. Then she laughed. It was humorless, that laugh, and bitter, and as she pushed by him, he searched for any sign of regret at uttering it. But her face was hard, her eyes stern.

"I'm sorry," he said to her back. She raised one hand in a casual goodbye. As Malia started after Peer, Gorham reached out and grasped her arm.

"Take care of her," he whispered. Malia nodded. She knew about grief and loss, and as Gorham watched them crossing the bridge, he felt comforted knowing that Peer was in good hands.

"Thank you," Nadielle said when the others were out of earshot. He had never heard her sound so vulnerable, and when she slipped an arm around his waist and kissed his cheek, he wanted to push her away, hear her say something cutting or derisive. He needed her back to how she always was, because weakness did not sit well with the Baker.

"What the crap is this, Nadielle?"

"I'm not sure. I have suspicions." She shivered, hugging her arms across her chest and nodding at the short woman. "She'll help us find out, one way or another."

"You say we're going deep. To talk to the Garthans? Is she chopped from one of them?"

"I've already spoken with the Garthans," Nadielle said. "And you're right, they're scared. That's why we're going deeper than that."

Gorham felt his stomach drop, and the hairs on his arms prickled. "Deeper . . ."

"Down past the deepest Echo. Deeper than history."

"To the Chasm," Gorham whispered.

"Something is rising from there. I have to know what."

Something is rising . . . Gorham looked at the chopped woman, her wide, dulled eyes, and wondered what in the name of every god true or false she could know.

They returned to the Baker's laboratories to gather equipment and so that Nadielle could secure her rooms against intruders. She went about things with a distracted air, and several times Gorham tried to speak to her. But events had taken on a weight of their own, and she remained silent and distant.

The two surviving Pserans were nowhere to be seen. The thin, slick man who sometimes welcomed Gorham was also absent, and as the Baker's womb vats bubbled and scratched into the stillness, it resembled a very lonely place.

The small woman sat on a metal chair close to one of the vats, seemingly unaware of her surroundings. Her eyes were wide. She appeared to be listening.

Nadielle called Gorham through to her rooms, then opened a trapdoor he had never seen before. "Go down," she said. "Fetch ropes, climbing equipment, and weapons."

He went to Nadielle and reached out to touch her face. She pulled back.

"Go," she said. Then she turned away and slipped out into the vast womb-vat hall.

Gorham glanced around, remembering sweeter times he had spent in here with Nadielle. She had always been a demanding lover, and it crossed his mind now that he had sometimes mistaken a base desperation for passion. All those times he had felt were keen and honest were now taking on a sheen of betrayal. He closed his eyes and tried to remember making love with Peer, but too much time had passed and it was like recalling the memories of a friend.

Cursing, he descended through the trapdoor. The room at the bottom of the short ladder contained a hoard of objects from the city above. He shook his head in wonder at what Nadielle could achieve and went about gathering equipment for their journey.

We're going down, he thought, and once again he shut off the terror that held for him. There were phantoms and Garthans down there, and other creatures less known. Places unseen, old histories built upon, pressed down, hidden away for many eons . . .

He found a rope, good and strong. He shouldered it and picked up a wire ring of crampons and a hammer. The most he'd ever climbed was the side of a two-story building.

The Echoes were places of darkness and forgotten things, and anything could exist in their blackest depths. There were tales of giant sightless lizards and serpents formed entirely from shadows that made the old buried places their homes; it was said that packs of wild dogs had gone blind in the darkness and found their way by smell and sound alone. And then there was the Lost Man. Some said he was a phantom craving the luxury of flesh once more. Others claimed he was an outcast from the earliest rule of the Marcellans, adhering to some ancient religion long since dead in the city above. Sent down, he had lost track of time, and time had lost him, his body adjusting to eternal night and eschewing the passing of days to give him a vastly extended life. This version of the story claimed that he was *happy* to live here—and that he delighted when an occasional meal got lost in the Echoes and wandered into his domain.

"Shit!" Gorham cursed as he dropped the hammer on his foot. He hopped several times, then retrieved the hammer and took some deep breaths.

Farther down, deep at the ancient root of the city, was the Chasm—bottomless, the place where the Falls and the city's dead found their end, and—

Something is rising!

"Weapons," he said, standing before the wall where all manner of martial equipment hung. He chose two small crossbows and several racks of bolts, a bag of poisoned dust globes, and some throwing knives. He carried his own short sword and gutting knife, neither of which he'd ever had to use, though he remembered drawing the sword one evening in a tavern three years before, just after Peer had gone and he drank each night to try to forget.

Something is rising!

"That's enough," he said. The room was darker than it had been, wasn't it? The atmosphere heavier? He glanced around and saw two doors he hadn't noticed before, one in each of the room's far corners, and without opening them he knew they led somewhere deeper, to rooms stacked with more things that Nadielle had stolen from somewhere in the city above. But right then he had no desire to discover those things.

"Nadielle?" He went back up into her room, looking at the unmade bed and remembering her chuckling against his neck, and from the vat chamber beyond he heard a sound unlike anything he had ever heard in his life. Perhaps babies being fed alive to rockzards would screech like this, or someone having their bones eaten from the inside, or people dipped into boiling oil—the terrible sound echoed and reverberated, gripping on to his mind with tenacious claws, though he would never want such a memory. He dropped the ropes and weapons and clapped his hands over his ears, screaming to try to drown the noise but succeeding only in adding to it.

Shoving through the door, the first thing he saw was the small woman still sitting on her chair, staring into the distance as if all were quiet. She blinked her heavy eyelids and licked her lips.

The sound was fading, and the room was filling with a haze that carried the rancid stench of innards. Gasping, swallowing hard to try to pop his ears, Gorham hurried to the side wall and looked along at the womb vats.

"Nadielle!"

"Here, Gorham," she replied, and he saw movement on top of the third vat. She raised one hand in a slow greeting, then waved at him. "You might want to stand back."

A hundred questions could find no release, because time would not allow them. There *was* no time; Gorham realized that now. He felt the urgency of the Baker's every action and movement, which had surely been translated to him much earlier but only now made itself known. Something was rising, and Rufus had arrived, and *of course* the two were connected.

The vat upon which the Baker sat began to change.

Though Gorham had never dared touch one, he'd always assumed them to be cast from some metal—thick and heavy and strong. The rough wooden buttresses holding them upright supported that supposition. Now the vat began to flex and crack.

Nadielle looked down into the womb vat, and Gorham wondered what she saw.

He blinked, convinced at first that his eyes were blurring from the stinking mist in the air. But then the vat deformed, something inside pushing out, extending the shell, and finally bursting through in a spray of foul fluid. An arm first, longer than a normal human's arm and tipped with an array of spiked bone protuberances. Its skin was milky and translucent and streaked with globs of thick red matter. The second arm slipped through the gap and worked at widening it, slicing with those bony blades. And then that terrible screeching came again, bursting up from the vat in another pressurized spray. Nadielle held her hands in front of her eyes, but she did not change position. As the cry died away, she looked down, and in her eyes Gorham saw the love of a mother for her child.

He pressed back against the wall, and when he looked at the small woman sitting farther along the room, she was looking at him at last. Her wide eyes were still blank, her hair framing her long narrow face, and a streak of spurted fluid had plastered her dress to her hip. But she seemed not to notice.

"Don't be afraid," Nadielle said, her voice carrying over the wet sounds from the tearing vat.

"If you say so," Gorham muttered, and he watched one of the Baker's creations being birthed. The vat opened, thick rips in its side spreading and allowing the thing inside to emerge. Both of its arms were in the open now, grasping at the air as if trying to gain purchase. Its head followed, then its body, hips, and legs. It fell to the solid ground with a wet thump, screaming again as it tried to stand. Fluid spilled out around it. The air steamed and stank. The vat spewed a thick flow of afterbirth, spattering down around the emerged shape.

It was the size of a big man, its hair dark, long, and matted across its shoulders and back. When it lifted its head and mewled, Gorham saw its face for the first time. It was a very human face, he thought, with an expression of startled delight at being free. He saw the fully formed teeth in its mouth, some of them longer and sharper than normal, and he concentrated on its eyes, because the rest of its body was far from human. Very far. It looked at him and smiled, dribbling slightly, and Gorham looked away.

"Gorham, don't be afraid," Nadielle said again. She slid down the side of the vat and landed with a splash. The vat hung open and steaming, but already the gap the thing had emerged through seemed to be shrinking. The huge container was repairing itself, as walls lifted and wooden buttresses shoved upward.

When Gorham looked at the newborn again, it was already on its feet. It was using its bladed hands to scrape the wet stuff from its hairless skin. Its legs were long and thin, ending in feet that sprouted thick spines. There were also spines projecting an arm's length along its backbone, flexing and spiking at the air as they stretched. Even as he watched, Gorham saw its skin darkening and hardening. The sound its blades made as they slicked moisture from skin turned from a clean, soft hiss to a harder scraping. In contact with the air at last, it was developing armor before his eyes.

Nadielle stood before her newly chopped creation. It was more than a head taller than she was. Gorham watched, fascinated and appalled, as the thing knelt on bony knees and rested its head on Nadielle's shoulder. She stroked its hair and kissed its head, glancing over its shoulder at Gorham and waving him closer.

He shook his head, but she persisted. "Come here, Gorham," she said. "Meet my new child. It's strong and hard, and it knows how to fight and kill. But more than that, it knows how to protect. I want to teach it who to protect, so come here."

As he went, fear was slowly merging with wonder. He'd just witnessed something incredible. "You've chopped a warrior?"

"I've been working on him for some time. Will you name him?"

The thing was looking at Gorham now, its eyes wide and dark. *Does it see me as a human?* he wondered. *Is there real intelligence in there?*

"He thinks," Nadielle said, perhaps seeing the questions and doubt in his eyes, "but it's a different kind of intelligence. You'll not discuss the finest points of philosophy and religion with him, but he could take a dozen Scarlet Blades and wear their scalps for hats."

"And you want me to name it?"

"Unless *it* is a suitable name."

"No," Gorham said. He paused a few steps away, and Nadielle leaned in and started whispering in its ear, all the while looking at Gorham. The thing never took its eyes from him. Even when it blinked, it did so with one eye at a time, so that he was always in its view.

"He knows you now," she said. "He'll never turn against you, and his life is dedicated to your protection."

"And you?"

"I'm his mother. Now, a name." She smiled sweetly, and Gorham thought she was enjoying this display of her strange, wonderful, terrible talent.

"How about Neph?"

"God of sharp things," Nadielle said. "Appropriate." She whispered to the thing again, and Gorham heard the name *Neph* mentioned several times. It closed its eyes, Nadielle pulled back, and it was named.

"So when we go down," he said, "what are you expecting?"

Nadielle's smile slipped a little. She touched Neph's face as it pressed against her like a hound twisting against an owner's hand. "Not knowing the answer to that is why we need him."

Neph keened softly, and as it stretched, its blades scored lines in the floor.

"So now we go?" Gorham asked.

"Yes, now we go. You leave first with Neph and the woman, and I'll catch up. I have to make sure no one can enter my rooms while I'm away. It's time to open another vat."

Later, with Neph stalking ahead as silent as night, Gorham asked what the second vat had contained. Nadielle would not tell him. She averted her eyes and smiled at the woman, and when he asked once more, Nadielle walked quickly ahead.

Gorham followed, brooding. He and Nadielle carried food,

climbing equipment, and other supplies, leaving Neph free to protect them, and already his shoulders were chafing from the straps. The thought that he would not see the sky again for days was harsh. The idea that Peer and Malia were up there now, searching for perhaps the most important person the city had ever seen, inspired a heavy sense of dread.

And Nadielle's strange woman watched him with her wide blank eyes.

Chapter 11

Rufus is not his name—he *has* no name, because as far as he remembers she did not give him one—but in memory, this is now how he thinks of himself. So Rufus, his younger self, is lying in the sand, and all there is for him to see is the low baking desert and the pale-blue sky, as if even that is scorched by the sun. And though only just born, Rufus feels that death is very close. There is no food, and the heat is burning the fluid from his body. *She'll be sad*, he thinks, not quite certain who *she* is. He swallows a mouthful of saliva, and the vague thought of *her* passes away entirely, replaced by a taste that brings a brief but intense recollection of a dark, cold stone wall. Then even that is gone, and Rufus thinks only of himself.

A long time passes, and then the shadow comes. Its touch seems to soothe his burning skin. He sighs, and his throat hurts. His tongue is swollen. *I'm almost dead*, he thinks, and those words feel strange in his mind. He knows how they are used and what they mean, but he is lost.

Rufus looks up into the shadow that blocks the sun, and the shape is unfamiliar to him. It comes closer, kneeling before him. It makes a guttural, deep rumble interspersed with clicks and hisses, and he realizes that it is talking.

"I'm lost," he says past his swollen tongue, and it's like talking through a mouthful of food. The corners of his mouth are split, and he winces, feeling blood flowing across his face.

The shape inclines its head, and now his eyes are becoming used to the shadow. He blinks a few times to moisten them some more. The shape smiles. It's a whole new experience for Rufus, and he wonders whether he can ever look like this.

It removes part of its face as it reaches for him, and his shock is tempered by the feel of something cool and wet pressed against his lips. He half-closes his eyes and sucks, and water flows into his mouth. He sighs and swallows, closing one hand around the hand of his helper.

Drinking, enjoying the contact of his skin on someone else's, Rufus searches his thoughts and shallow memories for something to relate this to. But though he feels something deep down begging to be released and revealed, his recollection is blank. This is all new.

His helper's face is dark and smooth, eyes deep and protected behind a transparent film stretched across a network of fine wire filaments. It's a woman—he can see the swell of breasts against the thin white gown she wears—and her full lips are moist and shiny. Her hair is long and glinting with bulbs of water. He's entranced by these droplets, because they seem to slip and flow as the woman moves, catching and casting tiny rainbows and shedding them again just as quickly. He lifts his hand from his helper's wrist and reaches up. She smiles—her eyes behind the film crease at the corners—and leans forward some more. Rufus takes in a deep breath and smells the woman for the first time. His child's brain is almost overwhelmed by the barrage of scents, and though his memory is not rich, he can still identify a sweetness and the heat of spices and warmth. He touches her hair, thick yet smooth, and one bulb of water makes contact with his forefinger. It breaks and flows across Rufus's skin. He sighs with pleasure as another burn is soothed.

The woman speaks again, but Rufus shakes his head. He cannot understand her. And then he sees that, though smiling, her eyes are also flickering this way and that as she examines his body. He's naked, and the relentless sun has scorched him terribly, stretching and reddening the skin all across his shoulders, back, and stomach. His legs and groin have escaped the worst of it, hidden as they have been by his stooped shadow for much of the time, but his ankles and feet are blistered and weeping. He sees sympathy in his helper's eyes, but also confusion.

He releases the wet thing in his mouth and lies back, careful to keep his face within her shadow. As he examines her some more, the rush of sensory input is exhilarating. Instinct gives him the ability to acknowledge and understand certain aspects, though there is little beyond that understanding—no reference points, no historical benchmarks. He recognizes much about his helper without recalling ever having seen anything like her before.

(*my mother wiped my mind, she made me a blank, and was it for me or . . . ?*)

The woman's robe is light and thin but looks strong. It is tied around her waist, wrists, and ankles with fine silver wire, similar to that which frames the clear film covering her eyes and face. Her skin is dark against the white robe, speckled here and there with pearls of perspiration, and the fine hairs on the back of her hands shine with the remains of some cream or salve. She wears boots with heavy bottoms, and around her waist hangs a loose belt. There are knives here and other things that Rufus does not recognize.

(*I know now, but I didn't know then, because even my mother could never have guessed at the wonders of the Heartlands.*)

While he examines his helper, Rufus is aware that she is drawing in the sand before him. He looks past her and sees the thing she brought with her. It is large and wide, steaming and breathing, and he cannot conceive of what it might be.

She taps her finger on the back of his hand until he meets her gaze again. Then she points down at what she has drawn. There are two marks in the sand; she points at them, then at him and her alternately. Rufus nods. The woman shuffles back, smoothing the sand she has disturbed until it is blank. She quickly makes marks and slashes, mounds and dips, creating a landscape before his eyes and marking it here and there with landmarks only she can know.

She draws something from her belt and whips it at the air—a long thin stick, appearing as if from nowhere. It's hollow and pierced at regular intervals with oval holes, and though Rufus cannot guess at its true use, his savior uses it now as a pointer. Again she indicates two small shapes, and then she moves back a little, thrusting the stick into the ground between a range of low sand humps she has made. A series of grumbled sounds comes from her mouth, which Rufus assumes to be a name.

A stab of pain slashes at his stomach. Thirst scorches his throat just as the sun burns his skin. He yearns to touch those water bulbs in her long hair again and for the wet thing she held to his mouth while he sucked the moisture from it. But her face has grown stern now, and he can sense a rising disquiet in her manner.

(*she took away my memories but left all my senses, all my human knowledge. She wanted me to survive . . . but turned me into nothing.*)

She holds the long pointer across the impromptu map, and Rufus knows what he has to do.

Taking the end of the proffered pointer, he climbs slowly to his feet. He knows he can be healed; he knows this strange woman will take him and do that. But first she wants to know where he has come from.

She is looking down at the rough landscape around her feet as he takes the first few steps. She glances up and freezes. Even her loose robe seems to catch the sunlight and pause, motionless in the still desert heat.

Rufus takes more steps back, eye on the map she has made, and he's aware of the drag marks his feet are making in that desert landscape. Soon he is walking across the marks he left coming here moments or days before, and the woman—his rescuer, his savior—has taken one of the several metal and bone things from her belt. She's holding it in both hands before her, raised as if to gather the heat of the sun, and something glints in the object's concave well.

She starts talking, and though he does not know the words, he recognizes the raised inflection of questions.

Back some more, back, way beyond what he can judge to be distance in the out-of-scale map she has made. But he knows that there's something staggeringly important about where he is, *who* he is, and what he has done, and suddenly he needs to make an impression. He's not just a young, naked boy dying in a desert. He is something far more.

(*if she'd told me I would still have come. If she'd trusted me . . .*)

He stops and plants the pointer in the sand between his feet.

His savior is shouting now, her strange guttural words stumbling over one another as she steps forward, stamping out her map as she moves closer.

(*she made me what I am . . . she sent me out to this . . .*)

Rufus turns and points his skinny arm out into the desert, back the way he has come.

(*whatever happens now is all her fault.*)

The shouting ceases, and now his savior is muttering again. He feels a sudden charge to the air. Every hair on his head stands on end. A thrill passes through him, aggravating every nerve and setting his whole body spasming, kicking up sand. As he turns fully to face her, there's an intense flash that is, for the blink of an eye, brighter and hotter than the sun.

And then a darkness and silence he has never known before.

Nophel soothed the Scopes, lifting their leather shrouds, rubbing ointment into their unnatural joints and creases, and his condition did not seem to bother them at all. Perhaps they did not even know that he could not be seen; their giant eyes, after all, were aimed out at the city. Or maybe this strange curse left in one of his mother's sample gourds did not affect their chopped, inhuman minds. Dogs and rathawks did not see him, but they were natural things whose minds worked in very defined ways. These Scopes were not conceived in the eyes or minds of gods known or unknown.

Just like me, Nophel thought. Though born a very natural birth, he considered himself offspring of a monster.

He had been watching for half a day, and Dane had not returned. He'd said that he needed to speak to the Council and, ever since he'd left, Nophel had sat in fear of what might come. His life had changed so much: the Blue Water, meeting the Unseen, and then the revelation that the Dragarians—not the Marcellans and their Scarlet Blades, as he'd always assumed—had killed his mother more than twenty years before. That disclosure had stolen some of the comforting satisfaction that playing a part in his bitch mother's death had always afforded him. Absorbing such changes was hard enough, but awaiting the inevitability of more change now was almost unbearable. *If he sends them to kill me, they won't be able to see me*, he thought. But Dane was not foolish. If he sought Nophel's death, he would lull him first. Unseen he might be, but he was as far from safe as ever before.

And then the Dragarian shouting, *Baker!* What did that mean?

Watching the viewing mirror for hours on end, his eyes had become sore and his mind jaded by some of the secret minutiae of Echo City's existence. Although guilty of matricide—at least, he'd once believed that was the case, and that belief had made him sleep easier—that had been an honorable murder, revenge for being shunned by the one woman who should have held his deformed face to her bosom and loved him unconditionally. The petty, sordid acts he sometimes witnessed from up here, and the resulting waves of effect that spread out from these acts, had planted a sickness in his soul. Most days he could purge that sickness by watching for only short periods at a time and then cleansing himself by longer moments of contemplation or study. But today he had been looking for too long. A visit to the roof, tending the Scopes, being among his own kind—though he was unchopped, they were products of the dead Baker, and bastard children to her—was already serving to erase some of those sights.

There was good, of course. Kind gestures, signs of benevolence, like the porridge kitchens set up around the many entrances and exits through the wall around Marcellan Canton, run by volunteers and renowned for the quality of the free food they gave away to the homeless, dispossessed, and streetwalkers of the great city. Such signs comforted Nophel immensely, and yet they sometimes troubled him as well. He could not watch a family playing in one of Marcellan's many lush parks—father and mother throwing catchballs, children scampering after them—without musing upon how his own childhood should have been. His life was missing a great part, a pivotal slice of existence. She had sent him away. He had been a bitter and angry child, and no one in the work-house had ever thrown a catchball for him.

He had finished creaming the Western Scope, working the oil-based soothing gel into the heavy creases around its elongated skull and eye socket, when it stiffened and grew still. He'd never seen anything like it before. The Scopes, he thought, were always static unless instructed to extend or divert their focus, but West's sudden reaction illustrated that motionlessness did not necessarily mean stillness. He'd not been aware of it moving, but as it stilled, the world around Nophel seemed to sway and flex.

The Scope turned to the north. He stumbled back, lest he be knocked to the ground by its enlarged and deformed skull. Gears and joints groaned and creaked in protest, old unoiled wheels shed rust and dirt as they traversed the uneven rooftop beneath the Scope's massive eye, and its body shuddered under the stress of moving so far, stretching too much in a direction it had not looked for years.

"What is it?" Nophel asked, almost as if expecting a reply. He crawled sideways and stood in the center of the roof, and it was only then that he realized the Eastern Scope was also diverting its attention to the north. Its complex support structure was not handling the shifting quite as well, and metal groaned and cracked as several bolted junctions gave way. Chains swung and clanged against supports, and Nophel saw the creature shifting its balance to compensate for the damage.

He turned around and stared into the glaring, flexing eye of the Southern Scope. "Do you see me?" he muttered, and then he felt the stirring dislocation of vertigo as its intricate lens shifted and changed. Perhaps if he'd seen his own reflection in there, it would have rooted him to the world, but he was looking at nothing, and he fell.

They've all seen something! he thought, closing his eyes and resting on his hands and knees for a moment. Never had he known the Scopes to act like this. They obeyed his instructions from the viewing room, turning slightly this way and that, extending and closing their vision, and projecting what they saw down to the viewing mirror. But this sheer act of will shocked him.

Nophel stood and looked north, but he could see nothing out of place. *It must be far away.* And as he ran for the steps down to the viewing room, he thought, *And far away in that direction is Dragar's Canton.*

He almost stumbled several times hurrying down the winding staircase, and once back in the viewing room he paused for only a moment to make sure he was alone. It was as silent as he liked it. Panting, unsettled by the Scopes' activities up on the highest rooftop in Echo City, Nophel ran to the viewing mirror and slumped in the seat before it—and he saw.

He saw what the Western Scope saw, with its head turned and body straining at supports, looking to the north at what its cousin the Northern Scope must have seen already.

One of the huge domes of Dragar's Canton filled the polished screen, but he had never seen it like this before. It resembled a nest in one of the ant farms of Crescent Canton, seen from a few steps away so that the industrious insects were shifting, hurrying specks.

"Something coming alive," Nophel whispered, unsure why he had chosen those words yet chilled by them.

He reached for the extension dial, tweaked the focus lever, then turned the oiled, worn scan wheel that sent a series of hydraulic signals up into that rooftop creature. Gasping against the inclination to hold his breath, Nophel stared wide-eyed as the image grew in the viewing mirror. The dome's roof closed in, the curve vanishing as the Western Scope focused on one part, and then Nophel knew for sure.

Across the dome, openings had appeared. Some of the creatures that emerged had wings, just like the thing he had questioned, and they took to the air. Others crawled down across the gray dome, soon disappearing from view. Hatches slid aside to reveal impenetrable darkness, and some closed again after only one or two darting shapes had emerged. Others remained open far longer.

As Nophel gasped in another breath, he shifted the source

for the viewing mirror onto the Northern Scope. It took a few beats for the swap to take place, and during that time the screen was painfully blank. *Must tell Dane Marcellan*, he thought, tapping his fingers against the instrument panel without actually touching any dials, levers, or buttons. Something momentous was occurring out there, and much as he saw himself as the keeper of the Scopes, he knew that this was so much more than him.

The Northern Scope saw the same view. He focused and panned, moved in and out, but however hard he tried to follow one particular shape when it emerged, it was soon lost from sight. It was like trying to track a single snowflake in a blizzard. He closed his eyes, cold, and then hurried from the viewing chambers.

All the way down to Dane Marcellan's rooms, he dwelled upon what he had seen and how he might reveal it. He passed several Scarlet Blades in the twisting corridors and hallways, a couple of them alerted only by the breeze of his billowing cloak. When he reached Dane's rooms, he burst through the door.

Dane stood quickly from an expansive desk in the corner, hand reaching for a knife as he scanned the empty room. Even as his panic subsided a little—perhaps he saw a shadow of Nophel's movement, perhaps he only assumed—Nophel spoke.

"The Dragarians are invading," he said.

Dane sank back into his seat, sighing heavily. He rubbed his face and then stared, blinking slowly as thoughts tumbled.

"Dane?" Nophel said, but the Marcellan did not even seem to register the improper use of his informal name.

"I hear you," the Marcellan said. "I hear you too well."

"Dozens of them. Hundreds! I tried to track them, but—"

"Nophel, I will grant you the White Water antidote, but on one condition." Dane shoved his chair back and stood. His brief moment of shock was over.

"What condition?"

"There is something you must do for me."

"If it's to do with the Council—"

"Nothing to do with them, Nophel. They'll know of this, of course, but the message I want you to carry is to someone very far removed from them. Someone else entirely."

"Then who?" And when it came, the answer, though perhaps expected, was shattering.

"The Baker," Dane said. "The *new* Baker. Your sister."

"Tell me about the Baker," Peer said.

"What do you want to know?"

"All of it."

"Really?" Malia paused, causing Peer to stop and look at the Watcher.

Peer smiled softly. "Her and Gorham," she said.

Dawn had broken across the mountain of spires, rooftops, and walls in the east to find them crossing the border between Crescent and Course once again. They chatted and laughed, trying to exude the image of strolling friends out to watch sunrise beside the Western Reservoir, but Peer was all too aware of the bulges of weapons beneath Malia's loose coat.

After what she had seen, she felt a long way from safe.

"Gorham is scared of her," Malia said.

"It's hardly surprising."

Malia took a pouch of tobacco from her pocket and shoved a good pinch into her mouth. She offered some, but Peer shook her head.

"He wasn't to start with," Malia said, picking leaf shreds from her lips. "First time he went down there after . . . after you'd gone, I was with him. He was broken. Talked about you in the past as if you were dead already, but I always saw the truth of it."

Peer wondered whether the harsh Watcher woman would mention her crucified husband. In a way she hoped so, because it would prevent Peer from feeling too selfish for asking about this. *Tell me about my old lover and this new woman*, she was saying, as if that was the only important thing.

"What *was* the truth?" Peer asked.

"Back then he could hardly live with himself. He helped me when things turned really bad after your capture, when the purge came. He was a real friend, and I sucked up all the help he gave, giving nothing back. He was grieving too. He spent a long time trying to convince himself that you were dead, yet all the time he held a spark of you inside."

"I'm not sure I believe that," Peer said, and Malia's strong fingers bit into her arm, surprising her.

"You asked me to tell you about him and Nadielle," she said. "That can only start by talking about him and you. So give me the courtesy of assuming I know what I'm saying."

Peer nodded but did not reply.

"Giving you up was the hardest thing he ever had to do. By then he was already working his way up what was left of the Watcher inner circles. He knew what your capture would do: protect the Baker, for a time. And he knew that her involvement with the Watchers was utterly imperative to provide us with what we've always sought."

"A way to escape Echo City when the city's end-time arrives."

"Yes."

"And she hasn't found it yet."

"The Baker's line is long," Malia said after a short pause. "You know that. Strange people. Their presence ebbs and flows through the city's history, from criminal to hero. This Nadielle and her mother before her—they were the first to offer such crucial help to the Watchers." She swished her hand through roadside grasses as they walked, releasing a cloud of feathered seeds to the air. "She's important."

"So betraying me helped Gorham save the Baker." Saying it so starkly made her feel sick inside. Had it been intentional? Had a history already existed between the two of them?

"Don't think about that too hard," Malia said. "He did what was best for all of us, but even that only delayed the inevitable."

"No," Peer said. "It saved the Baker. I suppose I'm a hero." The bitterness in her voice was so sudden and intense that Malia laughed out loud. Peer felt a flush of anger . . . and then she, too, laughed. It was the only way to hold back the rage.

I shouldn't continue down this path, she thought. *It's not my place to pry*. But now this *was* her place again. She'd come home, and however dangerous it was, and however temporary her homecoming might turn out to be, there was part of her history missing. Knowing what had happened after she was taken, tortured, and banished might go some way to filling in those blanks.

"And after I left?"

"The purge," Malia said, and in her voice Peer heard a sense of relief. Perhaps this was something she needed to talk about to keep her memories, and her fury, fresh. "The Scarlet Blades were sent out by the Marcellans—and their Hanharan-fucking priests—to stamp out the Watchers' organization once and for all. They'd already destroyed our political side, with you and the others being killed or . . ."

"Tortured," Peer said lightly.

"Yes, that. So they went after the rest of the organization. Announced it as a banned group, dangerous to the well-being of the city. Bad times. They swept through Course, killing and arresting as they went. Some of us escaped, some hid, a few fought. But fighting wasn't the thing back then, and it likely never will be. We're the sensible minority in a city of unreason."

"How did you escape?"

"Bren and I went down into the Echoes around the water refineries. We thought we'd be safe, because it's endless down there. And he hoped that after long enough we'd be forgotten and could return topside and live again. But there were Blades waiting down there. Maybe it was luck on their part, or more likely they'd already tortured favored hiding places out of Watchers they'd caught. They took Bren, but I slipped away—"

"From Scarlet Blades?" Peer winced instantly, ashamed at the doubt her voice betrayed. But Malia saw Peer's regret and looked down at her feet as they passed from unsurfaced paths onto a road of condensed gravel.

"Bren fought them," she said. "Gave me a moment to flee and hide. Just enough time, the edge I needed, and I ran and ran. I heard him shouting from behind me, a long time after I'd started. Heard them following, like rats scampering through the Echoes. And something . . ." She trailed off.

"Something?"

"Something saved me."

They stopped walking and Malia sat on a low wall beside the road. "There's a safe house not far from here," she said. "Devin and Bethy will hopefully be there. We need to start spreading the word about Rufus."

"Yes," Peer said, "but what saved you?"

"Phantoms."

Peer frowned. Shook her head. "They're echoes of Echoes."

"Some say they're unsettled wraiths of people killed by Blades in the distant past and that they hate them still." Malia shrugged. "But something covered me down there, smothered me from view, kept me still. I saw three Blades pass within stabbing distance of me, and if I'd been able to move I'd have gone for them. Might've taken two of the bastards with me, at least. But it kept me from moving."

Peer looked across a field of blooming fruit trees at the reservoir and let the brief silence grow.

"They sacrificed Bren on the wall," Malia said at last.

"I know. I'm sorry." Peer saw the glitter of tears in Malia's eyes. An uncharitable thought came—*So she does feel*—and Peer glanced away in shame.

"As far as I know, the thing with Gorham and Nadielle was all her," the Watcher woman said, wiping angrily at her eyes. "And I suppose he was feeling . . . vulnerable. Don't know what she sees in him, frankly."

Peer glanced at her, frowning, but then she saw Malia's expression soften somewhat, the creases around her eyes and mouth defined in the morning sun as she almost smiled.

"Yeah," Peer said. "Lousy in bed too."

Malia chuckled. Peer laughed. And then Malia stood quickly as something flitted overhead, flying low and fast toward a spread of buildings to the south.

"What is it?" Peer asked.

"Messenger bat. We use them, but only in emergencies. Too easy to trace. Come on."

Malia led them toward the safe house, and Peer hoped it would remain safe for a little while longer.

*   *   *

It took a while to reach the house, buried as it was far up one of the sloping streets leading toward the walls of Marcellan Canton. Malia jogged steadily, but soon Peer found herself out of breath and sweating, her old hip wound aching. All those long days harvesting stoneshrooms must have detracted from the fitness she'd once enjoyed.

The streets were busy already with people on their way to and from their places of work, and Peer and Malia attracted more than a few curious glances. *We should slow down*, Peer wanted to say, but something had Malia unsettled. So Peer stayed quiet, concentrating on the pounding heels of the woman ahead of her, and hoped that chance favored her this morning. Hers was not an especially recognizable face, but since breaking out of Skulk she was more than aware that a death sentence hung over her.

"Not far," Malia said over her shoulder, and Peer knew that the Watcher must have heard her panting.

They reached a small, sloping square where a group of musicians had set up their instruments on a leveled timber area. The musicians stood and sat with their backs to the Marcellan wall, their gentle strains serenading people rushing here, there, or somewhere else. Few stopped to watch, but the musicians seemed unconcerned. Peer had seen their like many times before, and from her time with the Watchers she knew more about them than did most Echo City inhabitants. Their music was designed to lull, written by songsmiths embedded deep within Order of Hanharan circles. *Listen to enough of that crap*, she remembered Malia's husband, Bren, saying across a table of empty wine bottles and spilled ale, *and you'll be paying homage to Hanharan's asshole by morning.* They'd laughed at the blasphemy and glared at any tavern patrons daring to throw a disapproving glance their way.

Past the square, along a tree-lined avenue of three-story buildings, and then Malia paused at a doorway and glanced back at Peer.

"Still with me?" she asked, smiling. Her breathing displayed hardly any sign of exertion, and Peer's respect for this Watcher woman grew some more.

Malia knocked at the door. A small viewing panel slid open and she exchanged words with someone inside. As bolts and chains were withdrawn beyond the door, she turned back to Peer, face grim.

"We should hurry," she said. "The bat's here and the reading's about to start."

Bats. Readings. Peer knew nothing of this. And as she followed Malia into the small, shady house, she wondered just how much the Watchers had ever confided in her. Being a part of their political wing, she'd believed that she had their beliefs and concerns at heart every time she'd confronted Marcellan politicians or the more fanatical Hanharan priests. The Marcellans had been entrenched, though, and although they were completely driven by their Hanharan faith, they had ironically viewed the Watchers' political face—the representation of a faithless belief—as fundamentalist.

But perhaps the Watchers had felt it safer keeping their true, deeper secrets to themselves. Having been banished and returned, she was now a part of something deeper and more covert. *Being used even back then*, she thought, but now was not the time for upset or recriminations. The past was past. The future had yet to be formed. And the higher the sun rose today, the more unsettled she feared their immediate future might be.

The woman was huge. Peer didn't think she'd ever seen anyone this size in her life—a bulbous mass of sickly gray and yellow flesh, with rolls of fat spilling from between swaths of damp leather. Atop this gently shifting mass was the woman's head, chinless and swollen, with a small tight mouth and eyes all but hidden in pits in her skull. Her arms and hands seemed unnaturally small compared to the rest of her body, and her legs were somewhere out of sight. The smells were rank and rich, and as the woman shifted to watch them enter, Peer heard wet and fluid sounds. It was disgusting, and it made her want to retch—but then she saw the woman's eyes for the first time.

"Hello, child," the woman said, staring directly at Peer. Her voice was high and light, lilting with harmonies that would have put a silk snake to shame. "Close the door behind you. It's cold."

Peer squeezed into the room behind Malia and closed the door. It snicked shut, and she had a moment of panic when she thought they might be locked in. But then she felt the warm, surprising touch of Malia's hand pressed flat against her thigh, a light tap—

that's the first time she's touched me.

—and she knew the Watcher was doing her best to settle Peer's fears.

"Peer, meet Blu. Ex-whore, ex-leader of the Bloodwork Gang in Mino Mont, ex-informer to the Scarlet Blades. Murderer, kidnapper, rapist, thief, and monster."

"Fuck you too, Malia," the huge woman said, and her body started to ripple as she giggled like a little girl.

"All that's true?" Peer asked.

"All but one," Malia said. She knelt beside Blu and smiled up at her, as though worshipping the fetid mass of flesh and bone this woman had become. *She probably can't even leave this room*, Peer thought, and she realized how safe this house must be. Anyone entering through the front door and not knowing what to expect would likely be scared right back onto the street.

"I saw the bat," Malia said. "I was coming to see you anyway, but the bat makes things so much more urgent."

"You want me to read and tell you, Malia?"

"Yes."

"And why should I do that?" Blu's voice was still high and light, but Peer detected the first hint of tension between her and the Watcher.

"Because we keep you safe," Malia whispered. Blu shook some more, but this time her laughter was silent.

"I'm only playing with you, Malia," she said. "Peer. You're very beautiful. I like beautiful women around me, but I . . . lose so many. I have my needs, you see. Places I can't reach. Things I can't do for myself."

"She's with me," Malia said, and those three words were loaded. Blu sighed, and a ripple of dejection passed around her body and lost itself in the clothes piled around her frame.

"Well, it was worth a try." Then the huge woman opened her hand, and curled in her warm, wet palm was a bat. Its wings were propped beside it, ears high, claws gripping lightly, and its nose twitched as its meaty prison unfurled.

"It flew in from the north," Malia said. "We're looking for someone, and I fear—" But Blu waved her words aside.

"Quiet, Malia. You've come to hear what I have to say, so don't taint the air with supposition."

Malia stood and backed away, standing close beside Peer where she leaned against the door.

"Now what?" Peer whispered.

"Watch and listen," Malia said.

Peer breathed lightly through her mouth, because tasting the stench did not seem quite as bad as smelling it, and her heart beat with nervous expectation.

Blu brought the bat up before her eyes. The little creature shifted in her plump hand, but only enough to maintain its balance. It was looking directly at the obese woman's face, and it seemed ridiculously small. *She can't reach her own head*, Peer thought, as Blu seemed to stretch her nonexistent neck a little, puckering her lips, pressing her arm into her side in an effort to bring the bat closer. *Should I offer to help?* Peer was about to ask Malia, but then Blu flicked her wrist, flinging the bat toward her. It landed perfectly on her wide shoulder, fluttering its wings slightly as if to shake off the effort of its short flight.

Blu settled again, and Peer had not realized how much Blu had been tensing her unnaturally large body until it slumped and regained its former, resting position. The huge woman sighed, belched, then tilted her head toward the bat.

Peer's stomach lurched and rolled, her eyes watered, and she could not understand how anyone could bear to be in here for very long. *I have my needs, you see*, the woman had said, and whenever Peer blinked she had brief flashes of what those needs must be. Her right arm ached in tortured sympathy with whoever had to fulfill them.

She saw Blu's lips shifting a little, and the bat's head tilting, and the woman muttered words and sounds almost too high for Peer to hear. In return the bat flapped its small leathery wings and squealed back. She felt rather than heard the conversation, and she was thankful that it did not take too long.

As the bat seemed to settle again, clawing its way down from Blu's shoulder to her expansive bosom, the woman's head snapped to one side and she grabbed the bat between her teeth.

Peer gasped. Blu bit. The bat squealed, its cries more than audible this time as its body popped. Blood streamed down the woman's wide neck. She bit again, jerking her head back like a wild dog as she drew the bat deeper into her mouth.

"Malia!" Peer said, an expression of disgust rather than a plea for action.

Blu chewed, crunching bone, dribbling blood, and her frown seemed distant and preoccupied. She started swallowing pieces of the bat, and each swallow made a revolting gurgling sound. She chewed some more, glancing at Peer and then away again, her frown deepening.

"What?" Malia said, but Blu ignored her.

When she had finished chewing, Blu opened her mouth and let a glob of glistening, blood-covered fur roll from her mouth. It struck her chest and rested there, spreading a pool of diluted blood across the cloth of her voluminous dress. She stared at it, unseeing.

"Blu, what?"

"Dragarians," the bat-eater muttered. "Many of them, streaming out of their canton. Some fly. Others crawl, run, and slither."

Dragarians! Peer had never seen one, other than in paintings and drawings. They were not quite as mythical as the deep-living Garthans—they were known to exist, beneath the cover of their massive domes—yet they were further beyond the reach of normal Echo City inhabitants. And Penler had respected, even honored them.

"What does that mean?" Malia said.

Blu looked at Malia, then at Peer. Any underlying humor had vanished, and the blood smearing her chin and bloated throat made her look monstrous. "That's for you to know," she said. "I'm just the reader."

"Rufus," Peer said.

"What about him?"

And though she needed to talk with Malia, she did not wish to do so here. Blu was still staring at her, those sunken, strange eyes piercing and animalistic at the same time. She was not chopped, Peer was certain of that. This staggering size was naturally wrought. But such a condition must have also affected her mind, giving her the ability to do what she had just done and perhaps also warping her in other ways. Malia might trust her, but Peer did not.

"Why did you eat the bat?" she asked.

Blu stared at her for a long moment before saying, "Evidence."

"But how did you—".

"Thank you, Blu," Malia said, and she turned to leave.

"But wait, Malia, what about . . . ? When do we . . . ?"

"Thank you." Malia reached around Peer to open the door, shoving her out into the corridor. She slammed the door behind her, closed her eyes, and leaned against the wood, sighing, then opened them again and stared at Peer. "Rufus arrives, and the Dragarians emerge from their canton overtly for the first time in centuries. Is there any chance that this could be a coincidence?"

Is she just going to ignore what we saw? Peer thought, and she felt dizzy with confusion. "Malia—"

"He comes in from the desert, and they stream out from their canton." She was staring at the floor now, where rotten skirtings were punctured with ghourt-lizard holes. "They've spent generations awaiting the return of Dragar. *From out of the Bonelands* are the words they used, before shutting themselves away from everything else. How the crap do they even know he's here?"

"Spies?" Peer said, shrugging. "People have all but forgotten them—it must be easy for them to watch."

"And now Rufus is lost in the city," Malia said, "and we have to find him before the Marcellans do, because they'll execute him as a Pretender. And we have to find him before the Dragarians do, because if they seriously believe him to be their damned prophet returned to them from the Bonelands . . ." She shook her head.

"If they believe . . ." Peer prompted.

"The Watchers know that the end is coming, and we strive to prepare for it. But to the Dragarians, their doomsday belief is a *religion*. They *crave* the end of Echo City, because according to their philosophies that's when Dragar returns to take them into Honored Darkness—whatever the fuck that means."

"It's the north," Peer said.

"The north?"

"Honored Darkness. A man I know was sent to Skulk because of his writings about the Dragarians. He respected their aims and their religion. Most think that 'Honored Darkness' means death, but Penler thinks it's the north, where the sun never shines and time stands still. And the Baker told me that Dragar, murdered five hundred years ago, was conceived in the desert and was immune to its effects."

"They think that Rufus is Dragar and he'll lead them north from the city," Malia said softly.

Peer nodded, and her stomach dropped. "And if they think he's returned early . . ."

"They'll do their best to fulfill the end-days prophecy themselves. Something might well be rising, but the Dragarians could be the immediate threat." Malia pushed herself away from the wall. "Flying things, Blu said. Crawling things. Who knows what the crap they've been doing under those domes for the past five centuries."

"Oh, by all the false gods," Peer muttered. "He's not just important anymore, is he? Rufus?"

"Not just important, no. He's dangerous."

I thought that the moment he killed the Border Spite, Peer thought. But Malia grabbed her arm and pulled her from the house, and events swept around her, dragging her onward, tugging at her fears and hopes, her pains and traumas from the past, and steering her toward some destiny she could not understand and would never have believed had she known.

As they ran back along the street, Peer asked about Blu.

"Believe me," Malia said, "it's better that you never know."

The sun was bright above Hanharan Heights, and the sky held only a few innocuous clouds. But Echo City suddenly felt darker than ever before.

Chapter 12

The three Gage Gang members usually worked only at night, but today they made an exception. They'd been following the tall man since sunup. He looked such easy prey.

Jon Gage—all gang captains took the gang's name in lieu of their family name—enjoyed working with the boy and woman he was with today. The boy was respectful, even reverential, and often in awe at some of the stories Jon told him about his last few years as a Gager. Most of these stories were embellished, and some were outright lies, but for Jon that was half the point. Slash took away parts of their lives that they didn't desire anymore or that caused them pain and left openings in memory and intention that could then be filled. The woman used to work as a whore in Mino Mont and was owned by one of the most vicious gangs there, though she had always refused to name which one. She'd escaped underground in a long journey through the Marcellan Echoes and ended up in Crescent, amazed at the intense farming that occurred there, letting her wounds and bruises heal, though her mind never had. Jon had found her one night shivering beneath a huge mepple stack, and they'd been friends ever since. She was comfortable with him, felt protected, and because Jon's preferences went the other way, there were never any sexual tensions.

So the three of them were friends, and this friendship worked well when they were hunting. They were a tight unit, a small part of a much larger organization whose main aim was

the procurement of slash. A very particular drug, slash stimu-
lated imagination and awareness, encouraging hallucinations
in the user, depending upon the grade of drug taken and the
concentration. Small amounts could be procured by anyone in
the city apprised of where to look for it, but the addicts forming the Gage Gang had realized years ago that the more money
they moved in bulk, the greater the amount of drugs they could
buy. They had shifted from being concerted users to organized
distributors. And there were those in the gang whose aims
were now edging even higher; they wanted to make a play for
the subterranean manufacturing plants.

But Jon had never been that ambitious. He was happy with
his daily fixes and the comforts that Gage membership
brought. The unpleasant side of such a business—the trans-
porting of meat offerings down to the rogue Garthan tribe that
ran the production plants—was something he thought about
only when he had to. He and the others would spend some
days sitting outside one of the rural cafés scattered across
Crescent, talking inconsequentialities, enjoying sunlight on
their skin and the feeling of slash massaging their minds, and
sometimes he even thought himself a moral man. Decent,
hardworking, he had certain values, and he let the slash construct and reinforce those beliefs as much as he could.

It was only when he had to hunt, collect, and transport
their victims down into the Echoes, then hand them over to
the Garthans who manufactured the slash, knowing that the
drug-addled underground dwellers would slow-roast them
alive, tearing off cooked chunks of flesh to feed their
babies . . . It was only then that Jon entertained an awareness
of what he really was.

The white-haired man was lost, that much was obvious.
He had been walking across the landscape in a vaguely north-
westerly direction since they first spotted him, and for most
of the afternoon they had been casually trailing him. They
followed at a distance, and once he wandered beyond a small
commune growing beans and lushfruit, Jon decided the time
had come to close in. Their traps had been empty for the last
few nights—not even a wandering wild horse or tusked
swine to offer in lieu of the preferred long pork. It would

bode well for the three of them if they could report a capture this evening.

"We'll wait until he's in the next valley," Jon said. "I know it well. There's a wide irrigation canal, no bridges for half a mile in either direction. Maybe he'll swim, or maybe he'll go for a bridge. Either way, we'll have him trapped."

"And then have time to take him," the woman said, her eyes wide with excitement. Jon knew that she'd suffered at the hands of the Mino Mont gang—she'd shown him her scars and injuries and where they had taken pieces of her away—and he was afraid that the mental wounds formed more-deadly scar tissue in her mind, places that could not be touched and tempered by slash. Sometimes, he thought she was mad.

"Can I take him down?" the boy asked. His eyes were wide as well, but this was a childish fear, not excitement. After each catch, the boy still cried. Jon always administered the slash to him first, and slowly he could see the drug working on the boy's concerns, burying and camouflaging them. But it always took some time.

"Well, it's daytime," Jon said. "We'll have to be fast. This is no time to let someone scream."

"I'm a good shot," the boy said, and Jon could not deny that. He'd once seen him take a rathawk out of the sky with his doonerang.

"Let the kid have a go," the woman said.

Jon smiled and nodded. "First shot, though," he warned, and the kid grinned and started forward.

They spread out and followed the white-haired man up a long, slow slope planted with countless rows of dart-root shrubs. The spicy smell hung heavy in the still air, warm and enticing. Jon brushed against leaves and sniffed at his fingers. He realized how hungry he was. After they caught this one and took him down—the Gagers maintained many hidden routes down to the exchange points in the Echoes, and he knew of one close by—it would be time to eat.

"Hey, kid," the woman said, and she started running.

"Wait!" Jon hissed. How could it have gone so wrong? The kid was darting through the plants, impressively stealthy and yet much too early. The man would hear him coming, turn and see him, and if he had a spit of self-preservation he'd be off, running into the endless miles of crops and making what should have been an easy catch hard. So Jon started to run as well, risking making more noise but offsetting that risk with the knowledge that they had to slow down. If he shouted after the kid now, all would be lost.

Something flew overhead. Jon stopped and looked around, but whatever it was must have been very low. The dart-root plants barely rose above his shoulders, but already the flying thing was lost to sight. *Rathawk*, he thought, but that felt wrong.

He moved on, keeping track of the kid and the woman. She was good, he had to admit, and he'd told her that many times. She was running faster than anyone and moving like a phantom.

Jon saw the tall man's outline as he reached the top of the hill. The man paused and looked around, lost but apparently searching for something. It wasn't often that Jon worried about what people were doing out in these fields—they rarely preyed on the farmers or pickers, because the Gagers knew how quickly suspicions and myth would spread among the farming communities—but this man had him intrigued. There was something strange about him, as if he'd taken a massive dose of slash and now was lost in the landscapes of his own mind. Jon had seen it happen before and had even experienced it once or twice himself. *Just what are you seeing when you look around?* he thought. He searched the memories of his own slashouts, but they were as vague as fleeting dreams.

Jon almost tripped on a ridge in the soil and looked down at his feet, and when he glanced up again the ground before him was red.

He should have stopped running, should have recognized what it was and what had happened, but he'd not taken slash for several days. His reactions were a little rusty, his perception skewed by thoughts of where and when the next smoke would come from. So he kept running, and it was the woman's uncoiled guts that tripped him.

Jon went sprawling, unable to contain the scream. Shock, disgust, grief, terror—they all came out in one piercing shout.

He held out his hands and they pressed into something warm. It splashed his face and neck, and then he rolled, feeling things crunching and bursting beneath him.

Her head, I see her head, and she's screaming, and there's no sound because—

Because her head had rolled away, and he was in her body. When he saw the hand, he focused intently on it, because it was the only part of her not touched by spilled blood.

Steam rose, and everything he touched was warm.

He was trying to take in another breath, but shock had winded him. *The boy*, he thought, because he always thought of him as Boy, and now he wished he'd shouted the kid's name one last time before he'd run away.

Jon managed to stand. His feet sank into wet soil, but he looked away. When he'd found her beneath the mepple stack, the woman had tried to kiss him, hands stealing to his cock because, in her gang, that was the only way she'd known to survive. When she'd felt no stirring there, she frowned, and then Jon had kissed her forehead and told her to tell him her story and that everything would be fine. Now everything was no longer fine, and he had to—

Something else flew overhead, wingtips and limbs skimming the uppermost plants and sending leaves drifting down. Jon flinched downward, closer to the ruin of the woman, and then he found his voice and screamed.

He stood and sprinted uphill. The tall man was staring down at him, skin pale and eyes wide, and, closer, Jon could see the boy's bobbing head as he closed on their prey. Plants all around the boy shook, and he disappeared.

Jon was about to shout when he heard the boy's terrible wet scream. It was cut off quickly. The plants stopped moving.

So did Jon. He was staring at the white-haired man, and he realized the man was not afraid. Confused perhaps, and a little bewildered. But the boy's dying screech, piercing and awful, had not seemed to perturb the stranger.

Figures appeared all around. Gray shapes, stooped like the few Garthans Jon had seen over the years, and he thought, *They've started hunting for themselves*. But then the shapes stood tall, and he realized that these were not Garthans. He didn't know what they were, though he had his suspicions. He'd read books about the Dragarians—speculative stuff concerning what that hermitic society had been doing for the last few hundred years, why they never came out, and why no one who tried to enter their canton was ever seen again. There had been illustrations, but most were merely projections of what they might look like now. They'd been human when they shut themselves away.

"But you've changed," Jon whispered, and the tall man met his gaze again.

Jon started to back away. His increased heartbeat flushed some slash dregs into his system and he felt a curious calmness descending, the terrible fate they had been ready to subject this man to vague and ambiguous now. He almost tripped over a dart-root stem but resisted the temptation to look back. *They're not looking for me*, he thought. *It's all him. Whatever this is about, whatever they want, it's all him.*

His vision swam and he closed his eyes, willing away the wooziness that sometimes accompanied his first slash of the day. When he opened his eyes again, one of the things stood before him. A Dragarian. And the very fact that it was humanoid made its indigo eyes even more alien.

"Wait," Jon whispered, and something flashed before him. When he went to speak again, no sound emerged. And as the thing turned away and sprinted back up the slope, Jon felt the rush of blood and knew that his throat had been cut.

He went to his knees, then fell forward onto the rich soil. His blood would fertilize, his flesh rot and give goodness, and his dying thoughts were fueled by slash. *Best way to go*, a fellow Gage Gang member had once said, *all slashed up*. Jon almost agreed.

As the world grew dark, he heard the sound of songlike worship, and the pain came in at last.

"You made me name Neph, because *it* was not a suitable name," Gorham said. "So what about her?"

Nadielle was walking beside him in the deepest Echo he had ever seen. Neph was somewhere ahead, patrolling beyond the reach of their burning torches and already making Gorham feel safe. Behind them came the woman. She neither spoke nor responded when he spoke to her, and he'd caught Nadielle watching him in amusement when he tried.

The Baker seemed uninterested. "Choose a name, if it will make you happy."

"Don't *you* want to name her?"

"No," she said softly.

"Why?"

"Same reason I had no wish to name Neph: I left that for your amusement. Besides, she's going to die."

Gorham wanted her to say more, but Nadielle walked silently on, staring down at the sandy soil of this older Echo.

"I'll call her Caytlin." He looked back at the short, slight woman as he spoke the name, but there was no reaction. She was following them like a sad puppy, and he wondered where her impetus lay.

"Fine," Nadielle said. She kicked at a raised rut, and the loose stones and soil clumps hissed down before them.

Soon after heading away from the Baker's rooms, they had been in a district of the first Crescent Echo that Gorham had never seen before. He was used to the ruined farmsteads and dead fields, visible only as far as torchlight penetrated. And he had been down into the most recent Course Echoes as well, which resembled that canton's built-up appearance. But the lifeless forest had come as a shock. The trees were stark and gray, leafless, petrified remnants of a place once teeming with life. He could not identify any of the species, though that was likely due to the amount their bark had degraded, most of it drying and turning to dust. The soil around their bases had shrunk away, revealing the agonized poses of old roots. And in the hardened flesh of several trees, he saw the carved proclamations of long-forgotten love affairs.

A thousand steps later, they'd reached a place where the ceiling had tumbled and the ground had reared up, and Nadielle had led them down through a series of caverns and tunnels to the Second Echo.

Now Gorham followed her and realized that he was completely in her hands. She knew these places. She had walked them many times before. If he became lost down here, he might never find his way out.

In the distance, he saw lights.

"Nadielle!"

"I see them." She did not stop. Caytlin walked past him and followed the Baker, not acknowledging his presence.

"Neph?"

"He's much closer than that. Those are . . . maybe a mile away?"

Gorham hurried after Nadielle again, passing Caytlin and walking by the Baker's side. "A mile?"

"This Echo is very flat," she said. "It's from perhaps twelve hundred years ago. Where we are now, they used to grow grapes and mepple roots."

"Mepples are grown in orchards."

"They are now, yes."

"So those lights . . . ?" he asked, but he already knew. He'd seen something like them before, but he was trying to shut the idea of phantoms from his mind. The deeper they went, the older the phantoms would be, and the more disturbing their existence.

"I think you know what they are," Nadielle said. "When we draw closer, they'll likely extinguish. Phantoms are only Echoes in themselves, but some have a strange awareness."

A shadow passed by on their right, moving quickly and confidently across the rutted landscape. Gorham caught sight of bladed hands and the sharp shadows of Neph's spines. If Nadielle noticed, she did not say.

"I never really considered the Echoes below Crescent," he said. "The fields up there now aren't too far above the Markoshi Desert levels. When you first took me to your rooms, it was the first time I'd been down, but now we're so much lower." He shook his head, unsettled by the implications.

"We're only in the Second Echo now, though they do become confused. There are more."

"You've been lower?"

"Much."

"But any lower than here must be *beneath* the level of the Bonelands."

"Maybe," Nadielle said.

"Maybe? What does that mean?"

"The Echoes are . . . nebulous. The deeper you go, the older the Echo, the more uncertain the geography becomes."

"But they're just levels." Gorham was becoming frustrated and a little angry, and he supposed it was due to fear.

"Just levels? Gorham, the past is a living place. The deeper you go, the further into history you travel. The city doesn't deal with history. It builds over its past, encloses it, shuts it off, and while tradition might persist, the real histories are soon forgotten. It's the present that matters to Echo City, while the past echoes below it, in some cases still alive. If you read the history books, one will contradict another, particularly as you go further back. So why should the Echoes be any different?"

The idea of landscape being altered by perceptions of the past was alien and disturbing, and yet it seemed to make sense. It could never be so simple as the city's past sinking beneath the weight of the present. Life was never that easy.

The lights in the distance—a weak and flickering blue, as if caused by cold fire—went out.

"How much farther?" Gorham asked.

"Not too far. The Marcellan wall is even thicker down here; we'll have to find one of the old gates."

"And then down to the Chasm."

"Does that scare you?"

"Of course!" he said, louder than he'd intended. His voice was swallowed by the space around them, even though the darkness and the knowledge that there was a solid ceiling somewhere high overhead made him feel very closed in. *I could lose myself down here*, he thought again, and his relationship with Nadielle had never felt so strange and strained. *Then I'd be just like the Lost Man.*

Behind them, Caytlin sneezed. Gorham jumped, and even Nadielle glanced back.

"It's a mythical place," Gorham said. "Unseen, unknown."

"And yet the city still drops its dead into the tributary of the Tharin that leads to the Falls."

"Just because something exists doesn't mean it can be understood."

Nadielle coughed a surprised laugh. "Gorham! You're a Watcher, someone who's supposed to appreciate reason above the irrational." She laughed again, shaking her head. "The Chasm is said to be bottomless. Doesn't that excite you? The idea that the river pours into it and that we're on our way to *see* it?"

"No," he said, "it terrifies me."

"Then why the crap did you come?"

"Because you asked me to." He knew that she was looking sidelong at him, but he did not want to give her the satisfaction. He stared at where the phantom light had just faded out, wondering what was there, what watched. He didn't want her thanks or her appreciation. But when she stroked gentle fingers across his cheek, he could not hold back the smile.

"It's some way yet," Nadielle said.

"Good."

"Yes, indeed. Plenty of other deadly places filled with monsters both known and unknown before we reach the Chasm."

"Thank you, Nadielle," he said, smiling.

"You're welcome."

They walked in silence, and for a while Gorham felt safer than he had for a long time. Up above, in Echo City, there was always the risk that the Marcellans would hear rumors of the Watchers' survival and regrouping after the purge. Whether they would stamp down on them as harshly as they had three years before, he was unsure, but the pressures were always there. There was the constant duty he felt as new leader of the Watchers and the stresses of maintaining an outwardly normal lifestyle—running a moderately successful domestic maintenance business, enjoying an unchallenging social life, and not doing anything to bring himself to the attention of the Scarlet Blades or their civilian spies.

Down here, it felt as though Nadielle knew exactly what she was doing.

It started to rain. The first few drops startled Gorham and he swept his torch above his head, the oil swilling in its small reservoir. Then he felt the water striking his upturned face, and when one drop entered his mouth, it burst sweet and fresh across his tongue.

"Rain," he said.

"Moisture condensing on the ceiling."

Gorham aimed his torch directly above them, Nadielle added her own illumination, and even combined the torches faded into a dull gray mist.

"How high?" he asked.

Nadielle shrugged. "I never really think about it when I'm down this far."

"More nebulousness."

"Yeah."

Gorham glanced back at Caytlin, and she was looking at Nadielle as if the Baker was the only focus of her life. Perhaps that was true, but Gorham could not forget what Nadielle had said about this small woman. *She's going to die.* He wondered what the Baker had planned for this particular chopping experiment of hers.

Neph appeared soundlessly before them. One beat there was only darkness, and the next there was Neph, large and sharp and covered with droplets of condensation.

"Near," it said, and its voice was like grit scraped underfoot.

Nadielle called a halt and they paused by the tumbled remains of an old roadside temple. Gorham could not tell which god or gods this place had been built to honor, and when he ventured through one of the ruptures caused by fallen walls, the insides consisted only of detritus from the roof and a few shreds of dried timber. There was no decoration and no signs of religious paraphernalia. Just as he turned to leave, a shadow moved.

He held his breath, then glanced back out to where Nadielle stood drinking from a water skin. Caytlin was close to her, as ever, and farther out at the limits of the lamplight crouched Neph, facing the darkness as if daring it.

The shadow moved again, and Gorham backed up against a cold stone wall.

A man emerged from a pile of rubble and shattered roofing tiles. He slipped through them rather than between them, the solid mass having no impact on his body. *Phantom*, Gorham thought, and the hairs on the back of his neck bristled. The man wore a simple robe tied around the waist, hood lowered, his bald head scarred across one side. Through his head and body, Gorham could see the far wall, but the splash of masonry seen through the phantom was different. More solid, more ordered, painted a subtle yellow and speckled here and there with small carved animals—offerings from long-dead worshippers to a god long forgotten.

He gasped, and the phantom paused.

They're just Echoes, he thought, repeating everything he had ever heard about these flashes from the past. But this phantom turned and looked at him. Its eyes were blank and unfocused, and Gorham thought the old dead man was looking through rather than at him, just as Gorham was looking through him. *Does he see me as a ghost a thousand years ago?* he wondered, and then the phantom left the temple through an arched doorway filled with the remains of the fallen stone lintel.

Gorham filled his lungs, aware only now that he had been holding his breath, and darted back outside.

"Did you—" he began, but he could already see that the phantom had vanished. Nadielle stood almost directly outside the ruined doorway. She raised one eyebrow.

"They probably won't hurt you," she said.

"I know that." Gorham tried to calm his breathing, hoping that the weak lamplight did not shine from the sheen of sweat he felt on his face and neck. For a beat he thought he felt Caytlin looking at him, but when he glanced her way she was staring at the Baker once again. If she'd had the ghost of a smile on her face, perhaps she would have spooked him less.

"We're very near the wall into Marcellan Canton," Nadielle said. "Of course, it's not guarded down here, not by Scarlet Blades, at least. But there are . . ." She smiled.

"There are what?"

"The history of this canton is a stormy one. The wall's roots are often the focal point for some of the many soldiers who've died in service to the Marcellans."

"You said they won't hurt us," he said.

"No, they won't. But they sometimes like to try. Just stay close, and we'll be through soon enough. Then we go deeper."

I'm not sure I should have agreed to this, Gorham thought, but he had no desire to show his nervousness. He hated it when Nadielle offered him that smile, like a teacher humoring a small child. The only time she smiled without condescension was in her bed after they had made love, when she liked him to stroke her stomach and she twisted his hair in her fingers, and she talked about the past as if it could save them all.

There were architects a thousand years ago who built with bone, and they made such wonders. A thousand years earlier, philosophers from Mino Mont wrote a series of books that are long lost but that supposedly placed us in a world much easier to understand and much less cruel. And three thousand years before that, the musicians of what would become Dragar's Canton could beguile with a note and possess with a word. Their compositions were as close to magic as anything the city has ever seen.

But even that would not last for long. Those times never stretched, because the Baker always had something to do, places to go, monstrosities to tend in her vats. And perhaps she feared she had told him too much.

His lovemaking with Peer had been purer and more honest, though his memory of it was still shaded by the full, terrible three years that had passed. He remembered her laughing cruelly as she'd walked away from him, the dismissive wave over her shoulder. She had not even looked around at him, however grave their situation. If only he could believe that it was because she could not face saying goodbye again.

He followed Nadielle and Caytlin, content for now to bring up the rear. He caught glimpses of Neph ahead of them—a shadow within shadows—and in the distance the darkness soon started to coalesce into something more solid. He wondered who had observed the Marcellan wall from this angle so long ago and whether they'd viewed its inhabitants with as much disdain as he did. The Watchers had a long but disorganized history, and until relatively recently they'd consisted of casual gatherings of like-minded people eager to shed the superstitions of the past. It was a painful irony that organizing had almost been their downfall. So he cast himself back, becoming a traveler venturing to Marcellan for some unspecified business, and the folly of its rulers, then as now, sat like a vague threat before him.

The wall emerged out of the darkness, catching some of their lamplight across its sheer surface. Before it lay the remains of many ruined dwellings, much of the timber used in construction dried and crumbled away to almost nothing. Among these places were a few stone-built constructs that had withstood the time better. But even these displayed areas of damage. As they passed, Gorham could not help thinking that some of the damage was intentional.

"There," Nadielle said. She'd paused to wait for him and, as he drew level, he saw the glimmer of phantom lights along the wall. In perhaps a dozen places from left to right, the weak blue lights clung like algae to the ancient stone, shadowed from within recesses in the wall's height and nestled at its base in several places.

"They weren't there a while ago," Gorham said.

"The phantoms here keep watch."

"But they're *Echoes*."

"Yes, but they'll be more . . . noticeable than some phantoms you might have seen before. I believe the deeper we go, and the older the Echoes, the more time the phantoms have had to become used to their continued existence."

"I don't understand," he said, his skin crawling at the memory of that phantom priest staring through him.

"I don't think we're meant to. I think they're just Echoes living in Echoes, but we choose to build upon the past instead of destroying it. Maybe it's inevitable that the Echoes of past lives will survive as well." Nadielle led them toward the wall, and Gorham could see Neph ahead of them, scouting its base. He paused at an opening—an old gateway with the remains of several flagpoles protruding from the stone façade above—and a vague phantom light glowed in the deep, dark route to the other side. Nadielle headed for Neph, with Caytlin her usual several paces behind. Gorham had no choice but to follow. It was that or stay out here on his own.

Neph had gone by the time they reached the gate, venturing into the Marcellan Canton of old. He'd left the phantoms behind. They were more blurred than others, yet their lights burned brighter and they interacted more with the subterranean travelers. They never actually touched him—Gorham wasn't sure he could have taken that without going mad—but they came close, faces manifesting from the glare, eyes searching, mouths opening in silent exhortations to stop, show their papers, where were they going, what was their business. And in the stark, ancient distance, he heard the whisper of metal on leather as they drew their weapons. He concentrated on Nadielle's back to guide him through; she walked without pause and without allowing herself to be distracted. *She's so strong*, Gorham thought.

The wall was thick down here, perhaps fifty paces wide, and it took an eternity to reach the other side. When they did, the first of this deep Echo of Marcellan Canton was revealed to them. And it was a ruin.

"What . . . ?" Gorham whispered, his question reverberating around the small square.

"War," Nadielle said. "Don't they say the history books are written by the winners?"

Gorham could not speak. These buildings had not fallen victim to the wearing effects of time but had been deliberately destroyed. Signs of ancient fires were still visible here and there, black soot stained across the pale gray stonework. Charred timbers poked broken ribs at the dark sky. And, close above the ruins, far lower than he'd been expecting, he could see the exposed underbelly of the Echo above this one.

"How deep?" he asked. "Two Echoes down?"

"More," Nadielle said. "As I said, there's no real judging of distance and time when you're down here."

"But a war between whom? How long ago?"

"I can tell you what little I know," she said softly, "but we need to keep walking. There's a place not far from here where we go deeper, and I want to reach it before . . ."

"Before?"

Nadielle gave him that annoying smile again—the one that said: *You're only a child compared to me, what I am, what I know.* And for a moment that shocked him with its intensity, Gorham thought of roughing that smile from her face.

"Let's just go," she said. "Neph will scout ahead and keep us safe." She turned her back on Gorham and started to walk. If he wanted to hear what she knew, he would have to keep up.

"There's no record of who fought this war, or why, anywhere for public consumption in Echo City," Nadielle began. "I suspect there might be writings buried deep in old Hanharan vaults or perhaps personal accounts handed down through the ages from Marcellan elders to their children. But what happened here is a whisper among shadows. Some of those phantoms we just passed might have been here when the fires came and went. Some probably died here. But even I couldn't ask them."

"Couldn't, or wouldn't want to?" Gorham asked, and Nadielle did not answer.

"All I know is what I read in my mother's books, and some of it she . . . passed down to me." Nadielle tapped her temple but looked only ahead, as if reassuring herself of something. "The Bakers might be the only line keeping some of the truth alive."

"But people come down here," Gorham protested.

"Not as many as you'd think. How deep do you travel into the Echoes?"

"Only to you," he admitted.

"And only because you have a reason to travel down. There aren't many who choose to venture into the Echoes. Criminals, perhaps, but they have only their own well-being at heart. Some explorers, yes. A few. But most who wish to explore history do so through their books. Actually visiting it—that's an experience any sane person would want to avoid."

Gorham had never thought of himself as any less than sane; he supposed his fear of being down there testified to that.

"So what happened?" he asked. They were walking between the ruined buildings now, following the route of what had once been a wide street. Ash, rubble, and other detritus littered the way, and protruding here and there above the mess Gorham made out the pale shapes of bones. The torchlight made them shift. He didn't look too closely or for too long.

"Have you ever heard of the Thanulians?"

"No."

"It's said they were watching long before the Watchers—an organized group who didn't believe any of the Hanharan teachings and who were waiting for the doom of Echo City. Their beliefs are shady and, much as I've looked, I've not been able to discover much about their outlook, their thoughts for the future, or what they intended doing should the end arrive. But one thing is clear: They claimed to have proof that Hanharan was not the city's firstborn but was a visitor from elsewhere."

"Proof?" Gorham asked, a thrill going through him. He'd always believed that Hanharan was a myth, but his conviction was founded only on what he thought of as his own good sense. The Hanharan story was wild and complex—a man born from a desert stone, shaping spit and sand to build, molding a wife from dusk's final rays, and founding the whole city. Gorham had always had trouble understanding how intelligent people could believe such stories, accept that one man had seeded and settled their whole world.

"Don't get excited. Whatever proof there may have been is long gone now."

"Destroyed in the war?"

"More like a massacre. The Marcellans at the time were mainly confined to the Hanharan priesthood—the city was a democracy then, and two main political parties juggled power back and forth as the years went by. But the Marcellans must have grown strong. There was a rout, the Thanulians were slaughtered, and all traces of their history were wiped away. Over time, with nothing written down, their existence faded."

"Left down here in the Echoes," Gorham said. Looking at the burned remains of ancient buildings, he could almost smell the fires. "They killed all of them? Every single one?"

"This is where the story gets interesting," Nadielle said. "Shall we stop for a drink?"

"No," Gorham said. He had never been anywhere like this. The surroundings felt so dead, but there was no stillness here at all. Things moved, and though any movement seemed to

be just beyond the edge of perception, his senses were alight
with evidence of activity. His skin was cooled by breaths of
moving air, he heard shifting sand or dust, and he could
smell something damp and old moving around.

Nadielle nodded, without offering him her smug smile. It
appeared that even she was spooked. Gorham glanced back
at Caytlin—still following, blank-faced and unresponsive.

"The Thanulians were peaceful. They wouldn't put their
hands on a weapon, even when attacked. Perhaps they saw
their slaughter as the beginning of the end, so to them death
was inevitable. But the Hanharans and their soldiers still
didn't get them all."

It took a moment for Gorham to recognize the importance
of what Nadielle had said. He stopped, and that secretive
movement around him stopped as well. *Almost as if it's following.*

"There are descendants?" he asked.

"The Garthans."

*The Garthans! Living down here for so long, feared by
some, almost mythical to others . . .*

"Of course!" he said. "I've never even wondered where
they came from. I just assumed they'd always been down
here, as we've always been up there."

"They were chased out of Echo City and fled below,"
Nadielle said. "No one knows much about them anymore.
Some speak to them—my mother conversed with them at
times, though I can't make any sense of what she wrote about
them in her journals. And I have limited contact with them,
when the need arises."

"They don't try to eat you?"

"You've heard that too."

"Just a rumor."

"No rumor. There *are* those who trade human flesh for the
Garthans' slash drug, which they refine from cave moss."

Gorham looked around at the ruined district they were still
traveling through, trying to imagine the terror, the pain, as the
Hanharan forces worked house by house, room by room. Piled
against one burned-out building was what he thought at first
was the tangled remains of a fallen tree. But it might also have

been the twisted, broken remnants of a whole family, killed and piled together so that their flesh would rot and their bones would degrade down here in the dark. He looked away and started to walk on, because he didn't want to know for sure.

Nadielle stayed beside him, and her enthusiasm for sharing this story was refreshing. Usually she held knowledge to her chest, perhaps whispering random facts about her own strange experiments into his ear as sweat cooled between their naked bodies.

"And then the Marcellans took control of the city?"

"Perhaps their domination of the order of Hanharan was the beginning, and this massacre showed their strength."

"I've never seen a Garthan," Gorham said, suddenly feeling an affinity with those strange subterranean dwellers.

"You probably will," Nadielle said. "If they choose to reveal themselves, that is. They're very secretive."

"That surprises you?"

She smiled sadly, shook her head, and Gorham reached out for her hand. Nadielle held on for some time. The contact made him feel safe. And then later, after they'd walked into an ancient district of that deep Marcellan Echo untouched by fire and violence, she turned to him and pressed him into the wall of a house.

"Nadielle?"

She was shaking. She dropped her torch, reached around his hips, and pulled him close to her.

"Nadielle?" he asked again, but she did not reply with words. She used her hands, pressing up over his chest, down his sides, delving between them. She used her mouth, kissing him with a passion he had never felt from her before.

Peer, he thought, but his lost love seemed a world away. He watched Caytlin over the Baker's shoulder, but the chopped woman simply sat and stared off to one side. *I can't*, he thought. *Not with her here.*

But Nadielle's hands and mouth were insistent, and he soon found that he could.

"What was that?" he gasped. She leaned heavily against him, one leg still curved around his hip. Her breath was fast and shallow, and he thought he heard faint sobs. She'd pressed her face into his neck. He felt her teeth against his skin.

"It's been too long," she whispered at last. "I'm so alone, Gorham."

"No." He didn't like this Nadielle. Nadielle was strong and confident, not needy and sad. *He* was the sad one. He needed her, not the other way around.

"Yes! I spend my time making people that aren't people. I live down here, and sunlight—it's rare for me. You're my . . ." She trailed off, and Gorham held his breath, waiting for what she would say next. Though he did not like her this way, he was still hard inside her; Nadielle's confession kept him there.

"You're my sunlight," she said. "And everything's starting to feel so dark." She fell quiet then, and soon after she pulled away and rearranged her clothing, not meeting his eyes. Gorham remained standing against the wall, feeling warm from what had happened, what had been said.

Caytlin stared with her expressionless eyes, untouched.

I'm the needy one, Gorham thought again. He went to Nadielle, and she relaxed into his embrace with a sigh of relief. Neither spoke, and they stood that way for a while until the time was right to move on.

Chapter 13

Just keep watch, Dane had said. That had been a message, as overt as any Marcellan could ever utter, even in the confines of his own rooms. He'd sent it with a stern look, and Nophel recognized the dreadful trust that had been placed in him. If he went to the authorities with the claim that one of the ruling Marcellan Council members was not a completely devout Hanharan, the resulting investigation would be long and damaging. It would be his word against Dane's—a deformed monster, who had attempted to betray his own mother, against a member of the greatest family the city had ever known. But once set in, the rot would be very difficult to expunge.

Nophel was starting to believe that he'd found a friend in Dane Marcellan. An ally. Even a fellow Watcher, though Nophel kept his beliefs to himself. And though a Watcher followed no gods, Nophel had always been a firm believer in Fate.

I have a sister, he thought. He paused again, leaning into the side of the circular stairwell and taking a deep breath. The news was almost too much. His mother—the bitch whore Baker who had abandoned him like a dog shunning a runt puppy—had chopped a child, and now that child had become the new Baker. He could barely conceive of such a thing, but Dane had assured him it was true. *Time is short*, he'd said, *but once you have handed her the message, stay with her. She will spare the time to explain what happened to you, and why*. The suspicion that Dane had not told him everything was rich, of course, because Dane was a politician. But Nophel could think of no reason why Dane should have lied about his having a sibling.

He pushed off and continued down the stairwell. He had far to go before he reached the first of Dane's contacts. The Marcellan had handed him a coded map, containing six places where Nophel might make contact with people who would be able to point him toward the Baker's rooms. And, after the map, came the vial containing the White Water.

"What is there between you and this new Baker?" Nophel had asked.

"A distant trust. An old understanding."

"Tell me."

"No, Nophel. I trust you as my messenger, but your mind is still corrupted with vengeful thoughts of your mother."

"But she's dead!"

"Yes, and I made the mistake of telling you that it wasn't your betrayal that led to that. Maybe you're angry. Unfulfilled. I need this message delivered, but I also need to trust that you won't harm her."

"Why would I harm my sister?"

Dane had stared toward him for a while, his eyes wavering slightly across the shadowy space that Nophel filled.

"Just go," the Marcellan had said. And he'd held out the sealed message tube for Nophel to take.

Descending from Hanharan Heights and making his way west, Nophel thought many times about breaking the tube and reading the message. But if the Marcellan had been in contact with this new Baker for so long, doubtless the message would be in a code or form known only to the two of them. Break the tube and he would shatter the trust Dane had placed in him.

He moved through the streets like a breeze or a whisper, turning heads here and there but never attracting real attention. He watched for more Unseen, but there were none. Perhaps they all congregated to the north.

North. What he had seen chilled Nophel like nothing ever before. The Dragarians streaming out of their canton, the way they had moved, and flown, and crawled . . . If it weren't

for the Scopes, he would never have seen, and whatever fate
was about to befall Echo City would have settled quietly
upon him in his sleep.

Perhaps that would have been for the best. He'd always
been plagued by the fact that he had no belief in anything but
eventual doom. And he did not trust that a method to leave
the city would ever be found, even if there were still those
searching for one. Had he been the worshipping kind—had
he a god—he would have prayed that the end did not arrive
in his lifetime.

Why would I harm my sister? he'd asked. He wondered exactly what she was and what her relationship had been with
their mother. She had taken on the dead bitch's mantle, after
all. The new Baker.

Nophel slipped unchallenged through one of the western
gates of Marcellan Canton's wall, then paused and looked
out over Crescent Canton; though green and lush, it felt empty.
And finding a hidden corner, he cracked the vial and drank
the White Water, because he wanted to be a part of this world
again.

"How do you find one person lost in the world?" Malia
asked.

Peer shook her head and took another drink. They were sitting on the street in front of a small tavern, Devin, Bethy, and
several other Watchers around them. She knew a couple of
them from her time before her banishment, but she had forgotten their names. They glanced at her as if she were a
ghost, and she shared their discomfort. She was nervous, un-
easy, frustrated. The drink did nothing to temper her sprinting
heartbeat. They should be moving and looking, not sitting and
musing, but she understood Malia's strategy. They had to de-
vise a plan; otherwise, they'd all be rushing around the city
like wingless wisps.

"Do you still have anyone in Hanharan Heights?" Peer
asked. One of the Watchers glared at her, and she wanted to
say, *I suffered too*. Her arm and hip ached in sympathy with
her memories.

"Not anymore," Malia said.

"What about the bat? You have ways of sending messages. There are doves and tailcoats. And can't·you access the Web?" Peer's mother had used the Web several times for her tax collecting—a vast network of pipes and wires through which messages were screeched and passed along by the chopped. But they were inexpertly chopped—not products of the Baker—and the system was frequently flawed. A message could change with its retelling, mistakes made.

"The Scarlet Blades monitor it like rathawks," Devin said. He'd met them there earlier, arriving just before Bethy; neither of them brought news. Rufus might as well never have existed at all.

"Right," Malia said. "Even if we could access the Web, it's far too dangerous. We alert the Marcellans or Hanharans to Rufus's existence, and we might as well give him up for lost."

"Might as well anyway," a male Watcher muttered, and raised his ale.

"No!" Peer shouted. She stood and knocked his hand aside, mug and ale spilling across the table. He sat back in surprise, one hand slinking down to his thigh, but she was over the table before he could do anything more, her arm across his throat. "There's hope," she said quietly. Eyes were on her now, and not just the Watchers'. Several people had paused in the street, and a group sitting inside the tavern observed through the wide open doors. She'd drawn attention to them all, but right then she didn't give a crap.

"Peer," Malia said quietly.

"Do they all know?" she asked, looking around the group.

"Yes."

"They all know everything?"

Malia nodded. Watchers exchanged nervous glances, and then Peer sensed the loaded atmosphere she'd somehow missed before. Some of them were drinking too quickly; others did not touch their drinks at all. Feet shuffled, eyes flickered, and there was a dearth of conversation. This was not a group of people out for a drink. It was a gathering of Watchers aware that what they'd waited for all their lives might have arrived.

"There's hope," Peer said louder. "We just have to find it." She eased back from the man and he picked up his spilled mug, nodding softly at her.

This is when we grow weak, she thought, and suddenly Penler's unspoken beliefs in a deity or deities seemed to make sense. *This is when faith in nothing makes us scared. We're rationalists and realists, but doesn't everyone need something to believe in?*

"Where?" Devin said. "Show us the hope."

"The Baker," Peer said, and she pictured that strange young woman's confident smile.

"You've seen her, Peer," Malia said after an uncomfortable pause.

"Yes." She was uncertain what Malia meant, troubled by the stillness that had fallen over the group.

"Well . . . she's mad."

Mad. Peer raised her own drink and took a long draft, taking the time to think about Nadielle, Gorham, and what the Baker could possibly do to help any of them. While she was venturing down to assess the dangers rising from below, the city itself was suddenly filled with threats.

"Maybe," Peer said at last. "But who wouldn't be, knowing what she knows? We take Rufus to her, and she can still help us. She *must*."

Malia sighed. Devin swallowed more ale.

"We have to look!" Peer said. "Start searching, and if that brings the attention of the Scarlet Blades, then we have to fight."

"Now *you're* mad," someone muttered.

"So this is it? All this time wasted?" She looked around at them, and her voice rose into a shout. "You're giving up?"

"Hush!" someone said, but she had their attention. She looked pointedly at Malia, lowered her voice again. "All those dead Watchers, nailed to the wall for nothing?" She pulled up her right sleeve to expose the ugly purple scars around her elbow and biceps. "All those people tortured, so we can sit and drink fucking beer while our last hope is lost out there somewhere?"

"You've heard the whispers," Malia said. "The Dragarians

are out. They probably have him already, and they'll take him back to their canton, and that will be it. We'll never see him again, and the next thing we know will be war with the Dragarians as they fulfill their own prophesies. And when they realize he's *not* their savior, they'll kill him."

"So it's hopeless," Peer said.

"Yes."

"Right." She stood and shoved her stool back. It fell onto its side on the pavement, and she glared around at them all. Those who knew her had believed she was banished to Skulk forever, and in some of their eyes she saw grudging respect for her escape. Those who did not know her saw only an intruder. It was sad that the Watchers' jealous protection of their outlawed beliefs inspired such paranoia. "Rufus is a friend of mine," she said. "I brought him into the city and exposed him to everything that's happened. So I'm going to go and find him."

"Into Dragar's Canton?" Devin scoffed.

"If I need to." *There's no way I can*, she thought. *This really is madness*. But it had gone too far for her to back down now, and she was too angry to even consider doing so.

"What about Gorham?" Malia asked.

"What about him?" She turned to leave, then glanced back. "At least I'll be doing something positive when the end comes." And their murmured conversation as she walked away could have been the distant echo of some subterranean thing coming for them all.

Rufus is moving, his body jarring against something solid, and when he opens his eyes he sees green.

He tries to sit up but he's bound. His arms are fixed tight to his sides, his head tilted to the left. When he attempts to move his legs, they are unresponsive. He tenses and flexes, but though he can feel a soft breeze against his naked skin, his entire body feels constrained.

The sky above the green is a burning blue, but this is no desert.

Then he opens his mouth to draw in a breath, and that's when he feels the film across his face.

For a moment he panics. He blinks rapidly, and though there's no impediment to his eyelids, he can feel his lashes brushing against something. He smiles and frowns, shifting his expression and feeling the film tightening and loosening across and around his face.

I can breathe, he thinks, but the panic is still there. Air moves in and out through his nostrils, but he's suddenly enclosed and cut off from the world, sensing that everything on the outside is dangerous, and all there is on the inside is him. *Am I dreaming?* he wonders, but then he realizes that this is a memory, and that when this happened he had no name.

He tries to lift himself to see where he is and what is happening, but he can barely move. He remembers the woman who found him, and that strange webbed mask she had been wearing. *She's wrapped me up in that,* he thinks, and starts to relax until he remembers what happened.

I showed her where I came from . . . across the desert . . . out of the sun and heat and Bonelands . . . and then she did something to me.

As if summoned by his vague memories, the woman's face appears above him. She touches his cheek, and the feel and heat of her skin are unimpeded by the constraining film. Those rumbles, clicks, and hisses come again, and there's something in their tone that comforts him. Her fingers do not scratch his face but soothe. Her eyes are wrinkled with a smile, not a frown. If she had meant him harm, he would be dead on those baking sands.

He can see green, and in his sudden rush of excitement he manages to sit up against his bonds.

The woman moves back a little but retains her uncertain smile. He sees her hand resting on the thing on her belt—

she did something to me with that

—but he looks around, shocked, amazed, and his delighted laughter seems to convince her that he means no harm.

It should be terrifying. But something about the lush green rolling landscape that is unlike anything he has ever seen is so natural that it holds no fear. The thing that carries him is moving along a rutted track, which runs along the bottom of a valley. The track side is speckled with swaths of blue bell-shaped flowers, and they spread out into the wide, wild fields beyond. He struggles to see order in the landscape but there is none, only randomness, and that amazes him even more. *No farming*, he thinks. *It's so bountiful here that they harvest from the wild!* In one place, the flowers give way to a low, thick plant spotted with a million yellow blooms. To his right, a woodland begins a hundred steps from the track, the trees short and squat, the canopy wild and untended—an uneven carpet crawling up the hillside toward its high, bare summit. Up there he can see the gray stains of rocky outcrops and a few white specks that seem to move slowly. There's a stream bordering the track to the left. It gurgles merrily, following his direction of travel, twisting and turning past rocks and through dips in the land. Bees buzz the flowers in abundance. Web strands drift on the breeze. Butterflies flutter across the fields, in colors and varieties that amaze him. Birds hurry through the air, taking insects on the wing, and high above he sees several larger, more-graceful birds drifting on the air without once flapping their wings. They circle, and he wonders what they must think when they look down upon him.

The woman is walking by his side, far enough back to allow him to see the view. And she's watching him carefully. The smile is still there, but so is a frown of concentration, wrinkling skin darker than any he has ever seen. The beads of water seem to have vanished from her hair. He is something amazing to her as well.

And then he sees so much more. The thing carrying him turns onto another track and heads up a gentle slope, revealing a fold in the land that previously hid the foot of another valley. As that valley opens up to his view, the things built across its floor and up its sides present themselves to him, and he catches his breath. *Even if I could remember everything from* before, *this would be something new*.

He snapped awake, shouting. Something pressed down over his mouth. He opened his lips, pushed with his tongue against the film, but there was something more solid there, tasting salty and stale, and when he opened his eyes he saw the face staring down at him in wonder.

Rufus sat up and looked around at the things carrying him. Ahead, across a canal spiked with spears of metal and wood around which sickly-looking plants grew, a gray stone wall rose before him. It curved into the sky, and to his left and right it curved away from the canal as well.

After they crossed a narrow bridge, they waited for only a moment before a section of wall slid open, and he saw inside.

Chapter 14

They walked through the dead city with movement all around. Gorham had never expected this. The phantoms usually kept their distance, but now and then he thought he saw someone rushing at him from the corner of his eye, and he'd spin around to be confronted by nothing. His only comfort was that Nadielle appeared almost as jumpy as he was.

Caytlin walked, and watched, and reacted to nothing.

Sometimes Neph came close and listened as Nadielle whispered to it. Gorham could never quite make out what she said, and perhaps she intended it that way. She had not mentioned their lovemaking since it happened. She was quiet. Something significant between them had changed, and Gorham was trying to decide exactly what it was.

His own guilt over Peer was richer than ever. He'd not felt it before when making love with Nadielle—but then Peer had been somewhere else. Now she was back in the city and his life, and he had betrayed her one more time.

Having passed the ruins of the Thanulian purge, Gorham was surprised to find much of the Echo still relatively intact. The buildings were of an older style, their construction rougher, and the materials used were more basic. There was a lot more wood, some of it dried and crumbled but much still standing. The stone blocks had been roughly cut, giving every building an irregular appearance, and nowhere did he see any glass. He checked several old window openings, always keeping one eye on Nadielle and Caytlin, but there was no evidence of these windows having ever been glazed.

Sometimes he shone his torch inside the rooms and saw the remains of what they had once been. Furniture was mostly crumbled away, but many of the houses still retained rusted wood-burning stoves on heavy granite hearths. He was surprised that these precious metal objects had been left down here and not recycled during the construction of the level above. Maybe after the slaughter, the Marcellans had represented the Thanulians as diseased.

"Here's where we start going down," Nadielle said, when they reached an open square. At its center stood a long-dried water fountain, and an entire row of buildings beyond had disappeared. They shone both lamps toward where they had been, and a gaping maw was revealed.

"What happened here?" Gorham asked.

"Who knows?" Nadielle started across the square.

"Nadielle." She'd hardly spoken since disentangling herself from him; perhaps she'd lowered her defenses too far. But he needed her to acknowledge what had changed between them. He felt like a fool, but her averted eyes were not good enough for him. After everything that had happened—after he'd sought some sort of self-forgiveness in her arms after Peer had gone—he wanted to hear her say that she needed him, as much as he'd once needed her.

His needs were becoming more complex as every moment passed.

"Can you hear it?" she asked softly, and her face had suddenly changed. Her mouth was open, head tilted as she listened, and her eyes glittered with wonder—and fear.

So Gorham listened. It was like blood rushing through his ears, but bad blood. Like the breathing of some far-off thing, but if so it was a series of final breaths. In truth, he wasn't sure whether he heard or felt it.

"What is that?" he asked.

Nadielle looked at him as if he wasn't there. Then she blinked and saw him, and nodded ahead. "We need to go and find out."

Caytlin followed her, and Gorham saw Neph's shadow

ahead of them, descending into the hole. He was fixing crampons and stringing the rope they'd brought, marking their
safest way down. Gorham had no choice but to follow. *Sometime soon she'll have to talk to me*, he thought. But as Nadielle
had already said, in the Echoes, time was ambiguous.

A while after they'd started down into the caverns, he realized that Nadielle was following Neph. The chopped fighter
carried a torch now, and it was never so far ahead that they
lost its glow. They passed through the tumbled ruins of homes
first of all, slipping beneath slanted ceilings, scurrying
through debris-filled basements, descending a set of stone
stairs that had remained remarkably intact. Then down, between massive stone beams that must have been laid many
thousands of years before. Neph kept moving, and whatever
means it used to navigate, Gorham was impressed. Here was
a chopped he had witnessed being birthed only recently, and
now it was negotiating its way into the bowels of the city.
They passed old sewers, long since dry, and then a sunken
street that flowed with stinking water.

"Don't get wet," Nadielle said, but Gorham did not need
telling. He could already smell the sickly stench from the underground stream; this was a small tributary of the Tharin.
The flow was minimal, and he saw no signs of objects floating
in it, so it could not have been the main tributary that led
down into the Chasm. When they found that, it would be
heavy with the city's dead.

Neph steered them beside the water for a while, then they
crossed a narrow rock formation that might have been natural. Past the small underground river, they entered a series of
catacombs that seemed to have been hollowed out by some
ancient cataclysm. Many of the walls and ceilings showed
the shorn ends of massive beams and columns, metal rusted,
stone shattered, and the walls themselves were pocked with
thousands of fist-sized holes.

"Those look like—" Gorham began, and as he was about
to say *sand-spider holes*, the things came.

"Back!" Nadielle shouted. She backed up, Caytlin behind
her, and Gorham staggered as he almost lost his footing.

It couldn't have been more than a hundred heartbeats, but to

Gorham it felt as though he and the others were huddled there for much longer. The things flitted through the shadows, uneven torchlight distorting their appearance even more. He saw wings, and long, trailing legs, and other protuberances whose uses were far less familiar. At first he thought the strange sound he heard was coming from them, and he covered his ears to keep out the high-pitched whine. But then, when several of the flying things swished past close enough to stroke or scrape his cheeks and forearms, he noticed that they were converging on Neph.

The chopped warrior held one arm in front of its mouth, and it was hooting through hollows formed in its bladed hands. The flying things spiraled around it in the constricted cavern, and Gorham perceived no collisions at all. Fast but controlled, these things were intelligent. Neph continued its hooting, drawing in more of the creatures. It lowered its head slowly, lowering the tone at the same time, and the things followed it down, settling finally on the uneven stone floor. Neph reduced the hooting and stood straight again. The sound stopped, echoing away into the darkness. Gorham held his breath. He could see the things more clearly now that they were still—insectile, spiked, glimmering.

Several of them flapped their opaque wings and rose. One darted at Neph's head, and the warrior leaned back and sliced it in two with its right hand. Two more went at Neph's groin, and it turned sideways and emitted spines from its hip. The things fell dead. Neph waved its arms several times, kicked out, and the remains of those that had dared attack fell among their cousins.

The carpet of creatures around Neph grew still and respectful.

Nadielle breathed in Gorham's ear, startling him. "Don't . . . move."

Neph was motionless again, torchlight glinting from the wet patches across its bladed arms. One of the attackers was spiked on Neph's left foot, writhing slowly as it bled to death. The warrior started hooting again, and this time the call was higher and more varied. *Almost like a language*, Gorham thought, and his skin prickled. The remaining things rose as one, the gentle flapping of many wings barely a breath through the cavern. Then they flew directly at the pocked walls, and Gorham gasped as every one of them disappeared.

Neph stood motionless for a while, then gently lowered its arm and turned to face them.

"What were they?" Gorham whispered.

"You can talk normally now," Nadielle said. She stood and brushed herself down, and Caytlin followed.

Gorham stayed down for a moment, eyeing the dark holes nervously. He aimed his light at some of them, but the only movement he saw was caused by the light. Whatever they were, they'd gone deep.

"We should move on," he heard Nadielle saying to Neph. "Some rebelled, which means others will follow."

"Nadielle?" Gorham asked.

"While we're walking."

Neph led the way as they departed the cavern, and though shocked and confused, Gorham was glad for that. Their route led downward, and after a time of negotiating treacherous conditions, they reached a wide, flat area. Torchlight touched nothing in any direction, and he felt the frightening pressure of space.

"Next Echo," Nadielle said, and her voice sounded different.

"So what exactly happened back there?"

"Garthan trap. They don't like visitors. They breed those things from sand sprites and cave wasps."

"And Neph can speak to them?"

"Of course. I chopped him, and he's part Garthan."

Gorham tried to absorb what she'd told him, working it through, attempting to make out what it all meant without reaching the conclusions that clamored for attention. It was the most she'd ever suggested about the chopping processes she used, but it birthed more questions than answers.

"You used—" But she'd already turned away, and he knew her well enough to recognize the tension in her shoulders. *Told me too much*, he thought. *Did she mean to?* Perhaps. Or perhaps the deeper they came, the more she was reaching out.

This new Echo felt very different from those above. There

were no buildings evident, for a start—strange, for an Echo of Marcellan Canton—but the darkness did not feel as empty as it once had. It was heavy and loaded, and it had Gorham looking over his shoulder as he followed Nadielle.

The ground was rough but even, vaguely soft underfoot, and each footstep crunched gently. He thought perhaps it was a layer of old dead plants, but the air smelled only of dust.

Nadielle led them unerringly onward, confident even though Gorham could not make out any landmarks. The mute and emotionless Caytlin followed the Baker like a shadow, and Neph was somewhere around them, flitting across their path occasionally without making a sound. *He's part Garthan*, Nadielle had said. Trying to imagine just how Nadielle chopped people in those womb vats made him shiver.

And if Neph was part Garthan, what were its other parts?

The shapes emerged quickly from the darkness—gray, motionless. Gorham's fear was held in check by Nadielle's confidence as she walked between them. They stood sentinel to the left and right, and Gorham recognized the forms of old statues. Around them the ground was more uneven but harder. *We're in a park.* He called Nadielle to a halt and went to one of the statues.

"We need to hurry," she said, standing by his side.

"A moment," he said, because he was trying to make out the statue's face. He held his torch higher, and the shadowy features jumped out at him. There was nothing unusual here—perhaps he'd been expecting something monstrous or unknown—but neither did he recognize the face from one of the many history books he'd read.

"Old city rulers before the Marcellans," Nadielle said. "This Echo might be from ten thousand years ago, when they used to have a park in every canton in honor of the rulers. As older ones died, they'd erect new statues to those who took their place."

"Sounds extravagant."

"Politicians have always liked attention. Nowadays they simply get it in differing ways."

Gorham looked around at the several other statues he could see, vaguer the farther away they were, and tried to imagine how many might be standing around them right now. They were perhaps the only surviving likenesses of many of these people, all part of the city's story and staring now into an eternal night.

"It really is the past down here," he said, as if that had struck him for the first time. The statues regarded him with nothing left to say.

The park seemed to go on forever. Gorham lost track of time, and when they heard the screaming man, they might have been walking for days.

The screams came from the distance just as Gorham became certain that he could hear something larger, and deeper. He'd been thinking that he could hear something for a while now, but Nadielle seemed unconcerned, and he hadn't wanted to mention it. If he ever stopped to listen, the noise did too, so he suspected it had something to do with walking through this Echo. Perhaps their footsteps reverberated through the dry ground, the land shaking in excitement at these first human visitors in an age. Or maybe whatever was making the sound stopped when he did and carried on to the rhythm of his pace. He opened his mouth to mention the noises to Nadielle, and then came the screams.

They were distant, their direction uncertain, and they sounded mad.

"Down," Nadielle said. Gorham knelt on the dry ground, and the Baker pushed Caytlin down and squatted by her head, protecting her.

"What the crap is that?" Gorham asked, but Nadielle did not turn around. The screams were coming from ahead of them. And they were drawing closer.

Just one person, he thought. The screams came in waves, pausing occasionally for an intake of breath, and as far as he could tell it was always the same voice.

Nadielle had drawn a knife from her belt, and in her other hand she nursed a round, flexible object. Gorham drew his short sword. It was keen and light, and he'd used it in anger only three times. He'd spent a lot of energy trying to forget those moments.

Something was running toward them. Their torches did not penetrate the darkness very far at all, but in the distance he could hear the steady *thump thump* of feet striking the soft ground, and he imagined lazy clouds of dust thrown up. As the thing ran, it continued to scream.

"Nadielle?"

"I don't know. Be ready."

"Where's Neph?" he asked, but the Baker did not have time to respond.

The shape that emerged from the darkness into shadows, then from shadows into light, was twisted and mutated, a bastardization of anything human, and the noise issuing from it was shattering. It slowed as it neared them and heaved itself up, growing even taller before it reared over Nadielle and Caytlin, twice their height and bristling with spiked weapons.

Nadielle lowered her knife and stood up, and then Gorham realized the truth.

Neph dropped the screaming man at Nadielle's feet. Dust coughed up around him, and shreds of ancient dried plants that had not seen sunlight for millennia drifted in lazy arcs. The impact drove the scream from him in a loud *humph!* and the sudden silence was shocking. He gasped in air. His face went from pale to white, and he writhed slightly as he tried to start his breathing again.

"Sprote Felder!" Nadielle gasped, and the man screamed again.

Gorham had to go close to the Baker to speak above the screams. "That's Sprote Felder?"

"Yes!" she shouted back. "I've met him a couple of times before, but . . . he's changed."

The man looked barely human. His clothes hung on a bony frame, his exposed arms so thin that Gorham could have encircled them with his thumb and index finger. His face was skeletal, eyes dim and sunken, and he was missing one shoe. There were remnants of finery about his clothes, but it seemed that he'd been soiling himself for some time. The stench was horrific.

He also had a broken leg. Gorham had missed it before,

but now he saw the blood-soaked rip in his trousers and the glint of pale-white bone protruding.

Neph took several steps back, then turned to face the darkness.

Nadielle knelt beside the screaming man, and it took a while for Gorham to hear the soothing words. He could not make out what they meant, but the tone was obvious, and it became audible only when the explorer's screaming started to lessen. *How can a man scream so much and for so long?* Gorham thought, but then he saw the way that Sprote's head kept twisting to look at Neph. Each glance would ignite the screams again, and it took Nadielle some time to calm him into silence. She stroked his face and held his hand, and at her single sharp command, Neph disappeared once again into the darkness.

Sprote Felder twisted to look at Gorham, then pushed backward with his feet so that he was curled into Nadielle's grasp.

"Should I go as well?" Gorham asked, but Nadielle shook her head.

"You're going the wrong way," Sprote Felder said, and his voice was surprisingly calm. He was still shaking and grinding his teeth together, but Nadielle's hand on his face and arm across his chest seemed to have soothed him a little.

"Which way *should* we be going?" Gorham asked.

"Up!"

"We're going down to the Falls," he said. "There's something . . . I've been hearing something." Nadielle looked up at him at this, and she seemed pleased that he was hearing it as well.

"It'll be the end of everything," Felder said, his eyes growing wider in his ravaged face. They looked nowhere in particular but saw something terrible.

"You've been there?" Nadielle asked.

"Not that deep. But deep enough."

"We found a Garthan trap but no Garthans."

"Some are still here," he said, "but most have fled. Out toward the city limits."

"Aboveground?" Gorham asked.

"Not yet."

"You say some are still here?" Nadielle asked.

"The old ones. The sick."

"Did they do this to you?" Nadielle asked gently.

Sprote shook his head, reaching around with his hand and touching her arm. The more contact he felt, the more he seemed comforted. "I fell," he said. "I was fleeing and I fell."

"Fleeing what?" Gorham asked.

"The Falls. What is rising." He shivered again, closing his eyes and trying to stop his teeth from chattering together. "*You* know," he said quietly, words meant for Nadielle. His hair seemed to stand on end and Nadielle held him tight, rocking him slightly while she looked at Gorham. He could not read her eyes. They seemed empty, as if she were waiting for him to say something to fill them.

"What?" he asked. But Nadielle shook her head.

"Every Echo is singing with its voice," Sprote said quietly. "You only need to know how to listen. Hear . . . can you hear? Low, like heavy footsteps over gravel. Can you hear?"

"I hear it," Gorham said, and Sprote fixed him with his gaze.

"That's the end coming for all of us, boy."

Gorham turned away and looked at Neph, a shadow standing against the darkness.

"Go on with him," Nadielle said. "Take Caytlin."

Gorham turned around, confused. Go on with Sprote? But then he saw that Nadielle was looking at Neph, and the wounded man in her arms looked smaller and weaker than ever. She'd put her knife back into her belt but had not fastened the clasp.

"How will you catch us?"

"I'll know where you are."

"How?"

"Really, Gorham, now is not the time."

Sprote Felder was looking at him. There was madness in those eyes but also a heavy knowledge that seemed to give the surrounding darkness weight. *We should listen to what he says*, Gorham thought, but then Nadielle frowned at him, nodded toward Neph, and Caytlin stood and came to Gorham's side. Her eyes were big and wide and empty. He'd rather stare into Sprote's madness.

"I won't be long," Nadielle said, her voice softening.

Gorham took one last look at the famed Echoes explorer, his broken leg, his drained face and mournful eyes, and then he turned away. They left one torch with Nadielle and took the other two themselves, but Gorham did not look back. Neph led the way—the chopped seemed to know where they were going, and he did not once hesitate—and Caytlin followed, never seeming to move quickly but always there behind him.

Without Nadielle, Gorham was colder and more afraid than ever. She'd called him her sun, and now he wondered what she was to him. He was unsettled that she was not walking beside him. He was nervous that he could not see her, acknowledge her control over what they were doing down here. But Nadielle was an absence, whereas Peer was still a warm, heavy influence inside. Time was running out for him to gain her forgiveness.

Later, when Nadielle caught up with them, she did not catch Gorham's eye.

"Did he say anything else?" he asked.

"No."

"Did you kill him?"

"No!" she said, aghast, but still she would not look at him. "No. I took him somewhere safe and told him we'd get him on the way back."

"He said you knew what was coming. *You*."

"He's mad, Gorham. And you're the Watcher. Don't *you* know?" She looked at him then, and the hard, derisory Baker had returned.

Gorham could only follow her. He stared at her back as they walked—the way her hips moved, the long, clipped hair hanging between her shoulder blades. He definitely preferred her in need of comfort.

The noises continued and grew. Faraway sounds, echoing through the Echoes, heavy and hard, and they carried about them a shattering sense of distance. The darkness became more oppressive than ever, now that it was no longer filled with nothing. Sometimes, the air itself seemed to shake in fear.

Gorham was fascinated with every breath he took. There were no living plants down here to make clean air, and yet it smelled and tasted as good as any he'd breathed up in the city. There were hints of age to it and sometimes a grittiness caused by their kicking up dust. But it seemed like good air, and it gave him strength. He wondered where it came from. It was something else that he would ask Nadielle, given time.

The huge park ended eventually, and they entered a built-up area. By his estimate they must be very close to the heart of this Marcellan Canton Echo, and yet the buildings were humble and small, not the gaudy sky-scratching spires and towers he was used to seeing. Nadielle pointed out several structures that bore signs of recent use, and in one place they found dozens of skins spread and pinned on timber frames to dry.

"Human," Nadielle said softly, and she told Gorham that they were passing through a Garthan settlement. He tried not to think about what they'd seen and who they might have been. The settlement seemed deserted. Gorham wondered what they knew that he and Nadielle did not.

Later, Nadielle called a halt and Neph built them a fire. The Baker produced some rolled bread from her backpack and started to warm it, and the smell of herbed butter wafted around them. Neph stood guard somewhere unseen. Caytlin sat. Gorham felt totally excluded, and when he tried talking with Nadielle, she shut him out.

"I thought you needed me," he said.

"I do."

"Doesn't seem like it."

"Don't be a child, Gorham," she said, and they did not speak again for some time.

Soon after the meal, they moved on and started heading down. Gorham caught the hint of moisture in the air, and as they descended through a series of narrow tunnels and crumbling stairways and emerged into the next Echo, he heard a steady, distant roar. It was a frightening sound, but it masked the mysterious noises that had been growing ever louder all around them—the sound of the rising thing.

What the fuck are we doing down here? he wondered more than once, but Nadielle's determination drew him on.

The roar was water, the tributary of the dead River Tharin that plummeted through the Echoes beneath Marcellan Canton and eventually, it was said, vented into the Echo City Falls. Though possessing such a grand name, the Falls was a hidden thing, buried deep where the roots of the city bound it to the land and where old history made way for even older. As recently as a hundred years ago, there were those who believed that the Echoes went on forever—buried histories and past times that not only should be forgotten but that could never truly be accessed. People went down into the Echoes then as now, but some in the city—followers of Hanharan, mostly, their religion tied inextricably to the city's lifeline—had believed that all they found were caves. Gases down there, they claimed, made people *imagine* streets and buildings, buried parks and the ruins of older times. And while explorers tried and failed to find them, the Echoes stretched back, and down, forever.

But Gorham liked to think that he lived in more enlightened times. There were still isolated pockets of believers who clung to outdated, more extreme dogmas, but now even the Order of Hanharan and their Marcellan politicians acknowledged that their new city was built upon the old, and the older, and so on. And this acknowledgment could never come without the understanding that there was a point, somewhere deep in the past, where the original city must lie.

This was the reason that deep exploring was strictly forbidden. Hanharan's birthplace would be way down there, if he had ever existed. But what anyone would have been able to tell from a ruined, rotting, crumbled wreck thousands of years old, he had no idea.

"That's the Falls," Nadielle said, and Gorham was unreasonably pleased to see a light in her eyes. He could not tell exactly what it meant, but it took away her expression of lifelessness.

"At least it masks the other noises," Gorham said.

Nadielle glanced aside, then back at him. "We have to go all the way down," she said. "And the easiest way to descend through the Echoes here will be through the holes and tunnels the Falls themselves have forged over time."

Gorham nodded. He knew that. He'd studied the old books, and he knew the alleged geography of the Falls as well as anyone.

"You know what we'll see, don't you?"

He nodded again. "The dead."

"The dead. And then the Chasm." For a second she seemed vulnerable and scared again, and Gorham grabbed on to it.

"We'll help each other," he said.

"I know we will." And Nadielle smiled. "But, Gorham— I'm not aware of anyone who's ever gone that deep and survived."

"Then why must we?"

"You know why. I have to know what's coming."

"So you can destroy it?"

She shrugged, such a hopeless gesture. "Just so that I know."

"Why don't you tell me?"

"I will. When I know."

"And Caytlin . . ." He trailed off. The chopped woman was going to die, Nadielle had said, and Gorham suspected it would be soon.

"Come on," Nadielle said. "It'll get louder. And you're right—at least it masks that other sound."

But as they ventured through this Echo toward the Falls that punched through them all, Gorham found that was not the case at all. The roar of water was thunderous, but the noises from below were insidious. The Falls sounded brutal and hard, but the thumps and whispers were defiant, secretive. Monstrous.

Closer to the Falls, the air was filled with a fine, foul-smelling moisture. The flames on their torches sputtered and flickered. Their clothes became damp. Exertion made Gorham sweat, but it was cool, and before long he was wishing for thicker clothing. *I'm breathing from the Tharin*, he thought, and took shallow, slow breaths.

They went down, still not within sight of the Falls them-selves. Neph led the way, and Gorham thought about that a lot. He'd seen the chopped birthed from the womb vat in the Baker's laboratory, and so whatever knowledge it carried must have been implanted while it was . . . what? Growing? Brewing? Forming? Nadielle told Gorham little, and he did not have a scientific brain that could surmise. So had Neph's knowledge of where they now were come from the Garthan it was part chopped from, as Nadielle had suggested?

Or did it come from her?

Deeper they went, time blurred, and at some point they must have passed the deepest Echo and entered the bedrock of the city itself. Gorham did not notice the point where this occurred. They were descending through a chaos of fissures and crevasses, past walls smoothed when the Tharin's water had flowed before finding an easier route down. But there were no more phantoms, and he felt the weight of the world all around him. He paused to touch the rock, and it shook with the power of the Falls. Shining his torch around, he tried to make out marks or structures that might have been man-made, but there was nothing. For some reason, he found that even more unbelievable than the receding Echoes of the past through which they had been descending.

I'm standing in a place that existed before the city itself, he thought, and he felt alone and lost. Nadielle glanced back at him, up the steep slope of a cavern floor, and Gorham pressed his hand harder against the rock. It gave nothing back.

He went on, following Nadielle and Caytlin, Neph's torch casting spiked shadows back toward him, and everywhere he desperately sought signs of humanity. He had never felt so connected with the city as now, when he was way below its very earliest part. But he saw nothing. And with the sound of the Falls thundering in his head so that he could not even hear himself shout, and the feel of them strong enough to shake the foundations of his world, he knew that the only people who came down here were the dead.

Shadows danced against the walls, giving the impression of movement all around. Even when Gorham held his torch still, he saw things flickering in tunnel mouths and holes, as if the ground were a living thing following his progress. All the while, Neph led and Caytlin followed—Nadielle's strange children obeying her every command, spoken or unspoken.

And at last they emerged onto a wide, wet ledge, beyond which was nothing but the Echo City Falls.

It plunged before them, a wall of water that seemed to suck in their torchlight and amplify it as a glow from within. The noise was almost unbearable, but the sight was astonishing, and Gorham could not tear his eyes away. He wiped water from his face and smelled its foulness, but that ceased to concern him. His stomach lurched when drops touched his tongue, but he pressed his hand against his gut and stared at the water. Its violence was incredible, its beauty mesmerizing, and Gorham thought: *All this is from beyond the city.* This water had traveled over the Bonelands from places where no one had ever been, crossed the city, separated from the river's main flow, and found its way down through Echo City's past until it vented here—flowing no more, only falling.

Nadielle shouted something into his ear, but the Falls stole her voice.

Then he saw the first body flit by. It was a blur, but its waving limbs were unmistakable. He'd known he would see them, and he'd been preparing himself, but it still came as something of a shock. *Someone's mother, someone's son*, he thought, and somewhere far above, a funeral wake was now taking place, as people stared into an unseen distance and remembered the sight of their loved one plunging into the lifeless river.

Nadielle held his arm and pulled, and Gorham realized with horror that he'd been edging closer to the Falls. The ledge dropped off maybe twenty paces from where he stood, and he felt a burning tension in his knees and shins, urging him forward. She shouted in his ear again, but he shook his head, touched his ear, and shrugged.

The Baker pointed back at Caytlin. The woman was farther back in the tunnel they had emerged from, leaning against the wall with a torch dangling from her right hand. Her face was as unresponsive as ever, but her eyes seemed

more expressive. Either that or the violent waters were reflected there.

Nadielle tapped Gorham's chest, pointed to his eyes, then
gestured to herself and Caytlin. *Watch us.* Gorham nodded.

Back in the shadows of the tunnel, Neph stood guard.
Against what? Gorham thought, but it was nothing he wished
to dwell upon.

Nadielle guided Caytlin out from the narrow tunnel mouth
and onto the ledge. The woman still had eyes only for the
Baker, but there was a hesitancy about her now, and perhaps
a slight tension against Nadielle's hand.

A sick feeling hit Gorham. *This is where she dies*, he
thought, and he glanced back at the Falls. Another shadow
fell past—another dead person plummeting down forever.
Members of his own family had come this way. He closed his
eyes and thought of his father, wished he could see him
again. Was he still falling, as the legends suggested? Or had
he found some unknown, unknowable fate somewhere far
below?

Something nudged him, hard. Nadielle. She glared at him
and frowned. *This is important.* Gorham held up his hands
and nodded sharply. He knew that very well. His whole world
was above them.

She eased Caytlin down to her knees and knelt before her.
Then she took a long, thin knife from a sheath on her belt and
stabbed Caytlin in the left forearm.

Gorham held his breath. The woman barely flinched, but
she did close her eyes as Nadielle jabbed her several more
times with the knife, leaving a trail of small puncture holes
from wrist to elbow. Trickles of blood flowed from some of
the holes, curling around her arm and then dripping to the
ledge. When the drips hit the rock, they seemed to disappear,
merging with the wetness already there.

Nadielle pulled up her left sleeve, glanced over her shoulder at Gorham, and then started jabbing at her own inner
arm. She pricked six times in quick succession, leaving a
line of wounds mimicking Caytlin's. Placing the knife on the
ledge beside her, she squeezed a couple of the wounds as if
to encourage the blood to flow.

Gorham knew that this was her talent, the Baker's work, but it still took everything he had not to try to stop her.

When her blood was dribbling from the wounds, she smeared her finger across the one closest to her wrist, then touched the corresponding wound on Caytlin's arm. She repeated this for the other five cuts. Then she rolled up the sleeve on her right arm.

Gorham stepped forward and slipped a hand beneath her armpit. He pulled, lifting her from her kneeling position, and noticed Caytlin's eyes flick open to stare at him. He shouted at Nadielle, voice lost to the roar of the dead river falls, but the sensation of venting his fear felt good. Her blood dripped onto his hand, warm and intimate.

She held the knife up in front of his face, shaking her head.

Gorham let go and stepped back. He bumped into Neph, and the chopped warrior's hands clasped around his biceps, squeezing hard. He struggled, but the grip was firm. And all he could do was watch as Nadielle repeated the process on Caytlin's right arm and then her own.

As Gorham wondered what would happen next, Neph released him. Gorham was relieved, but the last thing he expected was for Nadielle to drape two enclosed torches around Caytlin's shoulders, march her toward the Falls, and then shove her from the ledge. The water grabbed the chopped woman and snatched her away, faster than a blink, so fast that he wondered whether she'd ever been there at all.

Shadows fell with her. The dead welcoming her in.

Nadielle backed away, dropped to her knees, and fell sideways. If Neph had not been instantly by her side, she would have cracked her head against the rock. Gorham went to her and saw her eyes roll up in her head, and a terrible understanding began to dawn.

The world fell away above her because her mother was gone. But though she could no longer see her, Mother was still present in her mind, flowing through her body, and there was a warmth inside that meant this was closer than they had ever been before.

To begin with, the Falls smothered her senses. The water's

roar was everything; the taste on her tongue was rotten and foul; it scoured her skin, it smelled of dead things, and all she could see was the dirty brown liquid. Battering her within its embrace, the water flipped the torches around her head, but their sheltered flames were tenacious. They flickered and wavered but never quite went out. And that was important. It was *essential*. Because she had been sent down here to see.

Surprisingly quickly, the thunder began to lessen. This startled her a little—more so than the incessant roar—because she didn't know what it meant. A sensation of floating changed into one of falling, and the waters around her started to part like torn curtains. *Spreading out*, she thought, and beyond the tears in the water she could see only blankness.

(*That's the Chasm. She's fallen so far already. Caytlin has fallen into the Chasm and she's following the Falls down, and soon I'll be able to hear—*)

She found that if she placed her arms and legs in just the right position, she could fall in a controlled manner. She reined in the torches and their brave flames and started aiming them about her. The Falls, darkness, and, through the veils of water, she saw a shadow matching her fall.

(*A body, someone who died up in the city recently, and I hope it doesn't drift closer, and I hope if it does, Caytlin looks away . . . looks down, because what I need to see is still* down there.)

She shifted again and looked down. She was suspended now, descending at the same rate as the water and therefore appearing not to fall at all. It was a strange sensation, sick and exhilarating, and it brought a brief flash of something she could barely recognize. Not fear, because Mother was still with her, and she could never fear anything with Mother there. Not even nervousness.

Regret?

She blinked that away and aimed the torches down, enjoying the fall, ignoring the stink and taste of this water and the knowledge that there was a corpse falling very close to her. There was a long moment of peace and comfort, disturbed only by the intimation of a shadow drifting closer and then away again. She knew about death, as any living thing did.

Time passed. She fell.

(*Look down again, Caytlin, always down . . .*)

She directed her attention downward again, frowning for a moment because it was becoming difficult to tell *which way* was down, or up, or sideways. And then she saw—

(*What is that, what* is *that, oh, by all the fucking gods,* what is that?)

—a place far below, where the falling water struck something and splashed outward, an interruption to the flow, and as she fell closer and the torches had more effect she saw—

(*Corpses—it's so large and wide that it's covered with all the fallen bodies, and there's a darker opening there, something*)

—something opening up. True fear hit her for the first time then, and she screamed for her mother—an unintelligible sound that was the first and last noise she ever made. But until the last, she remembered her reason for being, her duty to her mother, and although it was still a long way to fall, because the thing was so huge, she held both torches before her so that they could illuminate the—

(*Teeth.*)

Nadielle was screaming, Neph hauled her back into the tunnel, and Gorham tried to grab her kicking feet to help carry her, but she was screaming, screaming, her expression made more grotesque because the sound was completely lost to the Falls. Her arms were bleeding again. And in her eyes, a black terror that even Gorham's torch could never hope to touch.

Chapter 15

What if it doesn't work? What if I'm like this forever, and the White Water is no cure at all? Nophel had been waiting for someone to see him and draw back, startled at his sudden appearance or fearful of his countenance. He could look down and see himself, but he was used to that now, his mind accustomed to his invisibility. Walking unseen, he so wanted to be a part of the world again. If it meant fear or disgust when people saw his blood-red eye and diseased face, so be it. He'd lived like that forever, and it was proof of his history.

He found the only address on Dane's coded map—an upper-class whorehouse close to the Marcellan Canton's walls. It displayed the scarlet wound sign on its name board, indicating that it served the Scarlet Blades, which Nophel knew meant that few others would use the place. He stood outside for a while, checking the map again to make sure he'd read it correctly. Invisible, he still felt a flush of embarrassment as he crossed the road and approached the front entrance.

"You're no Blade," the woman at the door said.

"What?"

She came closer, down the stone steps to his level, and even then she was a hand taller. "You. You're no Blade. Unless they kicked you out because of that." She pointed at his face, and Nophel felt the familiar, liberating flush of anger at what he was.

"You can see me," he said, smiling.

"My girls will suck a chickpig through a straw," the woman said, without an ounce of sexuality in her voice.

"But you can *see* me!"

"You'd have to pay extra if you want me to watch. For you, a *lot* extra."

It had been a long time since he'd been out into the city like this. If he ever had cause to leave Hanharan Heights, he usually wore a heavy robe with a wide, deep hood, and people seemed to understand that a person so clothed desired to remain hidden away. Perhaps some attributed the style to one of the lesser, more obscure cults, but that did not concern Nophel. Hiding away fueled his anger, which in turn held shame at bay. *Just show yourself*, he'd once thought, but he was unable to do so.

"I need to see Fat Andrea," Nophel said.

The woman—he thought perhaps she had been a Scarlet Blade once, and wondered what had happened to her— stepped aside, waved him in, and chuckled to herself as she closed the door behind him.

The corridor was poorly lit and strung with decorative flags from several chords of the Blade army. It opened into a large room where several women lounged, drinking wine and smoking slash from a communal pipe on the central table. They perked up a little at his arrival, posing and preening in their minimal clothes even though their faces remained impassive. Then they really saw him, and some winced.

"Fat Andrea?" he asked. A lithe, strong-looking woman stood and approached. She wore layers of fine material wound tight across her curves, and her red hair shone in the weak lamplight.

"What's your pleasure?"

"You're Fat Andrea?"

"What's in a name?" She shrugged, and she was avoiding his face—looking over his shoulder, at his throat, blinking slowly and alluringly so that she did not have to see his deformities.

"Where can we go?" Nophel asked. The woman turned and beckoned him after her, and already he perceived a relaxation in her pose. *Perhaps she already knows why I'm here*, he thought. *Am I really that obvious?* She led him through a warming steam curtain and into another corridor, this one curved and confusing. At its end she opened a door and welcomed him inside, standing back so that he could pass. Still she averted her eyes. The room was small—bed, chair, a bath in the corner, shelves adorned with all manner of oils and soaps. It stank of old sex.

"Dane Marcellan sent—" he began, but Fat Andrea cut him off.

"I was hoping. So?"

"Six wisps play their mepple strokes." He remembered it from the map, and speaking it aloud made it sound no less foolish.

The woman relaxed, sighed, and sat down on the bed. She held her head in her hands for a beat, then rubbed her face and looked up at him again. She had changed. She looked older, more weathered, and he knew he was seeing Fat Andrea for the first time.

"What does the fat old bastard want?" she asked.

"He said you could lead me on toward the Baker."

The woman smiled. "I can send you on your way, but I can't lead you. I'm too busy here. I need the money for . . ." She laid a hand on her stomach and looked away, but not before Nophel saw her skin fade to a painful gray. She looked sicker than sick.

"I have money," Nophel said.

"Good. Then pay me for your hour and I'll tell you the way to Ferner's Temple."

Nophel went to object—Dane had said these people would lead him, not send him—but the woman's pain was almost a heat in the room, the atmosphere redolent of wretchedness.

"I'll pay you for two hours," he said. Fat Andrea did not protest, and a few beats later he went back out through the gloomy corridors, past the ex-Blade, who sent him on his way with a few mocking remarks. At the end, Andrea had looked at him with those hooded, enticing eyes again, and perhaps she'd seen past his deformed face to the man inside. Or maybe his generosity had made that possible. But he'd felt no pangs of desire, and he had no wish to take anything from Andrea other than a way through the streets.

He followed that way, and by the time the street cafés were filling for lunch, he found himself at Ferner's Temple. He'd not expected to find a real temple. But the last thing he'd anticipated was a tavern.

Through the early part of that afternoon, Nophel was passed along a route of contacts and places that, if what Dane said was right, would lead eventually to his sister, the new Baker. Dane's message tube sat heavy in his pocket, and though he still felt moments of temptation, Nophel did not open it. There was a sense of loyalty to Dane and also the continuing belief—more proven with every contact he made and yet more confused as well—that Dane was more allied with the Watchers than with the Hanharan religion that had controlled the city for so long.

But there was also the alleged sister whom Nophel had never known about. He had spent a lot of time studying the Baker's long ancestry over the years, and everything he read made him more satisfied that his treachery had been a good thing. Always feared, rarely fêted, the Bakers were an oddity in Echo City's history that had persisted despite the many factors standing against them: lack of fealty to any government, practitioners of arcane arts, blasphemers, loners, and wielders of powers that would intimidate the powerful. As with any family, their history was checkered, with criminals, philanthropists, and monsters all holding the name of Baker for a time. Across the space of twelve thousand years over which he had managed to trace their ancestry—and though there were large periods in that extensive span when their line had become untraceable—they went from publicly visible to rumored as dead. People loved some and hated others but were always fascinated.

And there was always someone calling for their eradication.

The more he researched, the more amazed he became that no one had killed off the Bakers' line long ago. *Perhaps they're too hard to kill,* he thought. *I believed it had happened in my lifetime, but now . . .*

One other factor—the decider for Nophel, the silver seal upon the casket of his betrayal—was that there were very, very few instances of a Baker's giving birth naturally. He was one such example, and she had thrown him away.

She's no sister of mine, he thought. Whoever this new Baker might be, however possessed of her mother's talent and knowledge handed down from the past, he had no doubt that she came from somewhere vastly different than he did. He was a Baker's child, and she little more than another chopped monster.

But that did not mean he had no wish to meet her. On the contrary, he was eager. Perhaps in her he would find an answer to the question that plagued him always: *Why did she cast me aside?*

He drove down self-pity. His bitterness toward his mother was rich, and though he had learned that it was not necessarily his betrayal that led to her death—the Dragarians had killed her, or so Dane claimed—the responsibility still sat well with him.

He wondered what this new Baker looked like, how she spoke, what her young life had been. Dane had told him little, feigning ignorance, but Nophel sensed in the Marcellan a wealth of knowledge that he was simply unwilling to share. Such was the prerogative of a Marcellan. Most of all, he wondered whether this sister knew of his existence. If she *had* known about him all this time, then she must have chosen to not trace him or contact him. He did not care. That only made things easier.

The day was hot, his mind was abuzz, the past was becoming a shady, misunderstood place. And with every step Nophel took, the future came closer, more exciting than he had ever hoped and perhaps offering the chance for some sort of revenge.

Ferner, landlord of Ferner's Temple, was a thin man with an abnormally large head, and he carried the veined tracework of a drunk across his cheeks and nose. He seemed not to notice Nophel's disfigurement, and he sent him to a chocolate shop close to Course's western extreme. It took Nophel a while to walk there, and, in the end, tiredness overcame him and he bought a carriage ride. The two small horses walked slowly, breaking wind and generally ignoring orders shouted at them by the driver, until finally the western wall of the city came into view. Nophel muttered his thanks and disembarked, walking ahead of the horses toward the wall.

The chocolate-maker was an incredibly thin woman with a huge nose and a chopped third limb protruding from her hip. Her right hand gathered samples to sniff and taste, while her two left hands measured, stirred, and poured into a vat of new chocolate. She said nothing when Nophel entered her shop, simply staring at his disfigured face and continuing to work. When he told her that Ferner had sent him, then repeated the code words Ferner had whispered into his ear, the woman halted in her stirring for a beat. Then she carried on, using her third limb to stir while her two natural hands carved something onto the back of a slab of dark chocolate. She wrapped it, handed it to Nophel, and, when he offered some money, shook her head and waved him away.

He left her shop and read what she had carved.

By late afternoon he had visited three more places, imparting code phrases to six people, and he was convinced that he was being followed.

It was surprising how quickly he became used to being seen again. People stared at him and steered their children out of his path, and some of them offered uncertain smiles of sympathy. Those he respected most were the ones who either ignored him or treated him as they would anyone else— trying to con him out of money, overcharging him for food or services, or shoving past him in the street with little more than a mumbled apology. They made him feel human, while the frightened ones and the smilers turned him into a monster.

The last person he was directed to was an old man sitting on a bench by the main canal leading from the refineries to the Western Reservoir. He wore a wide-brimmed hat and heavy coat, even in the heat. Beside him on the bench were a fishing rod broken into three pieces, fishing paraphernalia, and a wooden bucket filled with water, in which a single fish swam in tight, slow circles. The woman who'd sent Nophel here had told him that Brunley Bronk sat on the same bench every day between the hours of noon and sunset, and most other times few people were able to find him. She said it was an old man's habit, but to Nophel it sounded like someone making himself available.

Nophel had doubled back several times on his walk along the canal, leaving the overgrown towpath and slinking between buildings, trying to make out who was following him. There was never any sign, but that only served to unsettle him even more. He felt eyes on the back of his neck. And since his experience with the Blue Water, he knew that not seeing someone did not mean no one was there.

So if the Unseen followed him, what of it? He did not know the rules and capabilities of his mother's potions, whether he would still be able to see the Unseen after taking the White Water. But he was also sure that such people would know of the Baker's continued existence, because they could sit in any shadow in the city and see, hear, and smell every secret.

Besides, caution was good, but paranoia would not serve him well.

He sat beside the man and looked down at the fish.

"You're from Dane Marcellan," the old man said.

"How did you know that?"

"Tell me."

Nophel muttered the code that the woman who'd sent him this way had written down for him. The old man nodded and scratched at his ear.

"Eat the paper," he said. "Don't want you dropping it so that just anyone can use those words. They have power. See this?" He held out his hand.

"What am I looking at?" Nophel asked.

"My reaction. Those words. They stop the shakes, because they make me excited. Something's happening. And you've come to ask me how to find the Baker."

He knows! Nophel thought. *I'm close now, so close!* The weight of Dane's message tube made itself obvious in his jacket pocket, as if aware that the end of its journey was near. He glanced back along the canal path, but the only movement was the splash of ducks and the scamperings of canal rats. They were twice the size of normal city rats, fattened on birds and frogs and water mice.

"What you looking for?" the old man said.

"Nothing."

"You thought you were being followed. You should have said." The man had turned to him now, and any lightness was gone from his voice. Nophel saw the seriousness in this man's eyes, and the startling intelligence, and he berated himself for forming foolish opinions. *I thought he was feeble*.

"So what do you want with the Baker?"

"It's not me, it's Dane Marcellan." *I hope he can't hear my lie*, he thought.

"Why?"

Nophel snorted. "I can't tell *you* anything like that! You expect me to—"

The cool touch of keen metal pressed against his throat. A hand curved around him from behind and clamped across his forehead. And, in the center of his back, he felt the bulky heat of a knee.

"One wrong move," a woman's voice said.

"So who the crap is he, Malia?" a man's voice whispered.

Nophel felt the woman lean in close and sniff at him. There was something animalistic about it, something brutal, and her voice purred like a serrated knife through flesh.

"Marcellan pet."

They took them farther along the canal to Malia's boat. It wasn't the safest place, but it was the closest. Malia and Devin guided Nophel, an arm each and a knife pressed into each side. They let Peer bring the old man Brunley. Brunley complained that he'd have to leave his fishing gear behind, but Peer assured him that they wouldn't be long. She could not inject any certainty into her voice. For all she knew, Malia was going to kill them both.

Inside the moored canal barge, Malia quickly drew curtains across the windows, while Devin tied Nophel into a chair. Brunley sat on a comfortable bench behind a small table, crossing his hands before him and watching the proceedings with a sharp eye.

"What are you mixed up with now, Brunley?" Malia asked.

"Fishing," he said.

Peer glanced from one to the other, and she could sense the long relationship between these two. Malia spoke to the old man without looking at him, bustling at a cupboard, and he answered in a lazy voice. *They've been here before*, Peer thought. *The questions, the deceits*.

"Fishing with the Marcellans' Scope keeper?"

"Is that who he is? I've never seen him before."

"Tell him," Malia said, standing before Nophel. Devin had tied his bonds good and tight and retreated outside, sitting on the barge's roof to keep watch.

"I'm thirsty," Nophel said.

"I'll throw you in the canal later." Malia turned back to the cupboard, and an uncomfortable silence descended.

This isn't finding Rufus, Peer thought. They'd been sitting in the tavern, dividing Course and Crescent into search districts on a large sheaf of paper, when the whore Andrea had arrived. She'd been running, she stank, and she'd grasped Malia's arm and dragged her into the toilets before any of them knew what was happening. Peer had not seen Malia controlled like this by anyone before. As she'd looked around at the others, eyebrows raised awaiting an explanation, Malia had come storming from the toilets, violence in her stride.

From there, to the canal, to here, and still Peer was as confused as she'd been at the beginning.

"What's the Marcellans' Scope keeper doing here?" Peer asked. Nophel looked at her—one good eye, and a face ravaged by growths. He stared, perhaps expecting her to look away, but she'd seen a lot worse in Skulk.

"Looking for the Baker," Malia said. And that was when Peer knew Malia meant to kill the Scope keeper. Talking about the Baker so freely before him—even mentioning her in his presence—meant that he would not leave.

"Who are you?" Nophel asked.

"I'm the one with questions." Malia turned from the cupboard at last, a bottle of cheap wine in one hand, a small velvet bag in the other. The bag moved. Truthbugs. Peer shivered at the memory.

"Do you know where she is?" Nophel asked. "I *have* to see her."

"So you can kill her?" Malia said.

"Why would I want to kill her?" Nophel's eye was wide, but his expression was hard to read; his was not a normal face.

"Because you work for the Marcellans." Malia squatted before him and placed the bag flat on her palm.

"Who are you?" Nophel asked.

"That's none of your—"

"They're Watchers," Brunley said, and Malia glanced at him, annoyed.

"So am I!" Nophel said. "A true Watcher, watching from the highest roof."

Malia placed the bag gently on the floor before her, drew her short sword, and pointed its tip at Nophel's good eye. He strained back in the chair, holding his breath, tensing, and several large boils across his jawline burst. Malia leaned forward, following him. The sword was never more than a finger's width from his eye.

"You've got only one good one," she said. "Choose your lies carefully, you fucking Hanharan pet."

Peer could feel the air in the small barge cabin thrumming with tension. Brunley was motionless, and Malia and the deformed man looked more like statues than like living people.

"I'm not lying," Nophel said at last. "And the Marcellan I serve—"

"Even *whisper* that name in here, and I'll cut its taste from your tongue!" Malia shouted. Peer stood, hesitant, but one quick glance from Malia told her to stay back.

There were times in Peer's life when she became very aware of the potential routes the future might take. One of them had been when she was fifteen years old, and three men in Mino Mont had approached her with a proposition: *Work for us, and your family will never be poor again.* Even that fifteen-year-old girl had been wise enough to see the gang markings on the men's ears, and her refusal had been a brave moment—but for a beat, she'd felt her life being squeezed into places she had no wish to go. Another time had been when the Scarlet Blades came knocking at her door. There were four of them, two holding back in fighting positions, and for a time after opening her door to them, she'd wondered whether she was going to be raped and killed.

This was another such moment. So many things hung in the balance that she felt faint, as if a series of waves had suddenly set the barge dipping and rising. Rufus was lost; Gorham and Nadielle were somewhere unknown; there were rumors of Dragarians abroad. The city was whispering with fear, from couples huddled in café corners to crowds gathered on the street listening to doomsayers. The world was changing, and she was at its fulcrum.

"Stand back, Malia," Peer said. "Killing's no good here."

"It was good enough for Bren," Malia said, not taking her eyes from Nophel's face.

"You think *he* hammered the nails into Bren's wrists?"

The Watcher breathed heavily for a while, muscles visibly tensed as if she were about to push.

Nophel could strain back no farther.

And then Malia eased, lowering the sword until its tip touched her trouser leg.

"What of the one you serve?" Peer asked.

Nophel closed his eye, trying to compose himself. She could actually see his shirt shift with the fluttering of his heart.

"He's not a Hanharan devout," Nophel said.

"I should believe you?"

"Yes." Nophel's hand massaged something in his lap.

"Peer, you've been out of this for too long," Malia said. "He can only be a spy, and as for Brunley—"

"I'd do nothing to harm you, Malia," the old man said, hurt in his voice. "We're *friends*."

Malia blinked at him but said nothing. Nophel squeezed the thing in his lap again. Peer caught Malia's attention, then looked down at Nophel's hands, and with a flash of movement Malia had the sword at the man's throat again.

Now what is this? Peer thought, hating the fact that she might have been wrong. Perhaps this man *was* a spy after all. Maybe he was an assassin.

"Enjoying yourself?" Malia asked. She pulled his hands aside, keeping the sword pressed to his throat, and delved into his pocket. Pausing, she smiled. "Is this a message tube in your pocket or are you pleased to see me, ugly man?" She pulled out the tube and lowered her sword once again.

"That's not for you," Nophel said. "It's private."

"If it's for the Baker, she'd want me to read it."

Peer wasn't sure if that was the case. The tension between Nadielle and Malia had been palpable, and if the Baker knew this Watcher was reading messages meant for her . . . But there was little Peer could do. This was Malia's home, Malia's situation, and the Baker was somewhere far away. And Peer was just as curious to know what was in the tube as she was.

"Nophel—" Brunley began, but Nophel shook his head.

"I'm the messenger, that's all. I serve Dane Marcellan, not because of his name but because of his beliefs."

Malia threw the tube at Peer. She caught it, surprised, and held it before her, aware that everyone was watching.

"Open it," Malia said.

Peer broke the wax seal and dropped it to the floor. Inside was a single piece of rolled paper, smooth and expensive. And on the paper, three lines. She read them aloud.

"Dragarians are abroad. The visitor might have arrived. I'm ready to help." She blinked at the sheet for a beat, scanning the words several more times to make sure she'd read them right. *The visitor might have arrived?* When she looked up, Malia was staring at her wide-eyed, and Nophel was glancing back and forth between them.

"A visitor?" he asked.

"Way ahead of you, Marcellan," Malia muttered.

And then, between the hastily drawn curtains, Peer saw a face pressed at the window. A face within a scarlet hood.

Dane Marcellan had watched many times as Nophel adjusted the Scopes' attitude and focus, shifted the viewing-mirror feed from one to the next, and aimed their monstrous eyes, but he had been only an observer. Sitting now with the control panel before him, he cursed his inexpert hands.

He thought he had connected the viewing mirror into the North Scope, but something must have gone wrong. The image on the mirror was blurred, out of focus, and gray shapes exploded across the screen in bilious, almost fleshy blooms. *Does it know I'm not Nophel?* he wondered, but that was absurd. He'd never ventured up to the roof on his own—those things spooked him, as had much that the old Baker worked on—and there was no way they could know simply through the remote touch of his hands on metal.

He caught glimpses but needed to see more. Needed to make sure, because if what he thought he'd seen was proven right, then the message he'd sent with Nophel—that risky message, sent with an unstable, perhaps mad man—was already too late.

"Curse you, Nophel, you'd better carry that message tube well!" He picked up his slash pipe and inhaled once more, closing his eyes to weather the rush. His blood was thick with decades of slash use, and the more he took, the more he needed to feel its effect. It was akin to breathing—a necessity, not a pleasure. He tried to present the acceptable face of addiction, and mostly he succeeded. But it was during these private moments that he hankered after the unbridled drug rush he no longer felt. He inhaled again, sucking deeply, and his lungs were like rocks in his chest.

When he opened his eyes, the image had clarified a little. Whatever had upset the Scope seemed to have settled, and Dane sat motionless for a while with his hand on the focus ball, afraid to shift in case the Scope sensed him again.

Dragar's Canton looked silent and still. The Scope was aimed at the shadowy junction between two massive domes, curving up to the left and right with the dark gulf at the screen's center. Dane could not imagine these shells ever breaking open—doors slipping aside, Dragarians streaming out. And there lay their deception, in the stillness they had presented over the centuries and the way they had removed themselves from the currents of Echo City. Dragarians were a thing of the past, beyond the memory of anyone alive today. Forgotten, they had become phantoms.

Dane blinked, breathed in more slash, and then something

moved across the screen. He gasped and shifted his hand, edging the Scope to the right. It moved too far and blurred, but he corrected the movement, not thinking too hard about which levers and slides he touched, simply relying on instinct. He'd seen Nophel at work here often enough; all he had to do was . . .

There. He stroked the focusing ball, the picture cleared, and a doorway was open in the left dome's shadow. Several shapes streaked inside, crawling across the surface of the dome like ghourt lizards on a dawn ceiling, and the doorway closed behind them.

"They're going home," Dane whispered, a haze of slash smoke obscuring his view. He turned away from the mirror and closed his eyes, hand clasping tight around the pipe in his right hand. It had once been the hip bone of a tusked swine, carved and smoothed by one of the most talented bone artists in Marcellan Canton, and it was only the quality of its manufacture that prevented it from crumbling in his hand. His heart thundered, sweat ran across his expansive body, and he tried to rein in his darting thoughts. His mind was rich and strong, but sometimes it went too wild. Sometimes, the slash took it that way.

They're going home, so they must already have what they wanted. That poor, wretched thing my love the Baker made and sent out—he's back, and they have him.

"We're too late," he muttered, and if he'd been able he would have gone to the new Baker then and there and cried at her feet. *The Dragarians have found the visitor already, and if he's who I hope—who I fear—they'll remain silent no more. And we have no idea what they've been doing under their domes all this time.* The Marcellans had sent spies, of course, hundreds over the centuries. But none of them ever came back.

Dane stood from the chair and staggered a few steps from the viewing mirror and controls. His legs shook. He felt sick. If the Dragarians believed they had their savior, they would do whatever was in their power the bring about the end of Echo City and usher in their prophesies of Honored Darkness. "We have to prepare for war," he said, and that word was beyond belief. "I have to see the Council, persuade those blinkered old bastards to go to *war*."

"Not all so blinkered, Dane," a voice whispered in the shadows. "Though most *are* bastards."

Dane caught his breath, looked around, and the darkness resolved into several swishing red cloaks. The Scarlet Blades came forward—two men and two women—and each of them looked terrified. They must have known already that they were here to kill someone they had served all their lives.

It was that more than the voice that convinced Dane he was discovered. Jan Ray Marcellan was there, and that was bad enough. But he had never seen a Blade look so afraid. "Jan Ray," he said, trying to level his voice. *I'm not afraid of her*. "I never thought to see you in this place."

Jan Ray came forward out of the shadows, tall and old and still as graceful as when she'd been a beautiful young woman. There were those who claimed that the Hanharan priestess was pure and unsullied, maintaining her birth-day innocence in deference to Hanharan and to better aid her total devotion to his cause. And there were also those who would whisper, given assurances of anonymity, that on occasion Jan Ray procured young girls from some of the worst rut-houses in Mino Mont and made them fuck her with chickpig hooves.

"I'm no great advocate of it," she said, looking around with distaste. "Hanharan guides our vision; we have no need of the Baker's . . . *monsters*. But it gives comfort to my kin. To see the city, they believe, is to own it."

"Haven't we always owned it?" Dane asked, offering a half smile in the vain, evaporating hope that her visit was innocent.

"We?"

The Scarlet Blades had spread around Dane, boxing him in against the viewing mirror and controls. They were not yet disrespectfully close, but neither were they too far away. Any one of them could be on him in a blink.

"I was just about to leave," he said. "I have grave news for the Council—"

"I can relay that news, Dane," she said. She paused before

him, and once again he was amazed at her grace. When she moved she seemed to flow, the loose black clothing of a Hanharan priestess a flock of shadows making her their home. And when motionless, as now, there was a stillness to her that was almost unnatural. Her expression never shifted; her mouth barely moved when she spoke. Such economy of movement was the mark of someone in complete control of herself.

And of the four Blades as well. He should not forget them. Inner Guard, highly trained, unendingly loyal to the Marcellans, these soldiers would nevertheless obey priestesses over politicians at any time of the day or night. That was the fruit of their indoctrination.

"It's news I should take myself," he said.

Jan Ray smiled. He rarely saw that. It was horrible. "Where is your deformed *bastard* today?"

How dare she? Insolent bitch!

"I'm not certain where Nophel is. I'll be reprimanding him when I find him; he should have been here, especially today, when—"

"I suspect he's been reprimanded already." Another of her habits—interrupting. It gave her control over any conversation.

"The Dragarians have emerged," he said. *Truth is best right now, just . . . be sparing with it.* "I'm not sure why, or what they've come for, but we should send—"

"Should we?"

"Send the Scarlet Blades north immediately. To protect us."

"Protect us from those unbelievers? They've hidden themselves away from Hanharan's smile for five hundred years, Dane. What could we possibly have to fear from them?"

Dane glanced at the Blades, each of them with one hand on their sword. Ready to draw; ready to move. He breathed deeply, wondering at his chances. *I'm fat and they think I'm slow. They know me as a slash user. That's all I have.*

"The ones I saw looked like warriors," he said. "Some flew, others crawled. They've been chopping in there for centuries. They were all heavily armed." One Blade fidgeted slightly, another glanced at her companions. That was exactly what he wanted. To unnerve them. He closed his eyes briefly, and when he opened them again he knew that his life was changing, here and now. This was when he paid for his beliefs, his passion, and his shunning of the god that had ruled his family and directed their actions for generations.

Doubt came, and he let it flow away once again. It was good to see it go. Its departure made him strong.

"You're a monster," Jan Ray said, voice filled with bitterness and distaste. "A traitorous, stinking, fat, disgusting monster. I've sensed your unbelief for years, Dane, but I never wanted to admit it, even to myself. Never wished to acknowledge that my second cousin could shun the god Hanharan, who made him."

"My parents made me," he whispered.

"And who made them?"

"Who?" Dane said, drawing strength into his voice. "Hanharan? Don't make me laugh." The Blades gasped, and he saw more ways to unsettle them.

He brushed his hand against his jacket pocket, uttered a subtle, deep hum, and something in there began to move.

"You'll be arrested. I sent men after your bastard, and I told them to bring back his ugly head for the wall. They'll follow until he reaches his destination and will kill whoever they find. So who is it, Dane? Watchers? There are many left, we know that for sure."

Dane scoffed. "Watchers? They're harmless ass-gazers. Why should I mix with the likes of them?"

"Because they're enemies of Hanharan. And when someone like you, Dane Marcellan, betrays his blood, any enemy will do. You can't do things on your own, because you're weak, and Hanharan has shunned your treacherous flesh. You need friends. You need accomplices."

"Jan Ray, there's no truth to any of this," he said, feeling the movement in his pocket, glancing at the Blades, and smiling inwardly when they averted their eyes. "Nophel is missing and will be punished."

"You think I don't know you've been feeding him that juice from the dead Baker witch?" she whispered.

Dane shook his head and slipped his hand into his pocket.

The contents were wet and warm, and he had maybe a dozen heartbeats before they would kill him. He closed his eyes and summoned his hate and rage, and he was pleased to find it close.

"You'll suffer, Dane," Jan Ray said, "and it will all be in the dark. Your name will be wiped from the family, and no one will ever—"

"You can suck Hanharan's cock while your bitches pig-fuck you," he said, closing his hand around the eggs, "and I'll happily hold my cock and watch."

The priestess opened her eyes in surprise, but it was the Blades' reactions he was watching. They stepped back, averting their eyes from such blasphemy and muttering prayers, and Dane pulled his hand from his pocket. Whatever the outcome of this moment, his time as a Marcellan was over.

He flung the scarepion eggs, flicking his wrist in four motions, letting one egg slip away each time. The first two found their targets, breaking across a Blade's chest and throat and spewing their screeching contents. The third bounced away and broke on the floor at a female Blade's feet, and the fourth missed altogether, disappearing into the darkness.

Jan Ray stumbled back from Dane, leaning against the viewing-mirror controls. The angle on the screen flickered and tilted crazily, and, high above, one of the Scopes would be screaming in pain.

The scarepion young—dozens to an egg—sought blood with their staggering sense of smell. They used their birthing horns to penetrate skin and inject venom, then clawed their way inside. In heartbeats the first two Blades were on their knees, screaming as they scratched and tore at their own flesh. The third Blade made the fatal error of leaning forward to look at the ruptured egg rather than stepping back. Scarepions could jump.

The fourth Blade came at him. His sword was drawn— a deadly weapon that had been handed down through his generations, scored with a record of kills, each scoring filled with dried oxomanlia extract that would turn toxic on contact with blood—and the man's eyes were wide with fear and disbelief that he was going against a Marcellan.

Dane had to turn that disbelief quickly to his advantage. If the fight began, the Blade's training would take over, and Dane would be cut down.

"How dare you!" he thundered. The Scarlet Blade faltered and blinked in confusion, his blade dipping toward the floor.

Dane stepped lithely into the soldier's killing field—his weight and build, as ever, belying his grace—and slid his knife between the man's ribs. The soldier's mouth fell open and Dane twisted, pulling left and right, wanting to kill quickly. The soldier groaned, and, as he fell away, warmth gushed across Dane's hand.

Dane kept hold of the knife and turned, looking for Jan Ray. She was going for the door. If she got away, the Scope tower would be crawling with Blades in moments, and Dane's only escape would be up and off the tower—an ignominious end, but at least one that would be in his control. He thought of Nophel, the poor bastard he had misled for so long, and hoped that his death would be quick and clean. And he thought of the old dead Baker—his friend, his lover, and the mother of his only child, whom Dane had taken under his wing and protected, bitter though the child had remained against the mother who had abandoned him to the workhouse.

"I'm so sorry, Nophel," he said, and he felt wretched now that they would never know each other as father and son. He should have told him the truth, but doing so would have doomed them both.

He could not take a blade to a Marcellan, though, not even this Hanharan priestess who had tried to kill him. He could not punish her for her foolish beliefs.

Jan Ray screamed. Dane looked toward the shadowed corner where she had fled, expecting to see the opened door but instead seeing nothing. And when her scream came again, he knew that fate had steered her to the fourth scarepion egg. And though he had spent his life consciously not believing in such things as gods, he closed his eyes and gave thanks to something, *anything*, for his fortune.

Dane Marcellan closed the door to the viewing room and descended the staircase. He had sprayed the room with barch oil first, hoping that it would kill most of the scarepion young before anyone else entered. That was the best he could do. He felt wretched at the deaths and sick to his heart at the betrayal.

But, in truth, the betrayal had been a part of him for decades. The Baker, his love, had opened his eyes to the folly of Hanharan beliefs. And when she'd had her own eyes closed at the hands of the Dragarians, he had vowed to see his way forward in the way she would have desired—as a disciple of science and truth. That vow had only now come to action, and it was Jan Ray's fanaticism that had led to those deaths. If only she could have let him walk away.

Now it was Nadielle, his old love's chopped replacement, whom he had to find. The Hanharan priestess said she had sent Scarlet Blades after Nophel. If what the old woman claimed was true, Dane doubted Nophel had a chance of reaching Nadielle at all. But his options were suddenly more limited than he had ever planned for. And Nophel was the only family he had left.

Traitor though he was, for a while he would still be a Marcellan in a city that feared his name. He would use that fear for as long as he could.

Beyond that, fate would decide.

Chapter 16

"You led them here!" the woman said, and Nophel shook his head.

They must have followed me all the way from Hanharan Heights, all day, keeping out of view and watching and waiting until . . .

"Malia, he's terrified!" the other woman, Peer, said.

Nophel could not look at either of them. He was staring at the window where the face had been, and he knew what would come next.

"Stop bickering if you want to live," he said. "They've come to kill us all."

Malia took control. Nophel had seen women like her in the Blades—harsh and cruel but with a discipline that meant they could focus under pressure and fight when the time came. And as she whispered orders to Peer, he started to work at his bonds.

"Back there, in the bedroom, under the bed. Weapons. Bring them all, and give one to Brunley."

"I'm not mixed up in—" the old man began, but Malia cut him off with a short, harsh laugh.

"You've been seen with us, old man. Tough shit."

Peer pushed past Nophel, glancing at him as she went by. Soon he heard the clink of metal as she rummaged under a bed in the barge's next room.

"How many are there?" Malia asked, and Nophel realized she was asking him.

"I don't know."

"How many?"

"Usually they work in fours," he said, and she glanced back at him. Was that grudging belief he saw in her? Right now it didn't matter. "They must have followed me, and whoever sent them wouldn't have risked them being seen. So, four. Any more and I'd have seen them for sure."

"What sort of a spy are you if you can't—"

"I'm not a spy, woman!" Nophel spat. With the immediate threat from Malia abating, their true position was only just dawning on him. Whoever had sent these Blades must want the people—or the person—Dane had sent Nophel to meet. The Baker. Who were they to know she was not here? Maybe they thought she was Malia, or Peer, or . . .

"Are *you* the Baker?" he asked Malia, and his heart skipped a beat. *I could watch her die, and then I'd die with a smile.*

Malia actually laughed. "I'm fun to be with, compared to her."

"They'll try to kill us all," he said softly.

"Yes, that's what I'm assuming."

Peer appeared with her arms full of weapons—several swords, knives, throwing stars, a crossbow, and a rack of bolts.

"They won't be heavily armed," Nophel said.

"Don't need to be with those blades of theirs," Brunley said.

"And I doubt they're wearing armor. Not if they were sent to track me. They'd have been running. Tired." He was thinking, trying to recollect anything about the Blades he saw every single day that might help them all survive this.

"Anything else?" Peer asked. She was hefting the crossbow, but it was obvious she had never fired one in her life. Her face was pale and slack, a fine film of sweat across her upper lip.

"Pull back, click, lock in a bolt," Malia said. Then she snapped up a short knife and squatted down three steps from the door, sword in her other hand, listening. "Here they come," she whispered.

"They're all right-handed," Nophel said.

As the door crashed inward, Malia dropped the knife and lobbed her sword into her other hand.

"Window!" Malia shouted, darting at the shape shouldering through the remains of the wooden door.

Peer ducked and turned, bringing the crossbow up, hoping she'd primed it and fitted the bolt correctly. Suddenly she was certain she had not, that it would misfire, and the woman shattering her way through the window—face flushed, teeth gritted, eyes glittering with a fury Peer could not fathom—would roll and bury her sword in Peer's stomach. She'd feel the warm rush of blood and see her guts spill, and before the poison on the sword killed her, she'd die of shock. So she pulled the trigger, fully expecting that breath to be her last, and someone other than her screamed.

The woman in the window slumped down and dropped her sword. Her face had changed. The fury had gone, and so had one of her eyes; in its place protruded the last third of a crossbow bolt. One of her arms flapped, thudding against the bulkhead. Her head lowered slowly and thick fluid dribbled from her face, pattering onto the wooden floor, and Peer knew it was the Blade's brains.

Peer had never killed anyone in her life. She heard the chaos around her but none of it registered. Her focus was narrowed and aimed entirely at the woman—the woman she had killed.

Malia shouted. Metal clashed on metal, and Peer was shoved aside as the Watcher backed into her. The Scarlet Blade who had come through the door pushed his way forward. Malia stabbed at him again, holding her sword left-handed so that it sliced in under his defenses. In the confines of the barge's small room, already filled with people, there was no finesse to the swordplay, only brutality. As Peer scrabbled backward and pulled herself upright against the table, Malia kicked out at the man's crotch. He turned sideways and took the kick in his thigh, punched her in the face, forced forward as he brought his sword around toward her unprotected neck.

"Malia!" Peer shouted, and then the soldier cried out as he tripped. Nophel jerked in his chair, kicking up and out with the foot he'd worked free of his bindings, shoving against the man's hip and tipping him over.

Malia drew back her sword arm, but Brunley had already buried a knife in the nape of the man's neck. The Blade hammered his feet against the floor, dropping his sword and reaching behind with both hands.

"Back," Malia said. Brunley did as told, and she thrust her own knife through the Blade's heart. "Two more." She went for the door.

"They'll be waiting for you!" Nophel hissed.

"Well I'm not getting trapped in here," Malia said. As if conjured by her words, a round smoking object smashed through another window. The curtain held it back against the sill, but a beat later it erupted in flames, fire splashing sideways and down across the wall. The flames spread too fast and gave off a pungent chemical stink.

"Flush-fire!" Nophel said, his eyes wide. Though his legs were free, his arms were still firmly tied to the chair.

Peer heard a shout outside and the clang of metal on metal. Brunley had followed Malia up through the door.

"Help me!" Nophel pleaded. Peer pulled her knife and started to cut the ropes binding him, the heat from the fire already shriveling hairs on her arm and stretching the skin on the back of her legs. As Nophel's first arm came free and she started working on the second, Peer thought she could see the wood of the chair through his wrist.

She paused, shook her head, and he grasped at her. "Cut!"

Fire flowed and wood started to crack.

She could see through his head now—the puddle of blood from the dead Scarlet Blade and Brunley's discarded knife.

"Cut!" he shouted.

"You're going," she said, still cutting.

Nophel looked at his hands, paused, then grinned. "Good." As the last rope fell away, he grabbed Peer's knife and shoved her toward the door. She crawled through and out into coolness, gasping in the fresh air. And when she looked around, Nophel was gone.

Malia was standing atop the barge, fighting a female Scarlet Blade. Their swords threw off sparks, feet thumped on the barge roof, and they punched and kicked and bit, trying to get each other off balance. It was a vicious confrontation that could not last for long.

Peer stepped across onto the bank and looked around frantically, fearing the impact of sharp metal against her neck at any moment. But then she saw the fourth Blade. He was sitting astride a struggling shape beneath a spread of bushes a dozen steps along the canal bank, right hand rising and falling, painting a bloody splash on the air. Beneath him, Brunley lay on his stomach, hands fisted into wet mud.

She took a couple of steps forward, hand going to her belt, but the knife was gone. *Nophel took it!* she thought. She backed toward the barge—there were weapons in there—but then a window blew out, gushing flame. Something inside exploded with a dull thud. Malia grunted behind her, and something heavy dropped onto the barge's wooden roof. Peer glanced back; the Watcher stood over the soldier, sword raised to deliver the final blow.

Peer heard the impact of booted feet on gravel.

Malia glanced up. The woman beneath her kicked, catching Malia in the crotch, and she gasped and fell sideways, trying to grab on to something but finding nothing. She splashed into the canal.

Peer was already turning back to the other Blade, ducking down as she did so, but she saw in a beat that she had no more time. The soldier was coming for her. His face was streaked with Brunley's blood, eyes wide, and he wanted her blood as well.

Peer froze. She wanted to roll to the right, stand, and try to run, but her body would not obey her brain's commands. *I killed someone*, she thought, and everything felt so hopeless and hollow.

The Scarlet Blade gasped and fell at her feet, hand reaching for his groin. He glared at her, frowning. Then his head tipped back and his throat opened, eyes going wide as blood sprayed and made the muddy path muddier.

Peer fell onto her rump and scrabbled backward, feeling

the fire's intensifying heat stretch the skin on her face and singe her hair. The soldier thrashed for a while, his arms waving but his body hardly moving at all, as if a weight sat on his stomach.

She heard splashing and the unmistakable *thunk!* of a crossbow firing. Then laughter.

As she stood and faced the burning barge, the Scarlet Blade still standing on its roof was turned toward her, priming her small crossbow and raising it in one practiced motion.

The boat dipped and creaked, fire crackling through rents opening in its roof. Flames licked at the soldier's feet, but she did not seem to notice. She was aiming at Peer, the shining tip of the bolt pointing directly at her chest.

Peer dashed sideways, tripping over the dead Blade and splashing down into his blood. She cried out and then thought she heard her voice echoing somewhere—but this was a different cry. The woman on the boat had her legs swept from beneath her and landed heavily on the barge's roof. Then she was thumped down into it, some invisible force pummeling her head and chest again and again; her waving arms were knocked aside and slashed open. When the flames erupted through the roof and enfolded her like grasping arms, Peer saw a shape jumping through the flames, a hollow where nothing burned. And then it was gone; and the soldier blazed. Her screams were terrible.

Peer moved quickly along the canal. Malia was swimming away from the barge. She seemed unwounded, pulling strongly with both arms.

"Here!" Peer called.

"Be careful!" Malia shouted.

"They're dead, Malia." She squatted by the canal and reached down, beckoning the Watcher to her. Malia swam in and Peer helped her up onto the bank. They fell together, gasping and wet, and then Peer noticed the wound on Malia's arm for the first time. It was dark, her clothing soaked with blood that still flowed.

"Crap shot," Malia said. She stood and stared at the barge—her home, burning now, popping and cracking and sending billowing smoke to the sky. That would attract the wrong sort of attention. The body of the Blade Peer had killed was still visible hanging through one window, fire dancing along her trousers and licking at her boots. The stench of cooking meat tainted the air.

Brunley and the other soldier lay dead on the canal path.

"Nophel," Malia said, nodding at the boat.

"No. I cut him loose, he got out, and . . . I didn't see him."

"He ran?"

"No. I didn't see him." Peer was shaking her head, because she didn't know how to say what had happened and was not sure herself. Something impossible, something unbelievable. When she blinked to clear her vision, she saw that soldier falling and his throat opening up as if sliced by sunlight.

"I'm here," Nophel said from behind them. They both spun around, and he was standing ten steps along the path. For an instant Peer thought he was a shadow, because she saw through him. She heard Malia gasp. Then she shielded her eyes against the sun and he was whole, both hands wet and the knife in his right hand still dripping, sticky and bloodied. He was shaking, and fire from the barge reflected from his wet clothes. *Been in the canal as well*, Peer thought. Then she realized the wetness was blood.

"We need to get away from here now," Malia said, then called, "Devin!" There was no answer.

"They must have followed me," Nophel said.

"Doesn't matter. Come on." Malia grabbed Peer's arm and pulled, still looking around for Devin. But for a moment Peer could not move. The fire's roar was growing, and the associated sounds of things cracking and breaking startled her. Still, she could not take her eyes from the dead soldier in the window. *I killed her*.

"Peer?" Malia said more gently.

"I shot her in the eye."

"And it was a good shot. If you'd missed and she got in, I don't know—"

"But I shot her."

Malia stood before Peer, blocking her view. "This is the first time I've killed anyone as well," she said. And the pain on her face was obvious now, the glitter of the open wound on her shoulder starkly colorful against her drab clothing.

"They came to kill us," Peer said. *That's our strength. That's how we'll get past this.* And then Malia said, "Oh, no," and Peer turned to where Malia was looking. She could just see the pair of legs protruding from beneath a clump of shrubs along the canal path. *Devin.*

"He never had a chance," Peer said.

"He and Bethy were . . ." Malia said.

"At least she wasn't here as well."

"So what happened to you?" Malia asked Nophel. Her voice suddenly had a cold edge, and Peer feared that the killing was not yet over.

"I . . ." Nophel dropped the knife. Looked at his hands.

"A first for all of us," Malia said bitterly. "Come on. There's somewhere nearby where we can lick our wounds and decide what to do next."

As they pushed through undergrowth and started to weave their way between some of the canal-side storage buildings, Peer felt a strange calm settling over her. Leaving the scene helped, the retreating fire and stink of burning flesh a fading reminder of what had happened. And there was also an irrational yet gratifying sense of satisfaction about what she had done. They had tortured her, and now she had killed one of them. It was illogical and brutal, but she held on to it for now.

"Nophel saved us," she said to Malia.

"I'll thank him later."

As they hurried away from the blood and the bodies and the rising pillar of greasy smoke, Peer vowed to make sure Malia kept her word. And she also promised herself an answer to what had happened back there. *If Nophel doesn't tell us, he's not on our side*, she thought.

The disfigured man followed, bringing all his mysteries with him.

The noise of the Falls had receded behind and below them, a distant rumble that still shook the ground, but Gorham was certain the sound was implanted forever in his ears. Around them were the caverns and crevasses of Echo City's roots, but he saw little, because he was concentrating on Nadielle's light bobbing ahead, which sometimes slipped from view entirely as the Baker turned a corner. They were heading in two distinct directions—away from the Falls, and up.

He was sweating, even though some of these caverns were ice cold. Only some of them—others were quite warm, as if they'd been home to something warm-blooded until very recently. That worried him, but he had no one to ask about it. They'd left Neph back at the Falls after Nadielle had shouted something into its ear and stabbed at its arms. And Nadielle herself was moving much too fast for Gorham to catch. He'd seen her fall a couple of times, and once he thought she'd broken a bone. But every now and then he heard her voice, an unconscious cry that ripped at his heart and set his skin tingling. He'd given up calling after her. He thought perhaps she'd gone mad.

After the screaming and the thrashing, she'd stared wide-eyed at the thundering Falls for a few beats, not even blinking when a knot of bodies shadowed by. Then she'd shouted to Neph, cut its arms, and left. Gorham had stared at Neph, hands held out in a *what's happening* gesture. But the chopped had only looked at Gorham dismissively before sitting down to face the Falls.

If Gorham had waited a dozen heartbeats longer, he might never have found Nadielle's light smeared across the darkness ahead of him. And if he'd followed her the second she darted away, perhaps he could have caught her and held her down, hugged the truth from her, shared his warmth to let her know she was not alone. *You're my sunlight*, she had told him, and he so wished to share his heat with her now.

Another scream. He looked ahead, panting hard, and saw Nadielle's shadow thrown back toward him from the narrow mouth of a smooth tunnel. She was staring away from him, head tilted up, but as he opened his mouth to call, she ran on.

I've got to catch her, he thought. *We're deeper than the oldest times down here, and if I lose her I'll never find my way out*. It didn't help that Neph and Nadielle had the only two remaining torches. When she was out of sight, he could not see his hand in front of his face. Every moment took her farther ahead—and closer to losing him. With her torch, she could scout her route over rocks and around potholes, while he relied mostly on touch. He could not become too careful, could not let fear make him any slower than he was now. The thought of being lost and alone . . .

"Nadielle!" he shouted, wasting a breath and a moment to pause and catch another. But his voice echoed strangely, swallowed by the darkness in one direction and sounding off to the deep in another. Nadielle's light flickered as though paused, but then she was away again.

Garthans down here, and their traps, those things bred from sprites and cave wisps . . . The Lost Man and his quest for a return to flesh . . . Other things, myths, monsters . . . There were a thousand ways for him to die down here and only one way to survive.

"Nadielle!" he shouted again, and hated that his voice broke.

The light ahead stopped once more, but he did not pause to look. He moved on across the smooth, sloping floor of a cave, into a wide crack in its wall, splashing through a puddle that felt too thick to be water and too warm to be natural, and all the while he drew closer to the light.

"Please wait!" He could see her now, her pale face yellow beside the oily flame. She was looking his way. He hoped her fear had calmed enough for her to be aware of him once more. As he approached, he heard her heavy breathing—part exertion, part terror. Her eyes flickered left and right, never quite centering on him. She stood in coiled readiness, ready to spring away at the slightest provocation.

"Teeth," she said, and that single word chilled Gorham to the core.

"Nadielle, please, just wait. Let me catch . . . my breath." He reached her at last, close enough to touch but careful not to do so. His breathing matched hers, but though exhausted she still looked ready to run through these caverns for another day, then up into the Echoes, toward sunlight. *You're my sunlight,* she'd told him, but she was now lighting the way for him.

"We have to go together," he said softly, shivering. He had

no idea how he had not broken an ankle, twisted his leg, dropped through a crack in the world. She held the light between them as if to share, but it could also have been a barrier. "Nadielle, what did you see?"

"Its teeth," she said, trembling, not quite catching his eye. "Neph will tell me when it arrives." Her voice was flat, dead. Her skin was pale and slick. He had never seen her like this.

In the distance, a low rumble ground through the caverns. Gorham closed his eyes but could not tell the direction from which it originated. *Behind us and down*, he thought, because that was the most obvious. He looked at Nadielle, raising his eyebrows. She looked sick.

"It'll be a while yet," she said. "But it climbs the water. It's been climbing for . . ."

"For?"

"A long time." She was staring into the darkness, and Gorham had no wish to see what she was seeing.

"Do you know?" he asked. "Is it something—"

"Something that shouldn't be. Something that should have *never* been." Then she looked directly at him for the first time. "We have to run." She moved away, holding the torch before her to light the way.

Gorham went with her, because he had no choice. He could have held her back, perhaps, to demand more from her. But, in truth, he had always been afraid of the Baker, and this just scared him more.

Nadielle seemed very certain of their route. Even without Neph, she moved unerringly through the underground. Sometimes they seemed to be heading down instead of up, but that would never last for long, and Gorham thought it was to reach easier routes or avoid dangerous ones. There was so much here that he was still afraid of, but being with the Baker went some way toward lessening those fears, because he was more afraid of her than of anything else.

They might have been underground for two days or five; all time seemed to have lost itself to the shadows and eternal night. They had paused many times on the way down, eating dried meats and fruit from their backpacks and catching brief sleeps before moving on, and though it went against his better judgment, Gorham had taken drinks from some of the pools they found in the caves. The water tasted heavy and salty but never rank. He always smelled before tasting.

Now he was exhausted and hungry. His backpack was empty, Nadielle had abandoned hers at the Falls, and Caytlin and Neph were gone. Caytlin had fallen, and if the legends of the Falls were true, she was still falling. Could she be alive? It was a horrific idea, but it circled him and kept presenting itself, and he could not help but imagine what she might be seeing or feeling.

As for Neph, he was sitting back at the Falls, awaiting whatever rose from them.

They walked and climbed for some time, Nadielle saying nothing. Sometimes he tried to prompt her to talk about the Falls again or simply to say anything. But she was silent, brooding, apparently concentrating on the ascent, even though her eyes were far away.

Finally, just when Gorham was considering how he would face Nadielle and force her to tell him what had frightened her so much, she paused at the mouth of a tunnel. Before them lay a deep blackness, barely touched by the torch.

"We've climbed into the deepest Echo," she said. "This is Echo City as it was in the beginning."

Gorham felt chilled, as if his bones had been touched by something terrible. They had not seen this place on their descent, because Neph had led them down through the caves and caverns around the Falls. But Gorham had been wondering when they would encounter the roots of Echo City and what they might find.

"How do you know?" he asked.

"Because there's nothing deeper," she said, as if explaining to a child.

"But this is . . ." *Old*, he thought. *Ancient*.

"What's wrong, Gorham? Expecting Hanharan to welcome you?"

"No," he said, but the darkness was thick and swallowed their voices. The depth of space before them felt immense, and he wondered how far he would see were this Echo to suddenly light up.

"We'd look for him if we had time," she said. He could see the dreamy look in her eyes—mostly hidden by the urgency of their journey, but still there.

"Hanharan? A god?"

"He must have been *someone*," Nadielle said. "Come on." They started walking, the bubble of light around them flowing across the dusty, uneven floor, and then they started to pick out ghostly shapes in the darkness. Buildings, Gorham guessed, but age had smoothed their artificial edges.

"I don't think I *want* to look for him," Gorham said.

"An architect, perhaps," Nadielle said, as if she hadn't heard him. "A philosopher. A carpenter. An experimenter. My ancestors all had their own ideas about who or what he might have been."

"None of them ever came down to explore?"

"No!" she snapped.

"Well, now *you're* here; you can find out."

"From so long ago?" Nadielle asked. She kicked along the ground, and a haze of dust weakened the torchlight. "Doesn't matter what he was down here. Up there, he's a god." She snorted, then chuckled.

"What's so—"

"Shh!" The sound was harsh and loud, and Gorham crouched, chill air cooling sweat across his body.

"What?" he whispered. He tried to peer into history-rich shadows, seeking those forgotten places where myths had been born.

But Nadielle had extinguished the torch. "We're not alone."

She was close enough to smell. He knew her scents, and some had always been mysterious to him, but he smelled them now and they were a comfort. If he held his own breath, he could hear hers. And, close enough to touch, he was sure he could feel the heat of her blood and skin passing across to his.

We're not alone, she had said, but she had not yet told him how she knew. That would come soon.

He listened for sounds of movement or pursuit but heard neither. When he started to become restless, Nadielle's hand closed around his arm and grabbed tight, then she pressed her face to his, sighing against him, and he felt the wetness of tears on her cheeks. He gasped in surprise but said nothing, and she turned his head with a hand beneath his chin so that she could talk into his ear.

"We have to survive," she said. "We must reach the surface. I might be the only one who can affect what's happening, so you have to help me in any way you can."

Gorham nodded, unsettled.

"*Any* way, Gorham."

She means me staying down here, he thought. *She means sacrificing myself, if I have to, so that she can go on.* He wondered if that was why she was crying but thought not. He nodded again, slower this time.

"First," Nadielle said, "we have to get past the Lost Man."

Gorham held his breath, and Nadielle's torch flared once more. She pulled away from him and shone the light ahead, out into the Echo that contained Echo City's earliest remnants.

Time had pressed down on this place with irresistible weight. Buildings were crushed and toppled, and close to where they hid lay a pile of rubble. Some of the stones might have been carved with images or even words, but dust stole away any impression.

Beyond this was a structure the likes of which Gorham had never seen. Built from stone and at least three stories high, it seemed to defy many of the natural laws dictating size and shape, with walls leaning outward and floors supported on one end. Perhaps shadows gave false images. Some of its blank window openings retained a gentle glow after Nadielle had passed her torchlight across their surfaces, fading only slowly, as if the windows wanted to hold on to their memory of light. Around the window openings were dark impressions of hands with index fingers missing.

"Garthans?" he asked.

"No, they don't build. They tunnel." She aimed the torch around them, picking out remnants of this Echo from so long ago and, here and there, evidence of those ruins that were used to build something new.

"How do you know it's the Lost Man?"

"I can't imagine what else this means," she said.

"You know everything. But not this?"

"I *don't* know everything! I know hardly *anything*. But everyone else knows even less than me."

"We have to go back," Gorham said. "We can find another way up, past the Falls, where the water's carved its tunnels. Avoid this place altogether." He'd heard stories about the Lost Man and always believed them to be apocryphal. Nadielle's merest mention of his name had made Gorham reassess those tales, and they were all bad.

"No," Nadielle said. "There's no time."

"But he's . . ." *A monster*, Gorham thought. *A killer. A ghost.*

"Don't believe everything you hear," Nadielle said. "He'll probably only watch." But though her words held confidence, she sounded as afraid as Gorham felt.

Nadielle went, and he had to follow.

"How do you know this is his place?"

"No one knows where he exists," she said. "Even the Garthans don't interact with him. He's as much of a phantom to them as to us. I'm just . . ."

"What?"

"With what's happening, I'm not surprised that he's this close to the Falls."

"What *is* happening, Nadielle? What *is* rising?"

"The end of everything," she said. "Follow me."

They walked out into the Echo. Gorham tried to guess how old this place might be—five thousand years? Fifty thousand? There were many estimates of the age of the city, and none made any real sense. Now its age and combined history were a weight, crushing down on him as effectively as the surrounding rock, compressing his thoughts and making them almost alien things. He tried to consider what this place meant, but even for a Watcher it was difficult. If Hanharan really had existed, there might be evidence of him here. If he was the founder of the city and its one true god, would his time here really have fallen into such ruin? In awe and terror,

Gorham eyed strange structures similar to the one they'd just seen, and he wondered how many more were spread through the Echo. Their torchlight picked out further faint images of a four-fingered hand—whether paint marks or impressions in the stone, he could not tell—and their randomness seemed to speak of ownership of this place. Whether Hanharan or the Lost Man had made these buildings from the rubble of history, there must have been a reason.

"I feel like I'm being watched," Gorham whispered, the sensation an itch on the back of his neck. Nadielle did not reply, and as he paused to look around, she kept walking. In the fading glow of her retreating torch, he thought he saw a face at a crumbled doorway.

He ran to catch up, heart racing.

"Keep moving," Nadielle said.

Another face, this time peering from a circular opening in one of the strange structures. Gorham wanted to point it out to the Baker, but between blinks it vanished. He was not certain it had been there at all.

Nadielle led them across this oldest Echo, and for the first time Gorham began to fear that she was lost. All the way down they had followed Neph, trusting his Garthan instincts from one Echo to the next. Ambiguous though these places might be, there still had to be set routes between one past landscape and another, and they were imprinted on a Garthan's memories. But going *up* was perhaps a different thing entirely. And now that Neph had been left behind, Nadielle was following some map that Gorham could neither see nor understand.

But he said nothing, because he did not want such a suspicion confirmed. To be lost down here on his own would be terrible; in some ways, being lost with Nadielle—whom he was trusting to get them from moment to moment—would be even worse.

They came to a place where the ruins were stacked high. Even in the weak torchlight, Gorham could see the smears of ancient fires across some of the rubble, and stones seemed to have been melted and reset under terrific heat. The dust of ages had settled here, but still the evidence of strife was clear.

"More wars?" he asked softly.

"Conflict is as old as the city."

There were no more of those strange structures. But the feeling of being observed did not go away, and every now and then Gorham caught sight of a pale face peering at them from atop a pile of tumbled stones or from the shadows beneath a fallen wall. It never lasted for long, but that somehow made it worse. If he had something on which to focus his fear, it would perhaps lessen it.

"Why won't he come out?" Gorham asked.

"He's been down here a long time. I doubt he knows how to communicate anymore."

"They say he craves flesh in which to return to the surface."

"And how could anyone know *what* he craves?" Nadielle said. "Even I have no idea. They're rumors and stories. Keep walking, Gorham. I know where I'm going."

"How?"

But she did not answer that.

The Lost Man watched them all the way through that ancient Echo. Sometimes he was blatant, his face appearing all around them as if he could flit through the space between breaths. And sometimes his observation was more sly, little more than a feeling. But he was always there, and when Nadielle started to scale a sheer rock face, torch slung around one shoulder, Gorham followed willingly. He could not see how tall the cliff was or where it led, but it meant leaving that haunted place. For that, he would have willingly climbed all the way up to daylight.

After ascending for a while, Gorham felt something grab the nape of his neck. It was a subtle, intimate touch, and he shrugged his shoulders and shook his head. But the feeling remained—and suddenly it was going deeper, as if an invisible hand were forgoing the physical contact to close its fingers around his mind. It drew him away from the cliff face.

"Nadielle!" he whispered, looking up. But she was hanging with one hand, waving the other around her head as if she felt the same. "No," he said, as he felt himself pulled farther from the rough rock wall. "No!"

He held on tight with his right hand and swept the left across the back of his neck. There was nothing there, but the feeling remained. It lured him, easing him away and tugging him down, gentle but insistent, and when he blinked he saw the Lost Man's image imprinted on the backs of his eyelids.

He had never seen an expression so wretched, hopeless, and lost.

"Leave us!" he roared. In this oldest of places, which had until now known only their cautious whispers and the hush of their footfalls, his shout was shocking. In the distance someone screamed, or perhaps it was the echo of his own cry. The deep darkness seemed to come alive, and there was movement all around. But in his struggles, Gorham sensed no life to the movement and no real purpose. It was as if the shadows themselves—settled down here for so many thousands of years and disturbed only by ghosts—were writhing awake at the sound of a living voice.

"Climb!" Nadielle said, and he needed no further prompting. Ignoring the sense of being pulled, straining against it, Gorham climbed hand over hand, trying to catch up with Nadielle so that he was closer to their single torch. Somehow his hands found handholds, his feet found footrests, and his panicked breathing became the only sound.

Slowly, the touch faded, washed away by sweat. Perhaps it was the altitude that lessened the contact, or their determination to shake it off. But, though relieved, Gorham also felt a terrible sadness at leaving that poor thing behind. *It only wants company*, he thought, and he let out a single loud sob. How often could history trap souls such as this? He was a traveler down here, an ignorant, an invader in the past who did not know his place. He felt a sudden overwhelming need to reach the surface again—however dangerous the present was becoming—and to find Peer, seek her forgiveness, and hold her tightly to him. They were alive, and they should revel in that. There was no saying how long it would last.

Nadielle climbed above him, but hers was a different touch. Desperation instead of passion. Convenience in place of love. She was as lonely as the thing they were leaving behind.

At the top of the cliff face, Nadielle did not pause for breath. She started to run again, not responding when Gorham spoke to her, and he had to save his breath just to keep up. She never seemed to tire, and he wondered whether she was secretly taking some unknown drug to keep her muscles warm and loose. They rose from one Echo to the next, and they might have been moving for a whole day without pause before she finally slumped against a wall. Above her, a painted portrait of an old Marcellan stared down, his eyes smeared over with black paint to give him a monstrous demeanor, Fangs had been added to his mouth. The defiler and the Marcellan were both long dead, but something about the defiance pleased Gorham.

He sat next to Nadielle without trying to speak. He drank water from his water bottle, realizing that he would have to find somewhere to refill it again soon. And then Nadielle broke her silence.

"I'm sorry," she said, voice breaking, tears starting to flow. "We're away. I can tell you what's rising." She took his water bottle and drained it before she began. "The Bakers have been here as long as history . . ."

Chapter 17

Nophel stared down at his hands. *I went away again, for a while.* When Malia came back she looked right at him, seeing him for the flesh and blood he was.

"You need to tell me everything," she said, "and quickly. Time's running out."

Nophel glanced at the woman, Peer, who had been left with him while Malia went for medicines. She had not spoken, though he'd felt the pressure of her questions.

"I can tell you only what I know."

"Peer, I'm sure you want to begin," Malia said. She closed the door and stood by the window, looking out onto the street, chewing herbs and pressing paste into wounds on her left hand and forearm. But Nophel felt all of her attention focused on him.

"You disappeared," Peer said. "When I was untying you, you . . . faded. Then you were gone."

"A potion from the Baker," Nophel said. "The *old* Baker. I told you, Dane Marcellan and she were friends."

"A potion to make you invisible?" Peer said. Disbelief rang through her words, and yet Nophel smiled, because she could not deny what she had seen.

"It's called Blue Water," he said. He closed his eyes, the good and the bad, and in doing so he brought back the images of those Scarlet Blades dying at his hand. It had been horrible, feeling his knife part their skin and flesh, seeing their eyes as they knew death had come for them. And yet he could not feel sorry. He thought of their families and friends, who would be told of their deaths today, and the people who had lost a father or brother, mother, or sister. But pity was something he had so rarely been shown that, when it did present itself, he hated it. Pity was for the weak and useless and those who had no aims.

"And he gave it to you so you could get this message to the Baker?" Malia asked.

"No, before that. Something came out of Dragar's Canton, and he wanted to know what."

"Did you find out?"

"Yes. And then I killed it."

Peer held her head in her hands, rubbing at her eyes. *She's been through a lot in a short time*, Nophel thought. Malia, the other woman, was harder and more dangerous. But even she was in a state of shock. For all their posturing, the Watchers had never been fighters. He was at an advantage here, and he had to remember that.

"I know who the visitor is," Peer said, staring Nophel in the eye.

"Who?"

"*We're* asking the questions!" Malia roared, but Peer held out both hands, as if warding the two away from each other.

Nophel looked at his hands, willed the Blue Water to act again. *I did it myself*, he thought, but however much he tried convincing himself of that, it did not ring true. It had been fear and danger that had forced the change, not a message from his own consciousness. Perhaps if Malia came at him with a knife . . . but he was not sure if even then it could happen fast enough. He didn't know how many people, if any, had ever been given the White Water antidote, but he possessed something amazing. Perhaps soon he would gain some control over it.

"A friend," Peer said, putting herself between Nophel and Malia. "A good friend of ours and the Baker. But we think the Dragarians have taken him."

"The Dragarian said he would go to the Baker," Nophel said.

Neither woman answered.

"So where is the new Baker?"

"Gone somewhere," Malia said, quieter now. "She'll be back soon."

"She knows about your friend?"

"Yes," Peer said. "But she also knows that things are stirring in the Echoes."

"What are you going to do with me?" Nophel asked. He was looking at Peer, but it was Malia who answered, wincing as she pressed the paste into a gash across her left forearm.

"I can't trust you," Malia said. "You're Marcellan, and—"

"I'm *not* Marcellan!"

"You work for them. You come from Hanharan Heights with a message tube, snooping around our business, and you can turn fucking *invisible*!"

"So you'll kill me, then?" Nophel asked.

"No!" Peer snapped, and when Malia looked at her, Nophel did not like the look in her eye.

"I'm with the Marcellans only because of the dead Baker," Nophel said, and the old bitterness burned at the back of his throat. "She was my mother and she abandoned me; the Marcellan I serve took me in. It has been the place where I've been safest. But I've always worked only for myself."

"Your *mother*?" Peer asked, aghast.

"Mother," he said, nodding. "So this new Baker is something to me as well."

Malia snorted, then returned to the window. There was a barely suppressed panic about her, the sense that she could unravel at any minute. She carried such an aura of violence that Nophel did not want to be near her when that happened.

"You say you're a Watcher," Peer said.

"It's my outlook, yes."

"The man we seek, our friend—"

"Peer!" Malia shouted, but Peer turned to face Nophel.

"He came in from beyond Echo City."

"No!" the Watcher woman said. But she did not come closer, did not interfere.

"Now I fear the Dragarians might have him, and there's something happening deep down beneath the city, and the Hanharans will do nothing to prevent what might come next."

Nophel gasped, the breath knocked from him. *Beyond the city? Dane knew . . . In his message, it's clear.* But there was no bitterness that Dane had not shared his knowledge with him. And then Nophel thought of the Unseen and their fading ways, and he knew what he could do. Helping the Watchers might be the only sure way to get him closer to this new Baker. Closer to true vengeance.

If only they would believe him.

"I can help," he said. "You might not trust me, but my convictions are strong. First, though, will you tell me about this visitor?"

Malia remained by the window, not as horrified as she had sounded. *She's in shock*, Nophel thought. *She lost friends today.* He could not imagine what she felt, because he had never had a friend. And what did that make him? Stronger than they were, or weaker?

"Malia?" Peer asked.

The Watcher woman shrugged. "You've told him too much already. See what he has." She coughed a harsh, humorless laugh. "Can't put us in a worse position than we're in."

Peer dragged her chair over and sat before Nophel.

"How can you help?" she asked.

"I know people who can get into Dragar's. People like me. Unseen."

"Good," Peer said, and Malia watched with interest. "Our friend's name is Rufus Kyuss, and the old Baker—your mother—chopped him just before she died."

She told him everything she knew. It did not take very long and, as she spoke, Peer felt the unreality of events washing over her. Nophel sat quiet and still as she talked, and his emotions were difficult for her to discern through the growths on his face. Yet what he had said was as confusing as what she was telling him, and trying to absorb it all gave her a headache.

Penler should be here for this, she thought, and thinking of her friend gave her a hankering for those simpler times in Skulk. An outcast she might have been, but at least her days there had rhythms and her nights had been for sleeping, not planning.

"So you can help?" she asked at last. Nophel sighed and rested his head back against the wall.

"We have to go north," he said. "Just the three of us. There are people I know in the north of Marcellan Canton who might be able to get us inside Dragar's. Once in there . . ." He shrugged.

"What?" Malia demanded.

"I've seen them," he said. "Through the Scopes. I saw them swarming out, and they were . . . changed. No longer human."

"They've only been shut away for five hundred years," Peer said.

"Many in the city try to mimic the Bakers," he said, shrugging. "They must have been practicing their own chopping. Preparing for when their Dragar returned, ready to fight anywhere to regain him—in the air, on land, in the water."

"But none can match the Baker," Peer said, thinking of the three-legged whores she had seen, the soldiers with blade limbs, the builders with four arms. With their strange attributes was always infection and pain.

"Maybe not out here, no," Nophel said.

"Then we go north," Malia said. "Sitting here frigging ourselves won't get anything done."

"Shouldn't we tell someone?" Peer asked, then she realized what she sounded like: a scared little girl.

"Devin's dead," Malia said. "I'll leave a message here for Bethy, but there's no saying she'll find it. And we can't wait for Gorham."

"Can't we?"

"Who's to say they'll ever come up again?" Malia said.

Peer knew she was right. They had to go, and now. Into Dragar's Canton with Nophel, this man who claimed to be the old Baker's abandoned, shunned child and who now worked for a Marcellan who, he claimed, was actually a Watcher. How dangerous could it be?

"It's a long walk," Peer said, "and we'll need a reason to be traveling through Marcellan."

"I can also help with that," Nophel said. And for the first time since they had arrived there from the bloodied and burning barge, he smiled. It was grotesque.

"You'd better not be fucking with us," Malia said. "I mean it, ugly man."

Peer offered Nophel a smile, but he was looking down at his hands, turning them slowly in his lap as if willing them to disappear again. There was blood beneath his fingernails.

Nophel walked with his hood up, hiding away from the world, and thought: *If this doesn't work, Malia the Watcher will kill me.*

He took them east toward Marcellan Canton, the gentle slope rising closer and closer to the place he'd called home for so many years. The wall was visible in the distance— a pale façade catching the setting sun and unmarred today by crucifixions—and beyond that the hill rose steeper toward Hanharan Heights. The Heights themselves were visible only as a thin sliver pointing at the sky, and, as he looked that way, he thought of the Scopes up there and hoped that Dane was taking good care of them.

I'm never going back, he thought suddenly, and though he was unsure where the certainty came from, it hit him hard. He paused in the street and stared ahead, hoping that perhaps the Western Scope was looking back at him right now. He almost dropped his hood—but that would have been foolish. Without him to direct them, the Scopes would be all but mindless.

"If you give us away—" Malia whispered at Nophel's shoulder, and he spun around, right hand up before his face with fingers splayed.

"Do you see the blood?" he said softly. "Dry now. But I can still feel its warmth."

Malia glanced away uncertainly, but by the time she had gathered herself, Nophel was walking again. *Foolish woman*, he thought, *and terrified*. His heart was beating hard, though not from exertion—ascending and descending the viewing tower's steps had kept him fit over the years—but from nervousness.

If the entrance has been sealed . . . if the Blades are guarding it . . . if word has spread already of the deaths at the canal and there's a clampdown . . .

There was so much that could go wrong, and in Malia's eyes any fault would be his. But it was all he had left. His drive now—his aim, his reason for being—was to meet this new Baker and ask her for answers that *her* mother had never offered. And then . . .

The Bakers were freaks, monstrosities, more deformed than his simple physical differences. Their deformities were on the *inside*. To kill her would be everything he had lived for.

As they walked—Nophel in the lead, Malia a threatening presence at his back, and Peer, a gentle woman, bringing up the rear—Nophel considered just how much and how quickly everything had changed. After years as an outcast orphan, he had discovered that his mother's line was not ended as he had believed. And not only that, but—

—there's another of my mother's monsters loose in the city!

He looked forward to meeting this Rufus Kyuss—a man who, if what Peer claimed was true, had spent years living out in the Bonelands. *And how could he have done that, if not for my mother's weird magic?* The Blue Water sang in his veins, a thrumming potential kept at bay for now by its antidote. In time, perhaps, he would learn to master it himself.

Closing on the Marcellan Canton wall, he sensed Malia growing ever more nervous behind him. Her hand grabbed his shoulder at last.

"Where are you taking us?" she asked, moving close. He was not used to such proximity; most people shied away from him. He smelled her breath, stale and spicy.

"Trust me," he said. "It's around the next corner. You'll both know it, though you might have forgotten."

"Forgotten what?" Peer asked.

"Just another part of the city passed into Echo," he said.

The streets were busy here. A market was set up in the center of the wide road, with food stalls hawking their produce to those trying to make their way home before the sun set. The smells that vied for supremacy were mouthwatering, and Nophel realized that he had not eaten since leaving Dane Marcellan early that morning. But though his stomach rumbled, now was not the time. He walked past the food vendors and breathed in their promise.

The building on the street corner was a tavern, its drinkers spilling out onto the sidewalks, where they sat at rickety tables talking loudly about fighting and fucking. Occasionally there were whispers of *Dragarians*. Two women were arguing, four men watched, and a tall fat man seemed to be asleep in the middle of it all. He wore the Scarlet Blades uniform, but he'd removed his sword and laid it across the table before him. Drunk though he was, scruffy, pathetic, and apparently sleeping, still no one dared approach. The Blades were truly respected, and Nophel felt a frisson of fear over what he had done.

They'll hunt me, he thought. *They'll find out who lived in the barge, and they're probably already hunting all of us.* But as they passed the tavern and he saw the entrance to the alley farther along the street, he realized the truth: The Scarlet Blades were the least of their worries.

He turned down the alley and walked quickly into the shadows between two buildings, one a three-story rooming house, the other a shop selling jewelry and trinkets. Malia and Peer followed without question, and that was good. They had to act quickly.

"Follow me," Nophel said. "We can't be seen, and these entrances are checked by special troops within the Scarlet Blades."

"What entrances?" Peer asked.

"Follow." Farther along the alley, Nophel kicked aside burst trash bags, spilling rotten food and thousands of broken and crushed trinket beads. They skittered across the alley floor, some dropping into drains, others gathering in cracks in the paving. Beneath the bags was a metal cover, and Nophel curled his fingers into the recessed handles. He pulled hard, straining, then the cover broke free from its surroundings with a wet sucking sound.

"Down," he said.

"The Echoes?" Malia asked. "You're taking us north through the Marcellan Echoes?"

"Nowhere near as deep," Nophel said, and he almost smiled. "Trust me, I know what I'm doing."

Malia and Peer swapped glances, and he saw an acceptance there, though unwilling on Malia's part. *I have them*, he thought. The sense of power was not altogether unpleasant.

"What's down there?" Peer asked.

"Bellowers," Nophel said. "Quickly now. I'll explain on the way." He glanced back at the alleyway's entrance, expecting at any moment to see the scarlet blur of soldiers rushing them. His heart thumped, and he followed Peer into the hole.

Nophel heaved the cover back over them and shut out the last of the light. It was as black as the Chasm. They waited for a minute, breathing heavily in the darkness, until Malia spoke.

"So I suppose you can see in the dark as well?"

"No. I can only turn invisible. Behind you to the left, there should be oil torches on a wooden shelf." He heard Malia rustling and then the sound of metal against stone. Moments later a flint sparked several times and a torch came alight, its diffused glow filling the small corridor. Malia passed torches to Peer and Nophel, then stared him in the eye.

"This way," he said. *She's staring at me. What does she see?* But he knew what she saw: a deformed man with pustulating growths on his face and one good eye, who had worked for the Marcellans most of his life. She saw someone whose arrival had led to the death of her friends Devin and Brunley, the destruction of her home, and her being on the run from the Scarlet Blades. *The only thing she can't see is who I really am.*

He had not been down here for more than a decade, yet the corridor still felt familiar to him. It was dark and hidden, damp and musty, and it smelled of older times; most of the places he had spent his life were like that. It curved left and down, and though they passed several doors standing ajar, he knew to continue onward. These doors led to empty rooms, where once people were supposed to wait while the Bellowers were primed. *I hope they're still alive*, he thought. *After all this, if we find them dead and the pods smashed, the women will not be pleased.* Displeasing Malia was not something he wished to do.

The corridor ended at a wide metal door. Nophel worked the handle, pleased to feel it move. It squealed open.

"There's a lamp system," he said. "I'll try to fire it up." That also worked. With a series of soft pops, seventeen lamps fixed to the walls of the large chamber came alight one after another, each giving off thick black smoke for the first few beats as the flames scorched away dried oil. That worried Nophel, because it meant that no one had been down here for a while. But as long as the fluid tubes and distribution systems had maintained their integrity, he hoped that the Bellowers would still be alive.

"I'm not feeling happy about this," Peer said. "What is this place?"

"Yeah," Malia said, "enough of the fucking mystery."

"It was built while my mother was still alive," Nophel said. He headed across to a wide channel in the floor in which a large tubelike apparatus sat. "You're aware of the Scopes?"

"Of course," Peer said softly.

"They weren't the only commissions the Marcellans gave the Baker. There are other things in this city even now, and many more that have died out. I know most of them. I've visited some. They . . . interest me. And these are called the Bellowers." He pointed at the wall behind them, glad that the heavy curtains were still in place. "I'll show you one."

Malia and Peer stood behind Nophel as he drew the curtains open. He sensed their fascination and their fear; he still felt both those things himself. It would be unnatural not to in the presence of such a creature.

As the curtains slid aside, the Bellower awoke.

Peer gasped and stepped back into Malia, desperate to run but not wishing to turn her back. The Watcher woman grasped her arms and held her tight.

"Wait," she whispered into Peer's ear. "Let's give the ugly man a chance."

It was huge. Perhaps it had once been human, but all facets of humanity had been chopped away by the Baker. *The Baker's mother,* Peer thought, *not the Baker I've met.* But she was becoming confused over such matters, wondering whether there had ever been any real distinction between the two.

"It looks like it's been dormant for some time," Nophel said.

The thing's face was huge, the height of three people and just as wide. Shadows around its bristly head indicated a deep hollow behind it. *And how large is the body on a thing like this?* Peer thought. *Do I really want to know? Could I even comprehend?* It had two small eyes—perhaps the size of her fist—which remained closed, though she could see their leathery lids moving as its eyeballs rolled in dreamy sleep. Its skin was wrinkled and hard like old dried mud, and small creatures dashed across it, trying to escape the light in crevices or up the several large nostrils that dripped slick fluid to the floor. Its mouth was a wide closed seam, almost as wide as the head. Peer dreaded to know what was inside.

"It's monstrous," Malia said. "Just . . ."

"It's genius," Nophel said. "I hated her, but she was a genius."

"Hated?" Peer asked. He looked back at her, his face dark, the single eye glittering with what might have been anger, or tears, or both.

"I told you," he said, "she abandoned me."

Malia stepped forward past Nophel, her hand stretched out.

"Malia!" Peer said, but Nophel shook his head.

"It's harmless," he said. "And it'll get us close to Dragar's Canton quicker than any other way. I need to prime it." He pointed to several thick pipes protruding from the wall on either side of the Bellower's den. "While I work, ask your questions."

"What is it, and what does it do?" Malia said. "That'll do for a start." Peer could hear the awe in the Watcher woman's voice, and she was glad. Malia projected the image of a hard, bitter woman, but it was good to know she still could wonder.

"I don't know the source of the Bellowers, other than who made them."

"More than one?" Peer asked.

"Eight, all around the base of the Marcellan Canton wall. It's a circuit. A transport system, designed for use by everyone, mothballed by the Marcellans after the Baker's death."

"They didn't trust her anymore," Peer said.

Nophel snorted. "Partly that. They knew she was allied to the Watchers, and—"

"We know all about that," Malia said quietly. "No politics here. Just this." She was touching the Bellower's face, laying her hand on softly, lifting it away, moving to another place to touch again.

"They live much slower lives than we do," Nophel said. He was connecting tubes to metal nozzles sunk into the ground, twisting connectors that squealed as they turned. "This one might have been asleep for many moons. I can tell you what they do, but that doesn't mean I understand it. I'm not sure anyone does, now that she's dead."

"Nadielle will know," Peer said, and Nophel glanced at her sharply. "The new Baker."

"Perhaps," he said, connecting another tube. "This is all done through fluids. The Bellower takes it in and expels it in a controlled motion. It's called hydraulics." He nodded back at the center of the large chamber. "We go in that pod, the pod goes in front of its mouth, and once the fluid is flowing, it pushes us along the route."

"All around the Marcellan wall," Malia said.

"From one Bellower to the next. At each junction we move to a new pod, into the mouth of a new Bellower."

"Amazing," Peer said.

"It's horrible." Malia stepped back from the face, wiping her hand against her trousers. "It's monstrous, making something like this. Where's its purpose? What are its thoughts?"

"I'm not certain it has any," Nophel said, pausing for a moment. "The Scopes seem content to do what they're made to do."

"But they were people before, and now . . ."

"I never said what she did was right," Nophel said. "Only that she was a genius. This new Baker does things differently?"

"Yes," Peer said, but Malia only frowned, and Peer knew what she was thinking about. The Pserans, those flying things down there, others—all given purpose and form by Nadielle but denied the one thing that any living thing must naturally desire: freedom.

"It's connected," Nophel said. "And it's awake." He backed away, and Peer saw the Bellower open its eyes.

They were as black as soot, glittering with moisture. They

rolled left and right, but such was their uniform darkness that she could not tell exactly where they looked.

"It sees?" she asked.

"I've never really known." Nophel walked along the wall a little, until he reached a series of large metal wheels. As he turned the first, the sound of rushing fluid filled the chamber, and the first of the thick tubes sprang upright as it was filled. The Bellower shivered and rolled its eyes again, and its whole body shifted in its massive hole. The ground shook.

It's enjoying this, Peer thought. But as Nophel turned the other wheels and the rest of the tubes started to pump fluid, she could not decide whether the creature was shivering in pleasure or pain. Its inhuman eyes gave away nothing.

Nophel moved to the pod and began to pull at a tall lever set in the floor beside it. Metal gears cranked, chains strained and buzzed with tension, and the pod shifted backward toward the creature.

It opened its mouth. The stench was horrendous, a stink so rich it was almost visible, and Peer pressed a hand over her mouth and nose.

"Smells like some of the taverns I've been in," Malia muttered.

Peer laughed. She couldn't help it, and it felt good. It came from deep in her gut, bending her over double, and it drove away circling memories of the dead Scarlet Blades, Gorham's betrayal, the Baker and her monstrous creations. It *sounded* good as well, filling the chamber with something other than awed whispers. As she looked up at the Bellower, its eyes seemed to roll toward her, and its mouth opened that little bit wider.

Malia stared at her with one eyebrow raised, one corner of her mouth lifted. Perhaps that was as close to laughter as she came.

"Into the pod," Nophel said, unaffected. "We don't have long until it bellows."

Peer composed herself, wiping tears from her eyes and wondering exactly what she had been laughing at. *Some madness in there*, she thought, imagining how Penler would have looked at her, his old, wise eyes seeing the truth. Once more she wished he was there with her, and as she approached the pod she felt an aching loneliness.

The pod was now positioned directly in front of the Bellower, its glass lid raised. Inside were nine flattened seats, footrests, and hand hoops; a series of small holes speckled every surface.

"Hurry!" Nophel said. He was becoming impatient, glancing back and forth between pod and Bellower, and his edginess did away with the dregs of Peer's humor. She felt flat and empty once again, and the future seemed darker still.

Malia climbed into the front seat, reclining until her shoulders and head were supported by the upholstered wooden rests. Peer sat behind her and stretched back.

"Press your feet hard against the supports," Nophel said, climbing in behind them. "Hold the rings on either side, settle your head firmly against the rest. When we go, it will press you backward. It'll be . . . strange."

"Have you done this before?" Peer asked, but Nophel ignored her.

"I'll hit the lever soon, but usually someone outside does it. The moment I hit it, the process begins, and I'll have beats to get inside and close the lid."

"Nophel?" Peer prompted.

"No," he said, "never. Always looked too dangerous to me." She thought perhaps she heard a smile in his voice, but she was already pressed against the seat. A staggering potential vibrated the air in the chamber.

"Deep breath," Nophel said. He shoved the lever and jumped into the pod behind Peer, setting it swaying. The glass lid closed on top of them, so close to her face that she thought she could stick out her tongue and touch it. It was dusty and gritty on the outside, obscuring her vision of the chamber. When she exhaled, her breath misted the glass.

"If you did believe in any god, now would be the time to pray," Nophel's muffled voice said. And then he giggled.

What the crap has he brought us into? Peer had time to wonder, and then her world was torn apart.

Once, before the Hanharans had declared Mino Mont's traveling fairgrounds blasphemous because of their artificial stimulation of ecstatic terror and awe, her mother had taken her to one. She was a child then, maybe ten years old, and the smells, sights, and sounds of the fair had remained with her ever since. She'd never seen anything like it. Men and women walked through the crowds on stilts a dozen steps high, dropping roasted nuts into willing hands, urging people to try this ride or that, or the phantom rooms, or the crushed-mirror swamp. Huge creaking structures of wood, metal, and rope rose all around, with oil lamps burning different colored and scented oils and casting their soft light over the whole scene. And it was one of these structures that had grabbed Peer's attention from the moment she first saw it.

Her mother told her it was called a drop ship. People paid to be strapped into a metal-reinforced wooden cart, which was then hauled to the summit by means of an intricate system of pulleys, ropes, and chains. The pulling was carried out by three tusked swine, and even that process was made into an entertainment, with clowns leaping from one creature's back to another and conducting a fake swordfight with silk snakes as they went. Once the cart was at the top, the clowns paused and began a countdown. Ten . . . nine . . . eight . . . When they reached one, a clown threw a lever in the hauling wheel's hub, and the cart fell to the ground.

The noise was tremendous. Ropes whipped around wooden spools, sending smoke hissing out of the ride. The people inside screamed. And as it reached the bottom, a high, whining shriek was emitted from the complex braking system. The riders emerged laughing and pale, shaking and whooping, and Peer had insisted that she have a turn. Her mother refused at first but soon relented. She'd been wearing a smile that day, and Peer was the center of her life.

The feeling Peer had in the pod as it was gushed from the mouth of the Bellower was similar—at least to begin with. Then it grew a hundred times more terrifying.

She closed her eyes and held her breath, but it went on too long and she had to breathe. She heard screaming and wondered if it was her own. Her body was both hot and cold, skin scorched or frozen in a hundred places, and she had never felt so sick without actually being able to vomit. The screams were swallowed as the terrible grinding, screeching sound from outside increased, shuddering through the pod with impacts that came so often it was difficult to discern one from the next.

Peer opened her mouth to shout, but something flooded in. She gagged. *Drowning*, she thought, *choking, dying*. But she did not vomit, and she did not die. The pod slowed, the noise lessened, and it took her a long while to realize they had come to a halt.

When she opened her eyes, Nophel was leaning over her, wiping a thick gelatinous substance from her eyes.

"Just scoop it away," he said, sounding as terrified as she felt. "It's exuded to buffer the body. There. That wasn't so bad."

"I'm going to kill you." Malia spoke from out of Peer's view. "Soon as I can feel my hands again, I'm going to kill you."

Peer sat up slowly, dizzy, closing her eyes until she found balance. When she opened them again, she saw another underground chamber lit by several oil lamps, another curtain lining an entire wall, and Nophel dragging coiled tubes across the floor. Malia turned in her seat.

"I think I shit myself."

"Don't worry," Nophel said, and he seemed cheerier the more terrified Peer and Malia became. "Two more like that and we'll be there."

Chapter 18

Gorham was beginning to understand Nadielle's terror. It was a fear born partly from knowledge and partly from the factors she still did not understand. But mostly it was composed of guilt.

He'd told her that she was not to blame. The mistakes of an ancestor born thousands of years before could hardly be laid at Nadielle's door. But then she tried to explain some of the background of the Bakers—information that, he was sure, was rarely imparted—and his own doubts had started to grow. All Bakers carried the successes and failures, and the triumphs and tragedies, of their predecessors. And though they were perceived as different people, in some ways their minds were one and the same. *Imagine being born with such knowledge*, he thought. *What could that do to a person?* But Nadielle, he was coming to realize, was more than a person. She was the culmination of her line. And everything she did, all her rights and wrongs, would also be passed on.

Such responsibility. Such *weight*.

Now he was following Nadielle again, up through the Echoes in a desperate rush to reach the present, see the sky, and make their way back to her laboratories. She was unsure whether there was anything that could be done, but she had to try. She *had* to.

All the time she'd told him her story, she never raised her voice above a whisper. He thought maybe the Lost Man's desperation had held a mirror up to her own.

"You've seen my mother's old books, Gorham, and many of them were handed down from generation to generation, hundreds or even thousands of years old. But you haven't seen *all* of them. Only I've seen them all, because I'm the Baker right now. I keep them hidden away. I add to them sometimes, when I improve the chopping processes or . . . something else. But some of the things my ancestors achieved put me in their shadows. They were explorers in arcane arts I can barely conceive of. I'm a nothing at the end of a long line of wonders. The Pserans are my greatest triumph, but I'm not sure they'll even merit an entry in the Bakers' diaries.

"I've always been aware of the Vex. It was legend thousands of years ago, something from the oldest times of the Bakers written in the oldest Baker diary. I've never questioned whether it was true. It was so old, it didn't seem to matter. The Vex was a creature created by the first Baker. Chopped, though I'm sure back then the processes were vastly different. The first Baker wrote about the Vex only briefly. I read the account just once, and that's all that was needed. I never forgot:

"The Vex was bad, and it would grow worse, so I threw it into the Falls.

"It was left to succeeding Bakers to write down what they knew. Some of it must have been word of mouth, though most of it is inherited memory. Gorham, I can't tell you, can't explain, how I know most of the things I know. It was in my head from the beginning. It's passed down, but not in the way your name is passed from your parents to you or the color of your hair. This is *knowledge*, as certain as the color of my hair or the build of my bones. And buried in that mass of handed-down knowledge, I see why that first Baker should have written so much more.

"The Vex was one of the first attempts at chopping—a new process, untested, the Baker ignorant of its power. She was attempting to create something that would watch over the city, be its heart and mind, its health and conscience, and take care of things, because the city back then was young and still in turmoil. But for reasons that are long lost to time, it went wrong. The Vex killed many people. It rampaged. In the vast scope of its slaughter, it wiped out so many potential family lines. Echo City would be a very different place if the first Baker had been more careful.

"So, yes, the Vex was bad. And it would have grown worse had she not thrown it into the Falls. It's been down there in the Chasm for tens of thousands of years. Feeding on the city's dead, perhaps. Absorbing the city's history of death, disease, and murder. Brooding, maybe, and from the glimpse I caught . . . it's been growing. And now it's climbing back up."

"Climbing?" he'd asked.

"Swimming up the Falls from the Chasm. And I saw . . . It has . . ." The tears had come then, surprising him. When he'd hugged her, she accepted his comforting, and he had wondered ever since just who she really was.

"I'm a monster," she'd said, gasping into his neck, the same way she had when they'd made love and she'd called him her sunlight.

"No."

"*Yes*. I was chopped, not born. No love made me, Gorham. Only a need to survive. The same need that makes every Baker—a determination for our line to continue. Whatever accident of nature made the first Baker is resounding through the ages."

"What *did* make her?"

"That's knowledge that was never handed down. Why would a monster recall the key to its existence?" she asked bitterly. "Someone could use it against us."

"You're just like me," he'd said.

"No. My predecessor knew she would die, and she needed to go on. Carry all our knowledge forward. In here!" She'd slapped her own head.

I'm a monster, she had said, taking on the blame for the Vex. And thinking of the Pserans and Neph, Gorham's uncertainty about this woman grew even more.

Now, the two of them close together as they climbed through the buried histories of Echo City, she was becoming more of a stranger to him than ever before. She was the

Baker, not Nadielle. In her mind, memories of old. In her heart, knowledge handed down through the ages. Behind and below them, rising from the unimaginable Chasm with the bones of millennia of the city's dead in its gut, came the Baker family's greatest mistake.

Nadielle was changing so much, and her fear was Gorham's terror.

Up through the Echoes, and Gorham felt eyes upon them all the way. Sometimes he thought he saw movement in old buildings and ruined streets, but when he looked, lights would blink out and darkness would stalk there once again. Other times he saw nothing but sensed things following them, slinking through shadows only just touched by Nadielle's oil torchlight, sniffing after them like hungry hounds. The feeling would go and then return, but he never mentioned it to Nadielle. She was very far away, and he was afraid to disturb her haunting thoughts.

And he wondered what would happen should her torch's fuel reservoir dry up.

Whatever observed and followed did nothing to interfere with their journey, and an unknown time after fleeing the thunderous Falls, Gorham thought that he recognized the Echo around them. Nadielle paused several times—from tiredness, he thought at first, but then he saw the alertness on her face—and all at once she seemed to relax.

"The laboratory is safe," she said. "Not far now."

"I recognize this place. These old fields."

"We'll approach from a different direction, but, yes. My rooms are guarded, Gorham."

"Guarded by what?"

But she was frowning again, distant, and Gorham wondered just how much of herself the Baker had left down at the Falls.

The land rose slightly, old farmland given over to the chaotic remains of wild forest, and soon Nadielle paused at a dip in the ground. There was a round metal hatch cast into the gulley's wall. She glanced back at Gorham, smiling uncertainly, then touched a succession of bolts and dials. A hiss, and then the hatch clicked open. She and Gorham entered, pausing to pluck two torches from the wall.

We're back, Gorham thought, and relief flushed through him. He climbed in after Nadielle and breathed in the familiar, mysterious scents of the Baker's laboratories. He held her arm and tried pulling her to him. She resisted.

"Nadielle?"

"Not now," she said, voice strained. "Don't you see that it's all changed? That I'm someone else?"

"No," he said, but he could not keep the lie from his voice. For a while, Peer's distant presence had been pulling him forward and upward, not Nadielle's.

"I've never had much of a cause," she said. "I've no memories of being a child. I don't even know how old I was when I was chopped. My first recollection is of things carrying me through the Echoes—and I *knew* what the Echoes were, even then. What child deserves memories like that? When they know everything? Ever since, I've been trying to find my sense of wonder. Sometimes the work I do is . . . just because I'm the Baker. There's never been much of a reason. But now I have to do what I can." She was distracted, uncertain, and could not meet his eye. "It's all that's left."

"And I'm here to help," he said.

Nadielle froze for a moment, then slowly lifted her head until she was looking right at him. He had never seen such soul in her eyes. "Thank you," she said. She turned from him and walked along the dusty corridor. "I hope you can."

He followed her. As they came to the end of the short corridor and she started to open another metal door, she muttered a brief warning over her shoulder, which did nothing to prepare him for what was inside. "They won't hurt you." Then she opened the door.

Her laboratory was alight with flaring oil lamps. It was also alive with stalking, crawling things—multi-bladed, many-fanged, their bodies muscular and trim, heads thin, eyes dark and large to make the most of the light. They hunkered down when Nadielle and Gorham first entered, then rushed to her like eager pets welcoming their master home.

They won't hurt me, they won't hurt me, Gorham repeated in his mind, because he had never seen anything like this. Neph was similar, but it was humanoid, its origins obvious. These things were part insect, part lizard, as large as a man but so obviously inhuman that he found them less disturbing to look at than Neph. But, unlike with Neph, Gorham could not read them at all.

Some hissed, a few clicked toward him on gleaming claws. Nadielle spoke words in a language he had never heard, and they held back, but he sensed a constant readiness in them to leap at him. He touched his sword's handle and almost laughed at how ineffectual it felt.

"Let's eat and drink," Nadielle said. "And you'll be wanting to rest."

"And you?" he asked, thinking of her bed, her warmth.

"No time for me," she said.

"Then let me help?"

"You?" she asked. When she turned around, it was as if she did not know him at all.

"Me. I'm not just an inconvenience, Nadielle. I went down with you to help, and I'm here to help now."

"I'm not sure what—"

"Don't cast me aside!" he shouted. The huge vat room echoed with the scrape of claw on stone, and shadows tensed.

"Gorham, this is beyond you. You don't know what I am."

"Yet you've tried to make me understand. How many others have you tried telling?"

Nadielle sighed, nodded, and they walked across the vat room together.

None of the womb vats was ruptured, but several still seemed to be working. The creatures—he'd seen maybe twelve, though there might be that many again concealed—patrolled the chamber, and he felt their attention focused upon him. *She's their mother*, he thought, and that realization led him to consider the convolutions of her strange, unnatural family history.

The more he knew, his fascination with her only increased. But the love he'd once claimed for her now felt different.

Lessened. In the face of the Baker, such an idea felt almost childlike.

Speaking again in that strange language, Nadielle entered her rooms at the end of the vat chamber, and Gorham followed. The sense of familiarity enveloped him, and he sighed in relief when he closed the door behind him.

"It's good to be home," Nadielle said, surprising him.

"I was thinking the same."

She looked at him quizzically, smiling. "You still . . . ?" she started, but words seemed to have left her.

"Trust you?" he finished.

Nadielle shrugged.

"Of course," Gorham said softly. He went to her, desperately hoping that she would not pull away again, but she turned and headed for the door beyond her bed. The last time she'd entered that room had been with Peer and Rufus, and Gorham had felt a stab of jealousy—he'd been in her bed but not her most secret room. Now she beckoned him after her, and he supposed that was some form of intimacy, at least.

He could smell her rich body odor, stale breath, and the fear and trials of their time in the Echoes. He wanted to ask her how long they had been down there, but he was afraid her answer might frighten him more. Peer and Malia had not returned with Rufus—or, if they had, those chopped monsters had kept them away. For all they knew Rufus might be dead, caught by the Marcellans and nailed up on their cursed wall as an offering to their twisted, stubborn beliefs. Peer and Malia might have been caught, and the pale stonework of that ancient edifice could be soaked with their blood also. It had seen too much sacrifice for too few reasons.

He was tired, afraid of everything he had discovered and everything that was to come, and as he passed through that door behind Nadielle, emotion took him. He tried to stifle a sob, but it burst out. His chest felt heavy, his eyes wet. He coughed, surprised, trying to disguise what had happened with a further coughing fit.

Nadielle did not turn around. *But she knows*, he thought, and that was the moment he realized she was beyond him forever.

The room was small and dusty, its corners soft with cob-webs. A table was pushed against a wall, one large book and a pile of loose sheets splayed across its surface. On the floor was another book, the cover ripped from its spine like a bird's broken wing.

"The thing my mother made to send Rufus into the Bonelands," Nadielle said, indicating the papers on the table, but she was not interested in this room. She went to the far corner and used her knife to scratch at the wall. She soon found what she was looking for and scraped the blade across the jambs and head of a door shape set into the wall.

"This," she said, " is my *real* library." She tugged at the door. It groaned, not eager to open, and Gorham went to help. The door ground across grit and its hinges squealed, and Gorham caught a breath of old books, hidden things, and something else. He'd never believed that eternal darkness could have a smell, but his time in the Echoes had told him otherwise.

"I'll bring them out," Nadielle said. "You go into my rooms and clear the table. Just sweep everything onto the floor; this is all that matters now."

"I'll come in and help," he said, but she looked back at him, close enough to kiss but so far away.

"Only me," she said. "This is Baker stuff."

Gorham left the small room and found breathing much easier in her bedroom. He'd never before felt claustrophobic; perhaps it was another way the Echoes had changed him for-ever.

He pushed everything from the table as she'd instructed, enjoying the brashness of it, liking the sound of crockery smashing when it hit the floor and the haze of dust thrown up by protesting books and sheafs of unsorted papers. He caught sight of some of what was written on the papers and recognized her writing. Numbers and formulae, sketches of things he had never seen, notes in some sort of personal code, and he realized once again just how far removed from the normal world she was. Perhaps genius was enough to do that to someone.

"Cleared a space?" She emerged carrying several large old books and twitching her nose as if trying to hold back a sneeze. "Take them, will you?" As Gorham lifted the books from her arms, the sneeze came, and she held both hands to her nose.

The door crashed open against the wall, and a black creature streaked in with bladed arms raised.

"No!" Nadielle shouted, and the creature settled like a cowed dog. It shuffled from the room without turning its back to her, and its long, waving tail caught the door and gently closed it.

"Remind me not to make you laugh," Gorham said, heart thundering. "Or cough. Or fart."

She chuckled, and it was a good sound.

"What do you need me to do?" he asked.

She instructed Gorham to spread the books flat on the table. They were bound in old, cracked leather, but they did not look damaged or fragile. To Gorham they appeared timeless.

"Well, I don't know about you," she said, "but I could eat a spitted swine and drink a vineyard."

So they sat together, eating cheese, dried meats, and stale bread, drinking good wine like water, and Gorham felt tiredness closing over him. Fear grew distant, held back behind veils of drunkenness. Nadielle drank at his pace, but she became more morose as time went on, talking less and spending more time paging through the books.

"I need to start," she said at last. "Need to look, understand. Find something."

"A way to kill it," Gorham said, nodding. Nadielle stared at him, her face a blank.

"Perhaps a way to slow it down," she said. She stared past him into a dusty corner, and beyond. "I think that's all we can hope for."

Gorham closed his eyes to blink, saw images of teeth and swimming things, and then exhaustion took him away for a long while.

When he awoke, Nadielle was slumped over the table. Her head rested on one of the old open books, hair hiding her face. One arm was slung across the table, the other hanging down beside her, and in that hand she clasped a pen. She breathed deeply and steadily, and her sleep seemed to be peaceful.

Gorham stood and stretched. He needed to urinate, his head thumped from the wine he'd drunk, and there was no way of telling how much time had passed. *How can she live down here in the dark?* he thought. He craved sunlight and vowed that, when she awoke, he would try to take her up, just for a while.

Then he remembered what she was doing and why, and he paused and closed his eyes to listen and feel. He could hear no sounds from below and feel no vibration. The Vex must still be climbing the Falls.

Nadielle stirred and sat up quickly, splaying her fingers over the page she had been writing on and glaring at Gorham.

"What?" he asked.

She shook her head. "Bad dreams."

"How long have—"

"I don't know. I drifted off, and . . . I *can't* sleep. There's too much to do. Too much! I've started, but we don't have any time at all. None!"

"Calm down; I'll help."

"Then go and help. Outside. Three vats need watering."

"Vats?"

"I was busy while you slept." She leafed through the book, her face made ugly by a deep frown. She muttered to herself, "I was looking for the seed, the root, the fucking *root* of it all."

"Nadielle?"

She looked up as if surprised he was still there. "Water. That's all. There's a pipe coiled beneath each vat." And she returned to her book and notes, effectively dismissing him.

When he opened the door, one of the blade creatures was standing there. It scuttled aside slowly, watching him with several sets of alien black eyes. He counted ten blades at least, stabbing things—spikes, thorns—and a sickly gleam to its dark skin that might have been poison. And teeth.

Another Baker creation with teeth.

The thing let him pass and he moved out into the vat room,

enjoying the feel of the wide illuminated space. Three of the vats were dripping with condensation and issuing a hazy steam from their unseen upper surfaces. He heard faint scratching and something smoother, like thick fur stroking against the insides. Remembering what he had seen when Neph was birthed, he looked at these womb vats now with different eyes. They appeared solid, but they could flex and shift to the Baker's desires.

Shadows moved around the hall, most of them sharp.

He approached the first working womb vat, found the pipe curled at its base like a sleeping snake, slung it over his shoulder, and began to climb the wooden ladder strapped to the side. Something thumped against the vat's insides— a strangely intimate sound that transmitted through the ladder as a stroke across his palms. The air was becoming damp as he breathed in the haze of steam and mist, and it left a familiarly arousing taste on his tongue. It grew warmer, and though he did his best not to touch the vat's walls, he could feel the heat exuding from them.

He stood on the third rung from the ladder's top. Before him lay the surface of the vat's innards. It seemed innocuous and unremarkable—an undisturbed fluid whose level was an arm's reach below the vat's lip. It was dark, heavy, and slick, and small bubbles rose and popped with thick, slow explosions. Whatever gas formed the bubbles was noxious, but the smell quickly dispersed to the air.

Gorham aimed the pipe's nozzle and turned it on. The water barely caused a ripple where it hit, as if something deep below the surface was drawing it down. He aimed it elsewhere, trying to cause splashes but seeing little disturbance.

"What the crap are you doing here, Nadielle?" he muttered.

He repeated the procedure for the other two active vats, where the water had the same effect. When he'd finished descending the third ladder, several bladed creatures were waiting for him. They were relaxed, close to the ground with their blades averted, and he felt no threat from them. But one of them licked its thin lips, another seemed to be staring at the pipe, and when Gorham raised it they instantly became animated.

He opened the nozzle and they drank the water down.

"Making friends?" Nadielle asked. She'd appeared silently behind him, and something about her had changed. The watering had calmed him a little, giving him time to think, and he'd hoped that the Baker would be more composed when he next saw her. Her work was in progress, after all. And being home must surely make her feel safe.

But when he turned to Nadielle, he was shocked. It was as if days, not mere moments, had passed since he'd seen her last; she looked older, more tired, and her skin had taken on a pale gray hue he had never noticed before. Her eyes flittered left and right. She had always been strong, superior in her position of greater knowledge—though he wasn't sure whether he'd placed her on a pedestal or if she'd climbed there herself—but now she looked like a lost soul.

"Nadielle . . ."

"It's all too much," she said. "Gorham, I can't do it on my own. Some of it, but not all. I need your help." She frowned and started talking almost to herself again. "There's so much to do. We'll need the seed, and then the ingredients, the formulae, and then . . ." She paused and glanced up at Gorham.

Did she really forgot I'm here? he thought. *Or did she forget where* she *is?*

"I'm here to help you, Nadielle. What do you need? I've watered the vats, and I'll do whatever else you want. They'll come back with Rufus soon, and—"

"Too late to wait for that," she said. She looked around at her vats, her chamber, her sharp creations. "Come with me."

He followed her to her rooms, closing the door behind him, and she went straight to her table. Books and papers were strewn across its surface, and at the mess's center lay one of the big books she'd brought in from that deeper room. Torn paper bookmarks protruded from it, and he caught sight of a smear of words and numbers where it lay open. It looked as if someone had passed their hand across wet ink, smudging the information across both pages.

"I can't do both," she said. "I can't fight the Vex and plan how to use Rufus, look at him, find out about him. It's too much for one person. My mother, perhaps . . . *her* mother . . . but not me, Gorham. I don't have it in me. Not with this happening. Not with the Vex."

"So what do you need from me?" he asked, sitting down across the table from her.

"Your seed," Nadielle said.

Gorham caught his breath. Her eyes glittered in her pale face. He smelled those vats, saw the strange surface sucking water down, heard and felt the gentle impacts against their sides as he climbed the ladder. And he knew what she wanted to do.

"How can another me help us?"

"It can't. But another me can."

"I don't understand," he said, but in truth he did. He simply did not want to acknowledge what she was thinking.

"I need to go back down *now*," she said. "I'm the Baker, and I might be able to slow it. There are ways and means." She waved generally toward the vat hall. "And maybe I can even reason with it." She ran her hand across the books again. "But I *also* need to be here, and to take *advantage* of the time I make by slowing the Vex to think of Rufus, and how we might escape."

He nodded slowly, her intentions dawning. *I've already lost one woman I love*, he thought, but the selfishness of that hit him hard, and he felt himself blush.

Nadielle must have thought the flush was because of something else.

"It'll be okay," she said, smiling wanly. "I've done it before. Don't you remember?"

He did remember. Before there had been passion and lust, heavy breathing from both of them, a need and a desire, and her stroking of his cock had been a preamble, a tender massage ensuring his hardness before she rode him or he rode her, and sometimes she'd kept going because she could feel how primed he was, how ready and desperate for the release.

This time it was joyless and harsh. Nadielle did not smile but worked at him hard and fast, keen not to waste any time. In her other hand she held the glass beaker, ready to catch his seed. He closed his eyes and tried to remember more-loving times, but he could not. It was so impersonal and cold that he did not even want to make a noise when he came, and he found it easy to spend himself with little more than a sigh.

She smiled at him when it was over—a sad smile that said so much—but they were both way beyond platitudes. She stood and went for the door, and Gorham stumbled behind her, buttoning his trousers.

"Gorham," she said, standing with her back to the door, "you can't watch me doing this."

"But I'm helping you." He looked at the beaker, clasped in both of her hands as if to keep it warm.

"You are," she agreed. "But no Baker has ever revealed her own special secrets. I'll not be the first." She opened the door, whispered something that sounded more like a hiss, and several bladed shadows manifested behind her.

"Please don't try to follow me," she said. "I'll tell you when it's done." And she closed the door on his bafflement and hurt.

He wandered the room for a while, looking at her papers and books and making sense of none of it. He sat on her bed. And when he heard a long, strident hiss—a vat being initiated, he guessed, or something more arcane that he could never even guess at—he lay back down and closed his eyes.

This time sleep would not come, so he lived his nightmares awake.

They help him. Give him water—sweet, pure, fresher than any he has ever tasted—but not too much. Fruit he cannot identify. A thick, rich vegetable soup that tastes of the ground and all the wonders within. He's settled on a gently swinging hammock strung between two tall, lush trees that are taller than any he's seen before, their tops scratching the sky and almost gathering clouds. The hammock is woven from soft rope. It's gentle on his sunburned skin. He's naked, and the woman who found him has tended his burns with a gentle, sour-smelling ointment that moisturizes his skin and eases the pain. There are blisters, and his skin is shedding from his shoulders and back, but he can feel his body fixing itself. All around him the rich green grass is crisscrossed with shale paths, and low buildings hug the landscape in the shadows of tall trees.

A group of children are playing away from the trees, throwing a ball to one another in a large marked pitch. Sometimes they shout and cheer as one of them scores, other times they argue good-naturedly, and he has spent some time trying to work out the rules of their game. The fact that he is no nearer to understanding than he was when he started watching does not upset him. This is a new place, a *different* place, and he's glad.

Some of the children glance at him now and then, and as the sun dips toward the valley's ridgeline, a few come to look. They stare for a while—long-haired and brown-skinned and glowing with health, their eyes filled with wonder and innocence. He sees intelligence in their expressions and the evidence of hard work on their hands. Perhaps soon they will let him play with them.

The woman comes and helps him from the hammock, wrapping him in a blanket and guiding him toward one of the buildings. He becomes aware of many other people watching him, observing with a frank curiosity that does not make him uncomfortable.

They don't know where I'm from, he thinks. *I showed her the desert and she was shocked. They must think nothing can live out there. Perhaps they think they're all there is.*

The building is like others he has seen in the settlement, made from baked mud bricks, strong and dependable. The windows are glazed with extravagant colored glass, the doors hung with strange sigils, and inside there are several rooms, all leading out from the central area. Here there is a roaring fire, and several people are seated on intricately carved wooden chairs. There's a peace about them, a calmness that puts him at ease.

They speak to him in that strange language, and the woman responds for him. Some of them blink in surprise. A couple look at him with suspicion.

Something strikes his arm, a harsh burning pain. He cries out and looks, but there's nothing to be seen here in this memory, only the woman's kindly hand holding him still.

He swam in darkness as his Dragarian captors drugged him quiet once again, and then he was somewhere else.

Rufus is drawing images from memory, using charcoal on fine white paper. He has been in the village for some time. He has quickly become a part of the settlement, welcomed in by people whose level of trust is great and suspicion low. There are still some who have difficulty believing where he has come from, because, to the Heartlanders, the desert is endless and inimical to life. But they do not hold that disbelief against him. His presence has encouraged a large degree of debate and discussion, and as he slowly learns their language he is beginning to take part in those discussions. It's amazing that he is there, they keep telling him, but they are a people to whom an amazing thing is a gift, not a terror.

They pay homage to the Heart and Mind and tell him that it keeps the Heartlands safe and peaceful. When he asks if he can see it, they go quiet, and this is when he feels most like an alien. *Perhaps one day*, his savior says, but there is uncertainty in her voice.

His sketches are becoming more elaborate. In the small room in her home where the woman has let him live—he learned early on that her own son and husband were killed several years before by a herd of marauding beasts, whose name he does understand—he is surrounded by his artwork. The early attempts were vague and unsure, smudged by faulty memory. The piece he is working on now is far more clear. It is a city on a flat horizon. Close by are bleached white bones half buried in the sand. There is nothing alive and nothing indicating life other than the city—a place of hills and walls, towers and buildings climbing the heights, all reaching for the sky. There's a haze in the sky above and around the city, and hints of a river to the west. The more times he draws this same image, the more detail he adds and the larger the city looks. When he blinks, he thinks the city could be the whole world.

The people study his artwork but do not interfere.

He draws a shape in the desert between the strewn bones and the city. And in this new language he is learning, he calls it *himself*.

There's a pain in his leg and he winces, scratching the

charcoal stick across the paper, grasping his thigh. There's no blood, no sign of injury, no smudge on the paper.

He swam in darkness again, his captors' drug in his blood, the pain of its gentle injection into his leg fading as this new memory cuts in.

Older now, fit and healthy and a full part of the settlement in the valley, he takes a walk with the woman who found him and who has become his guardian. She has been promising this walk for some time. He has been asking more and more, and as adulthood approaches, his need to see, know, and understand has grown. It is a long walk, past neighboring villages in other valleys, across a wide plain where different-looking people live in stilted buildings, tending walking plants that provide balms and medicines for everyone in this land. He has seen these people before on trading trips, and he stops for a while to converse with them. Their language is as alien to him now as his guardian's was when he first arrived out of the desert. Some of them try, however, and they call him Man from Sand. He is, it seems, something of a legend.

The walk opens his eyes to how vast the Heartlands are. From the top of one hill they can see the next, and the next, rising toward an uncertain horizon, and he understands that this place is much larger than the vague place he came from. Perhaps he could walk another ten days before reaching its far edge, where the desert would enclose it with its fiery landscape. He hopes they do not have to go that far. Man from Sand he may be, but he would happily never set eyes on the desert again.

"Why is everyone so fascinated with me?" he asks his guardian as they continue on their journey.

"Because you came out of the desert, and there is nothing beyond."

"There's the city," he said. "Sometimes I still dream of it."

A troubled look crosses her eyes. Even with age settling in her skin, she is as beautiful now as when she found him.

"Those dreams are nightmares," she says. "And those drawings . . ."

"No one believes them," he says, because no one ever has. Sometimes even he thinks of them as only a dream—a city built entirely in his mind, a hundred times larger than their largest village, which will fade over time. But sometimes he can almost taste the dampness of its stone, smell the market streets, and see the towering spires rising toward its center, hear the excited chatter of its many inhabitants echoed between buildings and down alleys. He can see the woman who might have been his mother back then, tutoring him in a language that stays with him now; he can accept the vastness of the place, the imposing concentration of buildings that are so close they seem to be constructed on top of one another. He can see the city and himself in it, and there is a sense of loss that he cannot comprehend, even in dreams.

"Only because they cannot be true," she says.

"My skin is paler than anyone's, even in the sun. And that language I can speak—"

"Is not one you should!" she snaps. A thousand times she has told him this, refusing his attempts to explore the language with her. He has been referred to physicians and mythmakers, and all of them have reached the same conclusion: that he was infected by a desert sprite, one of the cruel phantoms that stalk the sands close to the Heartlands, and it has jumbled his mind. Sometimes, in his darkest moments, he even believes this himself. These physicians and mythmakers have done their best to cure him of the affliction, but still the words come to him, and with the words are images, and those images carry the weight of memory.

He's confused, and his guardian says that this journey will help cure his confusion.

They walk for several more days, passing many small settlements and accepting the hospitality of their inhabitants. It's an exploration of food and drink as well, because everything here is affected by landscape. Wines taste different from valley to valley, and fruits and vegetables pick up diverse tangs from the soils. The land is rich and lush, and Rufus's strange memories of the city are sour and tainted in comparison.

At the pinnacle of one hill, he looks to the east and sees a stain on the landscape. It is miles distant—such distances that he is still becoming used to—but even from here its scope is huge. It is many shades of gray, smothering the landscape in that direction, filling valleys, crushing hills. The sky above it is similar in color, as if leached of blue vitality by what lies beneath. He can see the shattered remains of giant towers reaching to the sky with skeletal fingers. Around their feet lie other tumbled ruins, and all his senses seem affected by the sight. He imagines the smell of ash and age, tastes grit on the clear air, and hears mournful whispers of faraway breezes. Around this unknown place, the hillsides are green and the trees proud and tall. Lushness surrounds the ruin.

He is shocked silent for a while. This is not his city, though its scale is staggering, yet it is the first time he has been aware of its existence—no one has mentioned it, and it appears nowhere in the Heartlanders' lives, songs, stories, or history.

"Where is that?" he asks, voice barely rising above the breeze. He imagines the breeze coming in from that ruined place and talking to him, but he does not know its language.

"Somewhere nobody can go," she says.

"You never told me," he says. "It's never been mentioned. All those drawings, my dreams, my visions of the place I came—"

"Because it is nothing *like* your drawings!" she snaps. "That is . . ." She waves one hand, eyes averted. "It's a skeleton of old times. There's only disease there, and death."

"Have you ever been?"

"Why would I?" she asks, and there's an innocence about her. "Why would *anyone*? The land around it is left unfarmed and wild, so that its badness can be locked in. And even from this far away, it's death. Look what we have here!" She indicates the beautiful countryside around them. "Why would anyone *want* to go there?" And they carry on walking without once looking back.

That place disturbs him for some time. A cancer in the Heartlands, a blank spot in the landscape's lush presence— and also in the consciousness of those living there—its solidity is a terrifying thing. He can understand the Heartlanders subconsciously steering clear of somewhere like that, but their denial is a conscious decision.

That's not my city, he thinks, and though it is often on his mind, he never speaks of it again.

Days later, sitting beside a campfire watching children from a small village putting on a dance show for them, he feels another pain, this one in the back of his hand. He cries out and raises his hand, but that confuses him, because it never actually happened—

—and there was darkness once more, and the distant whisper of Dragarians in wonder, and more memory.

"This is it," she says. "Last time I came here I was not much older than you." There are travelers and traders in the Heartlands, and he has spent enjoyable days back in the village mingling with them. But there are also those who choose not to travel, and his guardian is such a person. Her life is full and rich, she is contented, and other than her pilgrimage to the Heart and Mind—the single journey that everyone *must* take at some time—she has hardly ever been far beyond her own valley.

This valley is very different. From a hilltop, he looks down and is amazed. On the floor of the valley is a giant structure—except when he looks closer, he sees irregularities and anomalies that indicate that it's something natural, not man-made. It is dome-shaped, its surface a deep red with darker, almost black striations webbing out from the center. Steam or gas is emitting from openings around its edge, and it is these rising and dispersing clouds that bring into context just how large the thing is. They drift slowly, their movement minute compared to the red dome, and because he's concentrating on one such steam column, he does not see the eyes.

"It sees you," she whispers. "It always recognizes a new visitor."

"It's amazing," he says, because even though she has told him about the Heart and Mind, nothing could prepare him for this.

It is the heart of our land, she'd said, *bearing the weight of the Heartland's health and well-being. And it is the mind of the land, our conscience. It keeps us well and safe. It is a physical thing, something we can see and touch. Dig deep*

*enough and you will touch it, because its breadth and influ-
ence underpin the ground itself.*

It's your god, he'd said in wonder, because he could think
of no other word to describe it. She had seemed amused,
perhaps confused, but she had not confirmed or denied his
observation.

Where does it come from? he'd asked another time.

There is history, she'd replied, and he'd seen the concentration on her face as she tried to answer his question while
keeping back knowledge that must yet be forbidden to him.
*And deep in history there is before and after . . . and the
Heart and Mind was created at the point when before became
after. One of the Heartlanders' saviors was called the Artist,
and he created the Heart and Mind to ensure our survival.
He was the only Artist. But his influence lives on.*

Artist?

A sculptor of natural things. She'd shaken her head then,
left him to his thoughts, and he'd wondered how and when
she had told him too much.

"Don't you feel it?" she asks now. "Don't you sense its interest? It knows me, and I can feel that too, but you . . ." Then
she trails off and gasps, going to her knees and grabbing his
arm to prevent herself from tumbling over.

"What do you . . . ?" he begins, and then he, too, gasps, because he can feel it, and he sees it as well. There are dozens of
openings across the dome's gentle concave surface, each of
them housing something that glitters and blinks.

Eyes. They're looking at him. He feels their interest, their
consideration, their shattering intellect. He's being analyzed
and assessed, and they are seeing much further than his skin.
He feels something deep inside, rooting gently in places he
does not know or understand, opening doors in his mind he
has never seen, feeling their way to consider what these
hidden places might contain. And he shouts, not through
shock or a sense of invasion, because both of those are gentle things . . . but from the sense that he can never look into
these rooms himself. They're buried away so deep that to un-
cover them could well make him mad.

"The Heart and Mind is knowing you," she says. "Now you're part of its world and part of ours."

"When do we go down?" he asks.

She stands uncertainly, still holding on to his arm to support herself, and he can feel the cool slickness of her sweaty hands.

"We don't," she says. "Only the Tenders ever approach closer than this."

He scans the slopes of the shallow valley, but there are no signs of any other living things.

"They hide unless they're needed," she says. "They're its *servants*." The stress she put on that word leads him to wonder whether she really means *slaves*.

She gasps and staggers again, short nails scraping the skin across his wrist and hand as she tries to hang on. "Ohhh . . ." she says, not really a word at all.

He goes to his knees as well.

The Heart and Mind surges with a rush of surprise at what it has found inside him. Several columns of steam vent, the landscape viewed through them stained red. The valley is no longer still and peaceful. There's no difference in the sounds and smells of that place, but the air is now loaded with a potential previously absent.

From several points across the slopes, yellow-clad men and women appear, hurrying toward the valley floor, stumbling as if awakened from a long slumber. None of them looks up toward the ridges; they only have eyes for the Heart and Mind.

But his guardian is staring at him. He has never seen an expression like that before, and she will never look at him the same way again.

Chapter 19

They sat on the wall until dawn, and Peer was already starting to suspect that Nophel was mad. He had brought them here
in those sickening Bellower transports, twisting their stom-
achs, crushing their insides, bruising their limbs, and promising that his Unseen friends could get them into Dragar's
Canton. And while it was true that she had seen him fade away,
she thought perhaps that was a madness rather than a gift.

He talked to himself as the sun rose across the Northern
Reservoir to their right, and what he said never made any
sense.

Malia was seated beside Peer on the bench, asleep. Her head
tilted forward, chin resting on her chest, and every now and
then she snored gently, startling herself into a new position.
Since the journey through the Bellower tubes, she had been
quiet and withdrawn, not the hard, forthright woman Peer had
grown to know in a few short days. Tiredness was some of it,
but there was also a quiet shock about the Watcher woman
now. She had been shown things about the city that she
had never suspected.

The rising sun splashed from the reservoir and smeared
across Dragar's Canton's domes. They were perfectly engi-
neered, and looked almost impossible rising beyond the northern finger of Crescent. There was little detail to them that
enabled her to judge their size, but the things around them gave
scale: flocks of red sparrows fleeting here and there, almost
lost against the structures; trees sprouting around their bases

where rainwater runoff made the ground particularly fertile; and the dry canal marking the canton's southern perimeter, little more than a vague line from here yet reputedly filled with all manner of traps and stinging things. The Dragarian domes were the most astonishing things in Echo City, and yet, lifeless and still, they were all but ignored.

"When the sun rises fully, we'll need to get away from here," Peer said. "If we're seen loitering, there'll be questions."

"I'm doing my best."

"You're just sitting there! You have been all night."

"I'm trying to find my way back to them," Nophel said, leaning in close. Peer was sure she caught a whiff of rot from the man's distorted face, and she saw several smears of dried fluids from where some of his boils had burst. She had to keep reminding herself that he had saved their lives.

"Look harder," Peer said. "The Blades will have our descriptions by now, and when one of their own is killed . . ." She let the sentence trail off, because it did not need finishing. *They won't take us into custody.*

Nophel sat up straighter. "Hit me," he said.

"What?"

"Strike me. I don't yet have control over this, but last time it manifested was in self-defense."

"I really don't think—"

Nophel gasped, turned away from Peer, and then she saw his shoulders slump as he relaxed. His head nodded forward, and for a moment she thought he'd fallen asleep or worse. She glanced back at Malia—still asleep. She almost laughed.

"And neither do I," Nophel said. "But, Alexia, we need your help."

"Nophel?" Peer asked. She stood and backed away, scanning around the disfigured man to see who or what he might be talking with. There was no one there. Nophel glanced at her.

"No, she's safe."

"Who are you—"

"She's a Watcher," he continued, nodding at the sleeping Malia.

"Malia!" Peer said. She glanced back and forth along the

wide head of the Marcellan Canton wall, at the benches and walls and small towers that marked the stairwells leading down. No one was there with them, but that would change soon. If Nophel was planning something, now would be the time. *"Malia!"*

Malia snapped awake and stood, drawing her short sword with a comforting hiss of metal on leather.

"Don't be scared," Nophel said. "She's here." He pointed beyond the end of the stone bench, to a place where the paved stone surface seemed shadowed with moisture. "And she recognizes you, Peer. She says to say sorry. Your torture is a weight on her mind."

"My torture?"

"She . . ." Nophel paused, head to one side. "Three years ago. She was the guide for the Blades who took you."

"What's happening?" Malia asked.

"We have to follow," Nophel said.

"I can't even *see* her," Peer said.

"But I can." He stood and smiled into space, reaching out one hand and clasping the air. "Really, you can trust them," he said quietly. "Somewhere private, and I'll tell you what we need."

"I can't even *hear* her," Malia said. She was still wielding the sword, but there was no threat in the air.

"*Could* we, in time?" Peer asked. Nophel nodded, evidently pleased that she'd acknowledged what was happening.

"I think so," he said. "I hope so."

"So we follow you?"

"Yes."

"We don't have much time," Peer said. "If you want to take advantage of the lead the Bellowers gave us, tell your Unseen friend to hurry."

"She hears you well enough."

She hears and sees us; we hear and see nothing, Peer thought. It was not a good place for trust to begin. But the sun was rising, time was passing, and she felt urgency plucking at her heart. Perhaps the time for caution was over.

Peer nodded. "We should go."

* * *

"I was watching you for a while. There's something strange about you. Those other two were like every other person we see and covet, their flesh glowing with substance. But you . . . A friend came and told me you were back, and I thought you'd come to join us. Thought you'd given in. But, instead, you've done something different. The Blue Water's effect is about you—I can smell it, taste it, and I haven't smelled or tasted anything in a while—but you're not Unseen. They follow you following me, and they can't hear a word of this, can they? They really can't."

"Not now they can't," Nophel said. "But maybe I can change that."

"How? Why?"

He thought about that as they followed Alexia's slight gray form around the central staircase column. They were almost back down to the street, and he could hear Peer's and Malia's nervous footsteps behind him.

"What's she saying?" Malia asked, but Nophel shook his head without turning around. He had the advantage here.

"Because I need the Unseen to help us," Nophel said. Alexia laughed a little, a gentle coughing sound that was barely audible. He guessed she did not laugh very much.

"The man beneath the domes," she said.

"What do you—"

"Somewhere private," Alexia said, and she spoke no more. She led them across a narrow street and into a bustling square, where traders and food vendors were jostling for space. She barged through without a care, and anytime she shoved into someone, it was Nophel they laid eyes on when they turned around. He was familiar with the expressions he saw—brief anger, turning into fearful disgust. No one would punch him even if they wanted to, for fear of dirtying their hands.

She's doing this on purpose, Nophel thought, angry at Alexia's behavior. But he supposed she had reason to feel jealous. He was flesh and blood again, after all.

They entered a building with one tumbled wall and a fire-blackened façade. Alexia had no need to be secretive, but Nophel signaled for the others to halt, making sure they were not observed. Alexia called something tauntingly from inside the open door, but Nophel could not quite hear her words.

The coast clear, the three of them entered the ruined building. It had been a large home once, but fire had gutted the insides, leaving only scorched walls standing. Timber floors were burned away to expose the sunken basement beneath, and, looking up, Nophel could see dawn sky through the remains of the roof. But he could make out no other Unseen, and for that at least he was glad. She had brought them somewhere deserted to talk, not a place where he would be surrounded by fading, sad remnants. He had no desire to be reminded of what he might become.

But I'm different, he thought. *Even she noticed that.* He looked down at his hand and willed invisibility, but all he conjured was Alexia's nervous question.

"Lost the talent, Nophel?"

"Not all the time," he said, and thought, *Has she ever seen anyone like me?*

Alexia was looking at Malia with undisguised dislike, and at Peer with uncertainty.

"Why should I trust them?"

"Why *shouldn't* you?"

Alexia regarded him for a few moments but did not reply.

"You mentioned the man beneath the domes?" Nophel said.

"Perhaps I shouldn't have."

"Peer," Nophel said, "could you describe Rufus?"

"Where is she?" Peer asked, and Nophel pointed. "Touch her face," Peer said. Nophel did so.

Peer came forward and narrowed her eyes. "I see . . . shadow."

"Now that you know she's there, you see more than most," Nophel said, and Alexia reached out quickly to touch Peer's face.

Peer pulled back, startled, and pressed her hand flat across her mouth.

"Rufus is tall," Malia said. "White hair. The greenest eyes I've ever seen. Wears strange clothes—light and strong but not leather. And if they haven't taken it from him, he carries a shoulder bag with unusual things inside."

Alexia was frowning at the description, and Nophel knew that she recognized it. So without any prompting from Peer and Malia—and without pausing to consider whether it was a good or bad idea—he told the Unseen who Rufus was and where he came from.

A loaded silence gripped them all. Nophel expected Malia to berate him, but she did not. He thought Alexia might laugh dismissively, but she simply stared at him.

It was Peer who broke the silence. "So you see why we have to get him back."

"And I should help why?" Alexia asked.

Nophel told the others what she had said, but already the answer was with him, obvious in his flesh and blood.

"There's a cure when you thought there wasn't," he said. "When he gave it to me, Dane Marcellan called it White Water."

Alexia did not act surprised, nor did she ask why a Marcellan would cure Nophel and not anyone else, but anger burned bright in her eyes. "Now that you've told us, the Unseen will look for it themselves."

"And knowing that, Dane will keep it where you can never find it."

"You think he'll listen to you?" Alexia asked, and Nophel knew just how far removed she was. It did not concern him that he was using her—there was very little guilt, even knowing that the chance of procuring the White Water for them was almost nil. But the fact that she actually believed there was a chance was a mark of her utter desperation. Accepting help from such a woman would be a great risk. He looked back at Peer and Malia, saw that they knew what he had offered, and then nodded.

"Yes. He listens to me. Help us, and I'll help you all."

"All," Alexia said softly. "There aren't many of us left. Only those like me, who hang on. Who still see themselves as part of this city."

"And that's how you know about Rufus?" he asked, probing for more information now that she did not seem so defensive.

But perhaps Alexia was not as damaged by her curse as he thought. She smiled at him—and at the others, as if they could see—then played her final card. "Your blood," she said. "Whatever was given to you is in your blood."

"Go on," Nophel said softly.

"A trade," Alexia said. "Think about this: You know what we are and where we can go, because you were one of us for a time. We have days to fill. The city hides fewer secrets from us than from most other people, but the enigma that has intrigued me and those close to me for so long is *apart* from the city—Dragar's Canton. We know the best routes in, the best out, the ones they guard and those they don't. And when they use guards, we know how best to distract them. We know some of the domes' insides, though they're not easy to know. The Dragarians suspect, but they're a superstitious people, and they consider us as phantoms of phantoms. So we'll lead you in and help you find your man, and we'll help you bring him out. But first you must offer some of your blood."

"They want my blood," Nophel whispered.

Malia advanced on him, drawing her short knife.

"No!" Peer said.

"Only a little," Nophel said, holding out his arm. "Only a little."

The Unseen watched hungrily as Malia's blade opened a vein. Then she cupped her hands and let the blood collect.

Malia left the room, but Peer had to watch. She wanted to understand. She had seen some of what the Baker could do—the Bellowers and Scopes, belonging to generations of Bakers past; the new Baker's Pserans and chopped fighters—but none of it compared with this. If she had not been educated enough to know that there was no such thing, she would have called this magic.

Blood dribbled from Nophel's nicked arm, but instead of splashing to the floor, it collected in midair, a small patch at first, and then a spreading, shifting pool. A few drops passed through and hit the burned floor. Most did not.

How will they do it? she wondered. *Drink? Or will they have to . . .*

Her question was answered for her. The Unseen began to appear. Contact with Nophel's blood seemed to be enough.

Barely a shadow at first, her hands manifested from nowhere—faint images that quickly grew more solid as they extended into arms, body, head. Alexia's amazed face appeared out of nowhere, and she looked up at Peer in fear.

"I see you," Peer said, and Alexia dropped the blood pooled in her hand. She stepped back, bloody hands held up to ward off an attack that was not coming. *She's been invisible for too long*, Peer thought, *and it's driven her mad.*

But Nophel calmed her, stepping in close, and the Unseen shook where she was backed against the soot-covered wall.

"How . . . how do you . . . ?" Alexia asked.

"I don't know," he said. "Last time I faded was when—"

The Unseen looked at her hands, frowning, and in moments she started to fade again. Then she snapped back to reality, and this time when she looked up at Peer, all the fear was gone. In its place, power. She smiled, but Peer could not smile back.

"You can control it?" Nophel whispered.

"Malia!" Peer called. "You can come in now." As the Watcher entered, she caught sight of the phantom in the corner, Alexia's smile just fading away to nothing.

"That is wrong," Malia said.

"Yet it works. You'll help us?" Peer asked.

"Yes." Alexia's voice came in from a distance, fading away more finally than an echo.

Nophel was wrapping a strip of cloth around his arm, stemming the flow of blood. He looked pale, nodding into the darkness as he listened to words that were little more than faint whispers to Peer.

"She's going to get more help," Nophel said, distracted. "She says it'll take three of them to get three of us in."

"But you're one of them," Malia said.

"She doesn't see it that way." He tried tying the cloth but it slipped off, and Peer went to help. She tied the ends across the small wound, noticing him wince as she pulled tight, and she wondered how much pain he'd gone through every day of his life. His facial growths were raw, one of them seeping a pinkish fluid.

"How does she control it?" Peer asked.

"I don't know." He stared into the corner where Alexia stood unseen. "Will you help me?" he asked. Peer heard no response, but Nophel smiled uncertainly.

"When are we going?" Malia asked.

"As soon as she returns with the others." Nophel stared at the bloodied cloth, nodding his thanks to Peer.

"That's some powerful blood," she said quietly.

"Yes."

"You knew?"

"I had no idea." He turned away and sat against a wall, head back, eyes closed. "She's gone."

Peer paced the room, passing close to Malia every time but saying nothing. The Watcher woman was checking her weapons. A tension hung in the air, but none of them could break it.

Almost magic, Peer thought again. What else could there be in Echo City that none of them had ever seen or heard of?

Later, Alexia's appearance in the doorway surprised them all. She was almost strutting, reveling in visibility, and she stood in the center of the room.

Nophel sighed, stood, and untied the cloth from around his arm.

"We'll go straight after this," the woman said. She looked at Peer and Malia, eyeing them up and down, dismissive and superior. "I wonder if his blood won't act the other way?"

"I'd rather stay seen, thank you," Malia said, her voice poison.

"Me too," said Peer. "I don't think I could . . ."

"Slinking through the shadows," Malia said. "Like *beasts*."

Alexia raised an eyebrow. "And you're asking for my help?"

"No," Peer said. "He is." She nodded at Nophel, the man who had brought them salvation, and Alexia's expression softened.

"I have an idea," she said, bringing out a small ball of twine. "I'll talk you through the plan while we're tying this."

Nophel broke the dried blood over his wound. Fresh blood flowed. Two other Unseen faded in, amazed. The room felt

smaller. And Alexia started to explain how they would infiltrate Dragar's Canton.

As they left the ruined house, Peer could feel their sense of
salvation. It was as palpable as the smell of roasting from a
nearby market. The three Unseen exuded it, each of them
visible for now so that they could experience the simple joy of
being noticed. Alexia was connected to Nophel by a wound
length of string—Peer had not understood the sense in that,
but he'd seemed happy—and she was walking with a short,
thin man who had yet to speak. His eyes were open with a
child's awe, and she wondered how he had been seeing the
world before now. His Scarlet Blade uniform was faded and
dirty, he stank, but his enthusiasm was infectious, and as they
followed the wall's route across the north of Marcellan Canton, Peer allowed herself to believe that they might be able to
achieve this.

You follow us, Alexia had said. *When we get close to Dragar's, we'll travel Unseen; the string will connect us, and
we'll be far enough ahead to spot any trouble before it happens. We know the routes in and out, and each of us has been
there several times. Keep the string taut. If you feel it go
slack, that means we've stopped and there's trouble.*

What's inside? Peer had asked.

Alexia had shaken her head softly. *Best just to see.*

They soon entered another building, and the three Unseen
laughed and chatted like old friends.

Alexia smiled at Peer and the others and said, "We have a
lot to thank you for."

"And you know how to show that thanks," Malia said. She
was tied to a tall man, his face still beaming from being noticed. In the streets, a group of children had pointed and
laughed at his unruly mop of ginger hair, and he'd ruffled it
up to make them giggle more. Even the children's guardian
had seemed unconcerned, so open and innocent was the tall
man's delight.

"The basement of this place has an entrance to a tunnel,"
Alexia said. "We've used it before, and we keep a stockpile

of oil torches inside. We'll be going down into the dark, then beneath the border through the first Echo."

"More darkness," Peer said. "More caves and torches. And the sun's only just come up."

"Hopefully it won't take long," Alexia said.

"They guard these places?" Malia asked.

"Most of them, yes. But there are cracks and crevices and old paths that even the Dragarians don't know." She smiled at Malia's obvious doubt. "Trust me. This will be our last time Unseen, and now we want to live as much as anyone."

The three Unseen faded from view, their faces masks of concentration, and the short man connected to Peer looked wretched as he slipped away. *It won't be long*, she wanted to say, but he had yet to speak a word to her. Communicating now, just as he was vanishing, seemed wrong.

Nophel watched them fade, and for an instant he shimmered in and out of focus. He caught Peer watching him and smiled.

"You can . . . ?" she asked, and Nophel nodded.

"Alexia told me," he said. "She's been Unseen for so long, her sense of self has distanced. If I view myself as others see me, not how I see myself . . ." He flickered in and out of focus again, and the power before her scared Peer more than ever.

Unseen once again, they went down. Nophel and Alexia left first, and Nophel kept himself visible so that Peer and Malia could follow him. Peer and the thin man were next, and behind her she heard the gentle footsteps of the tall ginger man as he led Malia.

Through an extensive basement, into tunnels, and then caverns, Peer and the others followed people they could not see into a place they could not imagine. Dragar's Canton had been hidden away from the rest of Echo City for more than five hundred years, and though there were written accounts about what it had been like *before* the concealment—a normal place, with buildings similar to those throughout the city, ruled by priests of the generally benevolent Dragarian religion—no one knew for sure what had become of it since. There had been conjecture for a while, and sometimes there still was, but it had become a silent part of the city, forgotten by most because it was as distant and unknown as the Markoshi Desert. *An enigma on their doorstep*, Penler had called it once, and he should know. His book about the Dragarians had resulted in his banishment, but even he knew little. It was a book of legends and myths, considered insidious because so few knew even them, he'd told Peer once over a bottle of wine. *The most amazing place in the city, and nobody thinks about it. It's just the six domes, that's all. They're regarded as sculptures now. Even kids don't dare one another to go out there and stand close to them anymore, because it's boring. Nothing can happen. Nothing ever does. At least, not that we see.* Pushed by Peer, tongue loosened by more wine, he'd smiled and leaned back, staring at the cracked ceiling of his adopted home in Skulk. *The Dragarians can't be fools,* he'd said. *They'll want to know what the rest of the city is doing. They might be closed off from us, but we're no mystery to them.*

And we're going there now, Peer thought. *Penler would be jealous. He should be here with me.* And she swore to herself that given even the slightest opportunity, she would see her old friend again to tell him everything she knew.

Down in the first Echo of Crescent's northern extremes, they found themselves crossing a dead landscape eerily similar to that which surrounded the Baker's rooms. It was strange being led by the Unseen, the string Peer held wound around her hand connected to nothing. The far end faded slowly. She shone her torch ahead and it illuminated nothing, swallowed by shadow where the short man must be. Nophel had told them that the Blue Water acted on the mind of the observer, and she wondered what that meant if the Unseen did not even deflect light. The word *magic* crossed her mind again, but she was a pragmatist, and the term held connotations she could never entertain.

It was a wide-open Echo, apparently flat, and they followed a trail north that must have been well used in times gone by. The track marks were deep, and here and there they were flooded with dark, thick water. Peer was certain she saw ripples in the puddles, but no one else seemed to notice.

They walked quickly, covering several miles to the canton's border without incident. She glanced back at Malia several times, but they exchanged nothing more than a gentle, nervous smile. Perhaps talking through someone was too much for both of them.

Eventually Nophel paused, head tilted to one side, and then said, "We have to extinguish the torches from here."

"It'll be black as the Chasm!" Malia said.

"The Unseen will lead the way."

Peer doused her torch and watched its pilot light fade slowly away. Malia grumbled but did the same, and moments later it was utterly dark. Eyes open or closed, Peer could see nothing, and she felt the gentle tug on her string. *Here we go*, she thought, realizing just how much they were trusting Nophel and, in turn, the Unseen. None of them seemed to have any love for the city. Rufus was possible salvation, but to them he might be simply another dispossessed, another wanderer of dark places whom they cared about as little as they seemed to care about anyone.

They could slit her throat at any moment, or steal her torch and cut her loose. But worrying could not help her now.

She followed and discovered that, with sight taken from her, her ears became more sensitive. Whereas before she had not been able to hear the short man's footsteps, now she could just hear the subtle, gritty whisper of his feet crossing the ground. He seemed aware of this, because the string slackened, and she found herself following only the confident steps of that invisible man.

Then things began to change. Their breathing became more audible, and the sense of distance around them was replaced by a feeling of intense solidity. When Peer turned her head slowly from side to side, her hearing changed, though standing still she was not sure she could hear anything. She reached out and touched rock, and a sharp tug on her string urged her forward. Still walking, two more quick tugs sent her a definite message: *Keep to yourself.* Wherever they were, the Unseen must be afraid.

Trying to regulate her breathing, Peer concentrated on following her guide. They kept the string quite taut again, which meant that he'd gone on ahead of her, and at the beginning she found it difficult to step forward with any confidence. She could walk into a wall, or a hole, or a Dragarian waiting to slice and kill. But if that happened, they were all discovered. Besides, there was little she could do to change the situation. If she lit her torch, she would give them all away. She was down here for Rufus, and for everyone else. For the first time in a while, she wondered where Gorham was and what he was doing, and she hoped that he was safe.

She would never have believed that blindness would inspire timelessness, but when Nophel's torch flared alight ahead of her and he signaled that they could do the same, she had no idea how much time had passed. She had little opportunity to find out. The curtain before them took her breath away, and any other thoughts fled her mind.

At first she thought it was fire, but of course she would have seen it long before now. Stretching up into the darkness above them, beyond the reach of her torch, the curtain was a shimmering, moving thing, rustling in an absent breeze. It could have been water, but she heard no splashing or pouring. It could have been metal, but surely it would have clanged and creaked where it bent and moved so much?

"What the fuck is that?" Malia said softly.

"We're beneath the canal," Nophel said. "When the Dragarians dug that, they were working down here also. Alexia says . . ." He drifted off, listening to a voice Peer could not hear. "She says they worked deep down through the Echoes, cutting even their history off from our own. Different barriers in each Echo. This is one of the hardest to get through, but also the quickest."

"But what is it?" Peer asked, unable to keep the quaver from her voice. There was something unnatural about the way this curtain moved before them, almost as if . . .

"Looks like it's alive," Malia said.

Alexia appeared before them, fading into existence and frowning in concentration or pain. *Maybe it* does *hurt*, Peer thought, and she surprised herself by hoping that it did.

"Not alive like anything we'd understand," the Unseen said. She sighed, rubbed at her face, then turned toward the barrier. "It's soul-fire. That's what we call it, anyway. I'm not sure it has any other name, don't even know whether the Dragarians *have* named it. Probably not. They just made it and placed it here."

"What does it do?" Peer asked, already filled with dread.

"Doesn't matter," Malia said. "We just need to get through."

"It steals your soul if you touch it," Alexia said, smiling. "But it doesn't kill you. Leaves you walking. There are several Unseen, on this side or the other, existing without a soul because of that . . . thing."

"How can that be?" Peer said quietly, almost to herself. It was a dreadful idea, fantastic, and something she had never heard of before.

"We know the way through," Alexia said. "All you have to do is follow."

"And you found the route how?" Malia asked.

"Trial and error."

"And the wandering soulless are your errors?"

"No, they're their own. Do you want to find this Rufus or not?"

"Of course," Nophel said. "We're working together, and there has to be trust." Peer nodded at him, but his single good eye could not convey any such emotion. It moved from sad to pained and back again, and she had rarely seen any other expression. She wondered what it must be like holding all that inside.

"Keep the strings short and taut," Alexia said, as she frowned and faded again. She closed her eyes as she went, and Peer wondered whether she was praying.

It struck her that she knew none of the Unseen's religious allegiances. Originally Scarlet Blades, they would have been raised Hanharan, steeped in that religion from a very early age and sermonized regularly once they were initiated into the Blades. And even three years ago, Alexia had worked against the Watchers, leading to Peer's imprisonment and torture. But since their transformation, surely much would have changed.

Now was not the time to ask. Indeed, if there had ever been a time, it was long past.

They approached the soul-fire. Peer concentrated, watching

the tight string before her, turning left when it veered that way and then heading straight into the shimmering curtain. It stank of a baby's skin and a rash-plague sufferer's final breath. She closed her eyes and breathed in deeply, and—

The faces scream and rage, their pain illimitable, the shrieks beyond any contemplation of sanity, and they surge around her like walls of stone flowing as fluid, always threatening to crush her, squeeze the air from her lungs, suck the blood from her veins, and she opens her mouth to scream but can taste only the soul-fire, rancid things, and fine grapes.

Why didn't you tell us? she thought, and then they were through. She went to her knees and heard Nophel's groan ahead of her, but her string quickly pulled taut.

"You could have warned us," she said, but if the Unseen responded, she did not hear. He tugged at the string and she stood, glancing back at Malia's pale face behind her.

"Well, that was nice," Malia gasped. Behind her, the soul-fire made no sound as it fell and burned.

They moved on, their Unseen guides not pausing. The ground headed upward, steepening sharply. They followed the slope, then at some unknown signal turned left, approaching a wall of rock that loomed from the darkness like the edge of the world.

Nophel glanced back over his shoulder and whispered, "Sometimes guards, sometimes not. She'll go ahead to see." His string relaxed and the end hit the ground, and Peer saw his head move slightly as he watched Alexia's progress.

She returned quickly, manifesting again as she walked and sighing when she stopped, resting her hands on her knees for a moment.

"Sick?" Peer asked.

"Been running," she said, but she was not out of breath. "It's quiet. But beyond the wall, some of their things keep watch. You have your swords?"

"What things?" Malia asked.

"Like hounds, except slower. Blind. Don't let them bite you." Alexia looked at where the other two Unseen would be standing. She gave a quick hand signal, then started to fade again.

"What was that?" Peer asked. "Alexia?" But the Unseen was already moving away, then she disappeared completely, the end of Nophel's string grasped in her hand. "Nophel?" Peer asked.

"Just telling them to keep watch," he said. "As must we all."

The gap in the stone wall was obvious only when they drew very close and she saw the end of Nophel's string pass inside. He followed, and then Peer was in as well, walls brushing both arms as the path narrowed even further. She held the torch in the same hand as her string and tried to reach her sword, but the little man pulled her on, and she could not turn enough between those sheer walls to draw her weapon.

From ahead, she heard a quiet, strangled shout. Nophel's torch danced about, then extinguished altogether.

"Here!" he shouted. "Peer!"

She ran, shoving the Unseen man aside and bursting from the short tunnel. Nophel was on the ground with a black creature standing over him, its jaws wide as it lowered its head toward his throat. As Peer was reaching for her sword, it screamed, darting its jaw to the right at the wound that had suddenly opened in its flank. Alexia withdrew her sword and buried it in the creature's shoulder. Nophel slid aside as the creature dropped dead.

"You all right?" Peer asked, and he nodded sharply.

"Watch for yourself," he said, standing. She did, shining the torch around as the end of her string led her forward again. She smiled uncertainly, hoping that if he was looking, the short man would see it as an apology.

Several shadowy shapes stalked them. Malia's small crossbow sang, a thud and a whine signifying a hit. Two more creatures came at Nophel and Peer. She gripped her sword hard and then stepped aside. The first thing snapped at where she'd been standing, and she swept the blade down across the back of its neck. It stuck fast in the thing's flesh, driving it to the ground. It died without a whimper.

Malia's crossbow whispered again, and then the things were dead.

"That wasn't too hard," Malia said.

"Alexia says there are usually Dragarians controlling them," Nophel said. "This is the first time she's heard of them being loose down here."

They moved on, heading upward through carved tunnels and encountering no more obstacles. Several times Alexia called a halt while she explored ahead, but the Unseen never found anything to concern them. At one point she and Nophel had a whispered conversation, which he relayed back to Peer and Malia.

"She's never known it so quiet down here. We're taking one of the main routes in from the Echoes. Usually the Unseen go in other directions, passing through guarded caverns or traps. But there are no traps set, and she's seen no guards."

"Which means what?" Peer asked.

"It means they don't care anymore," Malia said. Peer closed her eyes as a shiver went through her, and when she looked again, Nophel was listening to Alexia's unheard words once more.

"We're almost there," he said. "A few hundred steps and we'll be able to see inside the first dome."

"And what's in there?" Peer asked, but Alexia apparently did not respond. Nophel headed off with his string taut before him. Peer and Malia followed, and for the first time Peer smelled something that could be described as fresh air. It carried the mouthwatering hint of baking bread, and she realized just how hungry she was. *Dragarian food*, she thought. *Might not agree.* But they had been removed from the world for only five hundred years.

How different could they be?

Alexia brought them up into the bed of a dried canal, hiding them where it passed into an area of raised ground piled against the inside of the dome. Here they could sit and watch with impunity, taking time to observe, to see, to *understand*.

And to wonder.

In enclosing their land, the Dragarians had made themselves aware of the air. Much of the ground that Peer could see seemed to have been abandoned—tall buildings had tumbled, and lower structures were fallen into disrepair. Windows were smashed and doors broken from hinges. The Dragarians had started building up and out, and from where they squatted she could see no large expanses of open space inside the dome. Elaborate bridges spanned between buildings that seemed to hang in midair. Rope ladders rose and fell. Networks of cables were strung at apparently random angles and places, and directly above where they hid she could see dozens of cables fixed into the inner surface of the dome structure. The wall curved inward above them, and it was encrusted with hundreds of small structures, many of them interlinked by walkways and bridges. Windows stared out upon the space, and lights flickered in some.

It was not dark inside. Great swaths of the dome were left clear of fixtures, and sunlight somehow shone through. Peer had no idea how. There had never been talk of the domes having differing materials in their structures—no glass sections, no area that appeared to slide open and closed as the sun rose and set—and yet here it was, warm fresh sunlight streaming inside and bathing the interior. It even found its way down to the ground, courtesy of the mirrored finish to many of the hanging structures.

Mechanical things slid across that massive space on fine wires, clouds of smoke hanging behind them and dispersing slowly to the air. Peer could hear the gently clasping wheels that must drag them along the cables and the rattle of cogs and springs.

On the way in, she'd had time to wonder what she would see. A continuation of what was outside, perhaps, an echo of Echo City yet on its own level. And there were some who believed that this society must have gone to ruin, that after the construction of these incredible domes, the Dragarians' isolation would have caused strife, war, and regression. These people expected the domes to be inhabited by the animallike descendants of Dragar's believers, and the ruins themselves would be a wild hunting ground.

Surely no one could have anticipated this.

"Where are they all?" Malia whispered, and Peer gasped. She'd been so amazed by the scenery that she had not yet noticed it was uninhabited.

"I don't know," Nophel said. "Alexia, will you . . . ?" She was already fading in again, her mouth open in surprise. The other two Unseen followed suit. They leaned against the canal bank with the others, looking pale and exhausted but most of all amazed.

"I've never seen it deserted," Alexia said. "It's always . . . alive."

"I don't like it," the thin man said, and to Peer he sounded like a frightened child.

"So if they've all gone," Malia said, "how the fuck are we going to find Rufus?"

Peer closed her eyes, breathing deeply and yet unable to drive down the burgeoning fear. "It's obvious," she said. "Don't you see?"

"No," Malia said angrily.

"You know who they think Rufus is. They think he's Dragar. We find where all the Dragarians have gone, and there we'll find him."

"Oh," Alexia said.

Malia snorted. "Right. That'll be easy."

"Easy or not, we have to do it," Peer said. "If we can't, we might as well decide now: die in here, or die outside."

Chapter 20

Gorham watched Nadielle work. Having a plan in mind and an end in sight seemed to have settled her a little, and she moved about the vat room with a sense of purpose.

Gorham sometimes followed Nadielle and sometimes explored on his own. Those many-bladed things remained motionless in shadowy corners. He avoided them but felt no threat from them anymore. She'd told him they would not hurt him. It was amazing how quickly he could get used to something like that.

And perhaps over time he had become too used to the Baker. Because, watching her work, he realized once again just how incredible she was.

On occasion he fetched food from her rooms—chopped fruit and salads and dried meats—and they would eat and sit on some of the boxes and benches set around the perimeter of the vat room. If she spoke, it was to comment on the meat's taste, the fruit's ripeness. She said nothing about what she was doing, and he guessed it was because she was uncomfortable being observed.

But this is the last time, he thought. *Soon she'll go, and I'll never see her again.*

She climbed a ladder beside the womb vat she was working on most diligently. Others were steaming and hissing, popping and scraping, and she tended them quickly and efficiently. But this particular vat—she put her body and soul into tending it. Gorham's seed had gone in there, and something of

Nadielle as well. He dreaded the times she asked him to climb and water, because he did not wish to see.

Soon, she had told him several times already. She was thin and pale, her face seemingly shrunken, and he wondered whether, by giving life to the thing in that vat, she was dying a little in the process.

When Nadielle descended the ladder and hurried through the door into her rooms, he dashed after her. At first he could not see her and he began to panic. *Is there another way out? Has she gone without even saying—*

But then there was movement in the corner of the room, and she emerged from the shadows carrying another book.

"I can't trust myself," she said. "My memory is . . . haunted."

"Haunted by what?"

"What I've seen." She dropped the book onto the table, and it fell open in a cloud of dust. "What I have to face."

Gorham coughed, wiping dust from his eyes. *The dust of her ancestors*, he thought.

"When will you go?" he asked softly.

"Soon." She did not even glance at him. The pages of the book were too important to her, and he left her to them, closing the door to the toilet room and leaning against the door as he pissed in the pot. His piss stank; he needed a drink. *We're trying so hard to look after everyone else, we've forgotten to look after ourselves.*

He wondered where Peer was right then and hoped that she was safe. Since last seeing her, he had been down to the deepest Echo of the city, seen things that few living people had ever seen, and discovered a monster that might mean the end of everything they knew. But if he saw her right then, his first inclination would not be to tell her these things. It would be to hold her.

Nadielle had never just let him hold her. There always had to be something else.

Outside again, Nadielle was leaning over the book, scanning its pages. She did not look up when he approached.

"I'm not sure I can let you do this," he said.

Now Nadielle looked up, expressionless. "You'd try to stop me?"

Gorham did not reply. Though there was no threat to her voice, she'd sounded so cold.

"No choice," she said. "It's happening now, and I can't turn it back." She returned to her book, and Gorham slapped his hand onto the table. The anger was sudden and unexpected, and it shocked him as much as it did her.

"Then include me, at least!" he shouted. "I'm wandering these rooms like a lost puppy, and you're working as if I'm not even here. As if I was *never* here."

"Are you serious?" she asked, smiling in surprise.

Gorham already felt cowed and embarrassed. He looked away.

"This is so much more than us," she whispered.

"Was there ever 'us'?"

For a moment so brief he wasn't sure he saw it at all, Nadielle's eyes softened and her lips trembled. Then she was hard again, flipping a page in the book and running her finger along the lines as she read.

"You told me I was your sunlight."

"It's *dark*!" she shouted. "Darker than ever. Get off your own ass and wake up!" She ran both hands through her hair, then turned the book on the table so that it faced him, spilling loose sheets and another book to the floor. "Here. You want me to include you? I need the chemicals listed on the top half of this page, in those exact amounts. Bottles and measuring jars are in my cupboards. All labeled." She leaned in close and he smelled her breath, knowing that she was already becoming a memory. "Don't spill a drop. Don't make mistakes. Don't mess it up, Gorham."

She left the room and he glanced down at the book, her family history written in a hand the Baker could call her own. Closing his eyes, breathing deeply, he wondered whether the next Baker could be so cold.

It took Gorham a while to collect the powders, fluids, and carefully weighed tablets. Carrying them all on a wooden tray, he went out into the vat room and spotted Nadielle tending the special vat once more. She sat on its rim, both feet on the ladder's highest rung, and she seemed to be whispering.

She glanced at him, then pricked at her hand with a small knife. She squeezed several drops of her blood into the vat and then sheathed the knife, climbing down the ladder mindless of the blood smearing its wooden rungs.

"You should bind that," he said.

"I'll be needing it again. Thank you." She took the tray from him and placed it on the ground, mixing and stirring, careful not to spill or waste.

"How long will it be?" he asked.

"No time," she said. "I'll be leaving soon."

"So this new Baker . . ." he began, but it was too confusing.

Nadielle stood and took his hands. The move surprised him, but there was no affection or warmth to her touch. *Just because she thinks she needs to*, he thought.

"What I'm about to ask you is a true responsibility," she said. "Not like leading some underground political group or trying to take on the guilt for bad decisions you might have made. A *real* responsibility. My mother chopped me before she died and birthed me herself, and virtually every new Baker is welcomed into the world by the old Baker that chopped her. That's part of our duty and part of the way we cope with how and what we are. But I'm handing this duty to you. Because I must, and I trust you, and trust that you want the best for Echo City."

"I do," he said. "I always have."

"And this *is* for the best, believe me. I know what I'm doing." She glanced aside at one of the bladed things sitting against the wall. "Here, at least."

"And down there?" Gorham asked.

"Down there, I'll do whatever I can."

"To right a wrong."

"Bakers never make mistakes, Gorham. They simply explore too far." She smiled softly, let go of his hands, and grabbed the glass mixing pot by her feet. Climbing the ladder, she nursed the pot carefully against her chest, then emptied it into the vat as soon as she reached the top. She dropped the glass pot and bit at the cut on her hand, squeezing out more blood.

"Is it happening now?" Gorham asked, because he felt a

sudden change in the chamber's air. The bladed things had gone from relaxed to alert and expectant, and it was as if their blades were held at attention, a potential of violence almost unbearable in its intensity. Some formed a wide circle around the womb vat, several more stayed back, going to the doors that led to the Echo outside. Guarding. Though guarding against someone coming in or something going out, Gorham was not sure.

"New weapons," Nadielle said. "My daughter will take a while longer." She was staring lovingly into the vat, her face softer than he had seen for some time. Not vulnerable, as she had been down in the Echoes when she demanded his intimacy, but strangely content, even with everything she had done and what she had to face. Right then she was beautiful, and Gorham mourned for the woman she might have been.

Three other vats began to bulge. Some unseen, unheard message must have been relayed to them, and they started to spout steam and gas, sides cracking, fluids gushing from the ruptures.

"Nadielle," Gorham said.

"You'll want to stand back," she said. She waited a moment longer atop the ladder, looking down into that one special vat before descending.

Gorham had witnessed Neph's birth, and through the fascinated disgust he had felt privileged. But watching these new things born from Nadielle's womb vats inspired only horror.

How she could have grown them so quickly, he had no clue. The talents handed down through the Baker's generations were so arcane and mysterious that they'd be called magic by most, though he knew that she vehemently repudiated any such descriptions. *Magic's for the frightened and the indoctrinated,* she'd told him once, *and for those without the imagination to see how amazing things can really be.* They'd been naked on her bed at the time, and recalling the conversation now, he recognized it as another moment when he had not really been there for her. She'd used his presence to talk to herself.

Perhaps the speed with which these things had been

chopped went some way to explaining the terrible screams as they were birthed. They came to the world in agony, three of them emerging from vats with the help of their many-bladed and spiked limbs, forcing their way out as if inside was torture, only to discover that outside was worse. They thrashed and rolled in the thick fluids that spilled around them. Gorham backed away, closer to the Baker's rooms but unable to hide himself away entirely. He was shocked and afraid in equal measures but still certain that Nadielle would allow no harm to come to him.

Unless she's rushed it. Unless, in her desperation, she's made a mistake.

But then she was walking among her new creations, and now Gorham could see just how large they were. He'd subconsciously been comparing them to the dozen bladed guards that slinked around the vat hall, but these things were at least five times the size of those, and there was nothing even vaguely humanoid about them at all. They were flesh, blood, and metal, monstrous mergings of soft and hard. Their blades glittered with sharpness, their spikes were slick with afterbirth, hands were heavy with studs, and what might have been their heads—he wasn't sure, but he thought each creature had at least three—bore vicious white horns as protection around their mouths and eyes. In those mouths were silvery teeth that already had shredded their lips and tongues, the blood adding to the terrible mix smeared across the floor. And in those eyes was nothing he could recognize.

Nadielle spoke, and a bladed guard darted toward each of the newborns. The giant creatures lashed out, piercing the smaller chopped, picking them up with blades or fists, depositing them in mouths that opened up where Gorham had not noticed them before. The sound of chomping was appalling—crunching, crushing, splitting, bursting, and brief cries as three lives were snuffed out.

When the newborns had finished chewing, they were somewhat calmed, and Nadielle repeated those words. Three more guards walked in, a little slower than the first. They suffered the same fate.

She turned from her new creations and walked toward

Gorham, unconcerned, turning her back on monsters that would give him nightmares forever. Just before she reached him, her eyes went wide, her mouth opened, and she collapsed to the floor.

As he rushed to her side, he saw her right eye suddenly flush red with blood. And the new monsters began to howl.

Neph had been sitting for so long, listening to the sounds increasing in volume and frequency, that it could no longer feel its legs. When the time came, it lit its torch and shone it at the wall of water. At the place where the water fell beyond view, a shadow appeared. Neph had seen many shadows already, the dead from a city it would never know. But they were always falling.

This shadow rose.

Neph stood, legs burning as blood circulation returned. It took one step back, and the wounds on its arm began to bleed.

The shadow manifested into a mass of corpses, some quite fresh, others rotting. Chunks of their flesh had been torn away by the powerful flow, leaving only their bones behind. The impact of the falling water was brutalizing, and many of the corpses had flowed into one another, limbs punched through guts and bones embracing another's insides. Punching through the bodies were heavy, thick spines . . .

Neph flexed its own spines, startled at the familiarity.

The shadow rose higher, pushing against the water. Huge flailing shapes swung into view, thrashing at the water and seeming to grab on to it, hauling the mass of bodies higher, higher . . .

Neph squatted in a fighting pose.

Beneath the piled bodies, a massive eye opened, regarding Neph without emotion. Water poured around and across it but washed away none of this thing's menace. The thrashing things—arms with massive spade-shaped hands that hauled it upward against the shattering liquid weight—moved faster, lifting the shadow higher above the edge of the chasm.

The water roared, and the rising thing added its own voice.

When Neph found its legs and ran at the abomination, it did not even see the whipping thing that took out its right eye.

Neph fell, legs still pounding into the rock because it did not understand. Something felt wrong with its head. A thick tentacle hovered above it, and Neph lashed out with its right arm. But the arm would not obey its orders, and the tentacle thrashed down, crushing, breaking, spilling Neph across the rock and leaving its few lonely memories to be washed away forever.

"It's risen," she whispered. "It's here."

Gorham knelt, Nadielle's head resting in his lap, and he stroked her cheek. Her eye was bloodshot and blind, but she seemed unconcerned. The other eye stared off past the chopped creations, large and small, that had gathered around them. In the shadows past them, Gorham thought he saw the two remaining Pserans watching quietly, and he almost called to them. But other than Gorham, the Baker was the closest to human here, and even she was far from that.

"What did you see?" he asked.

"The Vex has reached the Echoes, clothed in the city's dead." She struggled into a sitting position, shrugging off Gorham's helping hands. "Tens of thousands since it fell, *hundreds* of thousands. It fed on them, and it grew so large that they litter its skin. Perhaps they can no longer fall past it. Perhaps it *filled* the Chasm." The Pserans came, shoving past the splayed blades and limbs of the chopped monsters as though they were tree branches blocking their way. They helped Nadielle stand. She swayed, then gently pushed their hands aside, staring down at the floor. She seemed physically lessened, but there was a strength about her that Gorham had never seen before. Previously she had been superior yet flawed, someone whose confidence went only so deep, he had always felt. He'd tried to touch her, but her front had held firm. Those insecurities had remained buried. Now she was the Baker, completely in control and self-assured, confident in what needed doing and how much she could do herself. When she looked up again, she had changed, in the blood of her dead eye and the power in the other.

"I must leave," she said, and she started for the end of the vat room. She passed the special vat without a glance,

walking taller the farther she went, and Gorham ran after
her.

"Nadielle! You can't just leave. You have to tell me—"

"There's no time. She's your responsibility." She paused
and stood face-to-face with Gorham, almost close enough to
kiss. "Water the vat regularly. Pay her attention; be here for
her. I've put accelerant into the mix, so she won't be long.
Maybe even today." She glanced past him at the vat, then
turned quickly away.

"But what about us?" he asked, hating the pleading tone to
his voice. He could not let her leave without another word.

"Goodbye, Gorham," the Baker said without even turning
around. She left the laboratory, with the Pserans following
behind. One of them looked back at him, cold and hard, and
in that stare was unveiled threat. The smaller bladed things
followed, and those three larger monsters disappeared behind the rows of vats, heading for the wider curtained route
he knew existed to the outside. In moments he was alone in
the Baker's rooms, left in charge of equipment, words, and
deed that he could never hope to understand.

Three years earlier he had sat at a table in a friend's home,
knowing that Peer was being taken by the Scarlet Blades. The
purge had not yet begun in full, and he and several others
were preparing to melt away as Watchers, allowing the Marcellans to think they had shattered the outlawed organization.
But for a while he had nursed a bottle of wine, staring into a
candle's flame and wishing he could be so consumed. The
guilt was a hard thing that weighed him down. There had
been a time when he had said goodbye to Peer, knowing that
he would never see her again, and he'd done so without giving anything away. A monstrous deception, a brutal betrayal,
and yet he'd believed it was all for the best. Every day since
then, he'd wished that goodbye had been sweeter.

He wished the same now. But Nadielle had left his life as
surely as if the door she'd passed through was a barrier between the living and the dead. She would not survive. And
though cold in passing, she had left him with the greatest responsibility.

Soon the new Baker would be born. He would be here to

care for her. In the space of a day he had gone from lover to father, and his insides ached as if an age had been impressed upon him.

He wandered the rooms for a time, watching the vat, watering, exploring. There was much about the laboratory that Nadielle had always refused to discuss, but looking on his own seemed an empty affair. He found small rooms he did not understand and corridors that seemingly led nowhere. He always returned to her living rooms, to lie in her bed and try to remember their good times. But already there was a bitterness, and strive though he did to shrug it off, he could not avoid feeling that he had been used.

And he could also not help thinking that he deserved it.

The rooms were silent but for the noises made by the vat. Sometimes he sang, but he could not find a tune to fit. He tried fighting songs from Mino Mont's gangs, but the martial aspects did not seem to fit the shape of these rooms, their echoes sounding all wrong. He tried some love songs that his estranged sister used to write when she was young, but she had grown into a woman whose belief in love was vague, and his own experiences made the lyrics seem naïve. So he whistled instead—aimless tunes that matched the path of his wandering around the rooms. Sometimes shadows drew him, sometimes areas lit by the oil lamps. He wondered why the oil never ran out. He wondered why there was always food in the cold store when he wanted it, and where the dried and smoked meats came from, and how he could be sure that the water collected in several sacs lining the wall in one small room could be fresh. It was all Nadielle's mystery. And more and more his attention was taken by the special vat from whence the new Baker would emerge. He spent more time sitting on its rim, watering when the levels fell and watching the thick fluid suck in the stream without a splash. Sometimes he reached out a hand to touch the surface but never quite got there. Fear, and respect for the Baker's talents, kept him away. He had seen but a tenth of them, and the loss he felt at her leaving was amplified so much more.

There were no timepieces in the Baker's rooms, and in

truth his concept of time had been shattered. He could not tell whether he had been belowground for days or weeks. His perception of day and night was gone, replaced with a need for food, sleep, and toilet, and that was how he tried to regulate his time waiting for the birthing. But there was no time for routine to form. It seemed an age since Nadielle had left, but in reality he guessed it was no more than half a day before the sounds from the vat began to change.

She told me nothing, he thought in a panic. He climbed the ladder fixed to the vat's side, and the liquid's surface was in turmoil. *I don't know what to do, or what this means, or whether I should be watching or running away.* Soon the vat began to shake and flex and the ladder's uprights cracked, sending several rungs spinning to the floor. He climbed carefully down and retreated from the vat, looking at the remains of the others, which had not repaired themselves after birthing those huge chopped warriors.

Helpless, terrified, he could only watch as Nadielle became the old Baker, and her descendant was born into a time of chaos.

The birth was not as violent as the others he had witnessed. The vat bulged and split, and the pale shape inside reached through with delicate hands, grabbing the vat's outside and pulling itself through. It gasped in a first lungful of air and vomited purple solids. As the rupture spewed the vat's innards, the shape fell and went with the flow, striking the floor softly and sliding a little until it came to a stop.

Gorham approached wide-eyed and amazed, because this was something of his. *I made that*, he thought, the idea ridiculous yet insistent.

Nadielle had told him nothing about what the new Baker would be like, how old, how possessed of knowledge, instinct, or fear. As he approached, he saw the body of a child approaching her teens. And when she squirmed around to look at him, he saw that she had his eyes.

Chapter 21

Peer and Malia waited in a small abandoned building close to where the dome met the ground. They did not like it, but Nophel and Alexia convinced them it would be the safest option. After all, they weren't invisible and had refused any suggestion that they sample Nophel's blood, insisting that they remain part of the world they were determined to help.

Nophel left the building with the three Unseen, and he was one of them more than ever before. Alexia had taught him the concentration required to control the White Water—it had given them more power than the Blue Water ever could, because fading away to nothing was no power at all. Now they could be seen or, with a little concentration, choose to be Unseen again. With that choice came salvation. Alexia and the others were ebullient, and Nophel enjoyed watching them rush invisibly across the base of this first Dragarian dome. They were like trapped animals set free, or confined prisoners given the run of the city. He only hoped they would fulfill their promise and help. Rufus was another of the Baker's victims and Nophel's only way to reach her.

The dome was all but silent. It was incredible—a whole city built to fill that massive space and yet resounding only with distant thumping. Nophel could not tell what caused this noise, but there was a regularity to it that suggested it was mechanical rather than man-made. It was like a massive heartbeat.

They made their way across the first dome without seeing any Dragarians. There were obvious signs of recent
habitation—lights were burning in some homes, and the
smell of food hung as a heavy background to the dome's
atmosphere—but they saw not one living thing. No Dragarians, but no animals either. If there were birds within these
walls, they roosted now. If there were hounds or rats, they
hid. The silence was haunting and intimidating, and Nophel
was pleased when they passed out of that dome and through
a huge, rose-encrusted arch leading into the second.

They had emerged on the rim of a vast, gently sloping bowl,
in which everything in sight was lush with plant growth—
fields of green and yellow, clumped trees with heavy
canopies, large areas of shrubs bearing all manner of berries
and fruit. The roof was similar to areas they had seen in the
first dome, letting in blazing sunlight and yet from outside
apparently made from solid stone. The engineering marvels
were astonishing, and Nophel found a sense of true wonder
dissipating his bitterness and drive for revenge.

"This could feed the whole of Echo City," Alexia said.

"Maybe, maybe not," Nophel said, "but it's more fertile
than Crescent. Do you see the color of those trees? The lushness?" He shook his head, marveling at what the Dragarians
had achieved in such secrecy. There were some outside who
believed they had all died out, but the opposite was true.
They were flourishing.

Then the first Dragarians came into view.

For a moment, Nophel was terrified. The Baker had made
Blue Water to work on the minds and perceptions of Echo
City inhabitants, but there was no way of telling whether
the Dragarians would be similarly affected and fooled.
Alexia said they had caught that flying Dragarian through
stealth, but maybe it had been injured when it landed, or
disoriented . . .

Or perhaps it had wanted to be caught.

He stood with his breath held, face itching in the sunlight,
and realized that if they were not invisible to those approaching, they would soon be dead. Because the natives of this place
were no longer people.

They were all humanoid, in the same way the flying thing had been. They retained their human basis, with torso, limbs, and head in roughly the correct locations. But they were altered in ways that made them amazing and terrifying to behold. Some walked on hands and feet, their necks curved upward to allow them to see ahead. Others flew, drifting above on wide membranous wings. A few crawled. And here and there some Dragarians slithered, their arms withered to useless dangling limbs, legs almost melded together, stomach and hips strengthened by musculature whose only purpose was to drag them forward across the ground.

"They're monsters!" the tall Unseen said, but Nophel could see the truth.

"No," he said, "they're chopped. No race could adapt like this in just five hundred years."

"Why would they want to be able to fly?" Alexia asked. "In this dome, perhaps. But in the one behind us, there's hardly any space. They've filled it."

"And why slither like a serpent?" the skinny man asked. "Strange."

The Dragarians passed within thirty paces of them. They headed down the gentle slope toward the grasslands below, mostly walking and talking together in a strange language. They seemed relaxed, not alert. And excited.

"Chopping of a different kind, perhaps," Nophel said. "Their own methods, their own aims. They've been isolated for so long, who knows what that can do to a race?" He shrugged. "We're not here to find out. We want the visitor, that's all."

Alexia nudged him and said, "Something tells me if we follow them, we'll find him."

Nophel nodded, then stepped ahead so that the Unseen were behind him. He wished he was on his own. This place was somewhere new, and these ignorants did not seem to realize that. Former Blades all of them, trained killers who'd turned bitterness into a disease instead of a driving force; he would happily have done without them if possible. But he admitted with regret that was not possible. Their task was huge, and, even Unseen, he had no idea how they would smuggle Rufus out of this place.

How do you possibly steal a god?

"So let's follow for a while," he said.

The grass felt good around his legs, cool and long and strong, and the ground below was soft but not muddy. A gentle breeze blew through the dome, carrying the scents of blooms familiar and unknown. The group of Dragarians was about one hundred strong, and they seemed to be moving with purpose across the bowl of this dome. Urgency pressed on Nophel, but he also enjoyed the walk. There was a sense of *wildness* to these manufactured fields.

The Dragarians passed a large lake at the dome's center and started up the far slope, heading for a distant arch that must lead into a third dome. The Unseen followed, and Nophel remained alert. There was no sign that they had been sensed at all, but in such a strange place . . .

Anything was possible. It was a rich, powerful feeling, which he was doing his best to shed. He hated it. Long had he denied the part of him—the part inherited from his mother—that saw wonder in the smallest of things. It made him believe he had her in his mind, and he could not live like that. It gave the impression that he had her sense of the wonderful, and so he had spent much of his life searching only for the mundane. The Scopes were amazing creations, but to him they were monsters, and he used their mutated lenses to spy on the rawest denizens of the city—the criminals, whores, slash sellers, and thieves, the lowest dirt in the crawling gutters of filth that he knew existed out there. For Nophel there *was* no wonder in Echo City, and when any sense of awe did creep in, from whatever quarter, he would close his eyes and not look again.

Now he could not close his eyes. His quarry might be close, so he viewed this place with the eyes of someone else—a new Nophel, given invisibility and thus the chance of a new life. He admitted the marvels here, and it was liberating.

He wondered if his mother had known.

They followed the Dragarians through to the next dome. This was almost entirely filled with a huge reservoir; several canals led off in various directions, and a network of refining rigs was set at regular spacings across the surface. The sound of water falling echoed through the dome, and Nophel could see pure water tumbling from the refineries' highest points. Birds swooped through the air, and flocks of ducks had made the lake their own. There were also many boats; close to the shore, down the small slope from where they'd emerged, a handful of craft were moored to a jetty. Smoke rose from several chimneys on the boats, and the scent of cooking fish was mouthwatering.

The Dragarians they had followed in were spreading out along the shore, joining hundreds of others already there. Many sat on the short grass covering the lakefront; others rushed through the crowds to hug people they had seen, gushing greetings and gesticulating wildly.

"I'm guessing that's our man," Alexia said, pointing toward the lake, and at first Nophel could not see. He scanned the crowd, glancing out at the moored boats and then back again. He followed a fat man, his webbed hands closed around a glass bowl containing something steaming. The man left the jetty and walked up the slight slope, and when he knelt before a seated shape, Nophel saw him.

Rufus Kyuss. He sat in a simple wooden seat, surrounded by a group of what must have been guards. They, too, sat, but were alert. They looked anywhere but at Rufus. And they wore long cloaks, beneath which glinted sharp things.

Nophel smiled, pleased to witness imperfection. It seemed that the Dragarians had made a successful contained society, but still there was a need for security.

"That has to be him," he said, and then Alexia fell on him, shoving him to the ground and flipping him onto his back.

"Nophel!"

"What?" She was *fading from view*! "Alexia, what are you—"

"Nophel, concentrate. You're *showing* yourself!"

Shocked, he closed his eyes and focused, slowing his breathing and imagining his flesh fading, his shadow brightening. Alexia's grip on his arms lessened and she stood away from him, and when he sat up, the others were looking at him. Though still ecstatic at what he had given them, now they appeared gray and wan.

"I . . ." But he didn't know what had happened. He glanced down the slope and saw no one looking their way.

"You'll have to stay here," Alexia said. "Keep low."

"What do you mean?"

"While we go to get him, of course."

Nophel stood, still shaken. "But we need a plan."

"No time," she said. "What, you want to go and hide somewhere, plan and scheme, and when we get back find he's gone?"

He looked at Rufus Kyuss, the visitor from beyond Echo City, survivor of the Bonelands, another creation of his mother's that she had simply let go. From this distance, it was difficult to make out the man's expression, but he seemed to be accepting the offerings presented to him—eating the food, drinking the wine. He did not appear to acknowledge those who prostrated themselves at his feet.

"He seems in no danger," he said softly.

"But those Watchers told us how urgent everything is," Alexia replied. "There's no time to waste."

"Maybe," Nophel said.

"Maybe? Are you . . . ?" She shook her head, snorting. "It's just as likely that they'll string him up and feed him his own balls as keep serving him. This could all be part of some sacrificial ceremony."

"You Blades should know," Nophel said coldly.

Alexia pressed her gray lips together. None of the Unseen looked like living people, and Nophel had to glance away.

"Stay here," Alexia said. "Keep watch for us. You have a good field of view. If there's any trouble, shout as loud as you can. They won't hear, but we will."

"Hopefully," the tall man said. "If he doesn't fade in again. Shouldn't one of us stay with him?"

"No," Nophel and Alexia said at the same time.

"I'm fine," he said. "I must have been . . . drifting. I'll concentrate." *I haven't come this far to lose out now. I have to meet him, talk with him. I have to know what he knows, and make sure he knows what I do.*

"You're sure?" Alexia said, and her voice was more friendly this time.

Nophel nodded. She smiled. And then the three Unseen started down the hillside.

It was strange watching Alexia and the other two pass unnoticed into the ranks of the Dragarians. When he'd followed Alexia through the streets of Marcellan Canton, she had moved with grace and ease, nudging or startling people only intentionally. Now that stealth had to come to the fore. The Dragarians were worshipping their returned god, and any suspicion that something untoward was happening could result in chaos.

Maybe that would help us, he thought, and for a moment he considered manifesting. Who would they bow down to then? But Alexia and the two men had already weaved their way through the Dragarian soldiers to stand before Rufus's wooden chair, and Nophel had an idea. He hoped that Alexia would be thinking along the same lines: use their fears against them. But the fact that none of them could communicate with Rufus without manifesting before the Dragarians and giving themselves away—therein lay the problem.

For a few moments the Unseen stood there as if confused. They swapped a few words, looked around, and then Alexia pulled a knife. She stepped forward and pressed it tight beneath Rufus's jaw.

He tensed in his seat, lifting himself upright from where he'd been slouched, eyes going wide and hands lifting toward his throat. The two Unseen men grabbed an arm each and held it down. And while they could not speak to him, Nophel knew for certain that Rufus understood the message.

The Dragarians had not noticed. But when the man they regarded as a god rose into the air before them, his wooden chair fading away to nothing, they started to shout. Some stood and backed away, tripping, sprawling, turning to run when they could. Others bowed down and pressed their faces into the grass. And several simply watched, their faces blank. *The fearful, the devout, and the doubting.* The last, Nophel knew, were the ones who might present problems.

The men used a shoulder each to carry Rufus through the crowd. Alexia kept a short sword pressed against his back, the point penetrating his clothing. To the Dragarians, he floated. They followed his progress, but no one pursued him.

Not yet.

Good, Nophel thought. *That might give us a chance*. But behind them lay two domes to cross and then the journey back through the Echo to the outside. And once the Dragarians realized where their god was heading, they would do everything they could to hold him back.

And maybe he won't want to leave. Nophel had not considered that. Probably none of them had. But once he managed to speak to Rufus—talk about their mother—he was sure the Bonelands man would be on his side.

They did not stop when they reached Nophel, and he followed on behind, glancing back at the chattering Dragarians.

"Move faster," he said. "This won't last long." And he was right. The observers who had only watched as their god levitated before them were leaving the crowd now, following slowly in their path. One of them had fine wings tucked around his arms and hips, another wore scaled skin, a third scurried through the grass, head raised and tongue flickering like a lizard's. These were the doubters, unafraid and questioning, and they would be the most dangerous. The devout would be too amazed.

"Run," Nophel said. "That's all we can do. Fighting won't be an option."

"We need to speak to him," Alexia said. She was still pressing her knife to Rufus's back, but running like that was awkward, and as soon as she lost contact he might start to struggle.

"Not yet," Nophel said. "We have to get completely lost first."

"I can't leave," Rufus said into thin air, but none of them could reply.

They ran silently for a while, breathing hard, and Rufus did not struggle. He sat motionless on the men's shoulders, looking straight ahead, neither helping nor hindering them in their flight.

Nophel kept to the rear, knife drawn. If it came to combat he would be lost, he knew that. And he was here for himself. If things went so wrong, he would flee alone, and perhaps later he would still be able to find the Baker on his own.

As they approached the huge arch leading into the culti-
vated dome, Alexia said, "By all the gods, how stupid we've
been!"

"What?" Nophel asked. They were being followed by at
least twenty Dragarians, and at present they were keeping a
respectful distance, easily maintaining pace with the Unseen. If the time came when they decided to close in—even
attack—there would be no easy escape.

"Your blood," Alexia said. "Or even ours. The White Water
in yours made us able to return to the world. But we *all* have
Blue Water in our blood, and—"

"Yes!" Nophel said, cursing himself for not thinking of
that. "And because he won't even see it—"

"—it'll be easy to make him drink it," Alexia finished for
him.

"But we have to get him out of sight first, somewhere we
can stop and do it."

"I have an idea," she said. "Here, take my knife, keep watch,
and do it as soon as you can."

Why me again? Nophel thought, scratching at the wound
on his arm. But Alexia's Scarlet Blade training was already
taking over. She threw him the knife as she ran past him
toward the following Dragarians, and the two men carrying
Rufus hardly broke pace. Nophel closed his eyes and
plucked at the wound with the knife, and it did not take much
to start the blood flowing again.

They passed beneath the arch and entered the huge green
dome. Smells changed from the tang of water to the perfumes of plants and blooms, and the short grasses around
their feet changed to a long, rough crop.

"Keep running," Nophel said, and he paused and turned
around.

Alexia stood just downhill from the arch, silhouetted
against sunlight reflecting from the wide lake, and something
about her outline was changing. There was a shimmer to her,
as though she vibrated against reality. And then the Dragarians rushing up the slope stopped and stared.

Alexia ran at them with her short sword drawn. She
was screaming—a murderous wail that set Nophel's skin

tingling—swirling the sword around her head, and uttering promises of pain in those unintelligible words.

Some of the Dragarians turned and fled this vision they had witnessed emerging from nowhere. One of them took to the air. It was a clumsy take-off, and his left wing caught on an item of clothing, pitching him heavily to the left. He emitted a cry not unlike one uttered by a rathawk and drifted low across the ground, the slope saving him from an ignominious landing. Another fell on all fours and loped back down toward the lake.

Three more picked up their pace and charged straight for Alexia.

"Not much time!" Nophel hissed. The two Unseen lowered Rufus to the ground, and while one of them grasped his arms to his sides, the other held his lower jaw and forced his mouth open. Rufus struggled, looking around wide-eyed and seeing nothing but green and the dome's roof. *He must be petrified*, Nophel thought, but there was no time for pity. He paused for a moment, taking a good look at this other abandoned child for the first time, this person chopped and cast out by the bitch Baker. Then he squeezed blood from his wound into the man's mouth.

Rufus could not see the blood, but he surely tasted it, gagging and coughing. The tall man forced his mouth closed and he swallowed reflexively, blinking hard as his eyes started to water. Then, somewhere in his fluid vision, he started to see the Unseen.

"We're here to help you," Nophel said, hoping the man could hear him already.

Nophel heard the clash of metal on metal and spun around. Alexia was fighting two Dragarians, while a third held back. They were soldiers, evidently, their muscled arms heavy and long, and the swords they carried were twice the length of the woman's. But though she had been Unseen for some time, she still retained her Scarlet Blade training. Fighting was what she had been bred for since childhood.

The first Dragarian went down, clasping a vicious cut across his chest, blooding spewing between his fingers. The second faltered, and Alexia drove in with her sword. Its tip pierced his shoulder and she twisted, eliciting a cry of agony and terror from the man's many-toothed mouth.

Alexia backed away from the wounded men and faced the third soldier—a woman with four arms and a blade in each. She looked vicious, but her lower two arms seemed weaker than the others, and there were wet, open sores where they joined her body. *Badly chopped*, Nophel thought. *Not as good as my mother*.

Alexia darted at her, and the woman turned and fled.

As she ran toward them, Alexia phased back to Unseen. She staggered a little as she came, blinking rapidly as if fighting off a faint. *It hurts her*, Nophel thought. *Maybe she was too far gone*.

"Let's go," she said as she reached them.

"Are you well?" Nophel asked.

"Fine, but we need to go."

Rufus Kyuss was staring at them now, the tall Unseen's long arms still wrapped around him. Though still visible, the differences in Nophel's blood—the White Water and the Blue Water—had worked on the Dragarians' god. He now had the potential to be Unseen, should they instruct him in its use, as well as the ability to see them in whichever state they existed. "Who . . . ?" he asked.

"Friends of Peer," Nophel said.

"Is she still with that *Baker*?" Rufus seethed, his hatred obvious, and Nophel felt his insides glow. He could not hold back a smile.

"Come with us," he said. "We've got plenty to talk about."

"I don't need rescuing," Rufus said. "They need me here."

"But this isn't all about you," Alexia said. "Come, or there'll be no Echo City left to take you to."

Rufus stood up straight and shook his head. "I belong here," I said. "Whoever you are, I can't leave with you. Rufus is not my name. My name—"

"Fuck this," Alexia said, and she struck Rufus across the back of the head. He fell, moaning, and rolled, and she hit him twice more before he grew still.

The two men picked up Rufus between them. Then they ran, crashing through the foliage, ducking beneath trees' low canopies, aiming for the other side of the dome and taking the most direct path they could. *That Baker*, Rufus had said. What did he know? Everything? Nophel kept looking at the mysterious man slung between the Unseen, and again he thought, *He looks nothing like me.*

They were halfway across the green dome, heading for the archway leading to the first dome, when a loud wailing noise filled the air. They paused beside a small pond, brushing flies and bees away from their faces.

"What the crap is that?" Alexia asked.

"Alarm," Nophel said. "There are similar ones set up on Hanharan Heights. It's a call to arms."

"War," Alexia said.

"Unless we get out of here quickly, yes."

"He could stop it," the tall Unseen said, nodding at the man they'd dropped to the ground. "Leave him here . . . let them find him—"

"No," Nophel said. "He's too important." *To me*, he almost said, but he bit his tongue. *Too important to me.*

"And we're not?" Alexia said.

Nophel smiled. His face was not used to the expression, and several of his sores split.

Sweating, exhausted, they ran again, hunted by a people who had found and lost their savior almost in the same breath. Nophel knew that if they were caught, there could be no mercy.

And Rufus Kyuss, unconscious, remained an enigma.

Echo City awoke that morning to a glorious day. There was hardly a cloud in the slate-blue sky, and the sun climbed from out of the Bonelands in the east with the promise of warmth and comfort for those who sought it. The sunlight illuminated the urban sprawl of Mino Mont, sending the slum gangs back into their shadows and splashing against the stark wall of Marcellan Canton. At the pinnacle of Hanharan Heights, the Eastern Scope stared wanly across the city, directly into the sunlight. Its enlarged eye did not water or smart from the brightness, and it did not lower the faceted lid that usually protected it from such glare. There was a small crater in the bottom curve of its eye, and the sun failed to scare away the ghoùrt lizard that picked at the organ's jelly.

In Course and Crescent, Marcellan's huge shadow was thrown as far as the city limits, its elongated spires and towers slowly crawling back across the city as the sun rose, like the retreating fingers of some vast phantom. In Crescent, blooms turned their heads to the sun and prepared to watch it cross the sky once again, while in Course Canton, the squares, courtyards, and parks bustled with early-morning traders, food purveyors, and people on their way to work or school. The smell of cooking soon drifted on the air, wafting away the sewer scents of nighttime and the metallic fumes from the smaller industrialized areas.

On the tall walls of Marcellan Canton, Scarlet Blades drifted to and fro in preparation for the changing of their guard. It would be achieved in shifts, so that there was never a time when the canton was not protected. Some of them were drunk, and not only those leaving their shift. There had not been a war for a long time. Soldiers grew bored.

At the end of one street in Course, a body was dragged into the shadows by three pairs of hands, its jewelry already stolen, its flesh and bones destined for the swine pits.

In the southern quarter of Mino Mont, nine corpses lay strewn across the steps of an old Hanharan temple, victims of a gang feud that had lasted for three generations. Such deaths were commonplace and barely merited a second glance from passersby. The feud was also expected, and expectation was one of the reasons it still existed. One gang would party all day in celebration, and tomorrow they would be the ones spilling blood and then seeking new recruits from the youngsters of that canton.

In Skulk, people drifted westward toward the stoneshroom fields. Others closed their doors for the day, preferring to sleep when the sun was up so that they could not look north and see the city that reminded them of lost times.

In Marcellan Canton, a group of old people passed laws that would mean nothing.

In Crescent, a farmer sowed crops that would never be harvested.

It was, all in all, a normal dawning to what seemed a normal day in Echo City.

But there were also those in the city who awoke to a painful truth—that things had changed, were still changing, and might never be the same again.

In Shute Fields, in the southwest corner of Course, shapes rose from places where the sunlight never touched. They were sleek, pale, and gray, and they raised their hands to protect their faces from the painful glare. Most remained in the shadows, hiding away from the sun behind walls, shivering in the growing heat of the day because they were so scared. Up was somewhere most of them had never been, but they could never go back down. Several were murdered by terrified people who thought they were monsters. Some fought back and killed their attackers, eating the fresh meat because it reminded them of home. Hunts proceeded, with the Garthans running through unfamiliar streets and existing for the first time in a place that was not an Echo. Though they were fewer than their pursuers, and disoriented, their custom of eating their victims meant that fear was on their side.

At the southern extremes of Mino Mont, where the canton narrowed down with the Marcellan wall on one side and the city wall, with the Bonelands beyond, on the other, the Bloodwork Gang was bettered for the first time in years. One of their main slash distribution centers had existed beneath an old abandoned workhouse for more than a year, storing enough of the drug to feed most of Mino Mont's addicts and a few of the more powerful devotees in Marcellan Canton. It was well hidden, its entrances and exits spread among neighboring buildings, and the Bloodworks had striven to keep it safe. Most knew not to interfere with them, and a thousand corpses could attest to this.

Protected and guarded against intrusion from above, the gang met doom from below. Fleeting pale shapes swarmed through the warehouse's rooms, spilling containers and setting fires. Perhaps it was surprise at finding the product that they made stored in such quantities. Or maybe it was panic. No one would ever know.

After the initial shock, the Bloodwork members guarding

the den fought back, but it was a short, brutal combat. The Garthans had no need of weapons; they hunted through stealth, stillness, and then fury. They killed anyone who stood in their way, chewing on human hearts as they charged onward. And the gang member who chose to hide—and who, later that day, would brag that he'd fought off a dozen attackers but instead had pissed himself as he watched his friends gutted and eaten—swore that these strange humans were terrified. They screeched as they attacked, but not in rage. It was fear that had driven them up, terror that gave them speed and strength. They rose into the streets and remained in shadows.

The Garthans emerged in many other places around the city. Sometimes there were large groups of them, but more often there were only a handful, and in places just one or two. In their terrified climb up through the city's Echoes and into its present, some had died, and many had lost track of their family and friends. The survivors did not care. All that mattered was escaping the thing rising from the deep.

Close to where the River Tharin vented into the desert, Bellia Ton had slept with her feet dangling in that dead river's flow. Her nightmares were monstrous, and as she woke to the sunlight burning her eyelids, the memory of them was rich. She could no longer discern whether what she heard, saw, and smelled were products of the fears already implanted in her or given to her afresh by the river. Bodies flowed past. Some of them were Garthans, and others had scarlet cloaks billowing around them like blood slicks. She tried to hear their voices, but there was one sound drowning out everything she needed to know: an insistent, throbbing impact on her soul. She heard and smelled it, felt and tasted it, and it was rising from somewhere deep—though not as deep as before.

She rolled from the river and her legs beneath the knees were white, skin and flesh soft as soaked mud. When she tried to stand, her legs gave way. There was no longer any feeling in them at all. She screamed instead, crying out all the things she thought she knew, but the only people to hear were the dead floating by. She always chose the deserted areas around the refineries to read the river. And hers were not the only screams sounding across Echo City that morning.

Readers across the city cried out, or ran, and some of them died where they worked, hearts riven with shock. Whatever the source of their knowledge—water, air, tea leaves, mepple flesh, stoneshroom visions, or rockzard-liver trails—their warnings were the same: *Something is rising*. They heard the sounds from below and spread word of them through the streets. Their warning dispersed, and no one who heard them could deny the sense of panic overlying the city. It started in the darkness and continued into the day, and sunlight brought no calming touch.

In Marcellan, a fat man approached the city wall, hoping that he still held power in his given name. Behind him trailed a small army of faithful soldiers, a score of Scarlet Blades whom he had been nurturing for years so that, when the time came, they would put the name Dane ahead of Marcellan. He tried to exude confidence and authority, yet he picked up the sense pervading the city that morning, and it was a wilder place. The wall guards stepped in front of the gate, and the fear in their eyes when they saw him gave him hope.

Where the Garthans rose—quietly and secretively in places, yet also interacting with the citizens in violent, startled ways that they never had before—word quickly spread of cannibalistic invasion from below. Many residents panicked and fled their homes, carrying their children and weapons and nothing else, and soon the streets were awash with people. The population spread out from those areas touched by the Garthans like ripples fleeing a stone's impact.

Scarlet Blades tried to contain the panic, and sometimes they succeeded. But here and there fights broke out and blood was spilled, not always the blood of civilians.

The Marcellan Council debated the news they were hearing from across the city. Hanharan priests advised the government, and their advice concerning the Echoes was always the same—Hanharan lives down there, and he exhales only goodness. They blamed the Garthans, and official word went out that an invasion was under way. Across the city, Garthan and Scarlet Blade blood mingled in short, brutal combats.

In the many places where news was vague and panic had not yet reached, and where people sat quietly eating breakfast or watching the sunrise, perhaps holding hands with their loved ones or smiling softly as their children readied for school, they heard a quiet, insistent noise from below: *thud . . . thud . . . thud*.

They frowned and wondered what it could be.

Chapter 22

Gorham sat and watched the girl come to life before him. *There is my daughter*, he thought, and yet she could never be. She was chopped, as much a monster as the Pserans or the Scopes, and she would not know him as Father.

He had carried her from the womb-vat room into Nadielle's bedroom. Naked, slick from the fluids that had nurtured her to such a size so quickly, she had already been looking around with those wide, curious eyes. Yet she had nestled into him, arms around his neck and head pressed against his chest. He'd felt her heartbeat, and that had given him pause. *She really is alive.*

Now he watched and waited, and it was amazing. He would never understand exactly what Nadielle had done here and certainly not how. But as the girl's awareness grew and her knowledge seemed to expand in her head like a balloon, so he believed he was coming more to terms with what she was.

The urgency was still there, crushing him like a giant hand bearing down on both shoulders. But Nadielle had left the girl here to prepare for Rufus's return. In a way Gorham felt useless, but he was also thankful that he could watch as the Baker's processes continued outside the vat.

She's the new Baker, he thought. She had the body of a girl maybe ten or eleven years old, but her eyes were already those of an adult. There was still confusion there and traces of fear, but at times Gorham also saw a striking wisdom and a depth of experience that would have been impossible in anyone else her age.

And yet her true age was measured only in hours.

He closed his eyes and breathed deeply, trying to settle the feeling that he should never have been here. He was a pragmatist—that had driven him since his early years, and it continued to guide him through his adult life as a Watcher. Yet what he watched here could not be real. Nadielle scoffed at the word *magic*, and Gorham had always allied it with the beliefs of Hanharans and the other, smaller religious sects throughout Echo City. Yet what more suitable word was there? If an act such as the Baker's chopping used talents, forces, and knowledge far beyond the understanding of anyone else in the city, wasn't that magic? It consisted of processes rather than spells or hexes, but he suspected they were processes that no one else but the Baker could perform, on the very edge of any science it was possible to understand. Nadielle had told him that much was passed down from chopped Baker to chopped Baker—he could see the stark evidence of that in the burgeoning knowledge before him now—but she had never explained how she did what she did. The Bakers had been practicing like this through the centuries, and that lent power to the concept of their own particular magic.

The girl was sitting on the Baker's bed, a gown tied tight around her waist, with Nadielle's books spread around her. There were sheafs of paper piled everywhere, notebooks, and those ancient books the Baker had brought from her secret rooms. The girl read as she ate—she had been eating ever since the birth—and she never once glanced at Gorham. He might as well not have been there, but he continued to bring her food and drink, and he knew that she was more than aware of his presence. Her hair was long and tangled. Her skin was pink as a newborn baby's. Yet it was her eyes—*his* eyes—that made his breath catch each time he saw them.

She ran her hands across one of the oldest books, turned a page, and touched the ancient words. She read and gasped. *She can read*, Gorham thought. *She's been in this world for mere hours and she can read, comprehend, understand.*

Crumbs fell from her mouth as she chewed, and she brushed them from the books with a gentle reverence. *She understands the value of knowledge, and that's something some people don't realize in a lifetime.* The girl was more amazing with every moment, and Gorham found himself observing from a greater distance. The first time she spoke, he was so startled that he thought he'd been woken from a dream.

"There should be another book," she said.

Gorham stood from his chair and backed away. He nudged against the wall, knocking something from a shelf. It smashed on the floor, but neither man nor girl averted their gaze.

"No," he croaked.

"She would have left it with you to hand to me."

"No," he said, firmer this time. "Not with me. She left nothing with me." That bitterness burned, and the girl's knowing smile stunned him.

She glanced around at the scattered books again, as if looking for one she had not yet seen.

"How much do you know?" he asked softly.

"Enough," she said. She rubbed her temple, then lowered her hand, the smile now gone. "Enough to know that something is missing."

Gorham shook his head, going over Nadielle's final words in his mind. He'd been angry, and perhaps sad, but he was certain he remembered everything that had been said. If she'd left something for the new Baker and told him about it, he *would* have remembered.

The girl keened and tipped to the side, resting her head against the open page of a huge old book. Gorham dashed across the room, and his every step closer made her more real.

"What's wrong?" he asked, reaching out but not quite touching. Though there were tears, her eyes were still older than they should have been. She gasped, sobbed, then pushed herself upright again. She seemed to be in pain, but when she reached out and took his hand, the touch was gentle, the hold firm.

"She rushed," the girl said. "But I'll be fine to do what needs doing." She had fine blond hair, and Gorham noticed a streak of white on one side. He was certain it had not been there before—he'd have noticed it when he carried her in here, surely? But his thoughts then had been in a mess, his senses distracted. *She took some shortcuts.* He wondered where else this new Baker lacked her creator's qualities.

"I think I know where the book is," the girl said. She pulled against Gorham's hand to help herself up, then closed books to clear a space around her. "Sit. I need to talk to you."

"Why?"

"Because the old Baker left you here with me for a reason. *You're* the book—her diary of the final days. You need to tell me everything you know and all the reasons why she chopped me while she was . . ." She smiled that knowing smile again. "I'm sure she cared for you."

"I'm not so sure," he said, but somehow the girl's words gave him comfort.

"The urgency is hot in me," she said. "I've no time to learn or research. You have to tell me what's happened, and try not to leave anything out."

"You're so *new*," he said. The deeper he thought about it, the more terrifying it became. "How can you talk? How do you know *all* those things?"

"No Baker is new," she said. "We're all continuations. I can tell you the color of the Baker's eyes from a thousand years ago. I can tell you what food the Baker from three thousand years ago favored."

"Then if you know everything, the name Vex will have meaning."

The girl paled, pressed her hand to her forehead, and grasped Gorham's hand to steady herself.

"The Vex is ancient history," she whispered.

"And all of Echo City's history is here."

"Then *tell* me. Quickly!"

"First tell me your name."

"I have none. Will you give me one?"

"Let me think."

"Think while you're talking," she said, and for the first time he heard a trace of Nadielle in the girl's voice, saw a glint of the old Baker's cool, detached humor in her eye.

So he talked, and some time into his story he named the girl.

"It's been too long," Peer said, hand pressed against her aching hip. Ever since the Unseen had left with Nophel, she'd been unable to sit still. She'd paced the two hidden rooms of the ruin where they hid, wearing a path back and forth across the gritty floor, and several times Malia had told her to fucking sit down. But Peer could not be still when everything else was in motion. So much depended on what happened here, and the responsibility she felt for Rufus Kyuss was almost crippling.

"There are six domes," Malia said, sighing because she'd said that a dozen times already.

"Still. It's been too long." Peer knelt close to one of the windows they were avoiding and looked at the incredible city outside. They'd seen very little activity since hiding themselves away. There were flitters of movement and now and then mysterious sounds that they could not identify—distant growls, an insistent clanging that had continued for hours, a long, low wail that rose and fell in random increments, and that thumping that seemed to rise from the ground. But there was no indication that they had been seen and no sign of the others.

Peer leaned back against the wall and stared across at Malia. The Watcher woman was sitting with her eyes closed, though Peer knew she was not asleep. She was meditating, perhaps, or simply thinking about what had happened and what was to come. The woman was Gorham's friend, and if put in this situation a few days before, Peer would have been quizzing her nonstop about her old lover. But that seemed so inconsequential now, compared to what was happening. Gorham had given Peer to the Marcellans for the good of the Watchers, and she had to accept what had failed between them for the good of the whole city.

Far too long, she thought.

"We should go," Peer said. "Make our own way in, look elsewhere. We can cover more ground than—"

"Than invisible people?" Malia asked without opening her eyes.

A distant wailing sound began—but this was different. The one they'd heard before had sounded like the cries of a wounded animal, but this was more regular. A continuous rise and fall.

Malia opened her eyes. "That's an alarm."

"They've been caught."

"Or they have him." Malia stood and approached the window beside Peer, sword in her hand. She was edgy, more animated than Peer had seen her in a while. Maybe she'd simply been preparing for this.

"We need to be ready to move as soon as they're here," Malia said. "We'll go on ahead, make sure the route out's clear."

"What about Rufus?"

"They'll be protecting him." She nodded at Peer, then clasped her arm. "He's more important to the city than to you, Peer."

"I know that," she said, but the truth hurt.

They watched the landscape outside, unable to see far because of the honeycomb structures filling the dome. And when the Unseen returned, it was not from the direction they expected.

"We need to move quickly," a voice said. Peer spun around and raised her short sword, and Alexia stood behind them.

"You have him?" Malia asked.

Alexia leaned against the wall and took several deep breaths, fighting off a faint. "Yes. I came on ahead."

"Is he . . . ?" Peer began.

"He's fine. Unconscious. I had to knock him out. I'm not sure he really wants to come."

"What?"

"Doesn't matter now," Malia said. "So, you're the soldier. What's the best way to go from here?"

Alexia grinned. "Well, when I was a Blade, in situations such as this we'd usually resort to running like fuck." The others entered behind her through a gap left by a fallen wall: Nophel, the two other Unseen . . . and, slung between them, Rufus.

"Back the way we came," Alexia said. "But, to stay together, we all need to remain seen, unless you two—"

"You'll have more of a chance on your own," Peer said. "Fade out again, and go as fast as you can. Malia and I will remember the way on our own. And if we trail behind you . . ."

"Yes," Malia said. "It'll be us they catch first, and that will slow them down."

"A drop of blood is all it takes," Nophel said.

"No," Peer said, and Malia also shook her head. It was no longer simply fear of the condition that made them refuse. It was the realization that they could provide a distraction.

"Fine," Alexia said without argument, and the Unseen began to fade. She placed her hands on either side of the unconscious Rufus's face and concentrated, and he, too, began to fade.

"What?" Malia gasped, surprised, and before Nophel flittered from visibility, he pointed at his bleeding arm.

They slipped from the building. Peer had never felt so naked and exposed. The dome sloped away above them, and without staring up it could have been just another expanse of gray sky. A thousand windows stared down at them, dark openings in the faces of incredible structures, and behind any one there could have been a Dragarian waiting for this moment. *Perhaps they've been playing us all along*, Peer thought, and it was an unsettling idea because . . .

Because she'd been thinking the same about Rufus. He'd killed the Border Spite and the Watcher easily enough, and he'd fled the Baker's laboratory as soon as he heard the truth—almost as if he'd *known* the truth all along, and this was all just a ploy to get here.

But perhaps her imagination was running away with her. If there was any truth in that, he'd have forced them to let him stay. He might talk like a child, but she had a feeling he had a much wider understanding of things than any of them gave him credit for.

They approached the dome's edge, dropped into the dried canal, and headed back down into the tunnels from which they'd emerged an unknown time ago. Sunlight still streamed through the hidden windows in the dome's roof, but it had taken on a darker, deeper hue, and she suspected that dusk was approaching outside. She wondered how much things would have changed when dawn next touched the city.

It was as they struck alight their oil torches that Peer first heard the sounds of pursuit.

She and Malia froze and stared at each other, heads tilted. The sound came again—a low, secretive grinding, like something dragging itself over the ground.

"You go on," Malia said, and before Peer could protest, the Watcher woman was climbing back toward daylight.

Peer moved deeper into the tunnels, alone and terrified, and looked for a place to wait. She could not simply leave Malia behind and flee, much as every part of her wanted to. And neither could she move on; even now she was unsure of whether she was going in the right direction. So she hunkered down behind the remains of a tumbled wall, wondered what the building had been, and soon heard footsteps pounding toward her from the direction of the dome. She thought of extinguishing the torch but decided to keep it alight. If the person running at her was not Malia, she'd need to see what she was fighting.

"We can't stay here," Malia said, rushing past. "Come on."

Peer ran after her, handing Malia the torch and trusting the Watcher's instinct. Malia moved this way and that without any apparent hesitation, and Peer only hoped she remembered the way correctly.

"Lots of them," Malia said. "We could wait and fight, but we wouldn't hold them up for long. Useless."

"So what?" Peer panted.

"We find somewhere narrow and try to hold them back."

"Just you and me?"

"Yeah. Narrow enough for one or two, and we'll do what we can."

We'll do what we can. That meant die. Peer felt curiously detached from the possibility, as if she'd already died once before and knew it was not so bad. Yet her will to live was strong—to see Rufus and help him as much as she could. To see Gorham again. He'd been afraid when she left him with the Baker, and the manner of their parting . . .

I could have said goodbye, she thought. *I could have given him some inkling of forgiveness, at least.* But that would have been a betrayal of herself. She had not forgiven him, *could* not. But that didn't mean they could not still be friends, of a sort.

And Penler. She'd made herself a promise to see him one more time. Failing in that would feel like letting him, not herself, down.

Behind them in the tunnels, echoes drifted in: growls and scrapes, the flapping of wings, the slithering of things across the ground. They merged with the sounds of their own footfalls. The sounds were growing louder, even though Peer and Malia were running as fast as they could. Whether they reached a suitable place of ambush or not, the choice to run or fight would soon be made for them.

Peer drew her sword, and it felt pathetic in her hand. Not long now. Not long until she discovered the truth about death and what lay beyond. Would she be taken down to Hanharan, in whom she did not believe, and welcomed into his shadowed embrace? Or would her senses blink out one by one until there was nothing to comprehend and no comprehension at all?

A Watcher all her life, right then Peer was no longer sure what she believed.

An arrow flicked past her ear and struck Malia in the neck. She grunted and fell, and Peer tripped over her flailing limbs. And then redness rose around them, and the sound of fighting and dying filled that subterranean place.

Sometimes Sprote Felder believed that the statues spoke to him. He did his best to listen, but their words were distorted by time and confused by languages he had never known. He thought he'd researched all the old dialects, reading them on inscriptions hidden from the sun for countless years, but perhaps he had been wrong. Perhaps there was so much more that he could never know.

The noise in his head was constant. Sometimes he screamed until he could no longer draw breath past the rawness in his throat, but that did nothing to cover the impact noises he heard from below. Other times he stuffed dust and dirt into his ears, wetting his finger and shoving it in as far as he could in the hope that it would solidify, cementing out the terrible truth. But then he'd slump to the ground and bang his head, and the plugs would fall out.

The tall statue before him was regal and aloof, missing one arm that might have been torn off by Garthans. They sometimes came and vandalized these higher Echoes, poor revenge upon the memories of those long-ago Marcellans who had wronged them when they were proud Thanulians. He had often suspected that one day they would marshal their forces, gather their anger, and rise up to exact true vengeance. It seemed that he'd been wrong.

Something else would be the end of Echo City.

He screamed again, raging at the pains in his throat and head. It had been a long time since he'd had a drink. Crawling from the small tomb beneath one of the statues where the Baker woman had dragged him, he'd cracked the water flask she'd left behind, spilling its contents into the dry dust of history. He'd lit his torch and watched it soaking in, amazed that things could still happen when there was no one here to see. *That's proof of the city's soul*, he'd thought. *That it continues on without us, and it'll move on, and on, even when this is all over. Even when we're all dead.*

Crawling, pulling with his hands, pushing with his one good leg, smelling the stench of his other leg, where the bone had ruptured flesh and set it to rot, he had no destination in sight. His only purpose was to move, because he had never stayed still.

Creatures ran past him, heading back the way he had come. A mass of small insectlike animals first, antennae waving at the air, ten legs scuttling across the uneven ground. They parted around him—smelling him, perhaps—though a couple came close and chewed chunks from his rotting leg. Larger creatures followed them, some flying, most crawling or running. He knew some of them from his long journeys down here, but there were shining diamondlike creatures that moved on cushions of gas that he had never seen before. Even now the wonder was there, and he reached out to grab one as it drifted by. His hand was slashed in a dozen places. It hissed as it passed by, absorbing his blood and glowing red for a few brief moments.

"Running from something," he said, and he started to crawl faster. Whatever they were running from, he had to see. He was dead but not yet finished, and curiosity and the search for knowledge were his prime motivators even now.

The ground thumped up at his chest and stomach, the regular rhythm of the impacts now ended. "Turning to chaos," he said into the shadows. They did not reply, because there was nothing left down there to hear. Even the maddest of the Garthans had gone—he'd seen no sign of them for what felt like days. "Chaos rising, and the city's reaping what it's sown." Crawl . . . crawl . . .

Something moved in the distance. Sprote paused and aimed his torch, but the oil had almost run out now, and the light beam was weak. Shadows shifted again and then dashed across the Echo before him—a huge, flailing thing that ran so fast he could not track its progress. Light reflected from lashing metal objects, and between them was only the darkness of a body built to hide.

This time Sprote did not scream, because he knew this was not the rising thing. This was something that had come down.

"Mounting a defense," he said, but this was not a creation of the Marcellans, and the Hanharans would not allow such bastardization. He knew who had made this, and why, and when he shouted this time, it was a cry of encouragement and defiance.

The impacts increased, the ground now shaking so much that each thump punched him into the air, and each fall drove lances of pain all through his body. From the far distance, across this Echo and from those much deeper, he heard and felt the steady rumble of roofs caving in, columns crushing, history imploding. The noise was immense, and at last, through the incredible volume, he started to distinguish one facet of the cacophony from another: here, the clash of metal against other hard things; there, the cry of something in pain; and elsewhere, a roar fractured by the teeth it was driven past.

The Echo smelled of death, and it was no longer only from him.

The ground opened up before him. The statue park, part of an Echo he had explored many times, split from side to side, and from the new rift something rose up. It was huge, a shifting tower of the dead and rotting, bones and flesh falling from it. His meager vision was clouded with the dust of crushed bones. Clad in the dead of Echo City, the thing beneath the corpses was visible in places—swaths of deep-red hide with cracks that glowed like lava bubbling in the Echo pits beneath Skulk.

Huge limbs the length of a hundred human arms thrashed at things clinging to its sheer sides. And these things—two of them, joined now by the one Sprote had seen rushing across the Echo—were hacking at the monster. Their bladed limbs rose and fell, scattering more bones of the dead and flicking countless body parts into the darkness, digging deeper until they encountered the monster's skin, slashing, rending, and moving on when gouts of fiery blood erupted from the foul wounds they had made.

Sprote's torch faded out, but the scene was lit with the blaze of combat. Old corpses flamed as they fell past the monster's burning wounds, disintegrating across the ground and setting a thousand bonfires. Fires burned on its ridged back. Gases ignited around the fighting things.

And then, far to Sprote's left, another upheaval, and another huge mass broke through the rock from the Echoes buried below. It tipped over and smashed onto the ground, shattering the statues of people dead for thousands of years and spilling a hundred corpses across the soil. At first he thought there were two monsters rising. But when he realized what he was actually seeing, and the ground between the limbs started to bulge as the thing's colossal head forced through, his heart stopped beating for the final time.

The Echoes around the turmoil collapsed, history fell, and Sprote Felder was crushed before he could utter one final, dreadful cry.

"Man from Sand," the voice says, and Rufus opens his eyes. He is in his small room in his guardian's house. Sunrise is near, and the only sounds from beyond are the soft calls of birds waking around the village. Soon the place will be bustling, but there is always that gentle, almost mournful time between night and day when the village seems to be holding its breath. Sometimes Rufus is awake for this and he stares from the window, wondering who he really is. Mostly he sleeps through to daylight. He is becoming comfortable, though afraid that the dreams will never leave him be.

"Who are you?" he asks, and then he sees the flowing yellow robes. *A Tender, from the valley of the Heart and Mind.* He has never heard of these servants leaving the valley, and he has seen them only once before, one moon ago, when he made his pilgrimage.

"My name does not belong to me," the man says. He is exceedingly tall and thin, his arms almost as long as Rufus's body, his head elongated, his feet large and flat. His face is somber and pale, but his eyes are bright. They glitter in the light of the small lamp he has lit. He sits in the chair beside the bed, and his knees are almost as high as Rufus's head.

"You're . . . tall," Rufus says, but the man does not react. He is removing something from a pocket hidden within his robes. He settles, and when he seems comfortable he begins to speak.

"Long ago, long before history, at a time when people passed events through song instead of writing, the Heartlands' ancestors fought a war. The causes of the war are long forgotten, but even now there is evidence of its ferocity and inhumanity—both to scales beyond our comprehension—in the eternally toxic desert. And you have seen the dead city deeper in the Heartlands, where only the ghosts of the past reside. There are more like that."

"More? I thought—"

"Our ancestors lost the war. But not as much as their enemies. Half the world died, and the other half struggled on for many painful centuries until it became the Heartlands. The Heart and Mind believes that you are from the world that died."

"But I—"

The man lashes out with the thin stick he has produced

from his robes, catching Rufus across the face. The impact is sharp, fast, and surprising. No one here has ever treated Rufus like this. There has been disbelief, and fear, and sometimes hostility. But never violence.

"Silence, Man from Sand!" the Tender snaps, and his voice carries so much more threat than before. "You must listen and do as I say. The Heart and Mind commands that you hear the truth and then obey." He arranges his robes again, shifting on the seat until he is comfortable once more. Then he stares at Rufus. "The Heartlands is the whole world. It stretches for a thousand miles south of here, and we are at its edge. The Heart and Mind was placed here long ago, at the edge of the rest of the world, formed and chopped by the Revered Artist. His was a tortured soul, and upon completion of the Heart and Mind, he let himself fade and die. He believed that he was not for the likes of us. But he will never fade from memory." The Tender looked sad, the first expression that had crossed its otherwise plain face.

"Why did he—"

"His arcane talents caused much suffering before the Heart and Mind emerged. But his purpose was finally achieved. It was based here to guard against future wars. That threat is . . . long past. But then there comes you."

The welt across his face is stinging, but Rufus holds back the tears. He is not weak. Confused, yes; often. Lonely . . . sometimes. But never weak.

"The Heart and Mind instructs that you are to return to the sands this coming night," the Tender said. "It senses deep, distant rumblings that trouble it and commands that you leave. No one must know. I will tell you where to meet me, close to the desert's edge. We will equip you, and you will go back to where you came from."

"Just because I'm not like you?" Rufus asks, flinching in expectation of another strike. But the man's face softens just a little, and he sighs.

"You are not like us, *any* of us. You're an upset that should not exist."

"I don't understand . . ." Rufus says, closing his eyes and seeing the city, and hearing a voice that might be his mother.

"And that is why you must return," the Tender says. "The Heart and Mind will touch you first, so that it can read you from afar. It is curious about you and where you came from. And it must know what the rumblings it senses forewarn. Knowledge gives it power, and it would have knowledge of your origins. What you see, it will see. What you experience, it will know. Thus it is with every Tender. You will become one."

"And my guardian?"

"She can never know." The man is sour and grim once again, staring at Rufus with a warning in his eyes.

"If I tell her, if I tell everyone—"

"You—will—not." The voice is like fire; the words spell death. Rufus shivers in his warm bed, and the man stands to leave. There is hardly any sound as he moves; no swish of his robes, no impact of feet upon the ground. He's almost a ghost, but Rufus knows for sure that he is real. He can smell a sickly-sweet odor coming from him that he knows has something to do with the Heart and Mind, and the man's shadow is cold.

"I'm afraid," Rufus says.

"Of going home?"

"I'm not sure . . ." he says, screwing up his eyes. He concentrates. "I'm not sure I really came from anywhere out there." The man bends down, looming over him like a carrion bird inspecting a victim as it slowly bleeds to death.

"But the Heart and Mind *is* sure," he says. "Sundown, by the Signal Rock."

Rufus nods, unable to speak. The man leaves. And as the sun rises soon after, and Rufus's last day in the Heartlands begins, the coolness of rejection settles over him.

There are no memories of that final day with the people of the Heartlands, because it must have been a happy one. Later, he is standing by the Signal Rock, its flanks scorched black by the hundreds of fires lit and doused there over the years. The Tender is there, as promised, and at his feet is a sled with several covered packages—water, food, the weapons he's been taught to use, a tent.

"I thought the Heart and Mind . . ." he began, and the ground at his feet began to stir.

". . . is everywhere," the Tender says. The tall man steps back, moving gracefully as the gritty ground breaks open. A shape appears, nosing from the soil, lengthening, its mottled red appendage seeming to sniff this way and that before steadying in front of Rufus. It moves in close, then becomes utterly motionless.

Rufus can hardly breathe. He glances at the Tender, but the man's eyes are closed, hands clasped before his chest.

The thing darts forward and touches Rufus's forehead. It spreads. Though terrified, he cannot move, can barely even breathe, as the Heart and Mind touches him outside and in.

Eyes still squeezed shut, he feels the weight of a yellow Tender's robe slung around his shoulders.

Later, when he starts out into the desert from which no living thing has ever emerged, he knows that the tall Tender is watching. But as Rufus pulls the sled and leaves the Heartlands, he does not once look back.

Chapter 23

Nophel sensed him coming before he saw him: Dane Marcellan, the man who had saved and doomed him, one of the city's dictators and also a Watcher. A man of complex contradictions, and now he was beneath the ground where no one ever came.

"Wait," Nophel said, and the others heard the urgency in his voice. *How can I know he's here? How can I?* "There's something . . ."

"What?" Alexia asked urgently.

He's close, Nophel thought. *And he's not alone*. However much he might trust the fat man, this felt wrong.

"We have to hide," he said.

"We have to go on!" the tall Unseen said. "We're through the soul-fire, but there's plenty of time for them to catch us yet."

"And why would the likes of us *need* to hide?" Alexia asked.

"You don't understand," Nophel said, and then lights danced in the Echo before them. *Oh, no*, he thought, partly because he had been right.

The Scarlet Blades streamed toward them, moving almost silently across the Echo, finding cover even when none seemed to exist. They were phantoms, their heavy red cloaks billowing around and behind them and deadening any small noise they *did* make.

"Move aside," Alexia said, and the band of Unseen left the rough trail they had been following south. She had relieved one of the men carrying Rufus. He'd awakened and struggled again, and Nophel had watched his every move, listened to his every word. *There's plenty going on inside that head*, Nophel thought. *Can he harbor such bitterness as I do?*

Following behind the Scarlet Blades came Dane Marcellan, with three soldiers surrounding him. The fat man was panting, but still he kept up with his soldiers, jogging comfortably in his finery. And something about him had changed. Perhaps it was seeing him in these strange surroundings instead of in the well-appointed Marcellan rooms back in Hanharan Heights. Or maybe it was because Nophel had spent more time out in the city than ever before, and his home and the Scopes seemed far away. But Dane looked different, lessened somehow, and Nophel smiled softly as his old master ran by.

And then stopped.

"Wait!" Dane said. His Blades obeyed. He looked around, shining his torch into the shadows, playing it across the Unseen without pause . . . and then holding it on Nophel, because Nophel had let himself be seen.

"Nophel!" he gasped.

"Dane."

The Scarlet Blades hovered uncertainly.

"Do you have him?" Dane asked, glancing left and right.

"Take them all," Alexia said quietly, and Nophel acted almost without thinking. He stood between Dane and Alexia, hands held up in both directions.

"We have him," Nophel said. "But the Dragarians are following, and if they catch us—"

"They won't," Dane said. "He's with your friends?" He nodded at the darkness where he could see nothing, knowing for sure that something was there.

"Yes," Nophel said. "Alexia, he's here to *help*!"

"Dane Marcellan," Alexia snarled, cursing the man who had doomed her and the other Unseen—and yet Nophel heard the hesitation in her voice.

"He's not like all the others," Nophel said, focusing on Rufus. *And he'll give us more time,* he thought. *More time to talk with Rufus Kyuss. To discuss. And to decide which of us will kill the Baker bitch.*

"Go fast," Dane said, waving his Blades forward. "Defensive line."

Alexia manifested, sighing and almost slumping to her knees. "Marcellan!" she growled, and Dane turned. A flash of recognition crossed his eyes. "There are two more behind us," she said. "Not Unseen. They'll not be expecting you."

"We'll watch for them." He glanced back and forth between Nophel and Alexia, eyebrows raised in surprise.

"We'll . . . move on," Alexia said, sensing the loaded air between the two men. She retreated into the shadows, fading again, and Nophel heard her and the others carrying Rufus between them.

"Why did you come?" Nophel asked.

Dane sighed, continuing to look for the retreating Unseen and the amazing man they took with them, but it was a distraction. Nophel saw the Marcellan's mind working, and he seemed to be at conflict with himself. Finally he lowered the torch and stepped forward, looking Nophel in the eye.

"To help you," he said.

"Why would you—"

"To help . . ." He seemed to struggle, chewing on words that might or might not come. "The Watchers," he said at last, but his voice was flat and unconvincing.

"And something more?" Nophel asked.

"I've always seen something in you I don't like," Dane said. "Bitterness. But whatever she did to you, she's dead now."

"It seems the Baker never dies," Nophel said.

"The workhouse was *her* idea!" Dane spurted, and Nophel had never seen him so out of control. "*She* couldn't keep you; you were a shock to her. And when you were born she tried to cure your affliction, but she failed. Weakened by childbirth, perhaps. You were too much responsibility for someone like her. And to begin with I agreed. If anyone were to discover I had a son . . ."

Son, he had said. Nophel's breath caught. *Son*.

"I've always wanted to tell you but never knew how," the Marcellan said.

"I'm your son," Nophel said. "You and the Baker . . ."

"She wasn't a good woman," Dane said. "Such unnatural

gifts, and they gave her a need for acceptance. Companionship.
But never love." Nophel had never seen Dane looking so sad.

"That's why you took me from the workhouse."

"When I could find reason, yes. We Marcellans needed
someone to tend the Scopes, and I volunteered to find the
perfect candidate."

"You took me because you cared."

"I took you because you're my son," Dane said, as open
and honest as he had ever been.

"Did she know?"

Dane blinked a few times as if he'd never even considered
that. "Maybe. But she didn't . . ." He glanced away from
Nophel, embarrassed.

"Care?"

Dane looked ahead at the shadows where his Blades had
disappeared. "I have to go," his father said, smoothing his
uniform. Three Blades waited a dozen steps behind him,
ready to protect him to their last breath.

"Why can't you come back with us?" Nophel asked.

"No," Dane said, shaking his head. "No. I can give you
time. I can help you, because you have to leave. To survive.
Don't be too harsh on the Baker. She's not like us." Dane
reached out and touched Nophel's diseased face, so gently.
And then he turned and started to run, and though Nophel
called after him—once, loud, risking discovery in these darkening places—the Marcellan soon disappeared into the shadows.

Nophel turned and rushed after the Unseen, the place on
his cheek where his father had touched burning, and as he
tried to absorb the news, a flush of fury washed over him. His
mother had abandoned him like a failed experiment, and
eventually his father had rescued him and kept him in a
tower, his shameful secret.

But the fury was a confused thing—hot and cold, rich and
weak—and the tears, from both good eye and bad, took him
by surprise.

Behind them, the sounds of death: screaming and hissing,
shouts and screeches, the harsh impacts of violence, and the

meaty *thunks!* of swords meeting flesh and bone. But Peer could not turn to see any of this, because Malia was dying.

The arrow had barely opened her skin, and the blood flow was slight. But it must have been dipped in poison, because the Watcher woman was thrashing on the ground, foaming at the mouth, and clasping Peer's hand so tightly her that Peer could feel her bones grinding together.

"Hold on!" Peer pleaded, but Malia could not hear. She'd dropped her torch and it shone ahead of them, casting only a small portion of its light across Malia's face. For that, Peer was glad. She had seen many people in pain before and had witnessed some dying in agony. But this seemed worse than any.

"K . . . k . . . k . . ." Malia choked, and one of her hands shifted quickly to the back of Peer's head. She pulled, and much as Peer resisted, she was no match for Malia's strength.

More screaming came from behind them as the Scarlet Blades fought with the Dragarians. The reasons and implications were far from her right now.

"Kill . . . me," Malia groaned, the effort immense. She let go of Peer and started to shake again, limbs and head pummeling against the ground, and the foam around her mouth grew darker. She was keening now, an unconscious sound of utter distress, and Peer screamed to try to drown it out.

Her short sword was on the ground next to Malia. Its blade was keen, its point sharp. With all her weight on the handle, it would take less than a beat to pierce Malia's heart and end her pain, but . . .

Peer grabbed the sword and stood, turning to view the violence behind her. She could make little sense of it— torchlight flickered here and there, illuminating a scene of confusion. Bodies darted and fell, the smells of blood and shit filled the air, and the screams were louder than any she could utter. *Because I'm not dying*, she thought, squeezing her eyes shut.

When she looked again, something was coming for her.

It flew, large diaphanous wings flapping rapidly in the confined space of this Echo, and it carried something in its hands—the curved shape recognizable as it drew closer.

Bow! she thought, leaping to the side, but Peer knew she could never dodge the arrow.

The flying thing squealed and fell, thrashing on the ground as it tried to dislodge a crossbow bolt from its underside. She never saw the man or woman who shot it.

"Peer!" Malia gurgled, hand closing around her ankle. She pulled, and Peer knelt at her side again. "S-send me . . . to . . . Bren."

"I . . ." Peer said, but then Penler whispered in her mind, words he'd said to her soon after her arrival in Skulk. *You're far from a coward*, he'd told her as she hugged a bottle of cheap wine, wallowing in self-pity.

She picked up her sword and rested it against Malia's chest. The Watcher woman tensed, controlling her spasms. And though blood still bubbled from her mouth and her eyes rolled with agony, the corner of her mouth turned up in her familiar half-smile.

Peer reared up, crossed her hands on the sword's hilt, and then dropped her weight on top of it.

Malia grunted once and then died.

Panic took Peer. She withdrew the sword, picked up the torch, and ran, fleeing the scenes and sounds of battle, the stench of death, the violence that seemed to stain the very air she breathed. And she craved the fresh air of reality, away from these past times that still echoed with chaos.

He had told her everything and named her Rose. It was his mother's name. Then she had fallen asleep, leaning her head against his shoulder, twitching, and mumbling things he could not understand. While she slept he smelled her hair, and she did not smell like Nadielle. He touched the skin on her face, and she carried a different coolness. He stared into the softened gloom of the Baker's rooms and wondered where Nadielle was, what she was doing, but any possibility that crossed his mind was a bad one.

The girl did not sleep for very long. When she stirred, Gorham was surprised to find that *he* had drifted off and her movements startled him awake. He'd believed that he *was* still awake, watching the walls of the Baker's rooms as they expanded and contracted beneath the breath and beat of her far-reaching influence. But seeing the solid walls again, he realized the flexibility of his dreaming. *She'll never leave me alone*, he thought as he surfaced, and the girl rolled from the bed and stretched.

There was a long, loaded moment when she looked slowly around the room. Gorham sat with breath held, watching the girl watching the room, and she had changed again. *Grown older*, he thought, though there was something not quite right about that. When her gaze swung back to him at last, he realized—her dreams had been her work, and waking had been the inspiration she needed.

"There's lots to do," she said. "Will you help?"

"Of course. I'm more than just a book."

The girl smiled, then scratched at her arms. The dried stuff of her birth flaked off and drifted to the floor. "I need to wash first," she said. "While I'm doing that, perhaps you can prepare some food?"

"Yes," Gorham said, feeling no qualms whatsoever about taking orders from a child.

While Rose bathed, Gorham rooted through the Baker's cold room to see what food was left. Whatever means she'd had of procuring fresh food must have gone with her, because the remains of older foodstuffs were all he could find. The dried meats and cheeses were still edible, and the sliced mepple fruits, though softening, were far from rotten. He prepared a few plates and left them on the table, and when Rose emerged in some of Nadielle's fresh clothes—the trouser legs and shirtsleeves rolled up to accommodate her smaller frame—they sat together to eat. The girl was distracted, staring intently at a plate of dried meat while her mind worked, and Gorham was careful not to interrupt. Finally, each of them nursing a glass of Echo City's finest wine, she started to talk.

"She cannot stop the Vex," she said. "She knows that."

"You can . . . ?" Gorham began, remembering the effect upon Nadielle when Neph had faced the Vex way, way beneath them.

"No," she said, "but it's obvious in her action. She chopped me as her successor, so she knew the end was close. She knew there were important things for you to tell me, which you have. And the Bakers don't . . ."

"Not unless they know they're about to die."

"Bakers have rarely coexisted." She stared into her glass. "She'll give us as much time as she can, but there's no telling how much that will be. We have to act quickly. But there are many assumptions. This Rufus has to be found."

"He will be."

"And brought here to me."

"He *will* be."

"You sound certain, but you can't be. You can only assume."

"Malia and Peer won't stop looking until they find him."

"In a city of countless people." The little girl drained her glass with the action of a seasoned drinker, sighing and licking her lips.

"He stands out," Gorham said carefully. *Is she already so pessimistic? Was she born this way?*

"Well, assume they *do* bring him," Rose said. "I'll then have work to do. And though I have ideas about what that is, there will be much preparation." She was talking more quietly now, as if to herself, looking around the room, searching for someone else.

"And what about me?"

"You?" She stared at Gorham again, her eyes piercing and intelligent. Her mother used to look at him like that. *A city of countless people, and that's far too small for you*, he thought.

"Do you want me to . . . ?" he said, waving vaguely at the books, the papers.

"I want you to help save the people of Echo City," she said softly. "I have ways and means for you to get your word out there. You still have networks? Watchers ready to spread information, should the need arise?"

"Yes, there are some. Though many have been silent for a long time."

The girl nodded. "Caution. That's good, in peaceful times. But now is no time for caution. Now is the time for chaos, Gorham. I want you to organize that chaos."

He shook his head. *Am I supposed to understand all this?*

"Everyone needs to go south to Skulk Canton. If all the assumptions come in just as we want—they bring Rufus here, he's amenable, my work progresses as fast as I hope, the results are successful—then we'll be on our way there too, as soon as we can. And we'll take with us the means for people to cross the desert."

"We will?" he asked, wide-eyed.

Rose smiled. And there again, in her eyes, Nadielle.

"Spread the word, Gorham. Come with me." She stood quickly, leaning against the table to steady herself, face paling.

"Are you—"

"I'm fine." She smirked at him. "I was just born, you know." She led him from the room, crossed the womb-vat chamber, and headed behind the three ruined vats. Nadielle had never let him go behind there, but he'd explored while waiting for Rose to be birthed. As well as the large curtained routes that led out into the Echo, he'd found three locked doors and one open. Behind the open door was a room with walls full of deep holes. No torch shone in there could reach the end, and he'd wondered what strange chopped things might have made them. Now perhaps he'd find out.

Rose unlocked each of the three locked doors by stroking her hand across a spread of moss on the door's surface. The moss changed color, the doors flexed and swung open, and when she shone her oil torch inside, she smiled.

"Very good," she said. "I remembered these were here, but I never knew how effective . . ." She trailed off, talking to herself again.

Everything she knows is like a memory, Gorham thought. *I wonder what she knows about me?* It was an uncomfortable thought—she was only a girl—but Nadielle had always claimed that her mind felt far older than her body. How confusing, how challenging to have experience and knowledge that did not match physical age. Indeed, in the world of the Bakers, what *was* physical age? A measure of time that they could contradict and tease. Their womb vats and what grew inside them *defied* time, and flesh artistry was only a small part of their talent.

"What are these places?" Gorham asked. The first room she had unlocked contained dozens of wooden boxes fixed to the walls, and shapes flittered at its shadowy extremes.

"These are our communications to the world," she said. "Bats in here." She pointed along at the other doors, naming each one. "Red-eared lizards, sleekrats, and . . ." She waved him over and they approached the final door together. It was open only a handbreadth, and the darkness inside seemed heavy and thick. There was no sound coming from within, but Gorham sensed a potential that was almost deafening.

"In here, more-unusual ways to send your message." She shoved the door open and shone her torch inside. The ceiling to the room was open, rising into a dense darkness that seemed to go up and up. Its walls were lined with what looked like flaking paper flicking in the breeze—and then Gorham saw that it was not paper at all, but wings. There were thousands of moths in the room, settled on the walls and apparently asleep. They seemed unconcerned at the light, and only a few took flight. The floor was scattered with dead moths, but only a small number. They clung, waiting, and he imagined the secret sound of thousands of fluttering wings.

"You should send the moths first. I'll tell you how they all work."

"And what will you be doing?"

"I have a vat to prepare," Rose said. "It's all up to time."

"Time and assumptions."

"Those too." Rose stared into the room for a while, lost and daydreamy again.

She's not even a day old and she's trying to save a world, Gorham thought. He reached out and took her hand, and she gave him a brief squeeze before heading back to her rooms. Her *rooms*. *She's the Baker now*. He followed, shivering when he thought of Nadielle, where she was at that moment, and what she might be facing.

Rose went to one of the many cabinets, opening and closing several doors, frowning as she looked for something. She paused, concentrating, then spun around and crossed to another cabinet. Behind the first door she opened was the bottle she sought. She brought it across to Gorham and unscrewed its lid. There was a new sense of urgency about her now. Even the act of sitting and eating together, so recently completed, seemed a world away.

"I'm going to give you—"

"You're *chopping* me?" he asked, stepping back. The bottle looked ancient in her young girl's hands, the glass uneven and distorted, coated in the dust of ages.

"No," she said sharply. "Aiding. Gorham, this won't hurt, it won't damage, and . . . even if it did, you can't think of yourself now. If I could chop you quickly enough, send you up with the message to spread yourself, I would. There are ways and means. But it would take far too long."

"But this?" he asked, nodding at the bottle.

"A gentle nudge in the right direction. Take this, sit in the moth room, repeat a short message again and again, and your voice will implant that message in the moths. They'll leave and spread it through the city. Same again for the other creatures. It'll be a dream in the ears of sleepers or an epiphany in those awake."

Gorham blinked, taking in what she had said. "Those rooms, they're always ready?"

"And they've been used in the past. That's how I know they work."

"But with methods like that, you could change the city. Steer events, influence . . ."

Rose stared at him, her silence speaking volumes. Then she tipped the bottle, spilling a splash of its contents into its upturned lid.

"The moths first," she said, "because they'll be most effective. Every message sent is one life saved, or a hundred if the listener spreads the word, or a thousand. And the only people who'll live past what's happening here will be those who take heed."

Gorham tried to comprehend what she was telling him. *I can't carry that responsibility.* But he realized instantly how self-absorbed that was. Rose was right—this was so much more than him. It was so much than all of them. That was why Nadielle had left him.

Rose swayed a little, and he saw the weakness in her. *She*

isn't going to last, he thought, and a momentary panic was subsumed beneath a determination to do whatever needed doing. They might not have very long.

"Will you know when . . . ?" he asked, thinking of Nadielle.

"Perhaps. I'm not sure." She held the lid out to him and he took it from her, swallowing the potion and tasting mepple petals, stale cheese, and vinegar. It was not altogether unpleasant.

"The moths," he said.

"Yes."

"I've always hated moths."

"That's because they want it that way." She smiled softly, then turned to leave. "I'll be working on the vat if you need me."

"Thank you," he said, unsure of what for. He watched her exit the room, then followed without pause. He suddenly felt part of—instead of apart from—this incredible place for the first time. And as he approached the moth room he felt a burgeoning sense of hope that had been absent for so long.

The terror is rising, go south to Skulk . . . the terror is rising, go south to Skulk . . .

He kept his eyes closed because his own fear was still there. He could sense them moving around him, approaching but not quite touching. He felt the soft draft from their wings and the soundless yet loaded movement of their bodies through the air around his head and face. Perhaps they were dusting him, but he could not quite feel that. What he did sense was that they were listening.

He spoke the same line again and again, and the potion Rose had given him did something to his words. They became abstract and meaningless, as though he were hearing them in an unknown language, yet the feeling as they were formed in his throat and left his mouth transmitted complete understanding. He saw the words in pictures that placed him anywhere in the city, yet always with the knowledge of where Skulk lay in relation to where he was. It was a mental map, and his words provided the route.

When he realized how thirsty he was and opened his eyes,

the moths had gone. He looked up into the endless space above him, and he knew that somewhere up there they flew. They carried his words with them. He hoped people would listen.

When he left the moth room, he could see Rose's feet where she stood beyond the nearest vat. She was motionless, silent, and he watched for a while, waiting to see if she moved. She did not. He thought of walking around the vat to see if she was well but decided against it. *What can she be making?* he wondered. *What can save all those people?* Nadielle had mentioned rackflies, their spreading of germs, but she had kept her ideas close to her chest.

Rose had set him on his task, and her own was something he could have no part of. He'd watched enough monstrous things birthed from these vats, and he had no real wish to see what she was making next.

So he went to the next room, the one with deep holes in the walls where the sleekrats lived, and started whispering his message again.

After the sleekrats, the bats; and after the bats, the red-eared lizards. These creatures he had never used before, and he approached them with caution. They had a reputation for being vicious and cruel, their surprising intelligence balanced with a hatred and fear of humanity that kept them deep, or in places where few people lived. But he trusted Rose and trusted what Nadielle had initiated here. The lizards watched him with their stark yellow eyes as he whispered. Then they left, flitting through cracks in the walls to the Echoes outside and from there up into the world.

He worked until there were no more creatures left. His throat was sore and dry, and the message repeated itself in his head: an endless, doom-laden echo.

Just before the last of the lizards had left, a distant impact shook the small room, dust drifting from the ceiling and stone shards pattering down in one corner. He'd paused and held his breath, but no more noises came. *Rose*, he'd thought, because she was working outside on her vat.

Leaving the room, stretching and craving a drink, he saw her sitting on the vat's top lip.

"Did you hear it?" she asked. "Feel it?"

"Was that you?"

She shook her head, then looked down into the vat. An array of bottles and pouches sat on a board beside her, and she picked up one bottle and dripped several splashes of its contents inside. Gorham went to ask her more, but it already felt as if she'd never spoken to him. *The Baker has a talent for being dismissive*, he thought.

As he stood at the toilet at the back of her rooms, rebuttoning his fly, another thud transmitted up through his feet. In the pale-yellow water below him, ripples.

He went back out to see how else he could help.

It had been a long time since Dane Marcellan had fought. As a young man he'd spent some time as an anonymous soldier in the Scarlet Blades—a rite of passage required of every Marcellan who did not make the shift into the Hanharan priesthood—and he'd been involved in the short but brutal Seethe War in the south of Marcellan Canton. Drug dealers and pimps had come in from Mino Mont, united to try to assert their authority over a small neighborhood. It had taken seven days of house-to-house combat before the last of them was captured or killed, and Dane had been at the forefront of the fighting, killing two men and a woman and being present at the impromptu execution of nine more. He had not enjoyed it, but it had been necessary. It had been *required*.

Now he had blood on his hands again—and his clothes and face, in his eyes and ears and mouth—and he fought with more fervor than he had felt in many years.

Those loyal Blades who had pledged allegiance to him also fought hard, and died hard. The force against them was staggering and inescapable, but behind them Dane knew the hope of the city was still fleeing, and he had to give them every moment he could.

And more than that, Nophel, his son. He had to save his son.

He sidestepped a sweeping blow from a Dragarian with blades for arms, ducked down, and buried his sword in the bastard's groin.

"Fight, you bastards!" he shouted. "For every mother and son and daughter and every fucking nephew and niece you have, fight for them all!" None of these Blades knew the story or why they were fighting. But every time he cried out encouragement, they roared their approval and battled that much harder.

They know this is death, he thought, *but they keep fighting. I'm fighting for Echo City, but they're fighting for me. For* me! He screamed and ran forward, reversing the direction of their retreat and engaging three Dragarians. These were regulars—unchopped but still trained for war—and they came at him with swords and knives, throwing stars and weighted wires that would take his head from his shoulders. He ducked and stabbed, kicked and bit, slashed and thrust. Something struck his shoulder and pain flared, but his scream was one of fury. Wetness splashed across his throat and chest, and he was unsure whether it was his. A sword jabbed at him and he fell back, straight onto another. It pierced his hip and he turned, kneeling, twisting the knife from the owner's hand, smashing his head forward, and feeling cartilage crunch beneath his forehead. The man stepped back, holding his nose, eyes watering as he looked in comical surprise at the blood pooling in his hand. Dane jabbed, and his sword's tip entered the man's left eye, wide blade jamming in his skull.

I'm leaking, Dane thought, and he caught a glimmer sweeping through the air toward him. He fell forward and rolled, crying out as the knife in his hip snagged on a fallen Blade's bloodied robe. The wire whistled by above him and he rolled onto his back, throwing a knife back at the wire wielder. It struck the woman's chest and rebounded from her thick leather armor. She glared at Dane, hatred filling her alien eyes, and her shoulder pivoted as she brought the wire around one more time.

Dane held up his hand to protect his face—and lost four fingers. They tumbled onto his chest. *The breasts I've stroked with those*, he thought, *the muffs I've felt, the slash I've smoked, the food I've eaten*, and the severed fingers curled as if stroking soft scented flesh one last time.

A Blade stepped astride him, warding off the woman,

dummying, stabbing her in the gut, and then smashing her face with a spiked fist.

Dane went to stand but could not. Something was wrong with his legs. He roared again, putting every ounce of strength into rising, but nothing happened, nothing moved, and when he sought the pain below his waist he found none. He grabbed the knife in his hip and tugged it free, feeling nothing. Its blade was sticky with his blood and, near the handle, dark with something else.

Dirty fighters, he thought. He had seen several Blades butchered as they lay motionless and helpless but had not let himself wonder why. But every moment he'd spent here had given Nophel a better chance to escape.

"Run," he said to the Blade above him. "Retreat, stand again a hundred steps back, fight until you can't fight anymore."

"I'll not leave—"

"Do as you're fucking well told, soldier!"

She glanced down at him, then disappeared from view.

A Dragarian with haunting indigo eyes and four arms stepped into view above Dane Marcellan. It blinked eyes lizardlike and expressionless. Dane imagined raising his sword and popping those orbs, seeing if the bastard thing had expression then, but none of his limbs would move.

"Eat me," he said, offering a final curse, and the thing's impossibly wide mouth hinged open to display horrendous teeth.

Chapter 24

Feeling and seeing the sky appear before her was the greatest breath of freedom Peer had ever experienced. The weight of the Echoes lifted away and she breathed easier, even though there was a stitch in her side and her lungs and legs ached. But she had to keep running. If she didn't and the Dragarians caught her, Malia's death would be in vain.

The moonlight was bright, unimpeded by clouds, and to the south, across this narrow finger of Crescent, rose the imposing mass of Marcellan Canton. Lines of lights snaked up its gentle hillsides where streetlamps had been lit, and window lights speckled the entire shadowy mound. At its pinnacle, the blazing illuminations around Hanharan Heights were there as usual, but there was a particular intensity to them tonight. It was as if every single light in that place was lit. The canton's outer wall was silvered by moonlight, and this was Peer's destination. For some reason, she felt that once she reached there, she would be safe.

We stole their god, she thought. *Nowhere is safe*. But she tried to shove that idea down as she ran. Grasses whipped around her legs, then she entered a vast field of whorn plants, tall as her shoulders and pungent with their burgeoning crop. Shoving the close-growing plants aside with outstretched hands, she ran as fast as she could, tripping over roots on occasion, her palms sliced from the plants' fine leaves.

She was desperate to reach Rufus again. He'd looked confused and bewildered, but deep down there had still been some measure of control. Whether or not he knew how special he was to Echo City now—*if* what the Baker said was true, *if* she could use him to help them all—Peer still felt responsible for everything that had happened to him. Discovering who he was and where he had come from had been a shock, to her as well as to him. But she wanted to help him learn more.

She sensed that she was no longer alone. Risking a glance behind her, she saw nothing, but she knew that the Dragarians were out now, flooding up furiously into the moonlight. Dane Marcellan and the Blades would be dead, and she only hoped that the others had taken full advantage of the lead they had been given.

Stumbling into an area of flattened whorn, she almost came to a standstill, looking around for whatever had made the rough path. But then she saw that it headed south across the fields and knew who had come this way. *It'll be easy to follow*, she thought, but surprise was no longer with them, and stealth could not save them. It all came down to speed.

Freedom from the oppressive belowground was good, but she had never felt so isolated. Peer ran as fast as she could, her breathing and footfalls the only sounds. She expected a poisoned arrow to strike her at any moment, plunging her into the same agonies that had taken Malia. She considered weaving to distract any potential killer's aim, but that would only waste time. *Fast*, she thought, *faster—just run!*

The wall loomed before her, and the path of beaten whorn she'd been following faded out. On top of the wall two shadows waved to her, and she heard a voice calling. Though it confused her, right then it was the finest thing she had ever heard.

"Go left!" Alexia called. "There's an open door." Peer did as she said, rushing diagonally toward a dark shape at the base of the wall, a newfound burst of energy carrying her across the rough ground. And that was when she heard the first of their cries.

Pausing for a moment to look back, she saw hundreds, perhaps thousands, of thrashing shapes forging through the whorn like a wave of darkness about to wash against the canton wall.

Above, other shapes drifted and flapped, low to the ground but faster than those on foot.

She rushed through the door and someone slammed it behind her, plunging them into darkness. Heavy metal bolts were thrown, then timber thumped against timber.

"Where's Malia?" Alexia asked.

"Dead."

"Oh. Come on, we don't have much time."

"I can't see—"

"Grab my hand. I know the way." Peer felt her hand grasped and she held on tight, following Alexia through a twisting corridor to the other side of the wall. They emerged into moonlight again just as there were shouts atop the wall, first of surprise and then alarm. Finally a scream of pain, and the sounds of combat rose again.

"Sleepy Blades getting a taste of the fight at last," Alexia said.

"They didn't see me coming in."

"Like I said, sleepy. Come on, Nophel is taking us to something called a Bellower."

"Good," Peer said, and the thought of sitting back in that claustrophobic pod while the Bellowers blasted them south was wonderful.

"And Dane?" Alexia asked hesitantly.

"I left him and the Blades fighting," Peer said. "I don't think . . ."

Alexia nodded. "Good. He's caused a lot of pain."

"He saved our lives."

Alexia shrugged, and they started to run again. Soon they reached the others, waiting in the shadow of a butcher shop's canopy. The shop was closed, but the smell of fresh meat still hung heavy on the air. They had all manifested, and Rufus leaned against the wall, head bowed. He was breathing hard. He looked up as Peer approached, staring at her with haunted eyes. Peer felt a rush of relief, and she suddenly felt safer than she had any right to.

"Your friend won't think himself Unseen," the tall Unseen said.

"It's not natural," Rufus said. "It's something of *hers*." Peer could sense a relief in Rufus that she had returned, and she went quickly to his side, grabbing his hand and glad that he gripped back. "I don't want it anymore," he said. "Get it out of me."

"Not sure we can," Alexia said.

"Maybe Nadielle," Peer said, and she felt Rufus flinch at the name. "Rufus, it wasn't Nadielle, it was the Baker before her who sent you out."

"They're all the same." He looked down at his feet, and Peer noticed Nophel staring intently at him, the deformed man's good eye glittering with tears or avarice.

"What is it?" Peer asked.

Nophel shook his head.

"Really, we need to get the fuck out of here right now," Alexia said. The sound of fighting at the wall had increased, and from several directions they could hear the familiar Scarlet Blades' horns as the call went out. Hundreds would be rushing to join the fray, but Peer was quite certain they would not arrive in time. Already she could see vague shapes flying above the city, circling here and there as they searched the warren of streets, squares, and alleys for their quarry. One fell, twisting and screeching as it flapped at the several arrows piercing it, but she didn't think the Blade archers would be so lucky again.

"They'll find me," Rufus said.

"Not if I can help it," Nophel muttered. "Come on." He led them along the street, dodging from shadow to shadow as they aimed for the route down to the nearest Bellower chamber. Peer knew that something had begun and that the Dragarians—emerging overtly from their canton for the first time in five centuries—would not cease in their quest until they found Rufus.

They followed the deformed man as he led them from street, to alley, and then down beneath the Marcellan levels. He knew where the tunnels were and where the oil torches would be kept. He knew which doors to open and which to ignore. As they emerged into the Bellower chamber and he immediately set about priming the chopped creature, she felt a distance growing about her, buffering her against what was happening. *Self-defense*, Penler's voice said, and she grinned without humor. At any other time she would have been curious, asking Nophel about what he knew, but today such curiosity seemed redundant. At the city's most dangerous time in history, now it was also at war.

What could be worse? she thought as they gathered around the first of the Bellower pods.

"I can't leave," Rufus said. "I belong back there."

"Oh, for fuck's sake!" Alexia shouted.

"Rufus?" Peer asked.

"My name is not Rufus," he said. "It's Dragar."

There was silence for a while, and then Nophel chuckled. "Er . . . fine. Can someone help me with—"

"They told me. I remembered. They paid the old dead Baker to chop me. She used her own essence and that of Dragar, the Dragarians' murdered prophet."

"The Blades killed a terrorist five hundred years ago, not a prophet," Alexia said.

"Then explain me," Rufus said. "They provided the Baker with his essence, stored for centuries in their holiest of holy shrines. She chopped me. And then she used me for her own ends instead. Sent me away. Cast me into the desert. Her *experiment*."

"So you're saying that you're . . ." Peer said, shaking her head, too confused to finish.

"Returned to the Dragarians from out of the Bonelands to lead them into Honored Darkness."

"I'm going to hit him again," Alexia said.

"The farther you take me, the more people they will kill to get me back," Rufus said. "Or . . . you can let me go now."

"We *can't*!" Peer said. "You're important, and the Baker needs you to—"

"She disposed of me once before. Why does she need me now?"

"*Because* you crossed the desert," Peer said. "You're immune to whatever's out there. Maybe Dragar was too, whoever he was, and—"

"No," Rufus said, "I'm much more than that." He smiled softly at Peer, and then there was a knife at his throat.

* * *

"You're no god," Nophel said. "And you're going to take me to see my mother."

"Mother?" someone gasped, but Nophel did not know or care who.

Rufus simply stared at him, calm and smug, and in his green eyes Nophel saw some of what the Baker must feel. With such knowledge must come superiority. With talents beyond those of anyone else in the city—in their world—there must be power and responsibility.

The air in the Bellower chamber thrummed. Rufus smiled.

"You won't cut my throat."

"No?" Nophel said, leaning in closer, curving his other arm around the tall man's back to pull tight.

"No," Rufus said.

There was movement behind Nophel and he turned, adjusting his position so that he held Rufus in front of him, backing against the Bellower pod, resting against it so that he could see the others. Peer was standing with her mouth open in surprise, as if the world had been pulled out from beneath her. The two Unseen men seemed to be glancing back and forth from Alexia to Nophel, obviously waiting to take their lead from her. And Alexia seemed to shimmer, her invisibility shifting unconsciously as her hand gripped her sword.

"I need to see her," Nophel said. "Need to talk with her."

"But she can't be your mother," Peer said. "She's barely twenty, and you're—"

"Age doesn't matter to them," he said. "They might look different or change bodies, but it's still the same mind. Still the same traitorous . . . bloody . . . mind. Right, Rufus?"

"We're going to her anyway," Peer said softly, trying to mediate. She held her hands away from her body, projecting calm. Alexia looked ready to slice Nophel's head off. Nophel almost smiled at the shock his actions had inspired in all of them.

Apart from Rufus. He seemed quite calm. Nophel could even feel his heartbeat—gentle, soft.

"She always has her reasons," Rufus said. "I don't know what she did to you, but I can guess. And she did the same to me."

"But you're not her *child*," Nophel said angrily. He pulled back on the knife and was rewarded with a satisfying stiffening of Rufus's body. The tall man, so composed, suddenly seemed afraid.

"Don't," he said. "Hurt me and you'll doom everyone."

"You think I care?" Nophel shouted, but his vision was blurring.

"I might not be her child," Rufus said, "but she treated me as a son for a while. I'm not sure how long. It's . . . confused. But I was with her—she taught me, and walked the city with me, fed and clothed me. And then I learned that it was all part of the experiment."

"I was her true son," Nophel said. "Hers, and Dane Marcellan's." Through his blurred vision he saw the added amazement on Peer's face, and even Alexia stood straighter, hand falling away from her sword.

"You're a Marcellan?" the Unseen gasped.

"No!" Nophel shouted.

"But did you find love?" Rufus asked. He eased back a little, lessening the pressure of the knife against his throat. "I did. Out there, past the desert. She took me in and loved me as her own son."

"Love," Nophel said, and he thought of Dane's final touch on his ugly face, and the way the Marcellan had taken him from the workhouse, given him a home, protected him. He'd been Nophel's point of contact among the Marcellans—a fat, slash-using monster who had treated the Scope watcher with disdain and disgust, but how must it have been for him? To know that he had employed the Baker's bastard son—his *own* son—in Hanharan Heights, and to know the terrible tortures that awaited them both if anyone there ever found out? Perhaps the only way to protect him had been to treat him like that. But in the end, when everything was falling apart . . .

"I can *see* you're not completely unloved," Rufus said. "I'm not sure anyone ever is."

Nophel lowered the knife, but Rufus stayed close, a harsh red line across his throat.

"I wanted to kill her," Nophel whispered.

"I understand," Rufus said, equally quiet. "But wouldn't

you rather just ask her why?" He stepped back from Nophel, and Alexia dashed past him, her sword drawn, hunched down, ready in case Nophel went for her with his knife.

But he dropped the weapon and pressed his hands to his horrible, disfigured face, the fluid from several open sores mixing with his tears. *Don't be too harsh on the Baker*, Dane—his father—had said. *She's not like us.*

"Us," he whispered, a single word that included him.

Nophel sensed a flutter of movement in the Bellower chamber, a shout, and then a dying scream. Looking up, he saw Dragarians streaming in, the short Unseen already dead on the ground.

"Wait!" Rufus said, but these were creatures ready for war. Some were wounded and bleeding, others wore hastily tied robes from Scarlet Blades they had killed, and one bore the slashed, blood-soaked remnants of Dane Marcellan's fine robe.

Alexia and the other Unseen went for the Dragarians. Peer seemed confused, looking back and forth between the attackers and Rufus. And Rufus stepped forward, hands held up as if to divert the assault.

They advanced quickly, two of them parrying the tall Unseen's sword and grasping his arms while a third drove a bladed hand through his face. He shook but made no sound as he died. They dropped him and moved on.

"No!" Rufus shouted, louder this time, and the sudden attack paused. The chamber seemed to echo with violence. "They haven't harmed me."

"That's my father's robe," Nophel said. The Dragarian wearing it was a woman, badly chopped so that her skin was hardened into chitinous armor, and she hissed at him. He pushed himself away from the Bellower pod, even then thinking, *Just what am I going to do?* But he had no chance to do anything. The *chunk* of a crossbow, a punch in his chest, and he fell, the rising chaos in the chamber suddenly very far away and no longer a part of him.

He saw his father's face as he had seen it only once—smiling for his son. And then darkness.

* * *

Everything was happening so quickly that, to Peer, it felt like a dream.

She brought up both hands as the Dragarian came at her. Its blades were raised, its eyes lidded for protection, its head lowered, and it moved sleek as a shadow and fast as starlight. *Penler*, was her last thought, and then she felt the cool kiss of metal against her throat.

"I said stop!" a voice thundered. She knew something in that voice, but it had changed, become whole, and now it sounded like the voice of . . .

I don't believe in gods, Peer thought as a hand rested softly on her shoulder. The Dragarians backed away, heads lowered slightly. The hand squeezed.

Peer turned and looked past Rufus. Alexia had approached Nophel hesitantly, sword still in one hand. Her edges blurred, but she remained seen as she knelt by the fallen man. He was breathing hard, one hand cupped around the bolt projecting from his chest but not quite touching it.

The chamber took a breath between deaths, and Peer wondered who would be next.

"Peer," Rufus said softly, and she turned to the tall man. "You've been my only friend."

"I wanted to help you," she said.

"And you did." His eyes flicked around the chamber, taking in the bodies of the two dead Unseen and the several Dragarians backed against the chamber wall. They all looked up but kept their heads bowed. *Their god has spoken*, Peer thought, and perhaps such power and belief was what it was about. Who needed real gods, if false ones could exert such control?

"I will return with you," he said to the Dragarians, "and no one will try to prevent that."

I'm losing him, Peer thought. *He's going*. She reached for his arm and he held her hand, squeezing gently.

"Doom hangs over the city," Rufus continued. "As Dragar I return, and my blood is as it was five hundred years ago—rich with the way to Honored Darkness." The few Dragarians muttered, shuffling their feet, glancing at one another. "But we will leave in peace. The city's end-days are here, with no need for us to hasten them. Our domes will close again, our warriors will be recalled, and there will be no more violence. This is no longer our home, and we have no more business here."

Alexia was now standing close to Nophel, glancing around uncertainly. When she caught Peer's eye, Peer nodded down at the short sword she held. The Unseen dropped the blade.

"Do you really believe . . . ?" Peer asked, but Rufus leaned in close and took her in a gentle hug.

"To them, I'm their god," he whispered, "and they'll use whatever is in my blood—whatever was in *Dragar's* blood— to help them cross the Bonelands. Honored Darkness awaits to the north. I find only honor in their desire that I lead them there."

"But Echo City *needs* you, Rufus!"

"This is not my home," he said, "and Rufus is not my name."

"Dragar *is*?"

He only blinked, and the Dragarians fidgeted.

"I don't believe in gods," Peer said. "We need your blood. The Baker needs it, and you can't just turn around and leave with them." She nodded at the chopped warriors, their blades folded and stained with drying blood.

"You'd fight them?" Rufus asked.

"Yes!" Alexia said, and she knelt to pick up her dropped sword.

"No," Rufus said. "No." He walked to Alexia and took the sword from her hand, and she did nothing to prevent him. He glanced down at Nophel, blood from the fallen man's wound spreading on the chamber floor. Then he sliced the sword across his own palm.

The Dragarians gasped, but Rufus stilled them with a glance. He told Alexia to empty her water canteen, then squeezed his wound above the container's neck, wincing, his skin turning pale as blood dripped. For a while it was the only sound in the huge chamber, and then Rufus swayed, and Peer dashed to his side to hold him steady. The Dragarians mumbled at her contact with him.

"This might not be enough," Alexia said, but Peer cut her off with a glare.

"Thank you," Peer said. Rufus nodded at her and let her bind the wound. "But you expected this?" she asked. "Ever since you arrived here?"

"I had . . ." Rufus said, frowning. "Feelings. And I had to follow them."

"And they led you here?" Alexia asked. But Rufus ignored her, looking only at Peer.

"They called me Man from Sand," he said.

"Who?"

"The people across the desert. Their world is called the Heartlands, and their Heart and Mind sees through me. It knows Echo City now. I hope it will welcome you."

"Tell me more!" Peer said.

"It's not for me to tell you," he said. "And I have to go."

"Please!" Peer said. She was pleading now, struggling to grasp the truth she had been seeking her whole adult life. "It's everything I've ever believed in!"

"Then have faith," Rufus said. He turned and walked to where the Dragarians stood in respectful, awed silence. They parted to ensure their bloodied weapons did not touch him, then followed him from that place without a backward glance.

The Bellower chamber fell almost silent; only Nophel's heavy breathing whispered against the walls.

"Well, that was intense," Alexia said. She stared at her two fallen friends, then knelt again beside the motionless Nophel, examining the injury.

"Is he . . . ?" Peer asked, still not looking away from where Rufus had vanished.

"It's not good," Alexia said. "Missed the heart, but he's losing blood."

Peer turned and looked at the water canteen Alexia had placed carefully on the ground. *That's the blood we can't afford to lose*, she thought. "We have to get to the Baker," she said. "As quickly as we can. We stop for nothing." She glanced up at the Bellower. "I hope I can remember what he did to make this thing work."

"I'm not dead yet," Nophel whispered. "Help me . . . into the pod."

"So she's really your mother," Peer said.

"My mother."

"Talk about mixed heritage," Alexia said.

And as she and Alexia lifted Nophel into the Bellower pod, Rufus's parting comment imprinted itself on Peer's mind forever.

Then have faith.

Chapter 25

He was pacing the vat hall, feeling helpless, silently exhorting Rose to acknowledge him again instead of just sitting on the vat, watching and stirring and watering, when she gasped and fell. She bounced from the shell of the vat, knocked her head against one of the large wooden uprights, and splashed in the warm pool around its base. The sound of her head making contact with the ground was sickening, and even as he ran across to her—fifteen steps, certainly no more—he was certain that she was dead.

He felt an impact through his feet, so powerful that he stumbled a little before regaining his balance. Accompanying it for the first time, a distant rumble . . . and a roar.

Oh, crap, oh, crap—and he knew how great events often turned on the pivot of a minor, pointless catastrophe. Kneeling beside her, he dreaded what he would see. There was no blood, at least not at first glance. No dents in her head. Her left eye flickered slightly, splashing droplets of water from her eyelashes.

"Rose," he said, reaching out but not quite touching.

Another impact, and dust came down from the ceiling. The vat rumbled and whispered, and he expected its sides to flex and burst at any moment. *What's she making this time?* He had seen the birth of Neph, and then those three fighting things, and finally Rose, so now what could Rose be making to better that? What monstrous creature would she send after the others to fight whatever was rising? It was like sending a bird after a spider after a fly . . .

"No!" she gasped. Gorham lifted her head from the water, and her eyes fluttered open. One was still pink and bloodshot, but they were both alert and conscious. She fixed her gaze on Gorham for a beat, then tried to sit up. He helped. She thanked him. Then she slowly lowered her eyes.

"She's dead," she said. "We don't have very long."

"Nadielle?"

Rose stood and held on to the wooden support. She wiped water from her face and looked at a smear of blood across the back of her hand. Her nose was bleeding.

"Are you sure?" Gorham asked.

"She tried to communicate with the Vex while her creations attacked it. Tried to reason with it. But it killed her. The chopped are still fighting it, but . . ." She shrugged. "Help me back up. I have to make certain the vat—"

"Don't you care?" *It killed her,* he thought. *She's gone—all that life, those gorgeous eyes glazed . . .*

"She made me because she knew it would happen," the girl said, confused.

"*I* care!" Gorham said.

Rose seemed uncertain, as if waiting for him to say more. When he remained silent, unable to speak, she turned away and looked back up at the vat.

Gorham walked away. *I ran over here to help her,* he thought. *And she never needed my help.*

"They'd better bring him soon," Rose said. As if to illustrate her point, there was another impact that shook the ground and made him stagger against one of the ruined vats. His hand slid into a sickly, thick mess, and he wiped it on his trousers without looking.

"If they do, they do," he said. *And if Peer is still with them, please, let her talk to me. Let her accept me.*

The distance roared, and he wondered what state Echo City was in.

* * *

The Bellowers bellowed, and Peer and Alexia traveled south in a pod with the injured Nophel between them. Alexia had administered brief first aid but thought it too risky to try removing the crossbow bolt. *At least it doesn't seem to be poisoned*, she'd said, and Peer's thoughts had gone back to Malia. It would be difficult telling Gorham about her death, but at least it had been a brave one.

And was I brave? she wondered. Whatever happened in the immediate future, she would never forget the feeling of her sword ending that tortured woman's life.

The journey passed quickly. At last they lifted Nophel between them and headed toward daylight, and he groaned as he walked, trying to help but losing a lot of blood. As they emerged into the dawn from the final Bellower basement— Peer welcoming the sunlight, reveling in the heat on her face, and yet convinced that something terrible was stalking them— the ground was shaken by an immense tremor. Peer staggered against a wall with Nophel, and Alexia went to her knees on the narrow path. Windows smashed, people screamed. The Unseen woman grasped the water canteen.

As the noise of the impact faded, a silence hung over the built-up area—a pause that invited more chaos. But none arrived.

"What was that?" Alexia asked.

"It's getting close," Peer said. "We have to hurry, Alexia. Fast as we can. We've got to get across into Crescent and down to the Baker's labs, and that's two miles away. And . . ." She looked at Nophel, with his head bowed. *We should leave him*, she thought. But he had helped them so much—the Unseen most of all—and before she could say more, Alexia had grasped his arm across her shoulders.

"Then we should go."

Smoke rose in the distance, and voices rose in panic again. This was not the usual morning chaos. This was the sound of a rout.

"What's happening?" Nophel asked.

"Come on." Peer grabbed his other arm and they walked along the narrow alley. The smoke she'd seen was thick and rich; the stink of cooking meat hung in the air. And as they rounded the corner and Peer looked down the sloping street, the chaos grew apparent.

The streets were thronged with people, carts, and tusked swine loaded with hastily tied packings, all of them flowing south. Arguments broke out here and there, fistfights flaring and dying out. Farther up the gentle hillside toward the looming Marcellan Canton wall, a building burned. Its windows gushed fire and the roof wore a head of flames, and from this distance it was difficult to tell whether the fire was being tended. One side wall had already collapsed, and burning brands were drifting westward on the breeze. Already there were smoke plumes heading skyward from a dozen secondary fires.

Someone called for their son. A woman screamed. An old man begged for help, somewhere out of sight. Children cried, men shouted, and a tusked swine was shrieking. It had fallen in the road, leg snapped where a hole had opened up in the paving. A family was hastily unloading the beast, and no one seemed eager to put it out of its misery.

Another jolt, and more glass broke and showered into the street.

"The moth said south!" a woman cried as she emerged from a building across the street. She was slapping at her husband's hands as he tried to hold her back. "Come with me!" she begged. "Please?"

"Moth?" was all he said, and the woman held his coat and tried to pull him with her into the throng.

"Moth?" Alexia asked.

"I don't know," Peer said. She grabbed at a woman walking by. "Wait! What's happening?"

"South to Skulk," the woman said. "Haven't you heard? That's what's best."

"The Marcellans have ordered that?"

The woman had walked on, but at that she paused and turned back, barely sparing Nophel a glance. "Ha! The Marcellans? You're joking, aren't you? They don't—"

There was another thud that traveled up through Peer's feet and set her teeth ringing. Somewhere far away, something fell, heavy stones tumbling and crushing. The flow of humanity paused for a moment, then continued on its way, voices a little quieter than before, a little more afraid.

"There's another one," the woman whispered. "If you've got your heads on right, you'll come with us."

"But who told you?"

"Who? People just . . . know. The terror is rising; go south to Skulk."

"We can't," Peer said. The woman looked at Nophel properly then, a spark of interest in her eyes. Then she turned and went on her way.

"Right, well, that's got me crapping in my trousers," Alexia said.

"Easy . . . for you to say," Nophel mumbled. "So are we going or not?"

As they set off for Crescent, across the flow of people, it felt as if Nophel was leading the way.

Beside the street at a major crossroads lay the bodies of three Scarlet Blades. They had been dragged to one side and left there, food for rockzards and other carrion creatures. People poured past, heading south for the Tharin. Though Peer could not see that far, she knew that the river crossings would be thronged, and beyond there would be streets filled with panicked, desperate refugees. Nothing like this had ever happened in her lifetime. The whole city was moving.

The terror is rising; go south to Skulk, the woman said, and it had echoed with the sound of something repeated.

The ground shook. The impact was so great that the air before her seemed to vibrate, and the shape and color of the city changed. *What* is *that?* she thought, stumbling into a wall to one side. She blinked, took in a deep breath, and realized that, in all the streets she could see, people had fallen down. They recovered quickly, and soon the flow of humanity was moving once again. But for just that moment the city had been still and prostrate.

A cloud of dust rose in the distance where a building had collapsed.

"Won't the Marcellans be *doing* something?" Alexia asked,

staring back and up the long hillside to the spires of Hanharan Heights.

"You tell me," Peer said. "You worked for them."

"They'll be debating a course of action," Nophel said, laughing, then coughing.

"They'll be doing something," Alexia said. But she did not sound convinced.

"We have to go against the flow," Peer said. She looked out across the northern parts of Course at the splash of green in the distance. Crescent. That was their destination, but between here and there were rivers of people flowing south. *Escaping something*, she thought. *We should be going with them*. But they had something important to do. These people could flee to Skulk, but that place was still a part of Echo City. If what was rising was as terrible as she feared—as terrible as it felt—they had to go farther. And the only person who might help them do that was the Baker.

"We could go down through the Echoes," Alexia said.

"You know the way from here?"

"From a long time ago," she said. "There was a time . . . With the Blades, we used the First Echo to bring people back to Hanharan Heights."

"People?"

"Dissidents." She glanced away, because there was a lie in her voice. Peer no longer cared. Perhaps none of that really mattered anymore.

"The city's going to change," she said, but at the back of her mind the change was greater than she could voice. *The city is going to die*.

"This way," Alexia said.

As they worked their way along the street, there was another terrible tremor. Tiles slipped from rooftops, injuring dozens in the streets below, and weaker buildings slumped in their foundations. The dead Scarlet Blades were already covered in a film of dust, and Peer noticed that Alexia averted her eyes as they passed them by. *Maybe she knows them*.

They pushed across the surge of people and made their way back up to the Marcellan Canton wall. *Go south to*

Skulk, someone kept whispering, and though Peer looked, she could not see who the whisperer was.

"It's history exploding," a man's voice said. Peer glanced around, and a short fat man was staring directly at her. He was well dressed, his skin was smooth, his hands soft and hair well cut. A lawyer, perhaps, or someone who worked in the upper echelons of the Marcellans' widespread governing network.

"What do you mean?" she asked.

"History. Down there." He nodded at the ground, whispering in case the Echoes heard. "Exploding. There's so much of it, see? We've been building on it forever, letting the old times sink down and fade away without saying a proper goodbye. There are phantoms down there that don't know they're dead, and they say there are whole civilizations, whole *cities*, just going along like they're the here and now. And the Garthans!" He waved one hand and gazed about surreptitiously, though they were surrounded by a hundred other people. "They're the players of the past. Explorers, they call them. But, no. Players. Manipulators!"

"You really think—"

"Hush, girl. I don't think; I *know*. It's history exploding. It's been under pressure for so long, and now it's all coming back." His face paled, and suddenly he did not seem to be enjoying his rumor-mongering anymore. "Coming back to haunt us." Then he was gone, pushing away from her as though he had contaminated Peer by telling her his ideas.

"Come on," Alexia said. "Through the gate, along the wall, next alleyway." They forced their way against the flow, passing into Marcellan without seeing any sign of the Scarlet Blades that should be guarding it. As they worked their way along the base of the wall, it was not long before they realized why.

The four Blades had been battered and crushed to death. Around them in the street lay the bodies of those they had taken with them—maybe ten people, around whom the crowds parted in silent respect. At least one of the bodies was that of a child.

"I don't want to see any more," Peer said.

"One thing you learn in the Blades: Civilization balances on a knife edge." Alexia tugged Nophel onward, and Peer went with them. "It's the alley behind those poor bastards."

"You won't escape them there." The short fat woman was

sitting ten steps from the dead Blades, a slashed red tunic around her shoulders. She bore a terrible wound across her stomach. Peer thought she must be bleeding to death.

"Escape who?"

"The outsiders. Haven't you heard? Dragarians—invading from the north. Garthans—from below." She rocked slowly back and forth, panting, and Peer wondered which corpse she mourned.

"Peer," Alexia said, and Peer was happy to be led away.

"Outsiders!" The woman's voice carried to them, and there were others shouting at her to *Shut the fuck up,* and *Keep it to yourself,* and *You're scaring my children.*

"Here," Alexia said, indicating a half-open door.

The ground shook, people screamed, and a building fell close by. *Whatever it is, it's really big.* Alexia steered Nophel inside first, and Peer followed, glad to be free of the crowd.

The Scarlet Blade house had been ransacked. Any spare weapons were gone, and someone had defecated on the dead Blades' table. Peer was amazed that, while fleeing for their life, someone would take the time to do that.

"Over here," Alexia said. "I remember using this one a couple of times before." Against the stone wall stood a huge wooden storage unit, shelves now swept clean of whatever they might have held. They waded through piles of smashed plates, torn sheets, and shattered storage jars shining amid spilled food, and Alexia pried with her sword behind the unit. "Help me . . . pull!"

Peer and the Unseen heaved and pulled, propping their feet against the wall to give added leverage, and, without warning, the unit suddenly tipped and fell. Behind it was an old door, bolted into the wall five times. It took several smashes from Alexia's sword handle on each bolt to get them sliding.

Behind the door was a spiral staircase heading down and, piled in a nook in the wall, several oil torches.

"We'll see daylight again soon," Alexia said. But hers was a forced hope, and Peer could see that. Darkness had never seemed so forbidding. The three of them stared down the stairwell, listening for the sounds of things rising below, sniffing the air, and wondering just how mad they must be.

Peer picked up an oil torch, lit it on the first strike, and handed it to Nophel. "We'll need our sword hands free," she said. The injured man smiled, ghastly and wan in the torch-light.

"Hate to say it," Nophel said to Alexia, "but do you know the way?"

The Unseen smiled softly, lit her own torch, and started down the stairs.

They traveled two miles through a time gone by, taking it in turns to support Nophel, and all the while the cloying silence was more terrifying than the noise of the crowds they had left behind. In the darkness lay a potential for terrible violence, and that potential was being realized more and more. They heard deep rumbles in the distance—behind them, they thought, though they could not be certain. Some of those rumbles seemed to echo as roars. And sometimes these roars grew and grew, and they had to try to find cover and lie down as the ground shook and dust and rocks fell from the shadows above them.

What are we really doing? Peer thought. The city was shaking to pieces, the population was panicking, and her only aim was to reach the Baker with a canteen of cooling, thickening blood. Rufus might be insane, and the Dragarians thought he was their god. Malia was dead. Many other people were dead. *Am I really that mad?*

Yet again, she wished Penler was with her. Dependable Penler, whose knowledge and intelligence would see him through these confusions. And, thinking of him, she realized that his life was about to be turned upside down as well.

"They're all going to Skulk," she said to the shadows, but Alexia and Nophel seemed not to hear.

The Unseen led them uncannily across Crescent, transposing Peer's memories of her journey to the laboratory above-ground onto the dead landscape they now walked. Old trails down here echoed the path of current trails above, and Nophel managed the journey without a single complaint. His wound had stopped bleeding for now, but the amount of blood he had lost was shocking. The Dragarian crossbow bolt protruded from his chest just below his collarbone, pinning his dirty cloak to his body. Even if he survived the internal injuries, Peer thought, infection might well kill him.

When they finally drew close to the Baker's subterranean rooms, Peer prepared for the welcoming committee. She glanced around nervously, listening for the sounds of flying things or the cautious tread of the Pserans, but the Echo was theirs alone. She found the door they had entered before, pushed it open, and was suddenly convinced of what would be awaiting them.

Gorham and Nadielle never made it back. They're lying dead way down where the deepest Echoes merge with myth and legend, killed by whatever's shaking the city.

She entered first, walking into the vast womb-vat chamber alone. Lights still shone, but several of the vats had broken and collapsed, slumped to the ground like giant melted candles.

One still bubbled and spat.

And then Gorham emerged from behind the vat. He froze when he saw her, but she had never been so glad to see anyone in her life.

"Gorham," she said, and ran for him. He seemed changed by whatever he had been through, but she would not ask him yet. He looked surprised at her eagerness to see him. Both of them had new histories to learn. But right then, the feel of the present when she held him was all that mattered.

Nophel looked through the wide doorway at the amazing room beyond. Peer hugged a man, Alexia stood inside the doorway looking around in amazement, shadows shifted, air moved, and scenes of destruction were countered by the presence of the single huge vat that still appeared whole.

These were the Baker's laboratories, and it was nothing like coming home.

He took a step forward and groaned. His vision blurred, and he tried to shout at the unfairness of things. *All this way, I only need to set eyes on her before . . .*

Nophel's world upended, and soft hands eased him to the ground.

Chapter 26

Gorham wanted to talk with Peer, discover what she had been through, connect with her again after being apart for so long. He had never believed that connection would be possible again, not after what he had done to her. But something had changed. And he was not foolish enough to believe that the change was only in her.

She told him about Malia. He told her about Nadielle and Rose. Alexia was introduced, Rose came and took the water canteen containing Rufus's blood, and the Pserans carried Nophel into the vat chamber.

"The Baker's blood son," Peer said. Rose paused for the briefest moment to stare at him, then walked away from them all. Peer stared after her, eyes growing wide as Gorham explained more.

"So she's your *daughter*?"

"I . . ." Gorham could not say, because he had not yet come to terms with the reality of that himself.

Rose had climbed the ladder beside the vat, and she sat there with her potions and mixes, carefully extracting blood from the canteen and doing something with it that none of them could see.

"I so need to rest," Peer said. "To wash, and eat, and sleep for a day. But it feels as if it's only just begun."

"The whole city's moving south," Alexia said. She looked tired and drawn, and already she was reminding Gorham very much of Malia. There was an inner strength to her that could never be touched by physical tiredness, and she looked like someone who would get what she wanted. Unlike Malia, her eyes held a restrained humor. He liked that. In the face of all that was happening, it made her seem so human.

"We're in Rose's hands now," Gorham said. "Every chance feels small, but without her there's no chance at all."

Nophel mumbled, still unconscious. The Pserans had quickly melted away after bringing him in, and Alexia crouched by his side, carefully examining his wound.

"It needs cleaning," she said. "And he needs medicine."

The new Baker returned to them, her girl's body and face already appearing older than any of theirs. *She's fading even more*, Gorham thought, and he only hoped she lasted long enough.

"Do you have medicine?" Alexia asked her.

The girl stared at the prone man, and there was something in her that Gorham had not seen before. Since her birthing she had been busy—either working at the vat, or thinking about what to do next, reading the Baker's books and charts, and making esoteric notes in a thick pad. Now, for the first time, she was still and contemplative.

"Carry him through to my rooms," she said.

"Seeing you is what's kept him alive," Peer said.

Rose looked at her, then turned and walked away without replying.

Peer took a step forward, but Gorham caught her arm.

"And you thought Nadielle was cold?" he said. She smiled at him, and that warm flush he'd felt upon seeing her enter the laboratory returned. They both had so much to say, with so little time.

"I'll tell you when I'm ready," Rose said from where she'd climbed back up to the vat's lip. "You should all rest. When the time comes, we'll have to go south, to Skulk."

"And then?" Peer asked.

The girl looked at her curiously, as if considering a specimen of something she had never seen before. "I remember so much about you," she said.

Gorham felt Peer shiver against his side.

"What will happen?" Gorham asked.

"Then we see whether any of this will work." Rose turned back to the vat.

"Come on," he said. "There's some food left. And wine. We'll drink to success." He helped Alexia carry the unconscious man through the vat chamber and into the rooms beyond, and the air buzzed with unspoken news.

Peer seemed changed. She held her injured hip, but there was a strength to her that had not been there when she'd offer him a dismissive wave goodbye. Her eyes were haunted, but she had a smile for him. He hoped that was a good enough start.

They placed Nophel on the Baker's bed, then sat at a table and passed around a bottle of wine. Before long, Alexia leaned back in her chair and slept, and Peer had to settle Gorham when the Unseen woman began to flicker from view.

Gorham and Peer lay together on the other side of the bed. He watched her close her eyes and sleep, but he refused to do so. This might be the end, and he wanted to spend every moment he had left looking at the woman he had wronged. But as her breathing deepened, he, too, closed his eyes, and he rested his hand on hers as dreams carried him away.

Come with me, the voice said. *Please, come with me*. It was a child's voice, yet it carried the weight of ages. Nophel saw the words in his father's mouth, yet his lips spelled something different, because he had gone against the Dragarians to save his son, not to doom him. There was a pain in his chest and his father frowned, but Dane could do nothing, because he was already dead. For an instant briefer than a blink, Nophel saw the fat Marcellan as he was now—taken apart in the darkness beneath the city.

His eyes snapped open, and his mother was looking down at him.

"Please, come with me." She was whispering. She looked in Nophel's one good eye, but her hands were elsewhere, sprinkling something warm and dry across his bared chest.

Nophel raised his head and looked down at the wound. The bolt had somehow been removed without him waking, and now the girl—the new Baker, two steps from his mother and yet still very much her—was tending the ragged hole left behind. It was red and inflamed, and the dust she dropped hissed slightly as it touched his skin.

"It smells," he whispered, voice harsh and dry.

"It will stop the pain." She averted her eyes.

"I'm dying." There was a weight in his chest, as if his heart had been replaced with a lump of rock.

"The bolt split a main vein. You've been bleeding into your chest cavity. I've seared the split, but it will reopen." The girl looked at him again, and there was something about her eyes that took his breath away. *One of them could be mine*, he thought. "Please, come with me," she repeated.

"Why?"

"Because you came down here for a reason."

Something thudded through the room, and a swath of spiderwebs hanging from the ceiling swayed. Scurrying shadows hurried across them, looking for prey that had not landed. The bed shifted, and by his side Nophel saw Peer and the man, both asleep. She looked exhausted and at peace. He only looked sad.

When Nophel held out one hand, the Baker took it and helped him up.

"Where are we going?" he asked.

"I think I have something to show you." She led him across the room, which was redolent with signs of the mother he had never known. The girl paused when he stopped, letting him lean against her as a faint passed through him. He bit his lip, and she pressed a small flattened nut into his hand.

"Sniff."

He sniffed, and the sharp scent brought his senses back.

In the corner of the room she opened a door, and they entered a much smaller room with a table, scattered charts, and a broken book on the floor. He leaned on the table as she opened another, lower door, and when she started to go down a small set of steps, he did not move.

"You abandoned me," he said, and though it was strange

talking like this to a little girl, he could see that she understood every word. "I came here to . . . kill you."

"I know," she said softly. "Please, come and see what I have to show you." And she descended out of sight.

She's luring me down to kill me, he thought. *And when the others wake, she'll tell them I ran raving into the Echoes.* But that was not the truth. *She's got my mother's corpse down there, hollow and dead with her mind passed down the generations, and she'll ask me to forgive it.* But that also seemed unlikely.

The Baker's face appeared in the small doorway again, pale and sad in the poor light. "Come."

I'm dying anyway, Nophel thought, and he went.

The staircase was carved roughly into rock. It curved out of sight, and it was only the sound of the Baker's footsteps that drew him on. Where the staircase ended, the darkness opened up around him. The girl stood a few steps away, but her oil torch could not penetrate the gloom.

"Where are we?" he asked.

"An old Echo. Hidden." She aimed the torch to their left, and Nophel saw a crumbling gray façade. "It was diseased, so they cut it off from the rest of the city."

"And this is about me?" he asked, anger rising. Diseased . . . cut off . . . forgotten. Could it really be that simple? He'd heard of wealthy parents in Marcellan Canton giving their children away to workhouses or chop shops if they were deformed, or simple-minded, or did not live up to their expectations in some other way—eyes too close, hair too dark. Was his story really that pitiful?

"My name is Rose," the Baker said, "and I am your mother only by blood. In memory, I am less so. So I've brought you here, because this is the Baker's place. No one has ever been down here, not even Gorham, who perhaps . . . perhaps I once loved. And there's something here for you to see."

The girl Rose led him through a doorless opening and into a dark room, placing her torch on a table and indicating a chair. Nophel sat, closing his eyes as another faint came over him. Something wet rattled inside as he sniffed the nut again, and he pressed one hand across the wound on his bare chest. It was blazing hot.

There was some basic furniture in this room, and Rose opened a wooden cupboard. She took out some objects and replaced them again, then moved to another cupboard.

"Lost something?" he asked softly.

"I was born only recently." She found what she was looking for and placed it on the table before him. It was a stark wooden box, rough-edged, undecorated. The lid above the simple hook-and-eye catch was smooth, as if it had been opened and closed many, many times.

"What's this?"

"This is your mother's real memory of you." She turned to leave, and Nophel experienced a moment of complete, encompassing panic.

"Please don't go!" he said. "I've been alone all my life, and now I'm dying."

The girl nodded, sat down on a chair close to the door, and rested her chin on her chest.

Nophel turned to the box and opened it without hesitation. Though he was a stranger to his own childhood, he knew that these things related to him. There was a shriveled, wormlike object in a fold of tissue—his umbilical cord, perhaps. A lock of fine hair. A tiny knitted boot—just one—snagged and dusty but still smelling fresh. Fingernail clippings. A simple but effective charcoal sketch of a baby, unrelenting in its honesty—one eye closed and, even then, growths on his face around his mouth and nose. As he examined the sketch, the charcoal darkened and smudged, and he realized that he was crying. He sniffed and wiped his eye, then started to take out other things.

Everything had a worn look, as if it had been viewed countless times. And when he finally piled it all back into the box—proof of his childhood, testament to his creation and existence—he closed the lid and sat back in the chair.

"So?" he said softly.

"Your mother loved you. That's good enough, surely?"

"She gave me away."

The girl nodded, then looked at her hands as if truly seeing them for the first time. They were not the hands of a child. "It's the fate of every new Baker to lose everything," she said. "She was incapable of looking after you, because of the things she did. She was dangerous, as am I. And she did what she thought was best."

"She gave me to a workhouse," he said, but he could no longer summon the anger that had always driven him. It had given way to sorrow, a hollowness inside being slowly filled with his own leaking blood.

"She did what she thought was best," the girl said again. She stood and left, and Nophel followed her back across the long-buried Echo and up the staircase into her laboratories once again. He felt drowsy, and sniffing the strange nut helped only so much. His chest was heavy and hot. And by the time he reached the room where Gorham, Peer, and Alexia still slept, his confusion was settling. As Rufus had said, he had found a trace of love in his father. Perhaps, in some way, there was some in his mother as well.

He asked how he could help.

Nadielle appeared above him, smiling what he had always thought of as a wry smile but what was probably just knowing. She reached down and tried to shake him awake, and when she spoke it did not exactly match the words her lips were forming. *You were always braver than you think*, he wanted to hear her say, but what she really said made Gorham sit upright.

"We have to leave," Rose said, her face and voice changed. "I've done all I can, but everything is getting worse."

"How do you—" he began, but then he noticed the constant shaking. Dust hazed the room, books slid from shelves, and it was only because he'd been asleep on the soft bed that the vibration had not woken him. He looked down at Peer, where she held his left arm, and across at where Alexia had slept. The Unseen was no longer there.

"She's helping," Rose said.

"And Nophel?"

"He's just left. And, yes, he's helping too."

"On his own?"

"He has a while, perhaps."

A harder jolt, and Peer stirred, mumbling Malia's name.

"Is it all the way up yet?" Gorham asked. "Is it risen?"

"I don't know!" the girl said, and it was the first time he'd heard her raise her voice. A glimmer of panic flitted across her face, then she was in control again, calm and efficient. "I don't know, but we can't wait to find out. I think I have enough."

"Enough what?"

"I'll show you. I hope you got plenty of rest. There's lots to carry."

Gorham gently shook Peer awake. She sat up quickly and looked around, then her shoulders slumped when realization hit her. Her eyes flooded with the knowledge of what was happening and the memories of what they had been through.

"It's time to leave," he said. "Rose needs our help."

Peer nodded and stood without speaking. He told her about Nophel, and they left the room and went out into the womb-vat hall, where Rose and Alexia were standing beside the vat.

What the crap is going to come out of this one? Gorham wondered. But there were no messy processes this time, and the girl Baker climbed the wooden ladder to sit once again on the vat's lip.

Alexia nodded at them as they approached, smiling slightly at Peer. Gorham liked that they were friends. That might not help a lot against that bastard thing rising against them, but in reality it meant the world. Arrayed around Alexia's feet were piles of a thin, wrinkled material, with string ties strewn like dead worms. At a signal from Rose, Alexia picked up one sack and threw it up to the Baker.

Rose leaned over the top of the vat and swept her arm down and up again. The bag came up bulging, throwing vague shadows that seemed to flit away into the darkness. Gorham was sure he heard a whispering, and he frowned and tilted his head to hear it better.

"Catch," Rose said, tying and dropping the bag without even looking. Alexia was there. She caught the bag, tested the drawstring, and lowered it gently to the ground. It looked oddly weightless.

Next time, Gorham caught the bag. He tweaked the draw-string and gasped as several small shapes flew from the bag's mouth, circling in tight circles before fluttering off into the darkness.

"What *are* they?" he asked.

"Bloodflies," Rose said. "Another." Alexia lobbed the bags up to her, Rose filled them, and when she dropped them someone was always there to catch.

"Do you really think these will work?" Peer asked.

"It's the best I could do," Rose said. She grunted each time she reached down into the vat now, and each time Gorham thought she was going to fall.

But he caught and tied the bags, and realization hit him— release the flies, hope they bite, and in their bites would be traces of Rufus's chopped blood. There was a terrible ran-domness to it and a reliance on the untested idea that Rufus survived the Bonelands because of something that ran in his veins. But Gorham also knew that Rose was right. It really was the best she could have done.

"Is this like the moths, bats, and lizards?" Gorham asked.

"They were proven," Rose said. "Used before, though on a much smaller scale. These . . ." She grunted, dropped an-other bag. "Bakers have tried things like this before, to spread cures in time of plague. But I have no firm memory of some-thing like this ever working."

"Marvelous," Alexia said.

The sounds resonating through the Echoes were now con-stant. They were accompanied by those staggering impacts, and Gorham feared that the ceilings would fall and crush them flat. He heard what might have been distant cave-ins, but he could not let them concern him. Their route was set, they were on their way, and it would take death to stop them.

They stacked the filled bags away from the vat. There were twenty in all, and they writhed and flexed with their insectile contents.

"So that's it?" Peer asked. "That's the hope of Echo City?"

"If Nadielle was right about Rufus's blood," Gorham said.

"She was right," Rose said, as she climbed back down the wooden ladder. "She made him, after all. She'd have known."

"But it was still a guess!" Gorham said, frustrated by Rose's pronouncements. "Nothing more."

"Lots of what the Bakers do is derived from best guesses," Rose replied, shrugging. "That's the basis of experimentation. It's all theory. We're just good at putting it into practice." She walked toward the main doors leading out into the Echoes, and when she turned and saw them standing there, she seemed surprised. "It's time to leave."

"Right now?" Peer asked.

"The Vex won't wait for us," Rose said. She looked like a corpse. Her eyes were sunken, her cheeks hollowed, and the shattering idea hit Gorham that she was only temporary. Nadielle hadn't had long, and she had chopped Rose to serve a purpose, nothing more. *Where will the* next *Baker originate?* he wondered. It was not something he wanted to dwell upon.

So they followed her from the womb-vat hall, each of them carrying several of the light, flexing bags. Gorham left last, and Rose was waiting for him outside the doors. She smiled softly and looked back into the rooms.

Leftover flies were rising from the vat in a swirling cloud, moving in beautiful synchronicity.

"We'll never return," Gorham said. *This is the first of many places I'll be leaving forever*, he thought, and he was as scared and excited as a little boy on his first trip out of his canton.

"No," Rose said. "But we'll leave the doors open for anyone else who might." She scratched at her arm, and he suddenly noticed the fresh blood speckled there. He grabbed her hand and twisted—the knife cuts were plain, on both underarms, and he had seen their like before.

"Nophel?" he asked.

"Yes. The city streets will be dangerous."

Gorham understood. "And who better to guide our way than the keeper of the Scopes."

Rose nodded, smiled, and seemed to be about to say something about the disfigured man. But Gorham guessed there was nothing left to be said.

They set off through the Echo, heading for the closest door that would take them to the surface. Their world shook around them, flinching away from the terrible roars and rumbles that echoed through the darkness.

And Gorham thought, *There's no way we can win.*

They looked at him strangely, almost as if they knew. *Perhaps they do*, he thought. *Perhaps they were there. There's no telling how old they are.*

She'd called them the Pserans, and they were guiding him across the Echoes. He'd only recently come this way with Peer and Alexia, but he'd been spitting blood then, in terrible pain and hovering on the boundaries of consciousness. Now he felt stronger, buoyed by the Baker's medicines, though he knew that he was dying. His senses were sharper and his purpose more defined, yet his breathing bubbled and he tasted blood when he coughed.

He'd be returning to Hanharan Heights a new man.

Nophel's arms stung where Rose had pricked them, but the pains had been offset by the touch he had been granted of her mind. The depth of that place had shocked him, the shattering extent of her knowledge exposed to him in a flash faster than thought, and he'd been left reeling. But then Rose had held his face in her hands and looked him in the eye, and he had seen the pain that went with such knowledge. *She is never a child, never carefree, and can never truly love.* In that, he found a closer tie to his mother than he had ever believed possible.

The two Pserans moved quickly, checking frequently to make sure he was keeping pace. They seemed unafraid but sad, and he guessed it was because this was the last task they would perform for the Baker. They passed a small group of Garthans, but the subterranean dwellers pulled back at the sight of the Pserans. Other things large and small approached in the darkness, fleeing the sounds reverberating through the Echoes rather than stalking prey, and the Pserans were always there to ensure his safety. At last they watched him up into daylight, holding back in the shadows, and retreating without a sound when he turned to give them thanks.

Nophel, Scope keeper for the Marcellans, bastard son of the Baker and Dane Marcellan, rose from the shaking Echoes of the past into a chaotic present.

Four people walked quickly through the Echo. Peer, feeling more fragile with every step they took, remained close to Gorham. Gorham, the leader of an organization whose worst fears were coming true, felt more lost than ever. Alexia, raised a Hanharan but whose beliefs had been taken advantage of, was now bitter and adrift. And Rose, who was mere days in this world but nonetheless possessed a mind almost as old as Echo City itself. They walked in silence because there was little left to be said. They walked with purpose. And, in all of them, doubt worried and bit, closing gentle fingers around their hearts and threatening to crush.

Peer had never been afraid of feeling insignificant. Even when she worked with the Watchers' political arm, she'd believed that most of what she did was trivial. It had implications, she knew, but hers was not a name that would ever be remembered. Then, in Skulk, banished and in pain, she had existed day by day on her own. Penler had been there, and his guidance, help, and support had seen her through many lonely times. But she had been one of many sent to that ruined place.

Now she was afraid, and some of that stemmed from loss of control. She had spent days doing everything she could to help a city unaware of its impending doom, but whatever might happen was out of her hands. She walked toward the culmination not only of the last few days but of *everything*. The city had been here for longer than anyone knew, and it was all about to change.

The ground shook. The air vibrated with potential. Something roared. Rose gave nothing away, and in that Peer recognized their true danger.

All she wanted to do was sit with Gorham and talk about old times, because events were far outpacing the differences between them. Though she still felt the physical pains of his betrayal, he was the last solid rock she thought she could hold on to, a love from her past who was so much more now.

There was desire, but that was a gentle feeling compared to the depth of connection she felt to him. And it was in the intensity of his obvious guilt that she found her own capacity for forgiveness.

This has always been way beyond the two of us, she thought, and that made them so much more important to each other.

"What are you thinking?" Gorham asked.

"That we're close to the end," she said.

"Or a new beginning."

"You really believe that?" They were approaching the route up out of the Echo now, and Rose was walking faster. *This girl's never even seen the daylight*, Peer realized.

"I *hope* that," he said. "This is everything the Watchers have waited for."

"Feared."

"That too, but it's been a practical fear. We've fought our concerns by trying to discover a way to move past them. The Marcellans, the Hanharans—they surround their fear with more fear, hoping to smother it. Those bastard priests think up more ways to make people feel crap about themselves, and we're persecuted for realism."

"All religions are real to someone."

Gorham scoffed.

"Really," she said. "You should have seen the Dragarians with Rufus."

"Let's see which one saves us from the Vex," he said.

"I don't *want* to see it," Peer replied. Gorham had described his and Nadielle's journey down, what had happened at the Falls, and how that had changed Nadielle. The Baker had not been able to truly convey what she had seen, but her fear had been enough. That and the guilt that bound generations of Bakers together.

Now Rose was feeling it too. That was why she fought against whatever weakness was trying to strike her down.

"Maybe we won't have to," he said. "By the end of today we'll be away from the city."

"And by tomorrow we might be dead."

"It's all just possibilities." Gorham reached out to take her

hand. He squeezed, she squeezed back, and she saw the grat-
itude in his eyes.

"Isn't that all the future can be?" she asked. Gorham did
not reply, and as they climbed up through the ruins of the old
farmhouse, she wondered what possibilities were about to be
realized.

At first she thought the Vex had risen and they were too
late. Crescent was deserted, but to the east and south, smoke
hung above the slopes and hillsides of Echo City. It drifted
toward the west, blown by the familiar easterly breezes of
late summer, and she could see a dozen flaming sources on
the high slopes of Marcellan. She and Alexia had left fires
behind, but now it looked as if the whole city was ablaze.

"Are we too late?" Alexia asked.

"No," Rose said, but she was not looking at the fires. Her
eyes were aimed at the pale-blue sky, streaked here and there
with wisps of white cloud. The sun was above the city, barely
obscured by the smoke this far out. To the northeast, the pale
ghost of the moon hung low to the horizon, biding its time.
Red sparrows flitted here and there just above the grass,
plucking insects from the air. A family of rathawks rode the
thermals high above. "It's beautiful," she said, and for the
first time Peer heard something human in the girl's voice.

"It's burning," Alexia said.

"Anarchy," Gorham said. "From what you described, the
Marcellans will be doing their best to halt the migration. At
times like this, there are always those who'll take the opportunity to . . ." He drifted off, shrugged.

"Settle scores?" Alexia asked.

"Maybe. Some just have chaos in their hearts."

"Peer and I saw plenty on our way here," Alexia said.

"Can we release them yet?" Peer asked. The bags strung
over her shoulders were bulging and shifting more as the
sunlight warmed them. The bloodflies were excited. Peer
was revolted, and yet she knew that each insect contained the
essence of Rufus's chopped blood. He was as close to her
now as he ever had been.

"No," Rose said. "Closer to the people. When we reach Skulk."

"That's almost ten miles," Alexia said.

"Then we should walk quickly," Rose said. "And we'll soon have help." She looked at Hanharan Heights through the drifting smoke, and for a moment she closed her eyes.

The smell of smoke hung in the air, and the farther south they went, the worse it would become. Then there was Course Canton to negotiate, the Border Spites, the Levels . . . and all the while, the city would shake with terror at the thing rising beneath it.

"How long until this Vex arrives?" Peer asked. "Where will it rise? What will it do?"

Rose turned to her, then glanced at Gorham and Alexia to include them in her reply. "I'm no god," she said. "There's plenty I don't know."

"But you made it," Gorham said, his voice cool with accusation.

"A Baker long before me—" Rose stopped when she saw Gorham's growing anger. In that instant, Peer loved him a little more. "But, yes. She made it, and then she threw it away, because it was imperfect and dangerous. She just didn't throw it far enough. Please, we need to hurry. We'll know when it arrives, and we must reach Skulk before then."

They started walking, Rose in the lead, the others strung out behind. It surprised none of them that a girl whose skin the sunlight had never touched knew exactly which direction to take.

Nophel thought about becoming Unseen, but that would have been no help. Whether people saw him or not, the streets were chaotic, and he would be moving against the flow. So he took a deep breath from the nut clasped in his hand and forged ahead.

As he saw the chaos and destruction, the bodies in the streets and the burning buildings, the fear on people's faces and the useless efforts by Scarlet Blades to temper the flow of fleeing humanity, his mind was on the contents of that old, worn box. They signified a pain in his mother's heart that he had never considered—he had always imagined her filled with hate and inhumanity, not sadness and loss. And they drove him on now, because he was doing this partly for her.

She's a little girl with an old woman's eyes, he thought of Rose, and in some ways she was the living memory of the city. Constantly reborn, her knowledge handed down, she was the echo of Echo City in blood and flesh.

Bleeding, coughing, Nophel made his way uphill toward Hanharan Heights. He passed dead people and fallen buildings, but they were invisible to him. He felt the city's doom constantly transmitted through his heels, and at one point, when a dreadful roar came from somewhere to the south, the ground shook so much that he believed this was the end. But the tremors settled, people picked themselves up, and Nophel started to climb again.

He cast his face upward in case the Scopes were watching for him. He would be with them soon. His breath bubbled and blood ran from the corner of his mouth, but after everything that had happened, he could not even consider failure. That would be the cruelest joke that Fate could ever play.

While much of the city fled, he climbed, and it was only as he reached the Marcellan wall that he went Unseen.

The first half of their journey was easy and fast. They crossed the southern border of Crescent into Course, passing the waterfront areas by the Western Reservoir where thousands once spent their leisure time eating, drinking, and sailing; the area was all but abandoned. There were some who had stayed behind, ignoring the strange warnings they'd received or heard from someone else. Several taverns were full to bursting with drunks. The overflow sprawled on the streets outside, fighting, sleeping, some of them fucking under the sunlight as if this was the last day they'd ever see. Perhaps some of them truly believed that, Gorham thought, but it never took much for a drunk to drink like the world was about to end.

There were bodies in the streets. Not many, but enough to show that the relative silence was far from normal. A mother and daughter lay dead beneath a second-story window, and a sprinkling of mepple blooms had fallen across their bloodied clothing. Several Scarlet Blades had been killed and stripped outside a large, faceless building that had once stored produce from Crescent. The warehouse now stank of fruit turning to rot, and the dead Blades were adding to the smell. Each of them had a sword handle protruding from the mouth. Farther on, in a small square where a water fountain still gurgled cheerily, at least thirty people lay dead, with hands tied behind their backs and throats slit.

"Bastards!" Peer said, and Gorham shared her rage. He'd seen this before, three years ago when the Marcellans were cracking down on the Watchers and needed the city to know how serious they were. Back then, most of those killed had been Watchers and their families. Here, he suspected those executed had nothing in common other than a wish to follow their instincts south.

"Why didn't the Blades get the message?" Gorham asked. He thought of those moths, lizards, and bats, drifting or running through the city and spreading the word he had given them.

"Maybe some did," Rose said.

"Not enough." He breathed deeply, taking some comfort from the fact that the Blades had been fed their own swords.

"We can't stop every time," Alexia said. "The city's in turmoil, and there'll be more. Peer and I saw the start of it, and it'll only have grown worse."

"You're right," Gorham said. *I'm not sure how much of this I can see without going mad.*

The ground shook. Things fell. They walked on.

Rose paused now and then and closed her eyes, frowning. After a couple of these occasions, Gorham asked her about Nophel, but she shook her head sharply and they moved on. *Not there yet*, he thought. *Maybe he's dead.* He had no idea what had passed between Rose and the deformed man, and right now he had no wish to find out. They all bore the weight of their own past; he knew that better than most.

When they reached the River Tharin and started across Six Step Bridge, the going became tougher. A group of Scarlet Blades had set up a checkpoint on the bridge, and they were charging people to cross. They were drunk and smashed on slash, and two of the female Blades wore what appeared to be male genitals on strings around their necks.

There were maybe a hundred people sitting across the bridge, some in front of the cafés lining each side, and others apparently camped on the road. Many were drunk. A couple appeared to be asleep, or dead.

Gorham sat down and the others followed.

"We can't let them slow us down," Rose said.

"No pay, no way," a teenaged girl a few steps from them said. She held an empty wine bottle in one hand and a bag of slash in the other. Yet her eyes were clear and her voice strong. She had been crying.

"What's the price of passage?" Peer asked.

"For you . . ." the girl said, lips pressing together. "Can't you guess?" She pretended to drink from the bottle, wiping her dry lips. Tears streaked her flushed face. "Bommy tried to protect me. He . . . stood in their way."

"They killed him," Alexia said.

"Threw him in the river. *The river!* They cut off his . . . They didn't even have the decency to cut his throat first."

Gorham closed his eyes, trying not to imagine Bommy's final moments.

"I'm waiting," the girl said, leaning forward. "They've been drinking all morning. One of them fell down drunk just now; the others dragged him away. So I'm waiting."

"If you try—" Gorham said.

"I'm not going to try anything. I'm going to do every one of them—with this." She pulled her jacket open, displaying rips in her shirt, scratches across her neck, and, in her belt, the cheap, dull sword she must have found in one of the taverns.

"Come with us," Gorham said. "We're going south."

"Your women going to give in peacefully, then?" the girl asked.

"Fuck them," Alexia said. "Watch this." Lying down behind Peer and Gorham so that she was blocked from the Blades' view, she started to fade away.

"What the—!" the girl shouted, stumbling backward.

Rose was by her side almost instantly, easing her to the ground and whispering, "You're drunk."

The girl—wide-eyed, scared, in pain and mourning—seemed to react to Rose's touch. She looked up into the young Baker's eyes and smiled.

Gorham did not even hear Alexia stand, but he felt a nudge on the shoulder as she passed him by.

"Come on," he said to Peer. "She'll need some help."

"I can't kill anyone else, Gorham," Peer said, almost manically.

"You won't need to." And he smiled at her, because he thought he knew what Alexia intended.

They walked up the slight rise of the bridge toward the roadblock, and the smell of bad wine and burning slash became much stronger. Gorham was careful to keep his hands away from the sword in his belt—in the shadows of a tavern's canopy, he could see a Blade resting a crossbow on a wooden privacy screen—and he tried to offer an appeasing smile. *They'll think I'm coming to offer Peer as our crossing fee*, he thought, and his smile suddenly felt like a grimace. *Relax . . . relax . . .*

"I don't like this," Peer said.

"When I point, just look that way." He hoped that Alexia was as serious as he thought. He hoped that she was still a soldier. And, most of all, he hoped that these murdering bastards were as superstitious as most Blades he had met.

One of the women with genitals strung around her neck staggered forward. She stopped ten steps from him, drawing her sword and pointing it. It had blood smeared across the blade.

"You wanna cross, she's gonna pay," she drawled, and Gorham saw a fleeting shadow appear and then disappear again behind the woman.

He raised his hand and pointed at the woman. "You pay first," he said, and her head tilted back and her throat opened up. The string bearing her trophies parted and they fell. Blood sprayed up and out from the slash across her neck. Alexia turned her so that the struggling Blade sprayed her companions.

Then the woman fell heavily, and several steps away Gorham caught another brief glimpse as Alexia manifested for a beat.

"He pays too," he said, pointing at the man closest to Alexia. His eyes widened and then his throat opened as well. He raised his hands and flipped quickly onto his back, gurgling as the front of his tunic turned red.

They panicked. Of the six left, five backed away from Gorham, swords forgotten, wine bottles slipping from their hands and smashing on the road. The last Blade stalked toward him but stared at Peer. He had hungry, mad eyes and an ugly lolling tongue. This time, Peer pointed, and the Blade's eyes burst as an invisible knife was drawn quickly across them.

"I'm blind!" he shouted, holding his hands before his face but not quite touching. "Help me, I'm blind!"

The drunk girl raced past Gorham and struck the man around the head with the wine bottle. It shattered, and he fell. Gorham was going to reach for her, pull her back, but then Peer grabbed his arm, and when he looked at her he could see the pain of memory scarring her face.

As the girl set upon the screaming man with the smashed bottle, they ran, Gorham trying to snort out the stench of blood. Rose was with them, along with a crowd of others, given the opportunity at last to cross the bridge and flee south.

"The terror is rising; go south to Skulk!" someone shouted, and Gorham gasped at hearing the words he had sent out.

Alexia was waiting for them at the other end of the bridge, manifested again and wiping blood from her hand. When she looked up at them, Gorham knew that nothing needed to be said.

"Not far to go," Rose said mildly. "And not long left."

It was not an easy journey. Being Unseen did nothing to ease Nophel's pain or prevent his wound from gushing blood again. The nut pressed almost constantly to his nose, he became light-headed with its effect, but he was convinced that he would fall without it. A mass of Scarlet Blades were stationed at the entrance to Marcellan Canton, standing close to one another as they stared south and west. In their eyes he glimpsed the reflection of chaos, but he did not want to look too closely.

If I glance back, I might lose all hope. So he crept between them. Some turned and frowned, as if at a memory. Others stepped back and raised their swords, and if they'd taken a swipe at the thin air before them, his head would have rolled.

He passed through the guarded gate into Hanharan Heights when it was opened to allow a group of Marcellans to exit. He recognized them—three members of the Council—and none of them had ever spoken to him. He'd always been a subject of their disdain. It was good to see terror in their eyes.

His journey from the gates to the viewing room was a blur of pain and darkness. Many oil lamps in the Heights had been extinguished, and the halls and corridors were all but deserted. *They'll be in the Inner Halls*, he thought. *Praying to their Hanharan god, hiding in his First Echo, begging for help, mercy, and salvation. Lot of good that will do them.*

In his viewing room, the mirror was cracked but not shattered. There were bloodstains across the floor where a body had been dragged. His father's actions, perhaps, but he no longer cared. All he cared about was seeing that small group on their way and seeing his mother one more time. His offer of help had been quickly accepted, and he had shushed her concerns about him remaining in the city. *I'll soon be gone*, he'd said; *I'd rather the time I have left is well spent.*

He tweaked the controls, but there was no reaction—no views of the city and no signs of life. Nophel groaned and went on, heading for the fifty stairs that would take him to the roof. *Don't stop*, he thought, *keep moving on*, and he felt the fresh slick of warm blood across his chest.

The Scopes were silent, awaiting his return and his tender touch. He went to the Western Scope and looked out over the city, scanning the tumultuous streets and wondering where Rose and the others were now. His arms itched, and when he scratched, he reopened the shallow wounds.

"Not long now," he said. "Not long, and I'll be able to help." He shooed away birds that were pecking at the Scope's eyes, washed fluid from its tense body, eased chains, and scooped handfuls of balm, working it into the folds around the Scope's head and neck. Leaving the roof, he looked back at the other three Scopes and felt a pang of deep guilt at not tending them as well. But the city had ceased being his concern. There was only one way left for him to look.

Back in the viewing room, he relaxed in his chair with a gasp, his vision swimming, arms and chest bleeding. And then he laid his hands on the controls and started his search.

Rose paused and closed her eyes again, and this time she smiled softly. "South of Six Step Bridge," she whispered, "at the junction of two roads."

Peer turned and looked up through the haze of smoke at Hanharan Heights, far to the northeast. She imagined one of those giant Scopes up there, extending its neck and turning its monstrous eye, and that brought a brief, unexpected memory of her mother. Long dead now. Peer wondered what she would think of her daughter. She thought she would be proud.

"And I see you," Rose said. She looked at the others, still smiling softly, and nodded. "We can move faster now," she said. "Nophel can see our way for us, warn us of dangers, and guide us along the easiest route to Skulk."

"How can you talk to him?" Peer asked, but Gorham touched her arm and rolled his eyes. "Oh," she said, quieter. "Baker stuff."

As they moved on, Rose was muttering to herself, an ongoing conversation with a man no longer there. Constant vibrations were rising through their feet, and as they entered the heavily built-up southern half of Course Canton, there were fewer and fewer unbroken windows. Glass speckled the ground, crunching underfoot. They passed a burning house. People ran, some screamed, and there were more bodies. *Could fear drive so many to this?* Peer wondered. *Was Echo City really built on such a thin crust?* They came to a place where a building had collapsed across the road, blocking their route completely. A few people were digging with their bare hands, calling names as they searched for buried loved ones.

Peer wanted to stop and help, but Rose steered them through an abandoned house and emerged in a small herb garden, climbed a wall, and veered left into a narrow, deserted alleyway. Still muttering, her arms still bleeding, the girl seemed hardly there.

They followed Rose through gardens and squares, wide streets and narrow alleys, and even though all around them they heard the sounds of chaos, they seemed to travel in a bubble of calm. Nophel steered them away from trouble and urged them south, as quickly and as safely as he could. Peer was humbled by the trust the Baker placed in that poor, brave man.

Everything Peer saw—every scene of random violence, goodwill, or heart-wrenching tragedy—brought home to her more and more that the city was at an end. When the Vex arrived, everything would change. The four of them bore the responsibility of ensuring that there was a future for some.

Gorham was keeping her strong. He was a constant presence beside her, and whenever she glanced aside he always seemed to be looking at her. There must be such a desperate need for forgiveness in him, but now he projected only strength and confidence.

The bags of bloodflies twitched and moved, a sickening sensation but one that drove her forward. *We can release them soon*, she thought. *Soon*. And then whatever this new, young Baker had done to the flies would be out there, and there would be only one way to find out whether they had worked.

She thought back to the day she had first seen Rufus coming in across the desert. Even rushing across to him and back again, she'd been reticent. *Will I be able to step out into that desert? Will any of us?* And then she realized that the decider would not be what might lie ahead but what was behind.

The streets and parks became more crowded the farther south they went. Many people had started the journey but ended it in a tavern or parkland, perhaps losing the urgency that Gorham's message had implanted in them or maybe just deciding that whatever was coming offered no escape. The Hanharans among them—most of them, she realized, because indoctrination was one of the Marcellans' greatest powers—would be praying silently to their deep prophet, asking him for salvation were they to die that day. Children cried and parents bustled, but there was a surreal air to the whole scene.

"Don't they *realize* what's happening?" Peer asked.

"How can they?" Gorham said. "The ground shakes, and that has happened before."

"Never to this extent. The fallen buildings. The fires."

"Most of the fires are started by people," he said.

After a while Rose guided them to a park where dozens of standing stones had been raised to signify important points in the city's history. It was called the Learning Fields, but today thousands of people were passing the stones without a second glance. Peer had come here once on a school trip when she was ten years old—a three-day journey, across the city and back to Mino Mont, that had opened her eyes to the rest of their world. The day spent touring the Learning Fields and being lectured by the historians who had made this place their life was one of the fondest memories of her childhood. Passing the rocks now only made her sad, because she could feel the rich history of Echo City being forgotten already. She wondered how many Echoes were left untouched below this place and whether any of them were even there anymore.

At the far edge of the Learning Fields, they found the long street before them thronged with people. They looked for another way around, but neighboring thoroughfares were equally jammed.

"Nophel says the streets are all like this between here and Skulk," Rose said.

"There's no way around?" Gorham asked. "No route through or below the buildings?"

"Even his Scopes can't see through walls."

"How far are we from the Skulk border?" Gorham asked.

"A mile," Peer said. "Perhaps less."

"The Border Spites won't let people through," Alexia said. "They're mean bastards."

"They're also cowards," Peer said. "Little more than

mercenaries. They'll have run at the sight of this many people. This must just be the line waiting to get in."

Skulk, she thought. *How unprepared was it for this?* It
could never feed and water thousands of people. The Southern Reservoir was kept mostly drained so that those who
lived in the ruined canton could be kept under constant threat
of thirst, and stoneshrooms could not feed the whole city's
population.

"How many do you suppose came?" she asked, raising her
voice above the crowd's hubbub.

"Not enough." Gorham was looking back the way they had
come, across the Learning Fields and past the imposing wall
of Marcellan Canton. On the slopes above, a whole sector
seemed to be blurring.

"What the crap is that?" Alexia said.

Peer squinted, rubbed her eyes in case they'd picked up
dust, sniffed the air for smoke. But nothing improved her
vision. And nothing changed what she saw.

A spread of buildings and streets almost a mile across sank
from view, sending up great billowing clouds of dust, explosions of rock and bricks, and a horrendous roar that swept in
across the Learning Fields like the cry of a dying god. The
Echoes were swallowing the present and making it history.

"Oh, by all the gods!" Peer said, adding her voice to a
thousand exhalations of shock and terror. "It's gone."

"Just sinking down," Gorham said, aghast. "All those buildings. How many people?"

Rose stood between them and held on to their arms, slumping down. The crowd was surging away from the park, as if
the cataclysm that had befallen the city several miles distant
could reach out and consume them all.

Perhaps it can, Peer thought, and, looking at Rose's face,
she knew there was no *perhaps* to it. This was the beginning
of the end.

"Vex?" she shouted above the crowd.

"Open the bags," Rose said. Though her voice was soft,
Peer heard every word. "Release the bloodflies slowly. We'll
make a path through the crowds. We have to reach Skulk's
southern walls. We don't have very long."

Penler!

Gorham hugged Peer around the shoulders, and she relished his warmth. But when Peer closed her eyes to lose the dreadful sight, she was presented with another—Malia, spluttering in agony, dying beneath her sword.

And she knew that she could not leave anyone else behind.

Chapter 27

Gorham went first, holding his initial opened bag up high before him. The flies spewed out and spread, thousands of them, hazing the air around him before darting off in all directions. Perhaps it was because they had been incarcerated for so long—or maybe because of something the Baker had done to them—but they spread and dispersed quickly. A few people cried out in surprise as they were bitten, but most pulled away from Gorham and the others at the sight of what they were doing, and a route opened along the street.

Peer came behind him, with Alexia and Rose bringing up the rear. *This is when we find out*, he thought, and the strangeness of their actions struck him. Releasing countless flies into the air might decide whether everyone he could see now lived or died. He wanted to explain, but they would never have believed.

He saw a woman swatting a fly on her arm, and he almost cursed her for a fool.

They moved quickly along the street, and when his first bag was empty, Gorham unslung another, pricked its corner with his knife, and hurried on.

"Save your last bags for Skulk," Rose said. The buildings around them were more dilapidated, obviously lived in but fallen into disrepair, and Gorham hoped that meant that they were approaching the Levels.

He had never been this far south. Skulk was another world, a part of Echo City that people knew existed but most tried to cast from their mind. Like Dragar's Canton, it was a section of the city cut off from the rest, though its purpose could not have been more different. He'd had many arguments with friends and fellow Watchers about the moralities of banishing people from the rest of Echo City, but he had always seen it as fairer than the alternative. A thousand years before, during the brutal reign of the first Marcellan family, criminals were banished to the Markoshi Desert, the city walls patrolled so that anyone trying to return would be captured and boiled alive in sleekrat oil. Banishment was surely preferable to that.

And there was still the Marcellan crucifixion wall for the worst offenders.

Then Peer had been tortured and sent to Skulk, and it had become more of an unknown land to him than ever before.

A fly landed on the back of his hand and bit. It was a sharp, brief pain, and when the fly fluttered away, he looked at the tiny wound it left behind.

"I've been bitten," he said above the excitable crowd's voice. "Will I feel a change?"

"I don't know," Rose said, sounding weaker than before. He glanced at her, and she was marching on with a determined expression, her face, arms, and hands speckled with dozens of fly bites. She met his gaze and looked away again. She wanted neither pity nor any more questions.

"You okay?" he asked Peer, and she nodded, turning her arm so he could see several bites across her wrist.

"I'm itching all over," Alexia said.

"You should wash more."

"Fuck you, Watcher."

By the time they reached the Levels, they had each emptied all but one of their bags. People behind and around them yelped and swore as they were bitten, and Gorham was amazed no one had tried to stop them. *Just another bit of strangeness in their lives today*, he thought. And then he saw Skulk for the first time.

To their right stood a watchtower, several people in its upper levels waving everyone on. To their left was the blazing ruins of another tower. He could smell cooking meat, and he blinked the smarting smoke from his eyes.

"Quickly," Peer said, and she was the first of them out onto the Levels. *This is* her *place*, Gorham thought.

The going was slow. Many people were crossing, though plenty seemed to be holding back, the ingrained fear of Skulk causing them to hesitate. *What must they think of the sudden idea to come here?* He thought of asking someone, but he felt apart from everyone other than his companions. They had come here not as refugees but as saviors.

He untied the last bag of flies and hurried after Peer. She seemed keen to reach Skulk. Maybe she thought of it as coming home.

I'll have to tell them soon, she thought. *I'll release the flies and then go for Penler. Make sure there are a few left in the bag for him.* She knew that he probably would not still be in his home, that he had likely moved on when she left, that what was happening today would have drawn him out, fascinated and afraid. But she also knew that she had to try.

"Peer, slow down!" Gorham called behind her, and she realized that she had broken into a run.

"I'm going for Penler," she said.

I left a man in Skulk, she'd told him.

"I know," he shouted, "but will you just wait?"

She paused and looked back at Gorham, Rose, and Alexia. They'd halted beside the hump of a burned-out building, and Gorham was leaning in close to Rose, listening to her soft voice. She seemed weaker than ever, but Peer still thought the new Baker had more strength left in her than most. Or was that wishful thinking? Right then it seemed to matter so much less. They'd done what Rose had asked of them, and now it was in Fate's hands.

Rufus had told them so little of what was out there, but perhaps detail did not really matter. What mattered was that there *was* something out there, beyond the murderous sands and lifeless dunes, and beyond the sun-scorched corpses of those who had tried before. *Their world is called the Heartlands*, Rufus had said, *and their Heart and Mind sees through me. It knows Echo City now. I hope it will welcome you.*

But that was vague and nothing that they could communicate

to anyone in the midst of such chaos. Instead, the people would need someone to lead them out into the desert. Someone to lure them. The idea of being the first to go out there and keep walking, seeing whether this new, young, fading Baker's ideas had worked at all . . . that would take someone special.

Peer sagged as realization struck her: *It would take Penler.*

"Gorham!" she called. "I've got an idea. I'm going to find—"

"Penler," he said again, nodding. "And I'm coming with you." He said something else to Rose and Alexia, then trotted over to Peer. "Better to split up anyway. Spread the bloodfly love."

"That's why you're coming?" she asked, smiling.

"Of course. Why else?" His feigned innocence made her chuckle, and she could not recall the last time that had happened.

"Welcome to my home," she said, indicating the first line of Skulk buildings not far away, and part of her enjoyed the flash of guilt in Gorham's eyes.

They waited until they'd crossed the Levels before pricking the final bags. Many of those crossing had been bitten already or were being bitten as the plague of flies followed the general direction of travel. But there would be people in Skulk who had yet to be exposed, and Peer wanted to give them as good a chance as any.

She kept glancing back toward Marcellan Canton. She reckoned that the area that had been swallowed down into the Echoes was five miles distant, and a pall of smoke and dust still hung over the whole site, obscuring the view. The glow of fires burned through here and there, and they must have been voracious to be visible from this far away. She tried to resist the feeling that they were relatively safe here in Skulk. Though the destruction seemed to be behind them, she could still feel the ground beneath her shaking. The Echoes below this place were fewer, the buildings here older than almost any in Echo City, but that did not mean they were safe. Whatever was rising—Rose had called it the Vex, muttered in hushed tones of abject terror—would have the whole city as its playground.

Nowhere was safe. The city was finished. She felt sick but also a barely veiled excitement at that. Everything she had always believed as a Watcher was about to be explored for real. In a matter of days, everyone in Echo City might be dead . . . or some of them could be somewhere else.

They ran where possible, and where there were too many people, they pushed through the crowds. Reaching the first of the buildings, Peer drew her knife and pricked the last bag, agitating it with both hands until the flies started pouring from the tear. Gorham did the same.

The streets of Skulk were awash with thousands of people who had never considered that they would be here. Some wandered in confused groups, aimless and seeking something more, casting fearful looks at their surroundings. Others were sitting along sidewalks or in the street, on fallen ruins or in the windows of the taverns and cafés that had been set up here over the years. Whole families sat together in protective huddles, and here and there single people roamed, lost and alone. Peer felt the urge to tell them what was happening—but if she stopped for one, she would have to stop for them all.

The crowds parted as she and Gorham rushed through the dilapidated streets, flies spewing from the shrinking bags. They left behind the familiar yelps of people being bitten. When Peer felt that her bag was almost empty, she pinched the slit shut and tucked it beneath her arm. *These are for Penler.*

"Done," Gorham said behind her. "Peer, wait."

"No time," she said, and Gorham cursed as he struggled to keep up with her.

The confusion was palpable. Encouraged to flee to this prison district by urges they could not identify, everyone was now waiting for whatever came next. Marcellan Canton was visible from most places, and where it was not, the people still seemed aware of what had happened there—what was still happening. The fear showed in their eyes.

This is not the place I lived in for three years, Peer thought, and she was glad for that. Skulk had never seen so many people, and even when she passed a small café where she sometimes drank five-bean while reading one of the books collected in a central library, it no longer seemed familiar. Only now did she realize that it was people who shaped the face of a place, not the place itself.

"How far?" Gorham asked.

"What's wrong with you?"

"Nothing," he said, panting hard. They paused on a street corner, leaning against a wall.

"You've let yourself go since I left," she said, offering a smile to show she was joking.

Gorham shrugged, looking around nervously. She felt protective of this place and what had been done here. The Marcellans sent those they thought were the worst of the city this way, and most of them had made a go of forming a functioning society.

"I used to live over there," she said pointing along a street. "Half a mile away. Small house, nice. Still had pictures on the wall."

"You don't need to tell me this," Gorham said.

"It's no problem," she said, looking back along another street at the imposing mount of Marcellan. Smoke hung heavy over that canton now, drifting west across Course. "We're becoming strangers to the whole city, and . . ." She trailed off. Gorham said something to her, but she could not hear. Blood thrummed in her ears, her heartbeat increasing, breath raking at her throat. She felt a fly land on the bridge of her nose and bite, and she welcomed the brief spike of pain, because it was the only hope she had.

Gorham grabbed her arm and shook it, and she raised one hand to point. Around them, the sound of panicked flight and frightened conversation subdued.

Something was rising out of Marcellan. Blurred and disfigured by the smoke and dust still hanging above the collapsed area, the shape was gigantic, pushing through the pale clouds and glittering as though wet. It was difficult to judge size from this distance, and Peer did not want to. She *could* not. It was unbelievable, terrible, and to try to judge the magnitude of the thing wavering above that hole . . .

"Oh," Gorham said, and it broke through her muffled terror. He held her hand and squeezed.

Now people were screaming and running. Some fell, others

trampled them. Peer and Gorham just stood. They'd been expecting *some*thing, but nothing could have prepared them for this.

The thing protruded above the city, shifting back and forth in the dust and smoke cloud, fires erupting around its base, a great column of flame spewing up and out from the hole in the shoulder of Marcellan Canton, and nothing of it was identifiable. For that, Peer was glad. It was a gray, glittering edifice, larger than any building, taller than Marcellan Canton's tallest spires, and if a great eye, or a mouth, had opened somewhere across its girth, she thought perhaps she would never recover from the madness that would bring.

"We need to find Penler," she said, amazed at how calm her voice sounded. Perhaps grabbing on to something rooted and certain was all she had.

Just before she turned to drag Gorham away, the thing tilted sideways. It fell with surprising slowness, but when it struck the ground, the violence was terrible. Buildings shattered, fire billowed, dust exploded in pressurized twisting torrents, and then the sound rolled in across the Levels, testament to the terrible destruction.

The shock wave came next. It knocked them off balance, and Gorham went down. Peer knelt next to him and covered her head with her hands. People cried, buildings fell, some screaming ceased.

As the rumble lessened, Peer said, "Gorham."

"Yeah. Penler."

They entered the rush of panicked humanity. Penler's home lay to the south, so they let the tide take them. But it was not long before Peer realized that they were just another part of the tide.

Nophel had watched them for as long as he could—as long as the Scope could extend itself that far, and the smoke did not obscure his view, and the rush of fleeing humanity did not swallow them. But then, inevitably, they were lost to him. And his last sight of the small girl who had once been his mother was as she leaned on the man's arm and let him help her along.

But the wounds on his arms still bled, and he could still touch her with his mind.

Sprawled on the floor, he looked at the bloodstains beneath him. He coughed again and added to them, and for a moment he panicked, thinking that perhaps this would be the last time he fell. But the Baker's ministrations had been skilled. His wound was a solid, burning pain in his chest, but still he managed to kneel, and then he took a deep breath before he turned back to the screen.

If the Scope was turned, its eye ruptured by flying debris, its mountings wrenched by the impact of that thing, I'll be blind until I draw my last breath. But the screen, though flickering, still showed an image of the city and the thing that had risen and fallen across it.

Nophel hauled himself back up into his seat, breath rattling in his chest. He kept glancing at the screen and away again, not quite believing, not able to acknowledge exactly what he had seen. But there was no denying the sight that awaited him.

He laid his hands across the controls and coaxed the best view from the ailing Scope.

Dust and smoke hazed the air, but he could focus through them, zooming in on the sprawled thing where it lay in a new valley of its own making. A thousand buildings had been crushed beneath it, along with untold thousands of people, and fires were spreading across the southern and western slopes of Marcellan Canton. Buildings folded, their walls exploding outward where the ground beneath them broke, and several fault lines progressed across the city like roaming monsters. One of them reached the tall Marcellan wall directly to the west and cleaved it in two.

Nophel grinned at the symbolism and wondered where the Marcellans and Hanharans were right then.

Two other shapes were rising slowly on either side of the massive fallen thing, pressing down against the ground and heaving, and he could barely believe that they were limbs.

The size of the thing was difficult to comprehend, because it was alive. So when Nophel saw the shapes parting from it— red dashing things that seemed to snake away from the fallen mass and steer themselves through the ruined streets—he tried to focus on one of them instead. He used the tracking ball to control the Scope, following one of the red things as it flowed along a sloping street like a globule of fresh blood. Nophel could only guess at its size—the girth of a tusked swine, perhaps—until it encountered a small group of people.

As it grasped them in its whipping appendages and pulled them toward itself and started to eat—*then* he could judge its size.

Nophel closed his eyes, and the Baker saw. He felt her fear and sadness, and that made him afraid and sad as well.

North, she whispered to him, and he urged the Scope to strain against its mounting, turning its eye toward the north as it had when the Dragarians first emerged. It did so more easily than he imagined, and he supposed it might be pleased to look away.

Working levers and dials, Nophel brought the northern extremes of Echo City closer. The domes of Dragar's Canton were as still as ever, but then the Baker whispered, *Beyond*, and he lifted the Scope's eye slightly and stretched it farther.

There was desert, the familiar bleached yellow of the Bonelands. And beyond the shadows of the domes, a tide of darkness washed out from Echo City.

"They're going," Nophel whispered. The Dragarians were leaving their retreat. He only wished he could coax the Scope to look farther, bring the distance in closer, because he wanted to see the Baker's other abandoned son one last time.

Back, Rose whispered gently. *Not long left now, so one last look* . . .

"I'm not afraid to die," Nophel said, hoping that she heard. And he drew the Scope back to the southwest, toward the risen mass of the Vex. Trying to shake the enormity of what he had seen to the north, he scanned slowly across the risen thing's surface. There seemed to be deep rents in its flesh, from which bubbled great gouts of blood-red fluid. And from these gouts manifested the dashing things, rolling and bubbling, crawling, and then running through the city's fallen streets.

The Baker could see, and Nophel felt her fear and resignation. But, with the sight of the Dragarians' flight, he could also sense her hope.

The building beneath him shuddered from a terrible impact. He almost slipped from the chair, such was the extreme of movement, and he heard the ominous crunching, cracking sounds of stone crumbling under tension. The image on the screen wavered, and then he heard a sound that was deeper and more terrible than the sound of the breaking city—a cry, a *scream*, and Nophel closed his eyes and felt blood dribble from his left ear.

The image shivered and veered up to the clear blue sky. For a moment all he saw was beauty, hazed by a thin skein of smoke that was all that indicated what was happening below. And he realized that the Scope had looked away because it was scared.

"One more look," he said, unsure whether he was talking to the Scope, or himself, or the child Baker. He touched the levers and dials and viewed the risen thing a final time.

Dust and smoke obscured much of it, and flames erupted here and there. It seemed unconcerned by the fires. It shifted and flexed, its countless appendages worming through the streets, destroying another hundred buildings with each movement. And then Nophel frowned. It was covered in . . . something.

He turned a dial and the Scope took him in.

The monster's hide was stippled, rough, and mostly pale. He focused in some more, stroking a guiding ball when the Scope began to shake with fear again, and then he realized what clothed the thing.

Bodies. Thousands of them, tens of thousands; skeletons and rotting corpses, some piled so deep that hundreds had sloughed off in drooping, skinlike jowls. They decorated the thing's hide like the pustules on his own, and Nophel put one hand to his face.

He could feel the Baker seeing through him, and her shock echoed back at him, a guilt that was not his own.

He coughed and blood flowed from his mouth, thick and dark. He guided the Scope to pan along the thing, moving inward all the time, sweeping its huge eye toward what he thought of as the Vex's head. He could sense that the Scope wanted to turn away, and he was sure that soon it would, denying his commands for the first time. And he would never blame it. But for now he had to see, because everything he saw, the Baker saw.

There were larger bodies pierced on huge spines lining the thing's hide. These were black and silver, and many-bladed, and looked fresh. Around them were dark, steaming scars on the leviathan's skin. And as Nophel moved on . . .

His breath stalled. He snapped a lever to freeze the image and saw a body that caught his attention. Surrounded by rot and bone, this body was new, pale and red in equal measure. He tried to push the Scope closer, unconcerned now at the discomfort he must be causing the wretched creature, ignoring the insistent prodding in his mind from the Baker to look away, look away . . . and then he saw the face, whose familial features he recognized. Its mouth was open wide in an endless scream. One arm was pinned high, as if waving.

The Scope died, Nophel's vision faded, and his body was lit by the mass of pain in his chest. He sat back in his chair, eyes closed. He welcomed the calming touch on his mind that did its best to see away the pain, though it was now beyond calming.

"Mother," he said.

And then he drove out that influence with a force of will, because he had no wish for her to feel his death.

Penler was standing on top of the ruined home next to his own. He was staring north while everyone else fled south, and for a moment Peer simply watched him. It felt as if she had been away from Skulk for years, not just days, and Penler's appearance lived up to that idea.

He stood like an old man. His thinning hair waved behind his head in the warm breeze washing down from the north, and she could see that he was squinting. *He can't quite see*, she thought, and she knew there was much to tell him.

Gorham stood close to her, one hand pressed against the small of her back. If she'd felt a shred of possessiveness there, she would have shrugged him away, but he was as scared as she was. Contact was something they both needed. That, and friendship.

Penler froze, then slowly turned. "Peer," he said, and grinned as if the world was no longer ending.

"Penler," she said. "I hoped I'd find you still here."

He took a final, long look north, then worked his way down the slope of rubble. Old he might be, but he was still sure-footed from half a lifetime of living among the ruins.

"Nowhere else to go, it seems," he said.

"This is Gorham," she said, and perhaps Penler heard a whole history in her voice, because his smile was uncertain.

"I've heard so much about you," Gorham said. "I think you saved Peer's life."

"She's a strong woman," Penler said.

"Here." Peer ripped her fly bag open and a handful of flies escaped, circling up into the air, darting left and right. Several landed on Penler, and one bit. He did not wince or make a noise. When the fly lifted away, he looked closely at the small speck of blood, touching it gently with one finger.

"What have you just done to me?" he asked, though with curiosity rather than suspicion.

"Hopefully saved your life," Peer said. "We have to go out into the desert, and—"

"And then we'll die."

"No," Gorham said, but he did not sound convinced.

"We think not," Peer said. "The Baker—"

"I thought the Baker was dead!"

"Oh, Penler," Peer said, and there was so much to tell. She closed her eyes, and fatigue hit her then, the darkness behind her eyelids luring her down to sleep. "I have some stories for you, my friend. So many. And there's plenty I think you'll be able to help us explain. But first . . ." She opened her eyes again, and Penler was staring at her in a way he never had before. *I really broke his heart,* she thought. *I shouldn't have brought Gorham with me.*

"First?" Penler asked.

"You've seen what's happening," Gorham said.

"I've seen something."

"The doom of Echo City," Gorham continued. "Rising

from the Chasm below the Falls." He shook his head, and Peer knew that none of them could adequately express what they had witnessed and experienced.

"Where's the visitor?" Penler asked.

"With the Dragarians," she said, and Penler's eyes opened wider.

"He came from the Bonelands," he said softly.

"There's going to be plenty of time to explain." A rush of enthusiasm almost overwhelmed Peer. "But right now we have to leave and take as many people with us as we can." She grabbed his hands and pulled him closer, then wrapped her own hands around his and put them to her chest. He felt her heartbeat, and she saw that familiar twinkle of humor and intelligence. She was glad it was still there. She'd feared her leaving might have extinguished it forever.

"And you think they'll follow *me* into the desert," he said.

"I *know* they will."

"You think they'd follow me?" Gorham asked, eyebrows raised.

"No," Penler said, and his smile seemed genuine. "Though they might line the walls to watch you die."

"Nice," Gorham muttered.

"Don't mind him," Peer laughed, "the old bastard has a way with words."

"Words are all we have," Penler said, and his smile turned sad as they all recognized the truth in that. "Is it really the end?"

"You saw what came up," Peer said.

"I saw *something*. I don't know what."

"The Bakers are to blame. But the latest is also to thank." She touched the swollen fly bite on his hand. "For this."

"Where is she?" he asked.

"Out there somewhere," Peer said, nodding into an uncertain distance.

"With an invisible person," Gorham said. Penler glanced at him, smile unsure, and then turned back to Peer.

"And this all began because of Rufus?"

"In truth, it began generations ago. I'll tell you everything."

"When we're away," he said, and Peer nodded.

"We'll need food and water," she said.

Penler stared at his house, unmoving.

"I'll go," Gorham said, and he dashed inside. They waited in companionable silence, staying close as they watched people rushing southward. Gorham emerged moments later with a water sack and a bulging backpack.

"Ah, stoneshrooms," Peer said.

Penler grinned and took Peer's hand. They turned south and headed for the city wall a mile distant, and Peer felt tears threatening. Penler had turned his back on his home, his maps, his studies, his books and projects and writings, and all because of what she had told him. All because of her. She felt a warm, rich love emanating from him that she had never felt from Gorham, and she realized he was the father she had never known, holding her hand and leading her away from danger.

"I've been waiting for you to come back," he said.

"Liar."

"No, really." He raised an eyebrow, maintaining his seriousness. "I always knew you found me irresistible."

Peer laughed out loud, and people around them stared at this madwoman amused by the end-times.

Sheltering along the base of the city's southern wall were several hundred Garthans. They shook in the heat of the summer day, shielding their eyes against the unbearable light, and people kept a good distance from them. They scratched at vivid red bites across their naked bodies. Peer hoped they would follow everyone else out into the desert but hated to think what effect the unrelenting sun would have on skin so used to darkness.

Gorham stared at them strangely, and Peer knew he would have a story to tell her later.

Penler led them to an open stone staircase, and they climbed to the top of the wall. It was wide here, arranged with seating that looked mostly inward, and she remembered sitting here many times with Penler, discussing, debating, and arguing. She felt an odd nostalgia for such good times.

The place where she'd first seen Rufus was a mile to the

east. She looked along the wall in that direction, and the mass of humanity stunned her. The wall was packed with people, and below them in the streets and roads that led along the wall's base were many more.

"So *many*," Penler said. "This used to be a nice quiet place."

"They're lost," Gorham said. "They're looking for someone to tell them what to do."

"Aren't we all?" Penler asked.

"No," Gorham said. "Not everyone needs that."

Peer raised her hands and smiled at both men. "Now's not the time for a religious debate."

"If not now, when?" Penler asked.

From the north came continuing sounds of destruction. A column of smoke and dust rose high above the city, thick and textured at its base, spreading and dispersing higher up where the desert breezes grabbed hold. It was rooted on the southwestern slopes of Marcellan Canton, but fires were apparent at many other sites across the city, from eastern Mino Mont to western Course. At the base of the cloud of dust and smoke—even from this distance—they could see movement.

"Later," Peer said again. "There'll be plenty of time later."

"It's good to hear your confidence."

"Penler, there's somewhere beyond the Bonelands," she said. "He didn't tell me much. He *wouldn't*. But it's there." She frowned, looking over Penler's shoulder.

"And?" he asked.

"And he said something there sees us, and he hopes it will welcome us."

Penler was silent for a few beats, glancing back and forth between Peer and Gorham. At last he said, "And you're the ones who cannot entertain gods," and then Penler turned to the crowds.

He stood with the grace of someone half his age. Peer knew that he commanded respect in Skulk, but she was also aware that most of those around them now had come down from the city. Their clothing gave them away, as did their smooth skins and the fact that they carried belongings with them. People in Skulk owned little.

This was the moment when they all had to cast differences aside and listen.

"Echo City is doomed!" Penler shouted.

"No shit!" a voice said from the street below. A man was crying, children were laughing and playing, and a hundred voices mumbled unheard replies to Penler's pronouncement.

"Look behind you and see what ignorance and blind faith will bring," he roared. "Fear and death with no hope for something more! What are the Marcellans doing to counter whatever this sudden threat might be?"

"I saw Blades raping a woman in the street!" a man yelled, and voices surged again, expressing disgust or offering other stories.

"That's because they're afraid. Fear breeds desperation, and from desperation comes such violence. They're afraid because the Marcellans offer them nothing else. They'll follow Hanharan because they're told to, not because they choose to listen to him in their hearts."

Peer shifted uncomfortably, but she knew what Penler was doing and respected the roots of his own beliefs. There was no way he could get the crowd on his side by expressing nonbelief, and even if that *could* help, she knew he never would. He was an honest man who would not deny his own philosophies. And that bullish honesty was why they would follow him.

"And what are you listening to, old man?" someone called.

"I'm listening to someone I call my friend," he said. He pressed both hands to his chest and looked out over the crowd.

"Who the fuck are you, anyway?"

"That's Penler. You can trust him."

"I don't trust criminals!"

A roar rose, the crowd surged, fists flailed. Penler glanced down at Peer and she nodded at him, giving him whatever encouragement and support he needed. *Someone I call my friend*, he'd said, and she smiled at his shrewdness. He could never lie—one of his weaknesses, but also his greatest strength—but he could let the listeners interpret what he said in their own ways.

He held up his hands and the crowd calmed. He had them, she realized. They were willing to watch and listen while the city fell behind them, because this was the first time someone had really spoken to them. They'd all woken with whispers in their ears, but now they could see and hear the person offering them advice.

"I'm told there's hope," Penler said. "I'm told you came here at the behest of your own inner voices. And look around—I see no Marcellan costumes here, no Hanharan priest's robes. That means we're *all* special. That means we've *all* been given a way to escape. To escape *that*." He pointed over their heads, over the top of Skulk's tallest buildings at the monstrous column of smoke. As if at a signal from him, another tremor shook the ground, and moments later the sound rumbled in, shedding tiles from rooftops and knocking people to the ground.

"And we have to escape!" Penler cried. "There's a way to defeat your fear. You have to trust in yourselves and trust in me."

"But how do you know?" a woman shouted.

"I've always known," he said. Then he stepped down from the parapet, crossed the wide head of the wall, and stood overlooking the desert with his back to the city.

Peer shivered. A chill went through her. The desert burned, dead and barren, and the thought of going out there terrified her. Gorham held her hand and pulled her forward. They shouldered past people until they were standing close behind Penler. And then Peer gasped as her friend started to descend a crumbling staircase leading down the wall's outer face.

She panicked. *Is this enough? Did he say enough? Will they think him mad? Will they turn their backs, on him as he's turned his own on Echo City?* She looked around the crowd and paused, seeing a face she recognized. It was a woman who'd picked stoneshrooms from the same rubble fields as Peer. The woman caught Peer's eye . . . and smiled.

She believes, Peer thought.

"Come on," she said, pulling Gorham after her. They stood on the wall and looked down at the desert below.

Penler was already halfway down. The treads cantilevered

from the wall, rough and never used, and he was pressed back against the stonework to avoid their crumbling edges. But still he descended with confidence, never once pausing, never once looking back.

Hundreds of people leaned over the wall to witness his descent, and hundreds more stood farther back, waiting to see what would come of this.

Peer looked at the sands that had played no part in the city's life other than to offer it a place of death. Gorham clasped her hand and kissed her softly on the cheek.

Peer went first.

He had found a form of forgiveness and a diluting of his guilt in the woman he had betrayed, and he would not betray her again. Though every scrap of flesh and blood and bone told him to turn back, he did not hesitate for a moment. Peer was already on the baked sand and walking out after Penler, and Gorham followed, feeling the change in texture beneath his shoes and biting down a sudden urge to vomit.

She did not look back at him, and there was intense trust in that. Likewise, Gorham did not look back at the city wall, and he trusted that the people would follow. *It'll take only a few*, he thought, *and then a few more. And then we'll be committed to discovering whether those fly bites were worth the prick of pain they gave us all*.

The sand was hot and hard, shifting slightly beneath him as he walked. Gorham looked at the bite marks across his hands and arms, but they were not changing. The sun felt hotter out here. It was late afternoon now, and soon dusk would be falling, and they would be out in the desert without anywhere to sleep, little to drink, and the city behind them would call and—

There was a noise behind him, the likes of which he had never heard before. It started low and far away, like a dog howling in the night, but it rose and grew louder—a howl that turned into a scream—and louder, and every hair on his arms and neck stood up, his balls tingled, and his legs grew weak. He paused but still did not look back, because he had denied himself the city forever.

The cry went on, louder than anything he'd ever thought possible, a shattering exhalation of rage and hunger, fear and triumph, and he was certain he saw cracks opening in the ground all around him as the land itself shook in sympathy, or shivered in fear.

As the cry faded, voices rose behind him. *I won't look back*, he thought, *I can't look back, I'll never look back.*

But he could look sideways.

Running across the sand toward him, fleeing the city at an angle, came Alexia. She was carrying Rose on her back, and the Baker waved. It seemed such an odd, innocent gesture that Gorham waved back, as if greeting a friend's daughter rather than the most powerful person the city had ever known.

"They're coming," Rose called as they grew closer. "They're following! Don't stop, Gorham. Don't stop walking for anything."

"What *was* that?" he asked, though he knew the answer.

"The Vex is risen." Rose looked more haunted than anyone he had ever seen. There was such knowledge in her eyes, but he wanted none of it. "We're the lucky ones," she said. "The lucky few."

The few, she called them, and Gorham walked on with Alexia beside him. The Unseen was sweating in her old Scarlet Blade clothes, and her hair was plastered to her head, but she wore an expression of grim determination.

The few walked on, and soon, from behind them, Gorham heard the many beginning to follow. There were footsteps and voices, shouting and crying, and even a few bursts of laughter. And as the sun dipped toward the Markoshi Desert's western horizon, Echo City already felt very far away.

Chapter 28

All through the night, they heard the sounds of destruction from behind them. Thunder rolled across the sands, and the city became a blazing pyre on the northern horizon. A breeze blew into their faces, drawn from the south by the conflagration, and at least that meant the stink of the burning city was kept at bay.

"What could cause such burning?" Gorham asked when they stopped to rest at last, and for a while none of them had an answer.

After a while Rose said, "After so long in the deep, climbing the Falls, perhaps heat is all the Vex seeks."

"You really believe that's all?" Peer asked, and Rose did not answer, settling down beside Alexia and closing her eyes.

But none of them slept. They huddled close for warmth, and all around them they heard the sounds of humanity uprooted—crying, sobbing, wild laughter, and groans of pain. When dawn came, the mournful tears began. Bodies lay here and there, causes of death uncertain. Peer could not even begin to entertain the fact that the desert had started to kill them.

They commenced their second day of walking with the city smoking far behind them. They were too far away to make out any detail, but the fires seemed to be dying down as morning passed into afternoon. The rising smoke grew lighter. And then the distant sound they had heard before leaving the city—pain, frustration, the scream of some mad

thing shown only more madness in its future—accompanied
them until dusk.

Peer had felt sick for a while, but that soon passed. Even
Rose seemed stronger than before, though the little food
Gorham had managed to grab from Penler's house would not
last them very long.

"People are dying," Peer said, as they sat around a fire that
night. Thousands more campfires burned around them, lighting up swaths of the Markoshi Desert—a place known for
time immemorial as the Bonelands. They burned clothing,
belongings, and wood gathered from the scattered remains
of old wagons and other constructs that had made it this far
in the past. Peer smelled cooking meat and tried not to imagine what it might be. Several groups of Garthans had accompanied them out, walking far apart from them.

They'd talked today about how many people they thought
had walked, and estimates ranged from Gorham's ten thousand to Penler's two hundred thousand. None of them had
any concept of such numbers or what that many people looked
like. No one would ever know for sure.

"Fear," Penler said. "Thirst. Hunger. Not everyone brought
food and water with them." There had already been fighting,
and late that afternoon they'd seen a father stabbing a man to
death after he tried to steal food from his children. Peer was
glad to have her friends around her. Alexia still carried her
sword, though she had discarded the tunic that identified her
as an ex–Scarlet Blade.

"Illness," Gorham said. "Maybe some are succumbing."

"There will be many people who weren't bitten," Rose
said, and Peer sat up straight, staring at the girl.

"I never even considered that," she said. She felt guilty at
finding hope in the deaths of so many, but, looking around
the fire, she saw the same hope reflected in everyone.

"Time will tell," Penler said. She'd told him everything
during that first afternoon and evening, answering his questions and bringing in Gorham and Alexia when there were
answers she did not know. When she told him what had happened to Rufus, he'd grown pale, and then Rose had revealed

what she had seen through Nophel. *A dark tide heading north*, she had said.

Everything I wrote about the Dragarians . . . Penler had whispered, but he would say no more. Perhaps he was seeing justification in a lifetime of belief.

Or maybe he was wishing he'd gone with them.

He had been quiet ever since, rarely contributing to their discussions. Peer knew when he was brooding. She also knew that he would talk when he was ready.

No one tried to take charge. Some looked to Penler—those who had been at the wall and seen him venturing out onto the sands—but his silence drove them away.

The people from the doomed city walked, and fell, and died beneath the sun and the moon.

They were five days out from the city. It was behind them now, below the horizon, evidence of its ruin little more than a pale smudge in the sky. Peer tried clinging to hope, and Gorham clung to her, slowly losing his way. Out here in the Bonelands, the past felt like it belonged to someone else, and she told him she forgave him. Hugged him close. It helped, for a while.

Their food and water were finished.

People died around them. They were left where they fell, after whatever food and drink they still carried was taken. Whispers passed this way and that of cannibalism, rumors drifting like the breeze that still blew in their faces. The Garthans had gone, either dead or drifted in another direction, and so the alleged flesh-eating was much worse.

Some people turned to go back.

It was not the desert killing people—it was exhaustion, hunger, thirst, desperation, and hopelessness. Peer was confident that the young Baker's chopping of Rufus's blood, and the bloodflies, had worked. But perhaps even that would not be enough to save them.

The walkers had spread out, not drawn in as Peer had expected, and for as far as she could see behind and around them, the desert was speckled with refugees from Echo City. But before them was only sand. Something in all of them drove them on—Penler most of all. He was old and weak, suffering badly and still mostly silent, and Peer feared he was grasping on to one small fact to keep himself going: He had been the first into the Bonelands, and he would be the first to reach their destination.

Where they were going could not be discussed, because nobody knew for sure. Peer had told her companions what Rufus had said about the Heart and Mind, but that meant nothing to them. His words echoed for them all: *I hope it will welcome you*.

For now they were just walking.

Rose spoke little, but when she did, Peer took note. The girl would never have a child's mind. "This is an adventure we've been waiting for forever," she said. And, "She did her best . . . she gave us time." And, "I'm sorry."

That afternoon, they took on a little boy they found crying over the body of his father. And, that evening, the little boy died.

Rose cried. That was what astonished Peer more than anything. The Baker cried for one death, while the destruction of a city and countless people had left her merely contemplating the histories buried in her mind. It made her seem almost human.

Rose started to fade next day. They waited with her while the sun passed its zenith, because she could not walk anymore, and even Alexia was no longer strong enough to carry her.

"I'm the last Baker of Echo City," she whispered to the heat, and when Peer tried to protest, the girl grasped her hand. "We've lasted too long already. After what we have done, do you think the Baker will be welcomed elsewhere?"

Peer remained silent, because she could not answer that honestly. So they stayed around her as others passed by, and no one else knew who the little dying girl was.

"Fading away," Rose said softly as the sun touched the horizon. "Nothing lasts forever." Gorham was kneeling beside her then, holding her hand. He seemed confused, but Peer held back because she sensed he needed space to be with the girl. He'd call her if he needed her.

And after Rose passed away, Peer was there for him.

Next morning, as they started to stagger across the desert for one more day, Penler was the first to speak.

"Last night I smelled something on the breeze," he said.

"What something?" Alexia asked.

"I'm not sure, but not desert. And I feel something. Something . . ."

"What?"

"Reaching out. Sensing. Don't you feel it too?" His eyes sparkled, but Peer had to shake her head.

"No," she said, saddened by his confusion. But Penler always had been amazing, and it was a hope she would cling to.

"Then we're getting somewhere?" Gorham asked.

"Maybe," Penler said. "Perhaps somewhere we never should have been. Who knows what made this desert what it is? The Baker has made us able to cross it, but who or what made the Baker?"

"Does it matter?" Peer asked.

"I think so," he said. "I think so very much."

She thought about the Baker as they walked, and what a mystery she really was.

Their skin was burned and peeling. Their tongues were swollen. More people died. They stopped that night, but only a handful of small groups found material to light fires. They tried sucking moisture from their clothes, and Penler chewed at his shoe leather before laughing and lying down. By the time dawn touched the horizon, there were no more fires left.

That morning, many people chose not to walk anymore.

Penler led them, and the others followed. Alexia seemed the strongest of them all, and Peer drew strength from both the woman and the old man. She could never stop as long as they walked.

"Do you still feel it?" Peer asked.

"Yes," Penler said.

Later, when she found enough strength for another question, she asked, "What do you think happened to Rufus?"

"You heard Rose," Penler said. "Honored Darkness. As we walk south, he leads them north. They believe in it . . . and that will be their strength."

"But what *is* it?"

"Perhaps it's exactly what the Dragarians believe—a place that is timeless and forever. Or maybe it's simply a place far to the north, where the sun never touches. Whatever, they have the strength of their . . . their faith . . . and . . ."

Penler went to his knees in the sand. It was almost a relief. Peer sat beside him and hugged his head to her chest. Gorham was behind her, his face split and bleeding from the relentless sun. And Alexia remained standing, and always would, as if to sit down was to give in for good.

Peer looked at the people around them, and most of them were stopping as well. *He didn't want it, but they've been following him all along.* There were thousands of them, still determined, fading, and dying, because Penler had told them there was hope.

Peer tried to ask Gorham what the Baker had done to them all, but she found that her throat was too dry to speak, her tongue too swollen. She rested her cheek on top of Penler's head, and Gorham sat beside her. It was too hot and painful to touch, but his hand in hers was all that mattered.

Virtually blinded by the heat, unable to speak, she squeezed his hand to show that she could love him. He squeezed back. And that made it easy to close her eyes.

In their dreams, a voice said, *The Heart and Mind has seen you, and you are welcome.* And later, perhaps only hours before they would have died, shadows fell across them.